Stephen Amidon was born in Chicago in 1959. He moved to London in the late 1980s and has recently returned to America. A regular contributor to the *Sunday Times*, he is the author of three previous novels, *Splitting the Atom*, *Thirst* and *The Primitive*, and a collection of short stories, *Subdivision*.

'Amidon brilliantly dissects a Watergate-era America shaken by public scandal, failure in Vietnam and the emergence of the Plastic Ono Band, interweaving the public and personal relationships of three families and two generations at one turbulent moment in history. By the end, belief in the Presidential myth and John Lennon's clothes are not the only things that have been lost'
GQ

'Large, impressive, highly intelligent . . . Amidon is a plain writer, in the best tradition of American realism that goes back at least to Dreiser, and includes also Sinclair Lewis, John O'Hara, John P. Marquand, the underrated Louis Auchincloss and Updike at his best . . . very satisfying. It is a pleasure – and a relief – to read a novelist whose prose . . . is free from flourishes, decoration for cleverness's sake, and self-admiration; a novelist too who is not afraid to tackle a big theme and who has the ability to tell a story and create convincing characters about whose fate one cares'
Allan Massie, *Scotsman*

'Amidon has a gift for creating characters and capturing the unstated, whether sexual social or racial . . . he uses the canvas of the American Dream, which never quite dies despite experience to the contrary, for a powerful exploration of race, wealth and ambition . . . There is an obvious comparison with Tom Wolfe. But Amidon's style is leaner, more measured. His characters are more complex, drawn honestly from life, rather than emblems of an age'
Toby Moore, *Express*

'Amidon drives the narrative forward with rare assurance, gripping his readers with a sense of mounting catastrophe . . . pathos combines with sharp social satire. Conceived and executed on a large scale, *The New City* is the sort of novel the Americans do rather well and we are generally too timid to attempt . . . the story has a sweep which makes those tales of adultery in Hampstead seem rather insipid'
David Robson, *Sunday Telegraph*

'Extraordinary . . . the most obvious comparison is with Tom Wolfe, although the novel is closer in texture to Dreiser's *An American Tragedy* . . . The novel is all the more impressive in that it manages to be about Watergate and Vietnam without ever making them its centre. It is as though these events have been absorbed by the characters on an almost molecular level, the effect being that their every utterance is a possible recording, their every movement a potential assault. The grand sweep of history does not need a life of its own; it has already consumed the lives of the people who live through it'
Graham Caveney, *Independent*

'A utopian thriller in which the best features of humanity are revealed as being uncomfortably close to the worst . . . it is this tension between perfection and the forbidden which reveals the essential vulnerability of the characters . . . Amidon's novel describes the sickness of a particular society. Obsessed with success, the avoidance of failure becomes a valid reason for corruption, hypocrisy and deceit. This is an ambitious book, but Stephen Amidon is a clever enough writer – composed, elegant and confident – to realize his own intentions'
David Utterson, *TLS*

Also by Stephen Amidon

SUBDIVISION
SPLITTING THE ATOM
THIRST
THE PRIMITIVE

THE NEW CITY

Stephen Amidon

BLACK SWAN

THE NEW CITY
A BLACK SWAN BOOK : 0 552 99915 6

Originally published in Great Britain by Doubleday,
a division of Transworld Publishers

PRINTING HISTORY
Doubleday edition published 2000
Black Swan edition published 2001

1 3 5 7 9 10 8 6 4 2

Set in 11/12pt Adobe Caslon by
Kestrel Data, Exeter, Devon.

Black Swan Books are published by Transworld Publishers,
61–63 Uxbridge Road, London W5 5SA,
a division of The Random House Group Ltd,
in Australia by Random House Australia (Pty) Ltd,
20 Alfred Street, Milsons Point, Sydney, NSW 2061, Australia,
in New Zealand by Random House New Zealand Ltd,
18 Poland Road, Glenfield, Auckland 10, New Zealand
and in South Africa by Random House (Pty) Ltd,
Endulini, 5a Jubilee Road, Parktown 2193, South Africa.

Printed and bound in Great Britain by
Clays Ltd, St Ives plc.

For Caryl

The New City

Part One

1

At first, the damage didn't look that bad. There was a jagged crack running through the front door's glass, but that could have happened in a hundred innocent ways. And the lobby's disorder – sand spilled from an upright ashtray and a scattering of drug awareness pamphlets – looked like the usual by-products of teen rowdiness. As Austin Swope stepped onto the metal staircase that helixed up into the converted silo, he began to think that maybe the security people had exaggerated when they spoke of a riot.

Hope disappeared when he reached the second floor. Unmistakable signs of violence were everywhere. Shattered glass and wads of bloodied toilet paper littered the pale carpet. A modular chair had been splintered and the crusted discharge of a fire extinguisher patterned the wall. There was an angry divot on the pool table's baize, partially covered by a forsaken sneaker. Swope sighed audibly. This would be impossible to whitewash. Chicago would hear about it, if they hadn't already. And they would not like it.

The third floor was even worse. He stepped gingerly through the debris, careful not to sully his custom-made wing tips. The wood paneling up here was pocked in several places by indentations, one deep enough to expose a cluster of electrical wiring. The Ping-Pong table listed on two bent legs like a camel ready for dismounting. Several windows had been smashed. A broken pool cue impaled the ceiling's acoustical tiles and the door to the director's office had been kicked off its hinges. Swope righted a toppled stool and perched gingerly on its edge. It's always the kids, he thought. They start, and then we have to finish.

He closed his eyes, suddenly wishing himself far away from here, deep in some distant election year, when his name was a household object and the dirty work of clearing up petty messes was left to lesser men. As a means of solace, he called up one of the imaginary commercials he deployed in times of stress. This one opened with him striding purposefully through some blasted urban landscape, a wasteland of smoldering storefronts, roof-scouring National Guardsmen and clusters of wary locals. He is moving with such resolve that his advisors must double-step to match his gait. Those churning opening bars of Mahler's Sixth provide the sound track. Suddenly, fearlessly, he peels away from his escort, heading toward a clutch of angry black faces. The camera circles as he engages them in direct dialogue. His tone is stern but compassionate. Snatches of the exchange can be heard through the swelling music. Words like renewal and responsibility. Citizenship. Hope. Those furious faces soften. He shakes a proffered hand, pats a young head. The music reaches a crescendo as the camera freezes on his face.

Austin Swope, the bass voice-over says. *Because in a crisis, we need a leader.*

Or maybe:

Austin Swope. Tough decisions for tough times.

He still hadn't decided which was better.

His reverie was interrupted by a scuffling footfall. He turned to see the EarthWorks security guard who'd admitted him, a young man with long, greasy hair tucked inconclusively into his cap. His uniform was a couple sizes too big, making him look like an inmate of some underfunded prison. In keeping with company policy, he was unarmed. He eyed Swope with a slack, vaguely defensive expression.

'Yes?'

The man recoiled slightly at Swope's stern voice. No wonder these kids run riot, Swope thought.

'I just wanted to see if you needed anything.'

'The National Guard.'

The man's brow folded in confusion.

'I don't suppose you know what happened,' Swope continued, realizing wit was not on the guy's agenda.

'I came on duty at seven. They said keep an eye on the place 'til you got here, was all.' The man sensed that Swope found this answer unsatisfactory. 'Though from what I hear there were cops everywhere.'

'Any idea where the center directors are?'

'They called in sick.'

'Sick? When?'

'Last night.'

'You mean the place was without any supervision when this happened?' Swope asked incredulously.

The man shrugged. He hadn't been on duty. Swope took one last disgusted look around, then led the guard back down the spiral stairs, feeling an unwelcome suck at his soles from a pool of stickiness cascading over the risers. In the lobby he paused in front of the portrait of the city's designer, benevolent old Barnaby Vine. A crudely drawn penis now tickled his jugged left ear. The guard awaited orders a few feet away.

'All right,' Swope said eventually. 'See if you can find some poster board upstairs in that office, a Magic Marker. Make a sign – closed until further notice. Then lock up. I don't want anyone in here until I decide what to do.'

The guard nodded with what he must have thought to be sober professionalism. Swope took one last look around the lobby, then strode through the cracked front door. All evidence of trouble disappeared the moment he left the silo. The covered walkway leading to Fogwood Village Center was perfectly placid. Muzak wafted sourcelessly through the trellised clematis and potted rubber plants. Citizens hustled past, searching out morning papers. Most nodded bright hellos, a few spoke his name. It was impossible to imagine that this place was full of brawling kids just a few hours earlier.

Swope walked back to his Town Car, parked in the fire zone at the curb. He shook a Tiparillo from the pack and fired it up, savoring that first mentholated drag as he leaned against the passenger door and stared at the converted silo. At

17

least there was no sign of wreckage from out here. The broken windows were invisible in their deep-set wells, the cracked door masked by foliage. Not that he worried all that much about the physical damage. Company builders could have the place as good as new by the weekend. It was the damage this could do to all those unsold lots that worried him.

When the call came at six that morning he'd first assumed it had been no big deal. After all, security would have phoned right away if it was serious. Or so he thought. It turned out the night duty man was new and didn't understand procedure. That was the problem with this place – everybody was so damned new. Swope wasn't contacted until the day supervisor arrived. The fight had in fact been a doozy, with a half dozen county prowlers responding. Five young men, all black, had been picked up on public disorder charges.

It wasn't until he'd hung up that Swope remembered his son had been at the silo. Terrified that something had happened to his beloved boy, he'd raced across the house to Teddy's room. But he'd been fast asleep, his concave chest rising and falling peacefully. His face had been unmarked, the clothes piled next to his bed free from bloodstains. Swope had considered waking him to get a report, though he knew it would take a half hour to get a coherent sentence out of him. Instead, he'd instructed a groggy Sally to have him report to the office as soon as he woke.

Swope took another drag from his Tiparillo, letting his eyes wander to the village center's sawtooth roof. He cursed himself for not being more aggressive in warning Chicago about this. A memo asking if he could hire an off-duty deputy to sit at the silo's door simply hadn't cut the mustard. He should have painted them a picture. Let them know how overstretched the county cops were. But he hadn't, and so the answer had been no. Cops at doors were not part of Barnaby's master plan. The city was supposed to supply its own order, all that greenery and light washing away any anarchic impulses its recently transplanted citizenry might bring with them from the world outside. How many times had Barnaby lectured him on this very subject back in the days when

Newton was nothing more than a stack of diagrams? Explaining how the abundance of public space and the equitable mix of housing would nullify the sort of invidious resentments and social alienation that led to crime. The Cannon County sheriff's department would be more than adequate to look after the occasional heart attack or domestic squabble. Vine was sure of it, as sure as he was that the traffic would flow and the pipes would carry water. And yet here they were, with five kids in jail and a couple thousand dollars' worth of property damage, plus a shitstorm of bad press darkening the horizon. The suburban stringers from the *Baltimore Sun* and *News American* would be all over this, having become avid students of the Cannon County police blotter ever since last month's seemingly endless article in *The Washington Post*, 'Will Race Woes Defeat New City Dream?' which cataloged in absurdly apocalyptic tones the recent confrontations between gangs of black and white youths. The scribblers would have a field day now that there had been actual arrests. The teen center, after all, was one of Vine's pet projects. Trouble there was not on the menu. In Barnaby's vision it was supposed to 'harmonize and homogenize' the kids, to serve as a place where proximity created peace. Tribal allegiances were to be a thing of the past. The notion of black boys and white boys going at one another with pool cues was definitely not part of the blueprint.

'Mr Swope?'

A young woman pushing a stroller stood a few feet off. Swope recognized her from the monthly homeowner meetings, though he couldn't come up with a name. She had a freckled nose and bobbed blond hair. Her bib overalls were immaculately clean. The thin strand of saliva dangling from her slumbering child's mouth caught the morning sun like a dewy web.

'Um, what's going on?' she asked, nodding at the silo. 'Somebody said there was a riot?'

Swope smiled tightly as he dropped his Tiparillo into a sewer grate.

'No, there was no riot,' he said. 'Just outsiders causing trouble.'

19

'Hasn't there been a lot of that recently?'

'I wouldn't say a lot,' Swope said gently, that smile still on his lips.

'But still . . .'

Swope knew he had to come up with something here. The woman was worried. Not that he blamed her. Five arrests just yards from where she bought her formula was unacceptable.

'I'm thinking about instituting youth ID's,' he said eventually. 'You know, to restrict access to Newton kids only.'

'That would be a start.'

'You get a nice new facility like this, you're going to get your share of undesirables in the early days.'

She nodded vague agreement. He could tell she still wasn't satisfied. These ex-hippies could be surprisingly testy about security.

'Well, I better get to work,' he said, reaching for his door handle.

She continued to stand her ground, looking like there was one last thing on her mind. Swope waited. He wasn't about to slight a homeowner. They were his core constituency. The launchpad to a stratospheric future.

'You know, Mr Swope,' she said eventually. 'After incorporation . . .'

'Yes?'

'People wouldn't mind seeing a few changes around here.'

Swope held her eye for a moment before nodding. Nothing more needed to be said. That was one thing he could guarantee – come summer's end, changes would be made. Satisfied at last, the woman smiled pleasantly and walked off, her child slumbering on.

Swope piled into his Town Car and fired up the big V-8. It was time to get to the office and manage this mess. He made a left onto Serendipity Way and joined the light traffic. After groping for his Foster Grants he rolled down the window, letting in some sweet morning air. The forecast said it would be hot later, but now, while the sun was still low in the salmony sky, it was mercifully cool. He moved through Fogwood's quiet streets, passing neatly sodden yards from which splintered saplings and preantiqued gaslights rose. The houses here were aluminum starters, three-bedrooms with modest garages and redwood decks. Unblemished phone booths and sturdy concrete mailboxes stood at regular intervals. The paved bike paths that ran among the houses like a nervous system were busy with dog walkers and joggers. A fine summery mist – not really a fog – shrouded low-lying areas. Barnaby's celebrated streetscapes were in full bloom. Planned and perfect, right down to the last blade of grass.

Swope joined Newton Pike, the four-lane arterial road that cut through the city from north to south. It wasn't long until the half dozen squat brown buildings of Renaissance Heights appeared, spread across a hill like the fecal leavings of some great beast. Swope's mood soured even further at the sight. Despite what he'd told the woman, he knew that it was kids from here, not outsiders, who'd been hauled off by the Cannon County sheriff's deputies. He pulled into the minibus bay across from the complex's entrance. Two black women waiting to clean houses up in Mystic Hills stared at him from the provisional shade of the nearby shelter. He nodded a general hello, then turned his attention to the parking lot, filled with dinged sedans, tarped pickups and a fetid-looking colony of overflowing Dumpsters. A dozen residents strolled wearily toward the minibus stop. Janitors and cafeteria ladies and landscapers. Minimum wagers. Barnaby's improvable masses. Their children no doubt sleeping off last night's fandango in the cinder-block boxes behind them.

Swope lit another Tiparillo, his fourth of the still-young day, realizing he'd better come up with a plan before arriving at the office. Nobody would be satisfied with 'I'm working on it.' He'd been given this job – and promised the big one to come – for one simple reason: he was a problem solver. The man they turned to in a crisis. The fire jumper. The late-inning closer. It was up to him to figure out how to keep trouble from happening. To protect the company's investment.

It didn't take him long to come up with something. Five drags on the cigarillo and he had it. He'd delay repairs. Indefinitely. Make up something about water damage. That way, he could shut down the silo until Labor Day without having to get authorization from Chicago. The kids would disperse, traveling into Baltimore or Washington to get their kicks. By the time the center reopened Swope would be city manager and there would be nothing stopping him from putting uniforms on doors. QED. Another problem solved. And he wasn't even at the office yet. As a reward to himself, Swope closed his eyes, letting another thirty-second spot form in his mind. In this one, he is seated at the head of a conference table – tie loosened, shirtsleeves rolled – where two raging groups of adversaries are going at it. Union and management. Cops and community activists. Whatever. Just when bedlam is looking set to descend he raises a hand through the gathered smoke. Silence falls. And then the camera moves tight on him as he begins to speak. Understanding dawns on faces where malevolence and distrust once reigned.

Austin Swope. Bringing us together for a new American century.

An inoffensive little horn sounded. Swope's rearview mirror had filled with the burnt sienna of a Newton Minibus. The driver, a long-haired man with the gaunt, hunted look of a returnee from the recent Indochinese fiasco, was in the process of realizing who he'd just beeped. Swope waved a benedictory hand and put his car in gear, slipping behind a Fury with a fading PEACE WITH HONOR bumper sticker. He punched on WTOP to catch the eight-thirty report. The top story was John Dean, Nixon's counsel, looking like he was about to pull a Judas. Swope shook his head. There was no longer any doubting it – the whole lousy crew was going down. With every bulletin he grew increasingly glad that he hadn't gone that route back in '68, when John Mitchell's people had directed feelers his way.

The pike followed the lake's contour along a gentle south-westerly curve. The vast geodesic canopy of Newton Woods Pavilion appeared. Beyond it loomed the Plaza's ten-story tower, its glass facade catching the morning sun like a great mirror. Muddy water flashed sporadically through gaps in the lakeside trees. To Swope's right was the mall, immense and windowless, surrounded by twenty acres of empty asphalt. A few hundred feet beyond that he turned into the Plaza parking lot. Other arrivals paused to let him race to his space by the door. Earl Wooten's neighboring slot was empty. He was no doubt already out on some far-flung site. Swope would get Evelyn after him – he wanted to square this teen center thing away by day's end. As general foreman, Wooten would have to back up Swope's water damage fable. Not that he would have a problem with a little white lie. He wanted this trouble to end just as badly as Swope.

He locked his car and strode toward the building's entrance, aware that dozens of eyes must be watching him through that looming wall of tinted glass. He straightened his back and put a little bounce in his stride. He'd almost made it to the revolving doors when he became aware of an unusual glimmering down by the lake, not unlike the burst of distant flashcubes. He wheeled and stared across the vast waterfront plaza. But everything seemed quiet down there, the forty acres of water perfectly still. Just a trick of the rising sun, he figured.

There were more people than usual milling about in the lobby, forming taut conversational clusters that fell silent as he passed. Sidelong glances were cast his way. On the elevator two engineers bailed out before Swope could start a conversation. By the time he reached the top floor he sensed corporate dread all around him – the quickly shut doors, the averted eyes, the hands cupped over receivers. Which meant that news of the fight must have already traveled through the building. Phones would be ringing in Chicago. Swope slalomed through the secretarial bullpen and joined the corridor leading to his own office. Color photos of earth-moving equipment decorated its paneled walls. Evelyn looked up from her desk as he entered his suite, her grey eyes perched on the twin horizons of her bifocals. After a nodded hello Swope picked up the stack of mail and began to flip through it. Most of the two dozen letters were emblazoned with the pompous calligraphy of law firms.

'Did Sheriff Chones call?' he asked.

'No. But your wife did.'

23

'And?' Swope asked as he continued to check the mail.

'She wants to know what kind of beer you want for your party.'

'Löwenbräu. Of course. Call her back for me, will you?'

Evelyn, long used to running marital interference for her boss, nodded once.

'But first get Chones on the horn. And track down Earl Wooten. See if he can swing by some time this morning.'

'Um, Mr Swope . . .'

Swope stopped shuffling and looked at his secretary. He recognized that tone.

'Have you seen the lake?'

'What do you mean?'

'This morning. Did you see it?'

That strange glimmering played through his mind.

'No.'

'I think you should take a look.'

He continued to stare at her, awaiting further explanation. But she'd already picked up the phone. Though he hated Evelyn's menopausal moods, he also knew that there was nothing he could do about them. He entered his own office, tossing the mail on his desk and then taking up a position in front of the long northern wall of tinted Thermopane. His first thought – that the damaged pier had finally slipped into its sink-hole – proved wrong. Everything seemed normal enough. The plaza directly below him glistened like arctic ice in the summer sun, its fountains and arches intact, the Gravity Tree unbroken and graffiti free. The shoreline town-houses and parkland were serene; the Pavilion and the Cross Keys Inn the same as ever. He was just about to buzz Evelyn and ask her what the hell she was talking about when he saw it again, that glimmering in the water, like fireflies on an August dusk. It took a moment to figure out what he was seeing. And when he did his heart sank even further than it had when he beheld the ruined silo. This was definitely turning out to be a shit day.

The fish were dying. All of them, from the look of it. Every last one. The suppliers had spoken of an attrition rate of 5 percent. But this was no 5 percent. Nor was it 50 percent. As far as Swope could tell, the entire generation had been wiped out. Three measly days after arriving in a convoy of gleaming steel tankers from the Pennsylvania hatchery. They were supposed to be easily catchable species, custom bred for novice fishermen. Crappie and carp, catfish and gar. He'd watched from this very spot as they'd been siphoned like slurry into the brown water, where they were supposed to feed and fuck and do whatever else it was fish did while awaiting the baited hooks of happy citizens.

But not die. That was the one thing the hatchery's men had assured him wouldn't happen. They'd made their final tests two weeks ago, absurdly serious geeks in lab coats and waders who'd measured the lake's alkali and acid levels, analyzed algae and fungus. The results were favorable. The bottom had sealed; the water was rich with microorganisms and flora. After a year's evolution, the lake was ready for life. Not the goldfish and newts and June bugs that had been here since the first, the Darwinian vagabonds that would pop up in a toilet if it went unflushed long enough. But a serious marine society that would turn what had recently been an empty ditch into a pulsating ecosystem.

Or so they said. Now, just seventy-two hours after the tankers had pulled away, the lake's entire surface was sparkling with brilliant extinction. Clusters of dead fish had formed near the creosote pilings of the boardwalk and piers, looking putrid and flyblown even from this distance. Unfamiliar birds had begun to congregate, big-winged scavengers already swooping at the surface. People were gathering as well, milling about the plaza to gawk at the spectacle.

Swope walked back to his desk and hit the buzzer next to his phone. It didn't take Evelyn long to answer.

'Any luck with Wooten?' he asked.

'He'll be out in Juniper Bend all morning. He can meet you some time after noon.'

'How about Chones?'

'He'll be calling just as soon as he gets in.'

Two more commas in an already overpunctuated day.

'Well, get me the goddamned hatchery, then.'

Somebody had to catch some shit for this.

Swope spent the rest of the morning on the phone. The people at the hatchery tried to maintain that some rogue pollutant must have made its way into the water. Swope suggested they back that theory up with immediate data or else they'd have a date with the Cannon County magistrate. Next came a testy conversation with Sheriff Chones. Normally an ally, he was clearly angry that his men once again had to deal with Newton's growing problems.

'Five arrests?' Swope hazarded after the usual persiflage.

'Misdemeanor public disorders. We cited and released four of them. The fifth gave us a bit of lip so we're going to hold him 'til that mouthpiece Spivey wakes up.'

'I understand they were all black.'

There was a pause. On the end of the line Swope could hear a squelched radio.

'Yeah, I guess they are,' the sheriff said eventually.

'How do you think that came about?'

'Well, Austin, I guess it happened like this – somebody called us to the scene of a fight in your city and when we arrived we arrested the guys doing the fighting.'

'Who happened to be black.'

'Black people have been known to mix it up. Ever hear that one?'

Swope controlled his temper.

'All right, Sheriff,' he said, his voice suddenly thick with conciliation. 'Personally, I couldn't care less if they were green. But Chicago, you know.'

Chones took the bait. His tone drifted from annoyance to exasperation.

'Austin, I got to tell you – this whole situation could be avoided if you'd let me take some preemptive steps down there.'

'I understand, Ralph. Just give me until the end of the summer. Things will change then. For both of us.'

'Summers can get pretty damned long, case you haven't noticed.'

The press began to call after that. As Swope feared, they were more aggressive than ever, no doubt because they'd

26

swallowed Vine's optimism whole in the early days, printing unchallenged his assertions that the city's design would provide a remedy for the social chaos gripping the nation. Put people in cages and they'll act like animals, he'd said time and again. Put them in communities and they'll act like human beings. Hard-bitten editors, desperate for something to counter the riots and assassinations and wars filling their pages, had lapped it up. Vine's idealism was so convincing that they'd even turned a blind eye to some of Swope's more questionable land acquisitions. Now, fearing they'd been had, they seemed almost glad that there was trouble. Though Swope held them off the best he could, he knew tomorrow's papers would make bad reading.

Finally, at high noon, came the dreaded call from Chicago – Gus Savage, EarthWorks managing director, firmly in control of the company since Barnaby's second stroke. An ambitious former New Frontiersman who'd been head-hunted from Bechtel, he didn't have the same regard for Newton's chief counsel as the company's founder.

'Austin, what the hell's going on? The press office just received a call from the *Post* asking if they would like to comment on last night's riot in Newton. Imagine our surprise.'

'First of all, Gus, there was no riot. It was a scuffle at the teen center. A few chairs were broken. That was all.'

'I'm hearing about arrests.'

'Five.'

'Word is they were all black.'

Swope paused, his silence a yes.

'Jesus.'

'Misdemeanor public order beefs. Nobody's going to prison.'

'As if that's the point.'

'Look, I really think we're in danger of blowing this thing out of proportion.'

Swope regretted the words the moment he spoke them.

'Austin, I don't think you have to explain the *proportions* of the situation to me. We currently have over eighteen hundred unsold units in the outer villages. And a lot more acreage waiting for the tractors to roll. Bad press is disastrous to us, even if you and I can convince one another that it is inaccurate or unfair. You know how far our necks are stuck out, PR-wise. We're selling a concept, not just land. Now, the role I see for you in all this is stopping that negative coverage from happening. And I seriously doubt that telling people they're blowing things out of proportion is going to get the sort of results EarthWorks wants.'

Swope was tempted to tell him he'd recently proposed measures that would have prevented the fracas, only to have them shot down by Savage's office. But there was no reason to start an argument he could only lose.

'Well, it looks like we're going to have to close the center for several weeks, anyway,' he said.

There was a staticky silence.

'That bad?'

'Yeah. Water.'

'Has Wooten looked at it?'

'Not yet.'

'All right. Report back to me once he does. And Austin . . .'

There was a long silence before Swope gave in.

'Yes?'

'Just so we're clear. There's been no final decision made on the manager's job. Not yet.'

And then, without another word, Savage hung up. Swope held the phone in front of him for a long while, as if he'd forgotten what it was. It wasn't until the beeping began that he slotted it back into its nest. Savage's parting comment howled through his mind. His heart began to pound and a cold film of sweat materialized on his skin. He couldn't believe the man had just threatened his job. The decision *had* already been made. Five years ago, when Barnaby hired him, Swope was to be the city's first manager. It was a done deal. They'd shaken on it. To deny him the title now would be criminal.

Savage couldn't mean it.

Swope instructed Evelyn to hold all calls, then walked over to the center of the office, stopping at the edge of the Newton

28

scale model. It was time to cool down. Take a minute and pull out of the nosedive he'd been in ever since that dawn call. He looked down at the model, taking comfort from its pristine, unchanging spread. Built by a team of Austrian artisans, it was the size of a regulation billiards table, covered with miniature houses and cars and people who, if you used a magnifying glass – and Swope had – had individual faces with distinct expressions. Everything in Vine's plan was here. The veinwork of bike paths and the village centers with their sawtooth roofs. The mall, the pavilion, the low-flung industrial parks on the city's outskirts – everything. Swope's own woody neighborhood of Mystic Hills. Even the carbuncular complexes of subsidized housing. At the exact center of it all stood the lake's simulacrum, its water-colored surface brilliant and unclouded, suggesting depths as infinite and mysterious as a Scottish loch.

He'd first seen the model in Barnaby's office in Chicago, back in late '67, when EarthWorks had flown him out for the big interview. Until then, he'd never really believed that the city would be anything more than a glorified subdivision. But on that day, as Barnaby spoke to him without interruption for over an hour, Swope's hard-won DC cynicism had crumbled like poorly mixed cement. Although he knew that Vine had given up a lucrative practice as one of the nation's most sought-after commercial architects to concentrate on the project, he had no idea how passionately the man believed in his new city. Newton would be no ordinary conurbation, Vine explained in a voice hushed by the weight of absolute conviction, no random collection of streets and houses and lives. This was going to be the place he'd been dreaming about ever since he came to Chicago in the early 1920s to serve as an apprentice architect at Louis Sullivan's old firm. The place where people would finally start living like they could. Look, he said, passing a conjurer's hand through the air above the model. No overhead power lines or billboards or factories to blot out the sky. With the exception of a single central building, nothing would rise above the trees. And Newton's citizens would work where they lived, in land-scaped business parks that housed new industries like

29

telecommunications and computers. They would shop in nearby village centers and worship under the discreetly steepled roofs of interfaith centers. Children would play in tot lots constructed of recycled tires and chipped wood, where every fall would be muffled, every knee remain unscraped. Most important, the city would contain a careful mix of middle-class and subsidized housing. People of different races and backgrounds would live together here. There would be no ghettos of poverty or privilege. And when Newton was done, Vine said with a matter-of-factness that sent a thrilled pulse along Swope's spine, they would build a dozen more cities. In the lowlands of North Carolina. Outside Dayton. Orange County. East of Augusta. North of Phoenix once the Salt River Project kicked in. All of them based on this perfect design.

By the time he'd finished Swope knew that he had to take this job. *This* was the future for him and his wife and his young son. Not in Washington or New York, but here, with this tall, straight-backed preacher's son from Nicodemus, Kansas, who believed he could create the perfect city with a T square and a pencil. Though a born doubter, Swope had been overwhelmed by the sheer, insane ambition of it all, the idea that Vine had built a model and now planned to make the world fit it. And when a hardworking black contractor named Earl Wooten arrived from St Louis a few days later to take up the post of general foreman, Swope could see he felt the same way, both of them believing that this was where all their toil and achievement had been leading – to this office and this man and his city.

They spent hours gathered around the model during that first heady year, Vine pointing out details with a long index finger as Swope and Wooten listened, hanging on his every word, both amazed at how the answers to their questions seemed to rise straight up out of the design. Some nights they were so intent that they forgot to eat or call home or even go to bed. Swope remembered one of these sessions in particular, during their first August together. The Democratic National Convention had come to Chicago, though none of them paid it much attention – it was a crucial phase for Newton, with

30

digging just begun on the first parcels of land. Gradually, however, a gathering wail of sirens penetrated the meeting in Vine's seventy-eighth-floor office, an incessant howl that seemed to come from every direction. Wooten, dressed in his customary outfit of pressed khaki pants and matching work shirt, strolled to the window to see what all the fuss was about.

'What is it?' Swope asked.

Wooten shrugged. He couldn't see.

'I'll tell you exactly what it is,' Vine said finally, his eyes never leaving the spread of blueprints in front of him. 'It's the past.'

It took Swope and Wooten a moment to understand. When they did, they shared a smile. And then they returned to work oblivious now to the sirens outside.

Those had been the best days for Swope. The Acquisition Phase. When life was simple. There was only one thing to do and he did it better than anyone else: buy land. The forty-four acres where Newton Plaza and its attendant lake now stood had been the first parcel. He'd coaxed it away from a bankrupt dairy farmer named Husted, who gladly signed over the deed when Swope offered to pick up his note. After that came the remaining 13,981 acres of contiguous soil, snapped up for prices that were a fraction of the going rate. God, what a time that had been. Traveling from farmhouse to farmhouse, sitting in those kitchens redolent of tired dirt, old Formica and yellowed wallpaper, he'd moved even the most intransigent of sellers. Most had been easy – the land was overfarmed, the market depressed. People couldn't wait to get their checks and hit Fort Lauderdale. And those who didn't want to sell were readily leveraged out by the pictures Swope painted of all those new houses and all those busy roads and – most decisively – all those poor blacks moving out from the Gomorrahs the locals referred to as Ballimore and Warshington. For those final few lacking the imagination to be scared off, Swope invoked liens and forgotten rights-of-way. It didn't matter that he occasionally had to play a bit rough. This was the future. Sacrifices would have to be made. And they were. Starting just a few days before they killed

Martin, he was able to wrap up his program by the time Buzz and Neil took their lunar stroll.

It was only then that things got complicated. In the intervening years Swope had to sweat every last legal detail involved in filling fourteen thousand empty acres with houses and schools and stores, with sewers and electricity and water. And with people – black and white, middle class and poor. Former hippies and hard-charging young bureaucrats; benumbed Vietnam vets and homebody engineers. It had been Swope who'd fought the zoning battles with the county and the road wars with the state; Swope who'd wheedled policing agreements out of Chones and low tax rates from the county commissioners. Four solid years spent doing what it took to make the model in front of him come to life. Drawing up leases with over six hundred separate businesses. Suing deadbeat suppliers and shoddy subcontractors. Getting social services in nearby cities and rural counties to round up enough poor folk to fill the HUD projects. He'd done it all. And now, come Labor Day, he would be the city's first manager. A three-year posting after which he would be a shoo-in for Congress in the newly configured Cannon County seat, kicking the hell out of the old-school Democrat who now slumbered his way back into office every two years with reshoveled New Deal horseshit. And after that, who knew? Senate. Governor. Or maybe even the big one, when a desolated party came looking for a savior.

Standing over the model, remembering all this, Swope soon realized that Savage was just blowing hot air at him. A little bit of managerial hardball. That was all it was. There was no way he could give the job to anyone else. No way. He knew what Swope had done. Could do. The threat was not real. The job was his. After all, it was to him that Barnaby had given his precious model when it came time to move it out to Newton.

'The Swope surveys his minions.'

He looked up from the model to see a scruffy teenage boy standing in the doorway. He was quite a sight, this kid. His long hair was limp with pubescent secretions; his small eyes almost invisible behind the purple-tinted granny glasses

32

perched at the end of his thin nose. His skin was so pale that it suggested bad diet and lurking disease. His chest seemed particularly meager, collapsed like a pothole where a breast-bone should have protruded.

His clothes were equally problematical. His army surplus jacket was emblazoned with a bizarre array of flags – Ecology, Union Jack, Skull and Bones, Old Glory, Rising Sun and, most baffling, the Republic of Panama. For equally obscure reasons, an alligator clip dangled from his breast pocket flap. Beneath the jacket was a T-shirt bearing the mirthless likeness of John Lennon and his demented-looking wife. The boy's Levi's were on the verge of disintegration, torn so widely that his bony knees poked through like twin skulls. If Swope didn't know better he'd have thought this was some kind of delinquent hippie dope fiend who should be immediately escorted from the premises.

But he did know better. This was his son and only child, Edward McDonald Swope. The flower of his generation, whose recently concluded high school career was the stuff of legend: 1590 on his SAT's. Awards up the wazoo: Moot Court, National Merit. Captain of the state champ High IQ Bowl team. Two separate scholarships to Harvard, where his admission to the law school was a foregone conclusion. This was no regular kid. This was his boy. Swope knew better than to sweat the clothes or the hair or anything else. All that would clear up, just like the acne. Leaving behind this amazing specimen. This miracle.

'Morning, Edward,' he said.

'Morning? I daresay not, padre.'

Swope checked his watch. It was already past noon. Jesus. He ambled across the carpet and settled in behind his desk, beckoning for his son to grab one of the leather chairs.

'So, Teddy – what the hell happened last night?'

33

2

Teddy stared at his clock radio with the single eye he was able
to pry open, waiting for one more minute to flip over before
he finally got out of bed. It was late: 11:19. This was the third
time he'd awoke this morning, starting with the 4 A.M.
stagger to the bathroom to void an evening's worth of Charles
Chips, French onion dip, Boone's Farm Tickle Pink and his
mother's famous lasagna. The second wake-up had come
when the phone rang around six, though he'd only been
conscious for a few seconds on that one. Since then his sleep
had been so dreamlessly deep that he'd left a residual puddle
of saliva on his pillow. His wrist was creased and humming; a
strand of long hair had become involved in the gunk gluing
his left eye shut. His tongue was dry and his bladder pulsed
painfully. It was definitely time to rise.

The clock moved, its number flipping like a lazily dealt
card. Ten more minutes, Teddy bargained with himself. In
return for that he would not do a single bong hit until 6 P.M.
Just as he closed the deal with himself a hot cell of headache
moved in behind his eye, reminding him just how insane
last night had been. True, now that it was summer every
night was supposed to be wild, a rolling party of wine and
weed and music whose master of ceremonies was none
other than Edward McDonald Swope. College loomed, and
Teddy would be damned if he didn't eke out every ounce of
hedonistic bliss from these last months of freedom. But
yesterday was no party. The fight had been a cataclysm, an
apocalypse that threatened the plans he'd so carefully laid for
a long valedictory bash before Harvard. Though fight was

34

perhaps the wrong word, suggesting a two-party scuffle, easily broken up and quickly forgotten. This had been a downright donnybrook, involving dozens of combatants gripped by deep tribal hatred. Teddy had watched in fascinated horror from the loft as they got it on, doing actual bodily harm with fists, feet and the martial arts weaponry that had become the rage since *Kung Fu* debuted. He and Joel and Susan had only narrowly escaped. If Teddy hadn't thought fast, who knew what those crazy fuckers would have done.

Though intense, the fight wasn't exactly a surprise. Trouble had been brewing at the teen center for weeks now. The converted silo had been getting increasingly rowdy, with new arrivals intent on causing mayhem showing up nightly. They were nothing like the old crowd, scruffy peace-loving kids who came in the cars their parents bought them, any riotous impulses they might possess muffled by Baggies of high-quality herb purchased with ample allowances. The newcomers were rednecks and angry blacks, brawling strangers who packed the silo like steer rustled from two genetically incompatible herds. The trouble had started in April, when the first ominous haiku of hatred had begun to appear on the walls. 'Fuck whitey suck my dick.' 'Niggers are assholes Allmans 4-ever.' Illiterate, but pithy. Toilets were clogged with tumors of paper; gum stoppered the drinking fountain. Stuff got stolen. The center's long-standing directors, married hippies named Josh and Merrie, had begun to go AWOL, leaving the silo to its own increasingly raucous devices.

The carefree integration that had existed since the center opened three years earlier vanished. Tough white migrants from West Virginia and Pennsylvania and their Cannon County cousins gathered on the top floor, where there was Ping-Pong. New blacks, not affable kids like Joel but remorseless boys and their gum-smacking girlfriends, congregated below them to play pool. There was no mixing other than in the bathrooms, which became a DMZ where one traveled at one's own risk. Which left Teddy and his crew nowhere to go but up into the silo's cramped loft, formerly used as a storage area for tumbling mats and surplus furniture.

Back when Teddy ruled the center, it had been a place where couples came to french and toke, an aerie that reeked of bongwater and Love's Baby Soft. Recently, however, it was the last place available to kids not part of the warring factions below. Their numbers had thinned recently, with old-timers seeking refuge at the mall or the slanting pier at the lake. By last night there were only eight of the original tribe left. They'd cowered invisibly below the loft's short wall when the melee broke out. As fists and furniture flew, Teddy finally understood that his days as king of the teen center were over.

The fight had started over music. A cacophony of private tape players had recently begun to fill the silo, replacing the Yes and King Crimson that had once echoed unchallenged on the center's big Panasonic system. After some records had been stolen a few weeks earlier the stereo was locked in the office, where it remained quiet until a half hour before the fighting broke out, when some rednecks Teddy had never seen before, hard-eyed crackers with stringy goatees and Confederate-patched sleeves, broke in and commandeered it. Their goal was brutally simple – to drive out the hated blacks by playing Edgar Winter's 'Frankenstein' as often and as loudly as the system could bear.

It wasn't long until the brothers stormed up the stairs to remonstrate, pointing out in their inimitable style that the inbuilt speakers drowned out their various small offerings of Stevie and the O'Jays. The whites, unmoved, bolted the office door. Teddy watched from on high, wondering if any of the black kids had actually *seen* the aptly named albino currently serenading them. In case they hadn't, the rednecks plastered the album sleeve to the window. The melanin-free Winter floated there, an apostle of honkyness for those proud African eyes to see. That was all it took. Converse-shod feet were aimed at the office's flimsy door, quickly splintering and dehingeing it. After a thirty-second scuffle a big black guy with a fisted pick in his hair broke through, tearing the needle off the record just as Edgar's synthesizer performed another rowdy breakdown. To Teddy, the ear-splitting scratch sounded like the end of more than just a song.

Shoves, kicks, punches. Pool cues were wielded, a Miller

quart chucked. Kung fu weaponry was deployed with vigor and skill. Teddy watched it all in astonishment. Although he and his friends had been the objects of menacing stares for weeks now, this was the first time he felt actually imperiled. Joel gathered Susan under his arm. Both looked scared and vulnerable. As the center's sole interracial couple, they'd been drawing dirty looks from both camps of late. Susan wanted to stop coming altogether after finding dried gobs of spit on her back when she took off her blouse one night. She'd been called a nigger lover once too much. And the ever-peaceable Joel had almost thrown a punch a few days earlier when a skinny black kid Tommed him. As Teddy considered whether or not to hold his ground a six ball flew over the railing, striking a gym mat with a dull thud.

'Comrades, let us repair to the drawing room,' he said.

'Affirmative, Will Robinson,' Joel answered.

Luckily, there was an exit on their level that led to the fire escape. Pushing open the door set off a gratuitous alarm – Teddy could already see the Cannon County sheriff's prowlers arriving in force. After reaching sea level the three of them ducked through the village center and out into the sleepy streets of Newton, where the hissing of gaslights intimated a ruined summer.

'Where to?' Joel asked once they were safe.

'I'd better get home,' Susan said. 'Curfew.'

'Yeah, me too.'

'Ah, children,' Teddy said.

They began to walk toward Susan's house. She lived in Fogwood, in one of the boxy aluminum houses her father sold. Teddy and Joel lived farther south, in Mystic Hills, where the houses were made of wood and the yards had trees.

'That was intense,' Joel said.

'It only confirms my hypothesis,' Teddy explained.

'Which is?'

'People are animals.'

'Animals are animals,' Susan said, flipping back a rogue blond strand. 'People are poeple.'

'Ah,' Teddy said. 'The tautologist speaks.'

'What did you call me?'

Joel diffused the brewing argument with the howled refrain of 'Let's Get It On.' Local dogs responded. They walked in silence until they reached Susan's house. Teddy watched from a few feet off as they frenched, right there in the road.

'I think I see Irma,' he said finally.

The couple broke apart as if they had been electrocuted. They stared at the house for signs of Susan's ever-vigilant mother. All was dark and quiet.

'Where?' Joel asked.

'I thought I saw a curtain move,' Teddy lied.

'I don't see anything,' Susan said, leveling a suspicious stare at him.

'Sorry. Next time I won't say anything.'

After she was inside Teddy and Joel continued on toward Mystic Hills.

'I wish you guys would get along,' Joel said, readjusting his omnipresent leather visor.

'Sorry, man.'

'It's just getting hard to hang with you both.'

Teddy felt a brief pulse of fear run through him.

'I said I'm sorry.'

'Yeah, well, anyway,' Joel said. 'You gonna tell your dad about tonight?'

'He'll hear. Prolly already has.'

'The Swope will be pissed.'

'Incanfuckingdescent.'

Joel smiled.

'I can just hear my dad,' he said, his voice going basso. *'Those kids have just got to stay in school. Educate themselves.'*

'The Earl.'

'Yeah.'

They made affectionate fun of their dads for a while, re-creating what would certainly be their horror at the fight. As they walked and talked Teddy couldn't help but think how much better it was without Susan around. They reached the top of his road. He was glad he'd left his car home. His head was spinning.

'Do you want to enter my humble abode and partake of the storied herb?'

'Better not,' Joel said. 'Got to get up early tomorrow.'

'Early? Egads.'

Joel kicked at a rare bit of loosened gravel.

'Nah, Susan and I were gonna spend the day in DC.'

Teddy suddenly felt a lot more sober.

'Really? Doing what?'

'Just hanging out.'

'Oh.'

They stood in silence for a moment.

'Well, have fun.'

'Yeah. I'll call when we get back.'

'Bring me one of those moon rocks everybody's talking about.'

Joel laughed and then he was gone. Teddy watched him for a moment before heading down to his own house. He couldn't believe that Joel was going to DC without inviting him. They always went there together. The Smithsonian. Watching the freaks on Dupont Circle. Drinking beers at the Rathskeller, where they never got carded. He hated the idea of Joel going with Susan and not him. It felt too much like getting ditched. And he swore he'd never let anybody do that to him again. Not ever. Sure, Susan had friends down there from her dad's army days, though that was no excuse for counting Teddy out. No excuse at all.

At home, he let himself in through the back door. His parents were asleep. He locked himself in his room, smoking one last bowl that quickly turned into three. He cranked up *Imagine* on the headphones, then *Plastic Ono*, then his customized Lennon-only Beatles tape. In between tokes he made his way through an entire pack of Hubba Bubba to quell his aroused taste buds, creating a brain-shaped mass on his nightstand with the spent pieces. As he smoked and chewed and listened he thought about what the teen center fight meant. The sound of that needle across Edgar's organ; the way the cops had stormed through the door, their night-sticks drawn, eager to apply wood shampoos. The days of the Fogwood Teen Center, the court of the great and sage Teddy Swope, were over. No more dispensing bowls of Panama Red as he told his friends about the *National*

Geographic documentary on the rope divers of Papua New Guinea or recounted the plots of *Siddhartha* and *The Crying of Lot 49*. Either his dad would close it or the place would be filled with so much security it wouldn't be worth the hassle. Despite the weed and Lennon's consoling voice, Teddy felt depressed. What was supposed to have been his last perfect summer before Harvard was suddenly looking deeply problematical. His hangout had been sacked by infidels. His best friend was otherwise engaged with a dumb blonde whose only virtues were an ass from heaven and a willingness to donate it to the cause of Joel's horniness.

Life sure could suck.

And then, because it was two-thirteen and you could only listen to 'Crippled Inside' so many times, he turned off the stereo, killed the light and hit the hay.

'Teddy?'

His eyes snapped open. Eleven forty-one. He'd somehow managed to fall back asleep. This had to be a record. Incredible. Sometimes Teddy amazed even himself.

His mother stood in the doorway.

'Hon? Sweetheart? Are you sick?'

'Only in my soul,' Teddy quipped.

Her pretty powdered nose wrinkled.

'What's that next to your bed?'

He looked at the mound of chewed gum.

'My brain.'

'Well, wrap it in something and put it in the trash, please.'

His mother slowly came into focus. She was dressed immaculately in one of her Mary Tyler Moore getups. Peach-colored pants suit. Matching hair band needlessly holding back spray-stiffened hair. Buffed jewelry, much of it shaped like seashells. Gooey black makeup.

'Do you want lunch?' she was asking.

'Surely you jest.'

'Well, I'll make a sandwich.'

'Go wild, Ma.'

In the shower he discovered a massive zit on his left shoulder. Sucker was a real ICBM. He launched it, sending a

40

dollop of creamy goo against the clouded glass door. He gave his johnson a few probing yanks but there simply wasn't enough blood this early in a hangover. Besides, he was out of pHisoHex, his lubricant of choice, as it not only provided optimum slickness but also fought the acne on his shaft. After showering he threw on some jeans and his *Two Virgins* T-shirt. It was the flagship of his wardrobe, custom silk-screened from the bootleg record he'd bought in Baltimore when he went for his interview at Hopkins, his number-two safety school. (Number one: Dartmouth. Three: Bowdoin. Four: Bucknell.) The front of the shirt showed John and Yoko buck naked, full frontal, Lennon's uncircumcised knob and Yoko's fun bags there for all the world to see. On the back you could see both of them bare-assed, just like on the record sleeve. Fairly fucking cool. It had been a month since he'd last worn it, having concluded it would not go down very well with the new crowd at the teen center. Today, he'd wear it in protest of his forced exile.

It was noon by the time he made it to the kitchen table, his hair wild and damp. His mother had been good to her word – a decrusted olive loaf sandwich rested on a mauve plastic plate, surrounded by a Vlasic wedge and a pile of chips. What you might call a culinary joke, Teddy thought. Beside it was a cup of scummy instant iced tea in which three contiguous crescents of ice melted. And a vitamin. Jesus. Here he was, almost eighteen, about to go to Harvard on twin rides, a National Merit and a Vernon T. Bagwell, whoever the fuck he was. And his mother still gave him a Flintstones vitamin. What's worse, it was Barney. She sat at the table, poking distastefully at a mound of low-fat cottage cheese that was speckled with pineapple chunks.

'I'm not eating that,' he said, nodding at his lunch from in front of the open fridge.

'I wish you would.'

Teddy grabbed a carton of orange juice and downed a slug straight from the wax spout. Watergate was on the small black-and-white. He watched as he drank, orange rivulets trailing down his chin. He wiped them away with the back of his wrist, then pointed at the screen with the carton.

'He's going down.'

'You think?' Sally asked.

Teddy mimed a flushing toilet.

'History. Ask Dad. He'll tell you.'

Sally pointed at his *Two Virgins* shirt with her fork.

'You're not actually wearing that thing, are you?'

'It would appear that I am.'

'Dear, it's pornographic.'

'Just like Adam and Eve were.'

'Well, look what happened to them.'

Teddy shrugged. His mom was Presbyterian.

'Would you at least put a shirt over it. It really is unbearable.'

'It's supposed to be.'

'Well, then, congratulations.'

He drank again. She gave him an exasperated look.

'All right,' Teddy said. 'I'll boil to death to make you happy.'

They watched the news for a while.

'Do you think Dad looks like John Dean?'

Sally tilted her head at the TV.

'Not so much looks like as brings to mind.' She speared a pineapple wedge and began to examine it. 'So did you have fun last night?'

Teddy shrugged.

'What did you do?'

'Stole a car. Drove to Vegas. Married a showgirl.'

'She nice?'

'Very.'

Sally bit off some of the fruit, then seemed to have second thoughts, retrieving the pulp between two painted nails and scraping it off on the edge of the plate.

'I heard there were fights at the teen center,' she said.

'Really? Who said that?'

'Your father.'

'Jesus, is there anything the Swope doesn't know?'

Sally searched the cottage cheese for acceptable fruit.

'Oh, there's things.'

A commercial came on. *It's not nice to fool Mother Nature.*

42

'Have you picked out a present for his birthday?'

'Not yet,' Teddy said.

'You should.' Sally yawned. 'He wants to see you as soon as you're up.'

'Why?'

'I imagine he wants an eyewitness account of the trouble.'

'All right. I was going to work on my novel, but.'

'Were Susan and Joel there last night?'

'We effected our escape together.'

'Teddy, I was going to ask you about that. I saw Irma at the bridge round-robin the other day and she said she thought the two of them were getting too serious.'

'Irma Truax is a Nazi.'

'Nonsense. What a thing to say.'

'Ma, the woman has a picture of Hitler in a scrapbook.'

Sally shot him a dubious look.

'I've seen it,' Teddy continued. 'Joel showed me. It was taken back in the thirties, when she was a tyke. Old Adolf came to her hometown and she was picked to give him a bouquet. She's got a picture of it. Hitler's bending over, patting her on the head.'

Sally stared at him for a moment.

'Are you sure it's Hitler? Mightn't it be one of his evil henchmen or something?'

'Mom. Please. Mustache? Three Stooges do? It's Hitler.'

'How strange. Though I suppose if she was just a girl . . .' Her voice trailed off.

'So anyway,' Teddy said, wanting to hear more. 'What did she say about Susan?'

'She said that they were thinking about breaking them up.'

Teddy looked at her for a moment.

'What the fuck does that mean? Break them up.'

'Edward, language.'

'Sorry. So . . .'

'Well, I suppose it means that she thinks the two of them are a bit too young to be so . . . serious.'

Teddy executed a terse, nullifying shake of his head.

'Never happen.'

'I don't know. She sounded pretty intent.'

'So what did you want to ask me about?'

'Well, I guess because you spend so much time together, I was wondering what you thought. I mean about them being so serious.'

They are, Teddy thought. Way too serious.

'They're dating, Ma. Isn't that what kids are supposed to do?'

'Well, anyway. She said she was going to have a word with Earl and Ardelia.'

They sat in silence. Teddy's mind reeled. Susan and Joel broken up. He knew that Susan's mom was weird about the two of them. And even Joel had begun taking flak from his parents, who were normally cool about everything. But Teddy had thought it was just the usual progenitorial bullshit. He never suspected for a moment that anyone was going to do anything as radical as break them up.

'Teddy?'

'Huh?'

'If you're not going to eat then you should go see your father. He sounded pretty anxious to speak with you.'

'Sure.' He smiled. 'I was going to hit him up for some change, anyway.'

It was a ten-minute drive to the Swope's office. Teddy raced through the quiet streets in the jet-black Firebird his folks had given him for acing his SAT's. New houses and new lawns and new trees flashed by. Japanese beetles kamikazed against his windshield. As he drove he smoked a quick pick-me-up joint he'd earlier leavened with the remnants of a gutted Camel. It was only after his second toke that he remembered his bargain with himself to lay off the herb until happy hour. Ah well, he thought. Tomorrow. Teddy had bigger worries, anyway. He couldn't stop thinking about what his mom had said about Joel and Susan. Normally, he wouldn't have paid it any mind. Sally was a sucker for gossip. But if Irma was making public threats, the situation must be serious. The possibility that his best friend might be forced to stop seeing the love of his life suddenly loomed. Joel would go nuts. For some reason, he was crazy about the girl. Not that

44

she wasn't a serious piece of tail, especially now that it was summer and she could let it all hang out. Long blond hair shining in the summer sun. Small firm tits bouncing under a halter top. Hip huggers cut just above her snatch. She was a honey, no doubt about that. It was just that she was so transcendentally stupid. She understood precisely nothing. Last night, before the riot, Teddy was describing the eighth chapter of his novel when he noticed Susan yawning, staring with bored and vacant eyes up into the smoky rafters. Which was something you did not do. Not to Teddy. Not in his loft. He'd tried talking to Joel about her brain deficiency a few times but the guy was thinking with his dick. He just couldn't see that the girl had pablum between her ears. Not that Susan's stupidity was a problem in itself. There were a lot of stupid people in the world. They served their purpose. They made up the curve. If there weren't stupid people then Teddy would have never got 1590 on his SAT's. Their *D*'s made his *A*'s possible. It was just that Susan didn't seem to understand that she was stupid. She was forever chirping in with her opinions, arguing with Teddy about things that were beyond discussion. Claiming, for instance, that McCartney wrote 'Revolution.' Unbelievable. Or announcing that she thought *The King of Marvin Gardens* was boring. And Joel actually listened to her, swallowing her insipid little pearls of wisdom without even the smallest gag.

It made Teddy yearn for the time when there had just been him and Joel, the summer four years ago when their fathers moved them out here to the middle of nowhere. At first, Teddy had hated leaving Potomac for this wasteland. Conditions were primitive back then. Strictly *Omega Man*. No more than two dozen houses were occupied when they arrived, each of them as isolated as frontier forts. The land around them was pocked and smoldering. It looked like a war zone, where two terrible armies had fought to a bloody standstill before withdrawing in shattered defeat. Churned earth, roofless structures and piles of rubble were everywhere. Instead of Potomac's comfortably worn houses there were timber frames and foundation ditches and big, scavenging machines that moved slowly over the land, leaving behind smudges of suspended smoke. You could barely move without tripping over a survey stake. The reports of hammers filled the air, sounding like the last, desperate fusillade of a retreating platoon. Newton Plaza and the mall had not even been built, while the lake was just a big weedy field.

But then he met Joel. Their fathers threw them together at the beginning of that first summer, a couple of thirteen-year-olds recently exiled to a place that wasn't even a place yet. Their first few minutes together were painfully uncomfortable. Joel was shy back then and Teddy had never even spoken to a black kid, except for that time he'd been mugged outside the Smithsonian, and then only to say sure, take the money, just don't hit me. But they soon discovered they had the same bikes – metallic-blue Schwinn choppers with sissy bars and banana seats. That was it. They were off, vaulting drainage ditches and daredeviling over mounds of dozed clay. They rode every day that first summer, from the crack of dawn until twilight. The city was transformed from a hostile wasteland into an exotic wilderness. The concrete foundations of schools became mazes; corrugated iron drainpipes were turned into tunnels they would penetrate with flashlit daring. The condemned houses of the locals his dad was evicting became hideouts where they would sometimes find left-behind magazines and photos and letters which Teddy would use as fuel for the elaborate stories he had already begun to weave.

They even invented their own game: house jumping. The rules were simple. They would stand together on the upper floor of one of the city's hundreds of unfinished house frames, surrounded by stenciled plywood and tape-crossed windows. Side by side, they would inch up to the edge of the abyss where stairs had yet to be installed. Two stories below, in the pitch-black basement, rested the bags of cement mix and bales of bubblegum-pink insulation they'd constructed into a big cushion before climbing the ladder to the top floor. Joel would grab Teddy's hand and count to three. And then they'd jump, falling at exactly the same speed, confirming what Teddy already knew about Galileo and gravity. Disappearing for a terrible moment into utter darkness before hitting the soft pile. Teddy could never have done it without Joel grabbing his hand. He would have been too scared, his mind too alive with the possibilities of fractured ankles or rusty nails. But once he felt Joel's cool dark skin around his it was easy. He could have done anything.

That first best summer ended on the day they were bused as freshmen to Cannon County High. It was an ordeal for them both. Teddy, accustomed to the property-taxed comfort of Potomac's schools, suddenly found himself in a brick warehouse surrounded by jostling farmboys and sullen, ignorant teachers. The things he had to offer, the precocious intelligence and sharp invincible tongue, had no currency out here. And Joel was tormented horribly by the Powdertown blacks, the sons of casual laborers and cleaning women who mocked his clothes and speech. Teddy would sit in dread on the long bus ride they took each morning, gripping the safety rail so tightly that its metallic stench clung to his hands all day. The screeching bell that seemed to ring through the school's halls every five minutes rattled through his synapses like an instrument invented to torture him alone.

But their tribulations made them even closer. Some days they cut school and wandered the unfinished city, buying lunch from one of the dimpled metal trucks that served the construction workers. They had to be careful – Joel's father could appear in his Ranchero as suddenly as a summer storm. But they were never caught. The school had bigger disciplinary problems than the whereabouts of a couple of scrawny freshmen. Any protests their parents might have at the number of unexcused absences were quickly stifled by the phalanx of *A*'s both boys achieved by simply showing up on test days.

Newton High opened the next year and everything changed. Suddenly, Teddy and Joel found themselves among several hundred kids just like them. A new school – no cliques or gangs or tribes. Even better, Joel's mother was vice principal, a daunting, blazingly articulate woman who was fearsome to those who didn't know her. Nobody was about to mess with Ardelia Wooten's son and his friend, the boy whose father sat behind those gleaming panels of mirrored glass on top of the tower just erected at the city's center. The first two years there were perfect. They ran the place. Teddy was the smartest kid, Joel the most popular. Teddy had no problem letting his friend be the one everybody liked. Other kids, he was beginning to realize, were stupid. Cattle, who listened to Top 40 and read the books idiot teachers gave them. He didn't give a shit what they thought. As long as he had Joel the others didn't matter. Things didn't even change when, at the end of their sophomore year, Joel began to get girlfriends. As he turned fifteen his voice deepened and his jaw broadened; he grew four inches and the awkwardness went out of his smile. The girls began to flock. White, black – it didn't matter. They all loved Joel. He treated them with a neglect that only seemed to make them more desperate. After he'd french or finger them he'd always come to Teddy, telling him about the stupid things they said, the noises they made. Once he let Teddy smell the pussy juice staining the end of the finger he'd slid into Veronica Teller's panties. Teddy had almost puked, though later when he thought about it he got hard. He never really had any girlfriends. All girls wanted to talk to him about was Joel. They were just a bunch of Cynthias, anyway. His Yoko had yet to arrive.

For two long and perfect years Teddy and Joel lived in this paradise. But then, during the fall of the senior year, Renaissance Heights opened. Bad kids began to roam menacingly through Newton High's unwalled pods. The school became charged with an undercurrent of violence. There had not been a single fight in its first two years – now there seemed to be one every day. Teddy could see the worry on Ardelia's face. Worst of all, his status as co-king of the school was ignored by this new wave of students. By Christmas he was dying to get out.

Making matters even worse was the advent of Miss Susan Truax. She'd appeared that September from Fort Meade, where she'd lived with her lunatic mother and ugly duckling sister while her father fought Charles in Nam. Her dad now peddled aluminums down at the model village. The other boys in the school went nuts with her arrival but Teddy decided to play it cool. If she understood, she could come to him. But she didn't understand. Instead, she just sat there in a corner of the cafeteria, sipping chocolate milk and flipping through teen magazines. Boys would come up and take their best shots but she'd just shoot them down. It was almost like she was waiting for someone. Teddy tried to make eye contact to let her know that he was different from the rest. But she never met his eye. She never met anybody's eye. She just sat there. Sipping and flipping.

Until Joel showed. He'd missed the first two weeks of school with the mono he'd caught from some bimbo at the teen center. He was sitting with Teddy at their table when she walked in, a big balloon of Dubble Bubble attached to her pouting mouth like some blimp towering her along. As she sat the bubble burst, a pink veil collapsing demurely over her face. She collected it with a single swirl of her finger and deposited it behind her frosted lips.

'And who', Joel asked, 'might this be?'

'Her name's Susan something. She has the IQ of a wombat.'

Joel simply stared at her. She flipped page after page of a magazine with Bobby Sherman on the cover, tiny bubbles detonating against her molars. For almost two minutes Joel eyeballed the girl. Teddy kept quiet. He'd seen this before. Her radar would pick him up eventually. Alarms would go off. Planes would be scrambled; the doors of the missile silos would slide open.

She'd look.

Finally, she tossed the magazine on the table with a bored sigh, then let her eyes travel aimlessly around the cafeteria. She saw Joel. When their eyes met he smiled. That simple, unfaceted smile Teddy had seen a million times. She smirked back defiantly, then rolled her eyes. Joel's expression remained unchanged. He nodded his head. Slowly. Once. This seemed to confuse her. She collected her books and walked quickly off to fifth period.

'Good God,' Joel said, watching her go.

'What?' Teddy asked.

By the end of the month they were going steady. She was Joel's first official girlfriend. From the beginning, Teddy could tell that this was different. Joel gabbed about her all the time. He'd never talked about girls before with anything other than dismissive indifference. Now, he'd bore Teddy to tears with stories of the little things she did or the clever words she said. At first Teddy tried to answer with sarcasm, but Joel always seemed to miss the slice and spin of his remarks. It was like her stupidity was rubbing off on him. For Christmas she bought him this hand-tooled leather visor down in DC, a ridiculous item, its brim decorated with black curlicues that looked like fossilized spermatozoa. But Joel, usually so cool, planted it on his sleek head like a crown. And there it stayed. Religiously. No matter how often Teddy pointed out what a doofus it made him look, he just wouldn't take it off. It was from Susan. Ergo, it was perfect.

This was what Teddy suddenly found himself dealing with as his senior year rambled on. What made things even worse was the fact that Susan disliked him. Intensely. From the first. She failed to laugh at his simplest jokes and even teased him about not having a girlfriend, laughing out loud when he explained the Yoko Principle. Their time together often degenerated into bickering sessions, with Joel standing silently by, failing, for the first time ever, to take Teddy's side. Some days Teddy would call the Wootens only to be told by Ardelia that Joel had gone out, and no, there wasn't a message for him.

And then, a few months ago, he'd overheard Susan say something. They were at their usual table in the cafeteria. Teddy had gone to get some Jell-O to quell a lingering uprising of the munchies but turned back after realizing he'd left his money in his ski jacket. Susan was sitting on Joel's lap. Their backs were to Teddy as he approached the table.

'So I suppose Mr Fag-Along will be coming,' she said, referring to their plan to see *The Poseidon Adventure* that weekend.

'Shut up, Susan,' Joel said.

But his voice was free of anger. He spoke the words wearily, as if he'd said them a hundred times before. Teddy froze, staring at the backs of their heads for a moment, a hot pulse of temper running through him. Thoughts of Michael

Corleone returning to the table in that Brooklyn restaurant ran through his mind. He quickly regained his composure, returning to his chair as if nothing had happened. But it had. And Teddy wasn't about to forget it.

That spring he got into Harvard, Joel to Bucknell. Teddy began making noises about maybe going to Safety School Four to room with his friend but his father had strafed that plan on the runway. Still, Lewisburg and Cambridge were only a few hours apart. Weekends were an option. And they had the summer together. Only, summer was suddenly looking precarious. Without the teen center it was hard to imagine where they could hang. There was the closed pier at the lake, though Susan didn't like it there. And the mall shut at nine. They had their respective rec rooms, though it was never the same with parents nearby. Teddy yearned for those first days in the city, when it was just him and Joel. Butch and Sundance. The Omega Men. Some nights as he sat in bed smoking and listening to John and Yoko he found himself wishing that they could go house jumping again. Just the two of them, falling into the darkness at the exact same speed.

He raced into Newton Plaza's parking lot, skidding to a stop next to the striped curb by the main entrance. The squeal of his tires echoed down to the lake. Heads turned. The shadow of a No Parking sign fell across the Firebird's hood. Some suit scowled at him. Teddy just nodded back. The first time he'd parked here a security guard had threatened to have him towed. Teddy had casually mentioned his last name. Nobody'd bothered him since.

He popped a Sucret into his mouth to mask the joint's reek, then slid out of the car, riding a released cloud of freon and dope towards the building. He glimpsed himself in the mirrored window, looking cool in his shades and khaki jacket. Only the tops of John's and Yoko's heads were visible – everybody could relax, there would be no gratuitous parental embarrassment. He pushed through the revolving doors and made his way across the lobby's marble expanse. It was crowded with EarthWorkers, many of them holding blueprint

51

canisters like relay batons. The air was filled with the hushed scuffle of rubber soles. There was Muzak as well, 'The Age of Aquarius.' He waited for an elevator beneath a portrait of Barnaby Vine. Teddy had met the old guy a couple times. He was all right. A genius, supposedly, though lately his plan for the new city didn't seem quite as hot as it had a few years earlier. He'd had another stroke recently. Not that it mattered. Soon, the Swope would be running things.

The elevator up was crowded. The little ditty Teddy had made up the other day started playing through his mind. 'Bebe Rebozo, can't blow his nose-oh.' Some of the other passengers started to titter and Teddy realized he was saying it out loud. He smiled. It *was* fairly fucking funny. He watched the riders in the door's polished brass, wondering what it must be like to work every day, to take orders and worry about getting fired. Harvard might be like that. Maybe things wouldn't be so easy up there. Though he doubted it. During his fall visit he'd spent the afternoon with some juniors who didn't seem all that hot.

He arrived at his father's floor, blowing past the receptionists with a nod. People said hello when they recognized him. It was a good feeling, being the boss's son. He started thinking about what it must feel like to be his father, coming up here every day knowing that you're the main man. Especially when you've pulled yourself out of the quagmire like he did. The last kid of a big, poor Michigan family, too young to be anything but a mistake. *His* dad a strike-breaking maintenance man at River Rouge, over fifty when little Austin arrived. All those drunk brothers and pregnant nieces. Teddy had seen the house where he grew up in Grand Rapids. An unloaded shotgun shack. He sometimes pictured his dad when he was his age, putting himself through Wayne State and then Michigan Law while his family and friends took jobs on assembly lines. Coming to DC because that's where the juice was. The only way he could have done it was to know that he was different. It was a knowledge that allowed him to see the same special qualities in his son. So even on those occasions when Teddy fucked up – that DWI mix-up down in Cannon City, for instance – he knew that his

52

dad, deep down, understood. Because, deep down, they were the same.

Evelyn was at her desk, looking more gargoylian than ever.

'Hello, Edward,' she said with a sour smile. 'He's expecting you.'

Teddy felt the usual rush of vertigo as he strode into his father's office. It was those two glass walls – they always freaked him out. Like stepping out of an elevator straight on top of K2. Other than that, the office was strictly corporate. A conversation pit at one end, sofas and a half dozen chairs. His father's big desk, catty-cornered where the glass walls met. The two Cross pens angled into a brass holder at the edge of the blotter looked like SAM missiles. His father stood at the model that centered the place, staring down at its toy houses and doll people with a worried expression.

'The Swope surveys his minions.'

He turned and grimaced.

'Morning, Edward,' he said wearily, pointing to a chair by his desk.

'Morning? I daresay not, padre.'

Teddy dropped into one of the chairs facing the desk. His father sat in his own leather seat, leaning back into the space where the windows met.

'So, Teddy – what the hell happened last night?'

'It was pretty hairy.'

'So I gather.'

'Hatfields and McCoys. These guys were out of control.'

'I'm telling people it was outsiders.'

Teddy grimaced.

'Not strictly true.'

His father shook a Tiparillo from the packet on his desk and lit it. He stared at his son through the resulting cloud of smoke.

'Go ahead,' he said softly.

'I recognized lots of them from school. Blacks *and* whites. Residents of our very own metropolis.'

His father blew out a thin cloud of smoke.

'I'm thinking of closing the teen center for the summer.'

53

'Well, *I'm* not going back there. Though I get the feeling . . .'

'Go on.'

'Well, I don't think it's the teen center that's the problem.'

'No. But still. It'll calm jangled nerves.'

'You know what the problem is, don't you?'

'What's that?'

'It's the plan.'

'Explain.'

'The projects. They were a bad idea from the start. From before the start.'

'But they're integral to Mr Vine's thinking,' his father said with zero conviction.

'Well, just 'cause something's integral doesn't mean it can't be wrong. Ever heard of the calculus?'

'I'm sure *he* has.'

'How is the old Vine Man, anyway?'

'Scuttlebutt is the second stroke was a doozy.'

'Well, whether *he's* integral or not, I think somebody's going to have to do some rethinking. There are some pretty nervous muchachos out there.'

'I know.' His father sighed. 'You want some lunch?'

'I'm not really that hungry.'

'All right.' His dad's small hands thudded down on his blotter. 'Well, I better get back to work.'

Teddy stood and looked down at his father.

'Hey, Dad,' he said tenderly. 'I mean, come the fall, you can handle this how you see fit, right? Vine and all them. It'll just be you and your infinite wisdom.'

'I guess you're right,' his father said wistfully.

Of course I am, Teddy almost said. But didn't.

3

Earl Wooten was driving fast. On the straightaways he pushed seventy; through turns he never dipped below thirty. Although his Ranchero's workhorse motor began to sputter and wheeze asthmatically after just a few minutes of this madness, he continued to power down the empty roads, ignoring the just-planted stop signs and freshly posted speed limits. At intersections he barely brushed his brakes. When he cornered, his tools slid across the vehicle's bed like a team of silent movie comedians. He didn't bother to check his rearview mirror – the only thing back there was a long cloud of reddish dust.

Wooten was driving fast for one simple reason: he could. These were his roads. Nobody would pull him out here. The law had yet to arrive in this part of the city. Back in the finished villages, in Fogwood and Mystic Hills and Juniper Bend, you had the overworked deputies of Cannon County to worry about, the vigilant eyes of newly arrived parents and even the EarthWorks security guards, lame as they were. Speed there and somebody would call you on it. And beyond the city limits there were state troopers, stone-faced men who didn't know Earl Wooten, who would only see a shine with a thousand dollars' worth of Craftsman tools in a late-model Ford. But here, in this no-man's-land of unpaved streets and unbuilt houses, this between place that was not yet city but no longer country, Wooten had no one to answer to but himself. He could go as fast as he wanted.

He had to admit – it felt good. After thirty years of driving with a feather between sole and gas pedal, Wooten had finally

55

found a place he could speed. Out here, cops could not pull him over for the unpardonable offense of doing five miles under the limit. They couldn't stop him for signaling right when he was turning right or coming to a complete stop at flashing red lights. He would never have to hand over license and registration to deputies who took them back to their cars for five, ten, *fifteen* minutes, only to return them without apology. The white men he worked with sometimes jokingly asked why he drove so fast on sites and so slow in the world. Wooten just smiled. His black colleagues – what few there were – didn't have to ask.

So on he sped, cutting across the unpaved parking lot of the soon-to-be-completed Whistler's Grove Elementary School. His wheels rattled through small ridges and gullies, bouncing Wooten like a baby on a footloose uncle's knee. At the lot's far end he jumped a curb, the giddy sensation causing him to whoop reflexively, though the celebration died on landing when the car lurched unexpectedly to the right. For a few seconds Wooten was close to losing control, saved only by the strength of his big hands. He eased off the accelerator after that, letting the car slow to a respectable speed. A solo wreck out here would be hard to explain.

By the time he reached the Newton Pike he was creeping along. As his car slowed, his mind sped up. There was still a day's work ahead of him. First came the snap inspection of Underhill. After that, the meeting with Austin to discuss the lake and the teen center. And then, provided there weren't any more gaslight explosions, home, where he would finally have that talk with Joel. There would be no more speeding today. And certainly no unit 27; no velveteen sheets and crackling fat and daylight slumber.

He'd had his little fun.

As if to remind him of this fact the naked frame of the Underhill project appeared on the eastern side of the pike. At first glance, the site looked abandoned. Wooten felt a brief swell of anger. He wondered if Vota and his men had finally gone too far, knocking off several hours early to visit a Cannon City bar or wherever else those ridge-runners got to when they weren't working. He hoped so. He'd been itching for an excuse to fire Vota. No union or government agency could protect a man who knocked off early. But then he saw a flash of stainless steel on one of the project's box girders. Figures began to appear. The Vota crew was still on the job. Doing as little as possible by the look of it. No more than a half dozen of the thirty men were working. The rest had gathered around a lunch truck. Wooten checked his watch. After two. Unbelievable.

He turned off the pike, his anger gathering as he passed the HUD sign. Vota was a goldbricker of the first order, a glorified ditch digger who'd been getting fat at the federal tit for twenty years. Wooten had been ragging him to get a move on for over a month now. Underhill was seriously behind schedule. But Vota was the most maddening sort of foreman, the kind who would agree to everything you said and then go off and not do it. He was an expert at hiding the sort of hard evidence of incompetence needed to dismiss him. Last week Wooten had spent the best part of a day breathing down his neck just to make sure he put the box girders up straight. And now he could see that next to nothing had been done since. The girders stood bare in the morning sun, the air surrounding them free of the dust that always hovered around a productive site. Vota's crew had the clean, relaxed look of men getting ready to start the day rather than reaching its end. And the foreman himself was nowhere in sight.

Wooten skidded to a stop thirty feet from the lunch truck. The workers watched him stonily as he approached. All of them were white. A rarity at EarthWorks. The old wariness made an unsolicited return, further souring Wooten's mood.

'Where's Vota?' he asked before he even reached them.

His voice came out louder than he'd intended. The few men working up on the girders stilled their tools and looked down. The goldbrickers by the truck exchanged glances. Wooten waited. Finally, one of them, a scrawny man with hair down to the middle of his back, gestured toward a Johnny-on-the-Spot with his Mountain Dew can, sloshing some of its coolant-green fluid onto the trammeled clay. Wooten stared at the portable toilet, uncertain how to proceed. There was no way he was going to call Vota out. That would be too much of a direct challenge. He was tempted to order the men back to work himself, but that would open the door for defiance. He realized with a sinking heart that there was nothing to do but suffer thirty cold stares as he waited for the man to finish crapping.

He looked around. Underhill was a nice site, shaded by the three surrounding hills that provided its name. In fact, all the city's HUD complexes were prime spots. It was how Barnaby thought. Streetscaping. The nicer the location, the better people who lived there would act. It was one of the few things about Vine's thinking Wooten found dubious. He'd spent enough time in picturesque Ozark countryside to know that it took a lot more than pretty scenery to stop people acting nasty.

Vota finally emerged from the plastic tank, a rolled magazine in his hand. He was a short, fat man whose already ample cheeks were further distended by a large plug of chaw. He waddled casually toward the truck, whacking his thick thigh with the scroll. The tools on his belt flapped like the wings of a flightless bird. His stride didn't break when he saw Wooten, though the magazine froze. A bland smile twisted lips that were flecked with tobacco.

'Earl, what can I do for you today,' he said.

Wooten was about to correct him about the uninvited use of his first name, but decided to let it ride. That's just how men like Vota worked. Got you looking at the small stuff so you'd forget the important things. There was movement in the corner of Wooten's eye. He marked it instinctively. But it was just the lunch truck driver, a wizened geezer with a paper catering hat, closing down his dimpled metal hatches, like some bit actor in a bad Western clearing the streets before the final showdown.

'You can put some fire walls on those girders, for starters,' Wooten said flatly. 'You can do the job you're being paid for.'

The smile on Vota's face was the sort you'd give a small child.

'Well, that's exactly what we're doing,' he said, his voice shot through with studied forbearance.

'I don't think it is, Mr Vota.'

'Well,' Vota said, still smiling. 'You're mistaken.'

'No.' Wooten said evenly. 'There's only one mistake around here and you're one more word away from making it.'

The smile finally disappeared. Vota held Wooten's eye for a moment. Then, with great deliberation, he turned and spat out a stream of rusty liquid. Wooten felt the anger move through him. Though directed away from him, that spit might just as well have caught him squarely in the face. Men like Vota knew what spitting in front of a black man meant. A few more glances were shared among the crew. No one spoke for several seconds. Even the lunch man had stopped moving.

And then it ended. A split second before Wooten threw caution to the wind and fired a man who didn't technically work for him, Vota pulled back from the brink. He shrugged, that smile returning to his stained lips.

'Well, boys, looks like the break is over.'

The men responded sluggishly, finishing off their drinks before tossing them toward the plastic bag hanging from the truck's flank. A few missed. They simply left them there, more trash on an already underpoliced site.

'I want those fire walls up by the end of business to-morrow,' Wooten commanded. 'Understand?'

Vota sighed and let his eyes wander across the wooded hills. After five seconds passed he nodded vaguely. Wooten knew that he wasn't going to get any more satisfaction from this man unless he spent the next two hours bird-dogging his sorry ass. And he didn't have the time for that. Not with the lake and the teen center and his own son to deal with. Besides, he didn't trust his response if one more drop of spit passed through that man's lips.

He was halfway to the Ranchero when he heard the laughter. A reedy, mirthless sound – the chatter of gorging scavengers. Vota's low growl was chief among them. Wooten was tempted to turn and ask if there was something he'd like to say. But he knew that was exactly what the man wanted – a futile show of temper that would either escalate out of control or leave him looking like some toothless fool. So Earl Wooten did what his mother had taught him nearly forty years earlier when faced with a battle you could not win.

He kept on walking.

It wasn't until he reached Juniper Bend that he felt his anger begin to fade. That was it. Vota was through. He'd inform Austin that the man had crossed the line. Swope would find a way to fire him, government rules or not. Getting rid of seemingly untouchable people was high on the list of the many things Austin Swope knew how to do. By the end of the week that fat hillbilly would be swallowing his own spit. Still, it rankled. Not just Vota's attitude but Wooten's own indecisive response. Challenges to his authority had become so rare lately that he was getting rusty at dealing with them. Ten years ago it would have been different. Back then, he'd faced down chumps like Vota twice a week, wielding an invisible power that men responded to like a dog to a high-pitched whistle. Authority, he realized, was something you had to keep working on. Like muscle. And, like muscle, it could go soft if it wasn't exercised enough.

Wooten fretted for a while that maybe that was what was happening here. He was going soft. Maybe the money and the respect were eating away at the very part of him that made his success possible in the first place. The cash, for instance. A decade ago hardly a minute would pass without him worrying about having enough to keep his family safe and secure. These days, however, he hardly worried about money at all. His 1972 performance bonus had been a staggering twenty-four thousand dollars, more money than his grandfather could have made in five lifetimes. But it wasn't just the green. There was the respect as well. He no longer had to fight for it. It was just there, like God's grace. Maybe that was why he had so much trouble dealing with men like Vota. Incidents like the one he'd just endured had become as rare as April snow. In fact, in the last few months the respect afforded Wooten seemed to be on the verge of going nationwide. There had even been two magazine articles, a short piece in *Look* entitled 'New City's Master Builder' and an embarrassingly complimentary spread in *Ebony* called 'From Mississippi Mud to Maryland Gold.' Phone calls had followed. Parren Mitchell. Vernon Jordan. Someone from the NAACP and a trustee of Howard University. Just to tell him how proud they were.

And then, just three nights ago, there had been another call, one that Wooten suspected might be the culmination of the respect he'd been banking ever since he left St Louis. Gus Savage, phoning him at home. Which was doubly unusual. Before that, he'd had scarce contact with the EarthWorks CEO. The man had more on his mind than housing starts or surface drainage problems or cement-vegetation ratios. For him to call Wooten outside office hours was unprecedented. But they'd wound up talking for nearly an hour. Savage had surprised Wooten with a series of vague questions. Things like 'Are you happy?' and 'Is our experiment working?' Wooten, who liked to deal in weights and measures, in costs and deadlines, had been warily tongue-tied at first, though he gradually began to unburden himself, speaking of his pride in what they'd accomplished as well as his unease at some of the recent strife. Savage listened intently.

'Earl, here's the thing,' he said when Wooten finished. 'We'd like you to fly out here next week.'

'Sure. Is there a problem?'

'On the contrary. We'd like to discuss your future.'

Wooten paused, waiting for more. But there was just an expectant silence.

'Well, yes, of course.'

'How about a week from now? Friday? You could catch a late plane on Thursday and then grab the red-eye home.'

'That would be fine.'

'We'll arrange the tickets on this end.'

'Any chance of my knowing what this is about before then?'

'Let's just say you'll be surprised and gratified. Very. Oh, and Earl – let's keep this talk between thee and me, shall we?'

'I'm not sure exactly what you mean.'

'Don't tell anyone you're coming.'

'Including Austin?'

'Including Austin.'

Wooten hesitated. He already had one secret too many in his life. The last thing he needed was another.

'Is that a problem?' Savage asked.

Wooten snapped out of it. If Savage told him to keep his mouth shut, then that was how it would have to be. He must have his reasons. You didn't get to be a man like Savage if you didn't have your reasons. Austin would understand if he found out. He was, after all, a company man. Just like Wooten.

'No, Gus. No problem at all.'

The phone call puzzled him for the next few days. Clearly something big was in the offing, though Wooten couldn't figure out what it might be. Even though he'd been with EarthWorks for five years, he was still not accustomed to the hidden grammar of office politics. That was Austin's domain. And then, just yesterday, he was grabbing a quick lunch in the Newton Plaza cafeteria when Richard Holmes, the young personnel executive who headed EarthWorks Afro-Am, stopped by his table.

'Just thought I'd let you know that we're behind you, Earl,' Holmes said, plucking out the unlit pipe he kept perpetually clenched between his lips.

'That's good to know, Richard,' Wooten deadpanned. 'What the hell are you talking about?'

Holmes made a show of looking around to see if anyone was watching. His voice dropped a dozen decibels.

'Your candidacy for the city manager post.'

'You've lost me, my friend.'

'I was talking to Hollis Watson back in Chicago and he said he heard it was in the works. All hush-hush, you know.'

Wooten stared evenly at Holmes.

'I guarantee you I do not have the slightest notion what you're talking about.'

'That's cool.'

Holmes's slang irritated Wooten.

'Richard, at summer's end Austin Swope will be named Newton's first manager. And at that time I fully expect you and everybody else in Afro-Am to get behind *him*.'

Holmes planted his pipe back between his lips and held up his hands in mock surrender.

'I understand,' he muttered. 'Mum's the word.'

Though annoyed, Wooten quickly dismissed the exchange. There was no chance of him being offered city manager. Holmes had got his information seriously wrong. Somewhere between Savage's office and Newton Plaza the message had become deeply distorted. Whatever they had in mind for Wooten, city manager was not it. The job was Swope's, period. Ardelia seemed particularly skeptical about the notion when he mentioned his conversation with Holmes.

'I don't know, Earl,' she said, leveling that look of hers over her reading glasses. 'I can't really see it, myself.'

'Why's that? You think I'm not smart enough?'

Wooten said the words with a smile, but there was something in them. Ardelia Wilson, daughter of a prosperous undertaker, valedictorian at Sumner High, had gained a BA from St Louis University back in the days when he was riding around in the back of exhaust-spewing pickups, a rusty shovel between his knees.

'It's not smarts you need, hon,' she said.

'What is it, then?'

'Craftiness.'

'And I suppose I'm deficient in that.'

'Husband, if you weren't I'd have never married you.'

Her words stung Wooten, raising the specter of the apartment 27 situation and all the craftiness he'd employed to keep her ignorant of it. He decided it was best to let the matter drop. Besides, the discussion was moot. City manager was Swope's job. Vine had promised it to him. Even in the unlikely event they really did want to give it to Wooten, there was no way he'd take it. He couldn't do that to his friend.

Which left open the issue of what Savage had in mind. After all, the main building in Newton was done. The infrastructure was laid, the big projects – the lake, the mall, the Plaza – completed. From now on it was just a question of chasing after goldbrickers like Vota. There had been talk about Wooten building the next new city out near Dayton, but he wasn't sure he wanted that. God knew he'd put up enough houses for one lifetime. From shotgun shacks to five-thousand-square-footers like his own, he'd built plenty. Each job leading to something bigger. When he was thirteen he'd left school to dig a ditch, a sewer line connecting a housing development in Florissant to the St Louis County mains. Before long he was carving foundations for cheap GI housing out of Mississippi mud. Then the bankers at Boatmen's gave him enough seed money to build the houses perched on those foundations. Two-fams, bungalows, even white-flight ranches on acreage out in La Due. Row upon row in the rubble of East St Louis. Until, finally, the great Barnaby Vine read about him in the *St Louis American* and asked him to build his city, teaming him up with a sharp-eyed lawyer and setting them loose on fourteen thousand acres of border-state clay. He was forty-four now, old enough to stop running around in a hard hat. Building Newton seemed to be a logical conclusion to an enterprise he'd started when he raised those first pink calluses on his hands back in 1942. A splendid conclusion. But still a conclusion.

Which still left the question of what Chicago had in mind for him.

Wooten entered the outer reaches of Fogwood, the first of the city's six villages to be completed. Everything looked righteous. Benevolent cumuli dotted the June sky. There were moving vans everywhere, a few of them navigating quiet cul-de-sacs, the rest berthed outside new houses, their gangplanks running to the edges of sodden lawns. Vista Cruisers and Country Squires bearing Ohio or Pennsylvania or Michigan plates were parked nearby. Still-slim mothers hovered as movers carried oak dressers and grandfather clocks up walkways that Wooten's men had poured just weeks earlier. Their husbands, men with just a hint of paunch – guys nobody was going to ask to pitch in and help tote the last of the furniture – kicked futilely at loose edges of sod. Boys drove their chopper bikes right off vans while their sisters formed whispering cabals with new neighbors.

Wooten passed some kids playing baseball on a just-raked infield that three years earlier had been bouldered pasture-land. Now it was as smooth as ice, able to carry anything with some mustard on it for extra bases. Just as Wooten looked a batter hit a frozen rope into the gap in left center. A skinny black kid took off after it, his sneakers kicking up blades of cut grass. At the last moment he stuck up his glove, shagging the fly just before it passed over his head. He stared at his webbing, astonished. The batter, rounding first, dropped to his knees. The fielders began to pirouette; gloves flew up in the air like a flock of flushed geese. The game was over.

In another part of the park he saw a man and his two sons launch an Estes rocket. The parachute blossomed like a sudden cloud in the midday sky. A few blocks later he saw a black family emerge stretching from a station wagon with Alabama plates, staring up at the house they were about to inhabit with unabashed awe. He rode by streets with names like Gandolph's Grotto and Barnaby's Folly and The Great Gatsby. There was no roadkill, no litter or graffiti. No billboards or power lines or fences.

It was perfect.

Wooten marveled at the city he'd built. The way the sun hit the forked mist of a sprinkler to create minor rainbows, or the bat kite that crashed down into a jungle gym but continued to fly inside the bars like a newly caged creature. Three boys perched in the upper floor of a house frame chucked rocks into a pile of unpoured concrete, each impact raising small clouds that looked like the dust kicked up when the *Eagle* blasted off from the Sea of Tranquillity.

And then he saw the silo and his good spirits vanished. From what he'd heard, the fight had been the worst yet. Chones's deputies, by all accounts, had overreacted, using their nightsticks freely on any nappy head that came into view. Luckily, Joel had been able to escape. Wooten was deeply relieved when he got the news from Ardelia after calling home this morning. Though the boy had a good head on his shoulders, Wooten still fretted about him getting dragged into a situation he couldn't control. Especially with that girl on his arm. Wooten felt the small flutter of dread that accompanied every thought of Miss Susan Truax. White as toothpaste and pretty as the spring day surrounding him. Wooten knew it was 1973, knew the city was supposed to be integrated and that things like Joel and Susan were exactly what Barnaby had in mind. But the first time he'd seen his son walking beside that gleaming blond hair and those little round hips, his borderline blood pressure just about went through the roof. Oh yes, she was sweet as the day was long, ma'aming and sirring and always offering to help Ardelia in the kitchen. And the girl certainly seemed to be crazy about the boy, hanging on his every word, jealously usurping his attention with all the usual pouts and prods. Her father was ex-army, working now as a realtor, many rungs below Wooten on the EarthWorks ladder. Which, he had to admit, made him feel secretly proud. And, well, as far as pretty went – which in Wooten's experience was pretty far – he had to hand it to his son. The girl was gorgeous. There were moments when he'd find his own eye wandering. Ardelia caught him at it once, those green irises of hers rising over her reading glasses like the cold light of a winter dawn. But the alarm that had tripped when he'd met her last fall still rang, slow and low and insistent, like a burglar bell on a neglected house. The battery may be about to run out but that didn't mean that anybody's given the all-clear. Not yet, anyway. And the fact that no one else could hear it – not his wife or his colleagues or, as far as he could tell, the girl's folks – didn't mean the thing wasn't still ringing. Wooten pictured his big, good-natured, brown-skinned boy and that snow-white girl caught between last night's warring factions of crackers and ghetto hoodlums. The thought chilled him to the bone. He was definitely going to have to talk with Joel. Tonight. Just to let him know that the situation wasn't necessarily as simple as young love. Just to let him know that he should be careful.

The familiar profile of Renaissance Heights' squat brown buildings came into view. The inexplicable jumble of feelings that always gripped Wooten at the sight of the place reared up inside him. The car seemed to lurch forward to get him past, his size thirteen steel-toed boot pressing down unconsciously on the gas pedal. It had been four days since he'd been. Four long days since his latest final resolution not to visit those velveteen sheets ever again. Breaking his own rule about speed, Wooten pushed the Ranchero up to thirty-five. Just to get him by that entrance.

You're a fine one to tell your son about being careful,

he thought as he put the place into his rearview mirror. A fine one.

A car almost hit Wooten as he pulled into the Newton Plaza parking lot. It appeared without warning, speeding heedlessly out onto the pike. Wooten had to mount the curb to avoid it. Only when the offending vehicle had vanished did he realize it was Teddy Swope's Firebird. Wooten shook his head as he drove through the crowded lot. He'd been meaning to speak with Austin about Teddy's driving, even though he doubted it would do much good. Although Swope was the smartest man Wooten had ever known, he was as blind as a mole when it came to his son. Not that Teddy was a bad kid. Just reckless. Neglectful. But there was no telling Austin that. He thought the sun rose and set on that strange child. Wooten had learned like many others in Newton that the best thing to do was just keep out of his way. He was secretly glad that Teddy and Joel would be separating come fall. Four years of Edward Swope was enough for anybody's lifetime.

He pulled himself out of his car, stealing a quick, reluctant glance down at the lake, where dead fish sparkled like floaters after a deep eye rub. He'd swung by first thing that morning, hoping that maybe the kill would be limited to a small fraction of the population. Fat chance. They were all going to die. The sight reminded him of how the hillbillies back home used to throw dynamite into a pond, killing every last thing just so they could get some dinner. He'd have to organize a crew to clean them out. The idea of using union men to row around the lake netting fish you couldn't even fry drove Wooten half to distraction. Worse still, he'd have to wait another month at least to get out there and do some real fishing of his own.

He recalled the lake's creation as he walked toward the building. Digging it had been, without doubt, the biggest construction project of his life. Starting with nothing more than a few tired-looking pastures surrounding a cow pond, he'd created this immense body of water. For most of the job he'd used the infernal machine EarthWorks had sent down from one of their discreetly owned Pennsylvania lignite mines, a bucket-wheel excavator that was able to gouge out forty acres of glistening clay and rock in just two weeks of merciless digging. What a machine that was, its eight-tread foundation nearly the size of a coal barge, its glass tower over three stories high. It took a team of four engineers to control the long steel claws that scooped clay from the ground like so much butterscotch ice cream. To fill the basin they'd cut a six-mile concrete aqueduct to the Patuxent. It had been opened last fall with a small ceremony, a frail Barnaby hammering away the chocks in front of a crowd of EarthWorkers and county elders. Wooten couldn't imagine what had gone wrong. Maybe the things just didn't take. Sometimes, that happened. No matter how much you planned or hard you worked, sometimes things just didn't take.

Upstairs, Evelyn passed Wooten into the office with a sour nod. Austin was in the process of hanging up the phone when he entered. He looked grave. Wooten lowered his big frame into one of the chairs facing the desk. It responded with a sound like cracking knuckles.

Swope nodded to the phone.

'Those were our friends from the hatchery,' he said.

'They have any theories?'

Swope shrugged.

'The best they can come up with is some sort of runoff from a site.'

Wooten shook his head.

'No chance. I'd know if there was effluent slurrying around.'

'That's what I told them.'

'I'll get a crew out first thing tomorrow,' Wooten said. 'We'll have to keep them out there for a few days. Some of those fish might take a while to die.'

Swope grimaced his approval, then looked out the nearest wall, his eyes tracking a rogue puff of cloud as it moved east.

'So I suppose you heard about the trouble over in Fogwood,' he said.

'Joel said it was pretty bad.'

'I was on the phone to Chones half the morning.' Swope finally met Wooten's eye. 'Five arrests.'

Wooten sucked air between his teeth.

'All from Newton,' Swope explained. 'And all black.'

'Now there's a surprise.'

'Chones swears that's just how it worked out.'

'Uh-huh.'

'I'll tell you,' Swope said wistfully. 'I can't wait until incorporation. We can get some of our own damned cops out here.'

'We always knew this would be a tricky time, Austin.'

'Tell that to Chicago. I've been getting memos up the wazoo from Savage about all this bad press we've been getting.' Swope looked at Wooten, a thin smile suddenly creasing his face. 'Well, most of us.'

Wooten scowled away the remark. He spent a long moment searching for the right thing to say. Discussion of headquarters with Austin had become difficult since Savage's call. Every time the subject came up he was tempted simply to tell him about his trip, just so there wouldn't be any misunderstandings if news happened to come out. But, once again, Wooten bit his tongue. Savage had asked him to keep quiet. And Savage was the boss.

'Well, what does Gus recommend be done?' he asked instead.

'Oh, he's not too forthcoming on methodology. He just wants results.'

'So what are you going to do?'

'I'm inclined to close the center for the summer.'

'Will Chicago allow that?'

'If we tell them there are structural reasons to keep it closed, yeah.'

'Are there?'

Swope met Wooten's eye. He shook his head in that slow, sly manner he had, his foxy face looking like it had just stumbled into an unguarded hatch of fat chickens.

'Ah.'

'Look, Earl – there's no way I want to have a repeat of last night's fiasco.'

'And Chicago definitely won't let it be closed for security reasons?'

'They think it'll look bad. And they're right.'

'But won't people see through this?'

'Not if it's you saying that it has to stay closed.'

Wooten's eyes traveled to Swope's blotter, filled with scribbles and half words, the residue of his busy mind. Another lie. They seemed to be adding up these days.

'Come on, Earl. Help me out here.'

Wooten met his friend's eye. As much as he hated to lie, there was no way he could deny him. Not with everything they'd been through together.

'All right.'

'Thanks, Earl, I owe you.'

Wooten remembered Vota's growling laugh.

'In that case, there's something I'd like you to do for me.'

'Name it.'

'Fire Joe Vota.'

Swope didn't bat an eye.

'Gladly. Why?'

'He's messing up bad. They're already two weeks behind.'

'Jesus. You talk to him about it?'

Wooten nodded.

'I think Mr Vota has a problem accepting instruction from a boss of a certain ethnicity.'

'Fuck him. He's history.'

'It might be hard, him being on a HUD contract.'

Swope smiled.

'Excuse me, Mr Wooten, but are you questioning my ability to terminate Joe Vota's employment in a manner both expeditious and absolute?'

Wooten returned the smile.

'No, I suppose I'm not, counselor.' He pushed himself up from his chair. 'Well, I best be getting back to work. Listen, Austin . . .'

Swope waited.

'It's summer. Be patient. Things will cool off.'

'Yeah. I know.'

70

Their business concluded, the men nodded an agreeable farewell to each other, just as they had nearly every day for these last five years. And then Wooten turned and made his way back across the big, sun-soaked office. By the time he reached the door he was hurrying. The day was getting old and there was still much to do.

4

'Something stinks in this place.'

'Ma'am?'

'That smell. What's that smell?'

John Truax had been just about to start the last droning stanza of his sales litany when the woman interrupted him. He pushed his right hand deeper into the pocket of his forest-green EarthWorks blazer, knowing immediately that it was the odor of his own putrid flesh snaking through the Ticonderoga's usual smells, the carpet shampoo and pine disinfectant, the freon and rogue motes of dust baked by the afternoon light. It must be getting worse. Usually, the ointment, muslin wrap and single leather glove were enough to keep the rot at bay.

'I don't smell anything, ma'am,' he said, staring right into the woman's eyes.

'Really? Because I thought there was something . . . funky.'

Truax nodded once, then turned back to the bedroom. For a brief moment he was tempted to simply walk away, leaving behind the stink and the shame and everything else he hated about this job. But of course he didn't. He stood his ground and pressed ahead with the sales speech they'd taught him, saying the words he'd said a thousand times before. But hurrying now. Wanting to get out of here before the stench became undeniable.

'Right, then. This is the master bedroom. You'll notice that there's an en suite bathroom and . . .'

As Truax spoke he secretly measured the couple, trying to

gauge the odds of a sale. Somewhere between poor and nonexistent, he guessed. They were younger than most of the people who came to him. Mid-twenties. No kids. Both teachers, just hired at Newton High. He was Social Studies, she was Math. He had narrow shoulders and a jackal's smile rimmed by a short scratchy beard. Turtleneck sweater, corduroy pants and Hush Puppies. Math was tall, no tits and long frizzy hair captured in a multicolored scarf. The skinny ankles sticking out beneath her peasant skirt were covered with fine down. It was obviously her idea that they walk through the models. Social Studies made it clear that he saw the visit as an exercise in comic futility.

They had strolled into his office just after lunch, Social Studies announcing that they were out to 'test the housing market waters.' After that he lapsed into a sullen, superior silence, letting his wife run the show. As she blabbered on he surveyed the office walls, his eyes coming to rest on the picture of Truax in combat fatigues at My Song. The jackal's smile tugged even harder at his lips. That smile remained fixed as Truax showed them through the Lexington and the Concord, the Gettysburg and the Bunker Hill, his expression suggesting that the walls and fixtures and carpeting were confirming something at once comic and vaguely sinister. By the time they reached the Ticonderoga, Truax was simply going through the motions.

He finished his spiel.

'The yards aren't very big,' Math said after a moment, moving over to the window.

'Well, no. But, in Newton, you're never more than a quarter mile from a playground or park.'

Social Studies snorted. Truax shot him a look. What the hell was wrong with this candyass?

'I like this one the best, though,' Math said, still at the window. 'What's it called again?'

'The Ticonderoga. Bought one of these myself.'

'Are there any lots left in Mystic Hills?'

You must be joking, Truax thought.

'Well, no.' He took a breath. 'In fact, this is the last remaining specimen.'

73

'What?' she asked, pointing at the floor. '*This?*'

'Yes.'

'But it's a model.'

'Well, yes. But identical to the others.'

Social Studies rolled his eyes.

'I don't want to live in a model,' Math said. 'I mean, what about all the buyers walking around all day?'

'Oh, no. The model village is closing. All the houses you've seen today are available for immediate occupancy.'

'Are they cheaper than the others?' Math asked.

'Well, there's a base price that we're supposed to work from, but they generally give us some leeway.'

She looked at her husband.

'Hon?'

Social Studies shrugged. He'd save his remarks for later.

'Are there any questions you might have?' Truax asked, hoping the answer was no.

'Could you explain that VOP thingamajig again?' Math asked.

'VOC. Absolutely.' Truax recited the words it had taken him days to learn. 'This is a feature exclusive to EarthWorks homes. The VOC filtration network is a household system which rids the dwelling of nearly all VOCs – that means volatile organic compounds – released from building materials as they undergo normal settling. It consists of a series of pleated filters located discreetly throughout the home which snatch mold and free radicals from the air. This, together with', he pointed to the window, 'our state-of-the-art weather stripping and insulation, makes for a caulked and sealed environment.'

'Wow,' Math said blandly. 'Sounds impressive.'

'It is,' Truax answered.

'I have a question,' Social Studies said.

Truax turned slowly toward him.

'Why are they all named for battles?' he asked, his eyes settling squarely on Truax for the first time.

'Come again?'

'These . . .' he raised the first two fingers of each hand to his hairy cheeks and wriggled them, 'these *homes* you've been

74

showing us. They're all named for battles in which people were killed.'

As opposed to battles in which people were not killed, Truax thought. But did not say.

'They're Colonials,' he guessed.

'Gettysburg isn't from the Colonial period. Nor is Ticonderoga.'

Truax held the man's gaze.

'I can give you the names of some people in the planning department at EarthWorks,' he said eventually. 'I'm sure they'd be able to field your question.'

Social Studies snorted.

'That I'd like to hear,' he said.

Truax looked from the man to his wife.

'Tell you what,' he said. 'Why not come on back to the office. I can give you some literature. We can kick around some numbers.'

'Run something up the flagpole,' Social Studies said in a thin, hectoring voice. 'See if anybody salutes it.'

Truax made sure his eyes stayed off the man. He took a deep, controlling breath as he turned to lead them out of the room.

'Wonder why they haven't named one for Khe Sanh,' Social Studies asked his wife in a stage whisper.

Just keep walking, Truax told himself as he made his way through the house. He focused on the things EarthWorks had installed to give the place a lived-in look. The small table with its glued down bifocals and snifter filled with two fingers of brandy-colored plastic. Cubes of family photos culled from a Sears catalog. The rows of *Reader's Digest* condensed classics. The desk laid out in a seductive state of disarray, with the bogus note he'd read almost every day for over a year now: *Get J from school at 2:30.*

Back on the cul-de-sac he put some air between himself and the couple. He walked quickly, a pleasant summer breeze ruffling his hair. It still felt strange to have hair moving across his scalp. After a lifelong brush cut he'd finally allowed his hair to grow in when one of the other salesmen had suggested it was a bit too severe for buyers. It came in thick and wavy as a child's. Behind him the couple were whispering, plotting their escape. They were goners. Either they'd hold out for the next phase in the newer villages or grab an out-parcel in the county to build on. Either way, trying to peddle them a model had been a wasted hour. Yet another in a series.

It had been like this for two months now, ever since the last of Fogwood's lots had been sold. The other salesmen were long gone, leaving Truax behind to hold down the fort and peddle the models. He'd yet to move one. People's reactions were always the same when he told them that this was all that was available. Disappointment and a vague distaste at being offered something that had been tramped through by a thousand strange feet. One woman had likened it to being offered display underwear at Montgomery Ward. This was the New City, after all. People wanted new houses. Truax had room on price but the houses were still proving impossible to move. Not that he was really in a hurry to get rid of them. Although he could certainly use the commission, once the models were gone he'd be out of a job. For the second time in three years.

He neared the sales office at the top of the gated cul-de-sac of model homes. Strangely enough, he was going to miss it, this nonplace nobody had ever called home. When he'd first come here it had seemed otherworldly, a colony of asphalt and aluminum stuck out in the middle of scarred pasture. Cow pies dotted the land just beyond lawns that looked like they had been lovingly nurtured for generations. EarthWorks had paid attention to the details, from the children's toys bolted to the front walks to the American flags hanging beside every door. Since his arrival Truax had spent nearly as much time in the models as he had at his own house. It had been a good place to be, a between world where he could come for eight or ten hours each day, a way station that had all the features of the society he was supposed to join but little of the aggravation. Having enlisted when he was seventeen, he had never learned civilian life. If Newton was the only place for him in America, then this cul-de-sac proved the perfect spot for him to get into the swing of Newton. Here, he could figure out how to stand in a room and talk with strangers. How to deal with people who had never been in battle or thought about honor.

But that was all to end. The between time was over. Whatever grace the models had held for him had evaporated in May, when he learned there would be no new posting for him in one of the city's outlying villages. His colleagues, men and women he had never really got to know, had either taken up these jobs or been offered spots with Century 21 down in Montgomery County. But not him. As soon as the models were sold he was going to have to find something else to do.

There would be no Century 21 for John Truax.

He led the couple into the sales office. The NOW SELLING dirigible tethered to the roof moved in the afternoon breeze like a fish in a tank. The multicolored pennants festooning the building clapped politely with each gust. Inside, Math accepted the information kit while her husband looked at his watch.

'Ready, hon?' she asked.

Social Studies turned to Truax, his jackal's smile suggesting he'd conjured one final quip. But then he saw the look in Truax's eyes. The look he'd learned twenty years ago and never unlearned. A sergeant named Mackey had taught it to him at Fort Bragg. Whatever was on the tip of Social Studies's tongue died suddenly. He looked away, startled by his own fear, then wheeled and walked out the door. Truax watched the couple slide into their Karmann Ghia. The high-pitched hum of the VW engine was reminiscent of the man's voice. The car made a sarcastic, squealing left onto Camelback Lane and was gone.

Truax went into his cubicle, where his Selectric purred on the steel desk like a fat, happy cat. He turned it on in the morning and let it run all day, even though serious typing would have been impossible with his bad hand. He took the logbook from the top right drawer and entered the visit, using the green Flair for no sale. Writing with the slow, childish left-handed scrawl he'd been teaching himself. There was a lot of green on this month's page.

Next, he removed the metal box from his lower drawer, the

one filled with ointments and unguents and antibiotics, the small vials of clove and mint aromatics, the yards of gauze. After double-checking that no new customers were coming, he took off his glove and examined the bandage. Small moist islands had appeared on the flesh-colored fabric. The odor was strong, peppermint and bad meat. He slowly unwrapped the dressing. As he worked he became aware of his family staring at him from the edge of his desk, their Sears photo-portraits lined up like a mute jury. On the left was Irma, the foreman, with her probationary smile and eyes that expected the good life after nearly twenty years of waiting. Next to her was Darryl, his youngest, once his baby but so distant at fourteen that she didn't even mean him when she said father. She spent nearly every night at Young Life meetings, clapping and singing hymns until midnight, getting fat on Kool-Aid and Oreos. She spent weekends at the Interfaith Center with Reverend Abernathy, a guitar-strumming draft dodger who once asked Truax if he wanted to pray for their sins in Vietnam. *Their sins*. Truax had merely stared the man down, earning two weeks of enmity from his daughter. Now, every time they met, Abernathy merely smiled wordlessly, having no doubt slotted Truax into the circle of hell reserved for Calley and Westmoreland. As if he knew anything. As if he knew one single thing.

He finished unwrapping the bandage, stuffing it into the plastic bag he'd leave in a Dumpster behind Giant. He examined his hand. The infection looked bad. Having started at the initial puncture near the base of his pinkie, it had made its way up to the tips of each of his four fingers and down to his lifeline, where it now paused, like an army at a wide river. If it reached the wrist then the hand would have to go. The risk of general infection would be too great. That was the one thing everyone was in agreement about.

He ran the fingertips of his good hand over the septic flesh, bloodless blue in some places, meaty and cracked in others. They thought it was just a bad case of pseudomonas at first, though it soon became clear that it was something much rarer. Other names were uttered. Necrotizing fasciities. Tenosynovitis. Brucella. Pastuerella multocida. Putrid Hand

Syndrome. Mycobacterium of various sorts. Sporotrichosis. None of them proved adequate. Various treatments were attempted. Antibiotics. Povidone-iodine solution. Exsanguination followed by radical debridement. But nothing worked. The infection was in the flesh and then it became the flesh, feeding off his blood. His hand still moved a little when he asked it and felt dully if he whacked it. But it was not his. It was not his body and certainly not his odor. The last doctor, a wizened old dermatologist at Bethesda Naval, had offered to take it off. No bullshit. No balloon juice. Just lop the sucker off. In his opinion, it would certainly not get better and it would probably get worse, so they might as well get it over with. For a moment, Truax had been tempted. Just for a moment. But tempted still.

He dried off the scummy ponds with a series of cotton balls, then began to apply the half dozen lotions he used, gently spreading each until it was a glistening film. Next, he wrapped the hand in fresh gauze, working expertly now, his left hand and teeth well practiced. After this he dribbled on the peppermint extract and then, finally, pulled on the glove. This was his umpteenth pair. He had a cardboard box in the basement filled with their unused mates. For some reason he couldn't bring himself to chuck them out.

As he worked he stole a glance at the last of the photos. Susan. The one member of the jury who hadn't decided on his guilt. Impossibly beautiful against the ethereal blue Sears background. A coltish little girl when he'd gone off to fight; a gorgeous dreamy teenager when he returned. Almost as old as Irma when he met her. For a moment he let himself get lost in that, the thought of his wife at eighteen straddling a battered bicycle, her cheap dress hiked up over her knees, revealing swatches of snowy thigh. God, those thighs. Staring at him, haughty and horny and not knowing two words of English, as he walked toward her through the hot German summer with two melting ice creams in his fists.

He cleated the dressing and called home, riding that wave of nostalgia. Irma answered on the fourteenth ring, her tongue thickened by schnapps.

'Ja?'

'Say *hello*, Irma.'

'Hello, Irma.'

Truax looked at her photo on the desk.

'So how are things there?'

'Just peachy.'

She laughed bitterly. Peach brandy was her current daytime poison. The whisky sours were for night.

'What are you doing?'

'I was looking at the Vatergate.'

'The girls around?'

'Darryl's out. Susan's in her room.' There was a pause, a sip. 'She wanted to go down to the jungle with the panther. I said no. So, she pouts.'

Truax said nothing.

'John, we really have to do something.'

'We've talked about this, Irma.'

She muttered something in German. Words he couldn't understand.

'What?'

'Say good-bye, Irma,' she said in an accent that was pure American.

Her phone rattled like dice in a cup. He waited for the dial tone, then replaced his receiver. His wife was beginning to frighten him. There had always been anger in her and he liked that. Always been a sharp tongue and he'd liked that as well, especially when she was young and hungrier than any woman he'd ever known. He'd figured you couldn't have one without the other; that anger was just passion that hadn't ripened yet. But now there was no hunger, no passion. Just bitterness, an emotion primarily directed against their eldest daughter. Irma's hostility toward Susan had shocked him upon his return. It was like walking into an ambush. The screaming fights and slammed doors; the piercing hateful looks and contemptuous names. There was no reason he could see for this war that had started to rage just as his own was ending. Irma saw evil in the girl's soul; claimed she was lazy and conniving and promiscuous. Susan reacted in kind. The true source of his wife's feelings hadn't become clear until this winter, when Truax had stood in his garage on a bitterly cold evening and watched Susan bicycle into the driveway, her hair tucked into a woven hat she'd found among Irma's old things. And it suddenly struck Truax that she was the picture of her mother on those frozen Sundays back in Frankfurt, when Irmagard Westphal and PFC John Truax would flee the city on the bike they borrowed from her postman father, looking for a place to make love. They would tumble into the first barn or bombed-out house they found, not caring how cold it was, generating so much heat between them that they forgot it was January in a country that seemed to have no warmth left. The moment he saw this he realized that Irma was standing next to him in the garage, watching their daughter as well. He could see from the twist of her eyes that she was thinking the same thing – that Susan had become the girl she once was. And Truax knew that she hated her for it.

So the girl had to be punished. At first the onslaught was limited to sarcasm and petty prohibitions, interwoven with hysterical eruptions of doting affection. And then, when none of these managed to sweep away the fact that Susan was young and beautiful, came the real attack. Irma's strategy was clear – she would stop her daughter from being with the charming, good-looking kid who was proving to be her first true love, a boy from a different culture who had become the object of the same rebellious passion Irma had focused on her American twenty years earlier. If Irma couldn't be young, then neither could Susan.

Only, there was nothing wrong with the boy. He was bright and clean and polite. And he was Earl Wooten's son. With any of the others Truax could have gone along with Irma simply to have some peace. The Steves and Lances with their long hair and slouching rudeness, their mysteriously runny noses and vegetal whiffs. But Joel Wooten was no Steve or Lance. And it wasn't just because his father was a big shot. Joel was everything you could ask for in a boy, especially these days. College-bound. From a good family.

But black. Deeply, radiantly, undeniably black. Not Harry Belafonte black. Not OJ black. No, he was Jim Brown black. It wasn't that Truax gave a damn – the thing about being in the service for so long was that you had to make up your mind about black guys. Either you had a major problem with them or none at all. Truax had gone the latter route. Sure, some of the bloods, with their head scarves and black power regalia, could be a royal pain in the ass, though truth be told they were no worse than the white draftees. Better – at least they could fight. Irma, on the other hand, had hit the roof the first time she saw Joel. Truax could feel her simmering rage as this amiable kid drank iced tea in their kitchen that day last October when Susan finally unveiled him. The strength of Irma's disgust had taken Truax by surprise. She claimed the idea of Susan kissing him made her sick to her stomach. As if she and her friends hadn't chased black GI's. When the schnapps flowed it all came out. Talk about black cock and jungle bunnies for grandkids. Her rage at Susan's youth compounded by the fact that the girl had chosen someone who was at once perfect and forbidden. Chosen, and then refused to apologize for it. Just as Irma did a generation earlier, spitting in the faces of her we-were-never-Nazi parents.

She could get nowhere with Susan, of course. Any common ground mother and daughter shared was too poisoned for even the most benign conversation about Joel. So she got to work on Truax instead. Telling him it was his duty as a husband and father to end this thing. Even though he liked Joel more every time he saw him, even though he knew that crossing Earl Wooten would be suicidal, Truax tried, simply to placate the raging woman who shared his bed. But it had been a miserable failure. Susan, usually so passive, suddenly had an answer for everything. She didn't want to see anyone else – was he really suggesting she go back to the Lances and the Steves? Yes, it was true, she was serious about Joel, but weren't they always telling her she wasn't serious about anything?

'Why is it now I've found something I care about, you guys want to take it away?' she demanded, forty-nine-cent mascara streaking her cheeks.

Which, she accused, left only one reason – skin color. If Joel hadn't been Earl Wooten's son, Truax would have toughed that one out as well. If the kid were some transplanted Baltimore brother up in Renaissance Heights or even the son of one of the dozen good black families he'd sold houses to this past year, he would have just gone ahead and given him the boot, taken whatever heat needed to be taken for a prejudice he didn't possess. If they wanted to call him a bigot, fine. He'd been called worse. But if he pulled a stunt like that with Wooten's son then he'd be finished at Earth-Works. This was the city of the future and the future, Truax knew, did not involve giving polite, respectful, college-bound suitors the boot because they were black. Truax had thrown in his hat with EarthWorks. It was his outfit. If he screwed up here then finding a decent job elsewhere would be impossible.

In the end, having run out of arguments and fatherly persuasion, he'd simply given up. Two weeks ago he'd told Irma that he saw nothing wrong with Susan and Joel dating. He explained that her reasons for disliking the boy were wrong and, even if he accepted them, his hands were tied. They would just have to live with it. Besides, Joel was off to college soon, while Susan still had her senior year left. Let them have their summer and then nature would take its course. He was the head of the family and this was the best decision for them all. Period.

Irma's reaction surprised him. She seemed to take the news in stride, saying nothing for the first few days. But then, one night in bed, after he'd wrapped a bandage on his hand and was just about to fall asleep, she started.

'They're fucking, you know.'

He raised himself to an elbow.

'What?'

'That buck nigger's fucking your little girl.'

Irma's knowledge of English improved markedly when the subject was hate.

'Don't say that, Irma.'

'It's true.'

'Of course it isn't.'

'Up the ass. In her mouth. You know them. They mark their bitches with cum.'

'How can you say these things?'

'I can see it in her eyes. She has fucked eyes. You know? Like this.'

Irma screwed up her face into a grotesque pornographic sneer.

'I don't believe you.'

'If they were, would you break them up?'

'I'm not going to talk about this.'

'Answer me, John. If you knew for a fact they were having the sex, would you put a stop to them? Or are you going to pimp for Earl Wooten?'

'Of course I'd stop it,' he said softly.

She said nothing more about it. Not that night, not the next day. Truax had begun to put the whole unhappy conversation down to just another drunken outburst when, three days later, Irma stopped him as he passed the laundry room on his way to the garage.

'John, come in here for a moment, please.'

It was that *please* that sent a chill through him. She stood next to a clothes hamper, holding a pair of Susan's panties. She raised them up to him.

'Smell.'

'Irma . . .'

'Riech doch mal!'

He had just begun to shake his head when she reached up with sudden ferocity, clinching the back of his thick neck with her left hand and pushing the underpants against his nostrils. She caught him just as he inhaled. He pushed her violently away, but not before he realized that this was not piss or shit he was smelling. He'd whiffed enough feces in his day to know it when he smelled it. Rising from poorly built latrines, the K-ration gruel smeared on *Stars and Stripes* or fat plantain leaves. Leaking from the trousers of dead or wounded or just plain scared soldiers. The enemy's sweet, rice-studded scat, smeared on the tip of a pungee stick. Buffalo shit and dog shit and rat shit and pig shit – Sergeant John Truax knew shit. This was different. A sweet organic rot, thick enough to chew. An odor he fleetingly associated with Tu Do whisky bars and the highland Quonset huts fronted by fast-talking teenage pimps. A heady cocktail of pussy, jism and sweat every soldier claimed to know as well as the stink from his own pits.

He pushed his wife's hand away.

'Do not do that to me again.'

'You know, John.'

He shook his head. Not thinking about this. Not ever thinking about it.

He checked his watch. Almost three. Time to close up and head home. Nobody would be coming now. Nobody serious. Not when there were brand-new houses for sale in the outer villages. He'd pick up a six of Schaefer at Giant after stowing his stink in the Dumpster. The Orioles were at home for twi-night against the Angels. Palmer and McNally on the mound. There were going to be some 0-for-8's in the visiting dugout.

But there was one more thing he had to do before calling it a day – phone Swope. He'd been putting it off long enough. He didn't want to arrive at Saturday's party without having made contact. That would look bad. Opportunistic. Besides, it had been almost two weeks since their meeting. The trail was growing cold. Other salesmen made follow-up calls when they were looking for new jobs. They were always yapping about how long you had to wait before making one. Evidently timing was everything. Truax knew nothing of this. In the army someone told you to do something and you did it. That was all the timing that mattered. And there were no follow-up calls.

He'd gone to Swope earlier in the month to ask for another posting at EarthWorks. Something with a steady salary. Something with a future. His army pension was shit and, besides, he was still far too young for retirement. Forty. Practically a kid. So after learning that they didn't want him selling houses anymore, he'd gone down to see the personnel people at Newton Plaza. A pipe-chewing black guy had given him some tests and then sent him up for a short meeting with Swope. The lawyer had been skeptical. Not that Truax blamed him. It was hard to see how he fit into the Newton puzzle. Even manual work was out with his bum hand.

Sitting there in Swope's big glass office, Truax suddenly found himself envying the grunts he saw around town, the long-haired, trouble-eyed men huddling at lunch trucks or slinging drywall. Keeping to themselves. Working for that minimum wage. Lurping through the day like ghosts; swallowing whatever they had to so they could make it through the night. Never having to wear company blazers or make small talk. But he could never be like them. His family kept him in the game. There were expectations. A mortgage and a job. Saturday afternoon barbecues with men he didn't understand, dinner parties where news of his service was met by embarrassed silence. And, most baffling of all, the need to raise two daughters over whom his authority had dissipated like fog from a lowland jungle.

At the end of their short interview Swope had spoken vaguely about keeping him in mind for something in security. Given his military background, that might be their best bet. And that was it. Truax had been shown the door. Leaving the building, he felt just as he had nine years earlier, when Irma had nagged him into asking his battalion commander for a promotion. She was sick of noncom life – the thousand slights visited upon her by officers' wives, the limited PX privileges, the dingy clubs and month-end cash panics. The meeting had been as short as his session with Swope. The major, a West Point burner younger than Truax, had cut him off after just a few sentences.

'John, I appreciate what you're saying,' he said, his oak leafs flashing. 'But I got to tell you, as far as the army is concerned, you're where you belong. You're a sergeant, John. Always will be. And there's all the honor a man could want in that.'

But he wasn't even a sergeant now. Not anymore. He was a house peddler with no houses to sell. And there was no honor in that. He plucked Swope's business card from the corner of his blotter and dialed the number. A grim-sounding woman answered after the first ring.

'May I speak to Mr Swope, please?'

'Who's calling?'

'John Truax.'

'And might I know what this references?'

86

'Our . . . we spoke a few weeks ago about a job.'

'Truax, is it?'

'That's right.'

Silence ensued. His family stared at him from the edge of the desk. Waiting. It took the woman more than a minute to return.

'Mr Swope asked me to tell you that he has nothing for you right now. But feel free to check back at a later date.'

'Yes,' Truax said. 'All right. Um . . .'

But she'd hung up before he could remember to thank her.

5

Susan was beginning to wonder what her mother was doing in there. It had been over five minutes since she'd entered the changing room. Maybe she'd passed out. Susan savored the thought for a moment, Irmagard slumped in a corner of the booth. Legs splayed. Dress twisted. Though it was too early for that. She hadn't been at the schnapps yet. Besides, with the buzz she was riding from that morning's coffee and Virginia Slims, it would be a long time before she lost consciousness. Maybe she'd accidently locked herself in and was too embarrassed to call out. That would be cool. There was no way Susan was going to lift a finger to help her. She could stay in there forever. Well, until closing time, anyway.

Susan looked around Newton Casuals. What a dump. Rags for hags. Cripple shoes. Prom dresses. The old bats who worked here wore the clothes off the racks, believing that enhanced the appeal. Susan shuddered at the thought of getting old. Chicken neck and varicose veins. Hair stiffening into a Brillo helmet. Tits down to there. But the worst thing was that your taste buds seemed to die on the vine. Like that lady by the door in the peach concoction. Jesus. She looked like a gallon of melted sherbet.

Susan caught a glimpse of herself in the mirrored alcove next to the changing rooms. It would be a long time before she got old. There were three views on offer, two of which, she had to admit, looked pretty decent. Straight on and the right profile. Her legs curving snugly up under her butt. Hair flying out just a bit. Nose so small you could hardly see it. It was the last profile that was the nightmare. She looked as bad as her sister from that side, her beak the size of Mount Rushmore, about ten chins bagging up her neck. She hated her left side. Keeping Joel from seeing it was a number-one priority. Especially since he was right-handed and liked to have her on that side. But eventually she'd trained him to hold her with his left arm when they walked. That was one of the best things about Joel. It might take him a while to figure out what she wanted, though once he did, he was only too happy to oblige.

Like getting him to slow down when they balled. Not that she didn't like him going wild above her every now and then. Those long muscles dancing beneath her palms. But that was only for once in a while. It was better to have him breaking like waves into her. One after the other. A whole ocean's worth. She closed her eyes and started thinking about that. It's what they should have been doing right now at April's place down in DC. If only her mother wasn't such a bitch.

'Susan?'

She opened her eyes to the sight of Irma standing in the changing room door, wearing some lavender monstrosity. Susan had known the dress was a disaster when her mom snatched it off the rack but had no idea it would be quite this bad. Layer upon layer of purplish chiffon, looking like they had been pasted together by monkeys. And what was that with the neck? It looked like a two-year-old's bib.

'Well?'

'Looks great, Ma.'

Irma touched her collarbone.

'Really? It's not funny here?'

Before Susan could answer, one of the old bats arrived, nodding neutrally, waiting to hear how the conversation was going.

'I was just asking my daughter if this neck was all right.'

The assistant looked at Susan. The woman clearly knew the dress was hideous. But she didn't want to contradict anyone. She got the same percent commission for selling ugly dresses as she did for the good stuff.

'I told her it looked terrific,' Susan said. 'With her coloring?'

'Oh, yes,' the assistant said. 'It highlights your cheekbones.'

As if that was an issue, Susan thought. Irma's cheekbones would only look good inside a burlap sack. These people will say anything.

'Then I buy it?' Irma asked in her worst cigarette voice.

Susan hesitated, then nodded. All of a sudden, she wasn't that sure this was so funny. Getting invited to Mr Swope's birthday party meant a lot to her folks. Especially her dad. But before she could think of a way out of it the deal was done. Her mother performed a quick once-over of herself in the triple mirror, then vanished back into the changing room. The assistant retreated, not daring to look in Susan's direction.

As her mother undressed Susan started to feel really guilty. Sure, Irma had been a bitch for stopping her from spending the day in DC. But she was still her mom. Making her embarrass herself in public was cruel. Hanging out with the Swopes was a dream come true. And her dad, who was looking for a new job with Teddy's father – how would he feel when people started laughing at his wife? Sabotaging their shot at the big time would be too cold-blooded. She'd have plenty more chances to be with Joel. Her folks, on the other hand, were running out of time. And her mother had looked so trusting standing there. So vulnerable. No, she couldn't let her do this. Susan unwrapped her long legs from beneath her and walked over to the changing room door, her sandals whispering on the new carpet. She knocked gently.

'Mom?'

Chiffon rustled for a moment and then the door opened. Irma held the dress to her chest. Her bra straps dug into the creamy flesh of her shoulders. A vague odor of sweat mixed with her Charlie. That vulnerable sheen was gone from her powder-blue eyes, replaced by their usual cool wariness.

'I was thinking – maybe we could find something better.'

'Better?'

'You know. A little less . . .'

90

Susan couldn't think of the right word. Irma's eyes narrowed suspiciously.

'But you said you liked it.'

'I know.'

Irma smelled a rat.

'Why would you say you liked it if you didn't? No, this I do not understand.'

'I just . . .'

Irma continued to stare suspiciously at her. Susan knew exactly what she was thinking. That her daughter was trying to talk her out of buying a nice dress. To wreck things for her. To get revenge.

'No,' Irma said eventually. 'I buy this one.'

Susan shrugged. She'd tried.

'Okay,' she said. 'It's your party.'

There were only a few diners at the food court. Store workers on break. Two well-dressed Mystic Hills women, surrounded by mounds of bags. Susan and her mom stood in silence before the counters, trying to choose. Tia Taco. Vesuvius Pizza. Nathan's. Orange Julius. Peking Palace. Kids with bad skin and paper hats watched them. Susan recognized some of them from school but didn't say hello. She never acknowledged anybody when she was with her mom.

'Chinese?' Irma suggested.

'Sure.'

Irma got the Number Three special. Susan ordered something else. They took their trays to a table at the mezzanine's edge. It had a view of the escalators and the big fountain. Shapes of light fell from the big skylights into the fountain's chemically blue water. They reminded Susan of the stuff they expected her to learn in geometry. Cosines and acute angles. Yeah, right. If Joel hadn't helped her she'd have flunked for sure. Not that it mattered. She wasn't going back to school in the fall. She was going to Lewisburg to start living her life.

'So, that's done,' Irma said, her voice fake-nice, as if that last exchange back at Newton Casuals hadn't happened.

Susan decided to give decency one more try.

'Are you going to get Dad something new?'

'I was thinking about him wearing his red trousers and that checked coat.'

Good God, Susan thought, picturing them side by side in those nightmare ensembles.

'You'll look nice.'

'Yes, well, I hope something comes of the party. Or else we have big problems.'

'Come on,' Susan said. 'Dad'll find something.'

The angles of Irma's eyebrows grew even more acute.

'With his hand all rotten like it is? And losing the war? I don't think so.'

'He didn't lose the war, Mom.'

'He didn't win it, darling.'

Susan looked at her mother's half-consumed meal. The egg roll's insides had spewed out like the innards of roadkill; the lo mein stuck together like tufts of wet hair. Whatever vague plans she'd had about eating her food vanished completely.

'You know,' Irma continued. 'If you were going out with that nice Teddy, then Mr Swope would be a lot more likely to help your father out.'

'Going out with Teddy? Are you for real?'

'Why, what's wrong with him?'

'Only everything.'

'Well, at least you could get Joel to talk to Teddy and see if he'll mention us to his father. *If* it's not too much trouble.'

Typical Irma – being nasty while asking a favor. Susan was tempted to tell her no but then she realized that would only be hurting her father. And she could never do that. Ever.

'Sure,' she said. 'Though it's sort of hard to ask Joel to do you a fave if I'm not allowed to see him.'

Irma and Susan met each other's eyes. A bargain was struck. Irma smiled sweetly.

'I never said you weren't allowed to see Joel, dear. I said you couldn't go to Washington with him.'

Susan smiled back at her mother. She most definitely had banned them from seeing each other for a week. Round two to me, she thought.

'I must have misunderstood you. Sorry.'

Irma shrugged and then pointed at Susan's plate.

'Aren't you going to eat?'

'Not hungry.'

'At least have your cookie.'

Susan plucked the fortune cookie from the edge of the Styrofoam plate and snapped it in half. It took her a moment to find the scrolled paper, lodged deep in the cavity at one end of the shell. It was blank. Both sides. Weird. Must have been a bad day at the fortune cookie factory.

'What does it say?' Irma asked, having broken hers as well.

'True love will prevail. How about yours?'

Irma read for a moment, then turned it over. *Nothing ventured, nothing gained.* Susan crumpled the two pieces of paper and tossed them on her untouched food. Mother and daughter sat in silence after that, munching their cookies.

At home, Susan tried calling Joel, but his mom said he'd gone out with Teddy. She felt a pulse of peeved jealousy. It wasn't fair. This was supposed to be her day with Joel. She very nicely asked Mrs Wooten to have Joel call when he got in, then locked herself in her room. Her mother knocked after a few minutes and asked if she wanted to practice bridge, but Susan wasn't in the mood to watch her pound the schnapps. Instead, she put on Carole King's *Tapestry* and stretched out in bed, snuggling the big koala her dad had brought her from Australia. She sometimes missed having him arrive after some long flight with another stuffed animal for her collection. Each new one seemed bigger and more exotic. She used to love the way he would feel when he hugged her after arriving. His arms so strong. Strange, spicy smells rising from his clothes and hair. His expression confident and happy, unlike the cowed look he carried around these days. But that was wrong, missing that. Because the only reason her father went to cool places like Sydney or Bangkok was because he had to be in the place whose name she would never again mention. And she never wanted him to go back there. Not after what it did to him, making him so tired and scared.

Think better thoughts, she told herself. Imagine being at April's pad with Joel. April had lived in the same compound as them at Meade. Though ten years separated them, Susan used to spend a lot of time at her apartment, talking trash and putting on nail polish. Listening to music. They both had long hair so they'd spend hours combing it. April's husband, Geoff, was a gunnery corporal who'd gone off to the war and got killed when a shell misfired. Luckily they didn't have any kids. That's what everyone said, anyway. Though Susan could hardly see luck in the situation. After that, April got real mad at the army and moved down to this hippie pad on Dupont. So now, when Susan and Joel wanted to be alone, they had a place to go where the only grown-ups around seemed younger than them.

Susan thought back to the last time they were there, just before school got out. They ran this great scam. April had called Irma to invite Susan down for the day, making it seem totally innocent. The best thing was that April wasn't even staying in town – she'd gone off to be with some freaks in Virginia. They'd spent all day there. Balling every hour. Walking around naked. Calling out for pizza and almost forgetting to put on their clothes when the delivery guy showed. It was so great. Like they were married. Only better than married, because there wasn't all the stuff that made parents miserable. Today was supposed to have been a repeat. April had once again offered to clear out. Only Irma was on her toes this time, giving her the third degree. And stupid April had finally spilled the beans about Joel coming. Though Susan couldn't really blame her friend. When Irma wanted to know something, she was like the Gestapo.

So she and her mother had it out that morning after her father left for work. They'd screamed at each other for almost an hour. Irma said Susan couldn't see Joel for a week because of it. Then she started to blubber when Susan said she'd rather be skinned alive than help her pick out a new dress for Swope's party. In the end, Susan wound up going just to shut her mother up. She was glad she had. Now that Irma wanted Joel to do her a favor there was no way she could keep them apart. Though Susan decided not to ask him to speak to Teddy just yet. She wanted to milk this thing. It wasn't beyond Irma to wait until Swope gave her father a new job and then go ahead and split her and Joel up anyway.

Not that it really mattered what she did. The days of Queen Irma were definitely numbered. Because, come September, Susan and Joel were out of here. In just over two months they would be living together in Lewisburg, a million miles away from her mother's whims. They had it all planned. Though Joel already had a dorm room rented out for his first year, Susan would still get a place somewhere near the campus where they could be together. She'd already saved up eight hundred bucks. And she could easily get a job waitressing, especially in a college town. That was one of the advantages of looking like she did. Greasy men always wanted to give her jobs. She could work while Joel went to classes. In the evenings they could do the stuff college kids did. And at night it would be like at April's. Only with no deadlines or curfews. Her mother would freak but there was nothing she could do. By the time she got the cops on it Susan would be eighteen. She never thought she'd be grateful for having to stay back in seventh grade. It would be perfect. Joel would be on his way to becoming a man every bit as great as his father. Only without all the hard times. And she would be right there with him. She could maybe even start to have babies, though that would be tough with no money. Besides, there was plenty of time for that. She wanted five. They'd have caramel skin and Mrs Wooten's green eyes and her father's strong chin and Mr Wooten's rolling laugh. And, okay, her mom's blond hair. They would look so beautiful. Four boys and a girl. The girl would be the youngest. Brandy, like the song. Her brothers would all look after her. The first two boys would be called Earl and John. There'd be time to think of what to name the other two later. Susan would read every book there was so she would be a good enough mother to not make the same mistakes as Irma.

There was one other good thing about going to Lewisburg. No Teddy. He'd be off at Harvard being an evil genius. There would be no more of his sarcastic remarks or his dumb novel or that awful Yoko music. No more of those stupid drugs he gave Joel that made him ignore her. No more having to sit in the back of his fucking Firebird, going wherever he wanted to go. Once they had a place of their own Teddy would realize that he wasn't the boss anymore. If he wanted to come visit he'd have to ask nicely. And then she'd probably say no anyway. Well, some of the time. She'd finally have the man she loved all to herself. All she had to do was keep it together for the rest of the summer. Just two more months and they'd be free. Last night's riot and this morning's fight with Irma showed just how hazardous this city could be to the cause of true love.

The phone rang. Susan went to her door to listen. She could tell by the bitterness in her mother's voice that it was her dad. A word drifted up the stairs. Panther. God, how she hated her mother some times. She fell back onto her bed, thinking of the tone Irma used with her father these days. It was so unfair of her to treat him like she did. After all, it wasn't like he was one of those creeps back at Meade who'd come home from the war with a jar full of ears and photo albums nobody was allowed to see. Her father was never mean and never drunk and he worked just as hard as Teddy's or Joel's dad. It wasn't his fault if they made him go fight that stupid war and then threw him out of the army because of his hand. Irma should stand by him. Adversity was the test of real love. Susan had read that somewhere. A magazine. Or maybe in English class. She'd never get that way with Joel. No matter what happened, she'd stick by him. She'd already proven she could, when those jerks called them Tom and nigger lover. She would never let him down like her mother did her father. Never.

She reached out and grabbed another of her animals. It was the white tiger her dad had brought from Tokyo. Her favorite. She closed her eyes and held it close, imagining it was Joel. Thinking what it would be like to be with him every night in a place far away from this stupid city.

Part Two

6

Susan was trying to dunk Joel. She leapt at him after he'd splashed water in her face, her pretty features twisted with bogus anger. Joel twirled away at the last moment, forcing her to land on his naked back. She placed her hands on his shoulders and tried to shove him down. He resisted, causing her to rise as gracefully as Olga Korbut. Her breasts shrugged against her bikini top and her legs scissored through the surface. Just as she'd risen as high as her rigid arms would take her Joel buckled his legs, pitching them both forward. Susan's scream was choked silent as she shot over him and belly flopped into the water. Joel grabbed her braceleted ankle and reeled her in, then went under himself. They stayed below for five seconds – writhing, entwined, bubbles roiling up from them.

Teddy watched from his chair, *Psychic Discoveries Behind the Iron Curtain* splayed over the straining zipper of his jeans. When they surfaced Susan was really pissed. She'd been under too long. She'd swallowed water. Susan hated going under. Joel moved close to comfort her, easily parrying a lame slap she threw at his shoulder. He said a few things. She pouted and he spoke again, placing a gentle hand against her cheek. She finally smiled and they began to kiss. Deep frenches, right there in the middle of the pool. Teddy's book rose a centimeter on his lap. This was amazing. It looked like they were about to get it on right here at the Fogwood Recreation Center. Although it had been just six short days since they'd cowered together during the teen center riot, they seemed to have forgotten how crazy they could make people.

A sharp shriek sounded from the far deck. It was the lifeguard, staring critically at Joel and Susan over a nose frosted with zinc oxide. He shook his head, gesturing to the mothers and children spread around the pool.

They broke apart. Joel waded over to the side, just below Teddy's deck chair. Susan stayed where she was, wringing water from her long blond hair.

'You comin' in?' Joel asked.

'I'm cool,' Teddy said.

Joel laughed quietly.

'That is one thing you most definitely are not.'

He lifted himself out of the pool, balancing on its guttered edge. He brushed out the multitude of drops that clung to his matted-down 'fro, then teased it up with his fingertips. The spindly black hairs on his calves had been flattened by the water – they looked like something you'd see under a microscope. The label stuck up from the back of his swimsuit like a lolling white tongue.

'Gettin' hot,' he said, squinting up at the midday sun.

'Summer.'

Joel located his stupid leather visor on the edge of his chair and put it on. God how Teddy hated that thing. Susan waded over. Beads of water glistened brilliantly on her lightly freckled chest. There was a blush of burn on her shoulders.

'I hate that guy,' she said petulantly.

Joel looked up at the lifeguard.

'He's just jealous,' he said.

'Of Susan,' Teddy added.

Joel's deep, rolling laugh cut through the ongoing pool noise. His father's laugh. He helped Susan out of the pool. They sat together in the chair next to Teddy.

'Yuk,' Susan said, chucking her chin at Teddy's *Two Virgins* shirt. 'I mean, look at her. Buy a bra, lady.'

'She's not supposed to be a *Playboy* bunny.'

'Then she should wear some clothes.'

'You're so bourgeois, Susan.'

'Hey,' Joel said, the admonition in his voice both gentle and absolute.

There was a long silence. Splashes and shouts echoed

around them. The pop of a wave caught in a nearby filter. A rogue breeze carried a Coppertone reek.

'Anyway,' Teddy said finally.

His word for sorry.

'So what weird shit are you reading now, man?' Joel asked, reaching for the book.

Teddy covered it with his hands before Joel could pluck it from his lap and reveal the tumescent ridge straining his jeans.

'What?' Joel asked, shooting his friend a quizzical look.

Teddy repositioned his legs, then handed Joel the book.

'*Psychic* . . . man, what is this shit?'

'It's pretty amazing,' Teddy said. 'It's about these Russian guys who can bend spoons telekinetically and read other people's minds.'

'Bullshit.'

'It's all here, man. I shit you not.'

'I don't believe in any of that,' Susan pronounced, leaning back into her deck chair and closing her eyes against the afternoon sun.

'I can read minds,' Teddy said after a moment.

'No way.'

'I can.'

'What am I thinking, then?' Susan challenged, opening one eye and leveling it at him.

Teddy had a funny idea. He leaned forward and placed a fingertip on her brow. It felt strange. He'd never touched Susan before. Her skin was hot from the sun and cool from the water.

'Uh, let's see,' Teddy said. 'You're thinking about . . . wait a minute, this is amazing. A first.'

'What?' she asked dubiously.

'You're thinking about . . . absolutely nothing. Your mind is a complete blank.'

She slapped his hand away. Not gently.

'Hah fucking hah.'

Teddy rubbed at his hand for a moment. She'd hit him really hard. It stung. He felt the anger percolating beneath his chest's deep concavity. For a few seconds he was tempted to slap her hand in return. But Joel was there. He could never do anything to Susan when Joel was there.

'So what *were* you thinking?' Joel, ever the peacemaker, asked.

Susan's eyes closed again.

'I was wishing you and I could go away somewhere,' she said. 'Ditch my fucking mom.'

'I don't know,' Teddy said. 'It's pretty rough out there.'

'Yeah, but I'd be with Joel,' she said sweetly. 'He'd look after me.'

Teddy snickered.

'People saw you two out in the real world there might be some serious lynching action.'

Susan formed a sour face. But real anger arrived in Joel's expression.

'Don't say that, man,' he said.

'What?'

'Don't talk about people getting lynched and shit.'

'I was just—'

'I don't care what you were just. You shouldn't be talking about people getting lynched. My dad knew about a guy getting lynched.'

'What, can't I make a joke? What is this, Russia?'

'No,' Joel said. 'It's America. Get it?'

Teddy held up his hands in surrender. Joel could be so sensitive about matters Afro-American. As if anybody cared. There was a long, tense silence. More pool noise washed over them – yelping kids and the scrape of a deck chair. Not knowing what else to do, Teddy checked the diver's watch his folks had given him last Christmas.

'Well, I better get going,' he said. 'You guys want a ride?'

'Yeah, all right,' Joel said, resentment still in his voice.

Susan shrugged. She didn't answer. She never answered. She just came along.

Teddy fired up a half-consumed joint with the Firebird's lighter. He offered it over his shoulder but there were no takers. Worried by the silence, he angled the rearview mirror to get a better look at Joel and Susan, huddled together in a corner of the backseat. Their wet bathing suits had soaked through their clothes. Both stared out the window. Occasionally, Joel would whisper something to Susan, and she would snuggle in closer. Knowing conversation was an impossibility, Teddy punched on the tape player. 'Scumbag' was just giving way to 'Au.' But Joel told him to turn it off before Yoko could get one good ululation out.

Teddy was beginning to regret that lynching crack.

The plan was to drop Susan off first. Teddy had hoped Joel would spend the night at his house, though judging by his current mood he was starting to doubt it. Tonight was the Swope's annual birthday party, a sprawling drunken bash where all rules were suspended for the duration. For the past three years Teddy and Joel had attended, sneaking drinks under the semi-blind eyes of their parents. Even Ardelia, usually so strict, seemed not to mind the sight of her eldest son knocking back a frosty Miller or three. Joel would sleep over and the following morning both boys would wake up with legitimate hangovers. It was one of the summer's highlights. This year, however, there had been no talk of Joel hanging out with Teddy. Instead, he'd be taking advantage of the Truaxes' unexpected invitation to the party to get some time alone with Susan at her house. No invite had been forthcoming to Teddy. Yet again. Pissing him off, which was probably why he'd made that slip about lynching. He was getting sick of Joel and Susan ditching him. This was not how the summer was supposed to be panning out.

Still, it had been a stupid thing to say. A very large red flag to a very touchy bull. It had been a long time since he and Joel had angry words on the subject of race. Over two years, in fact. The last time had been Christmas Day, 1970. The Wootens had swung by for a late afternoon drink. The boys had fled up to Teddy's room to assess their presents. Joel had been given a high-powered telescope, Teddy an electric typewriter. He mocked the sweater Joel was wearing, a motley monstrosity knitted by some aunt. Joel responded by leaping on Teddy. Their wrestling had a playful ferocity. It didn't take long for Joel to get Teddy on his back.

'Now, say, "I've got a tweezer dick," ' Joel said, echoing

the insult Teddy had recently scrawled on the wall of the Wootens' tree house.

'Ne-ver,' Teddy gasped.

'Say, "I eat dingleberries in a delicious sauce of hot and spicy cum." '

Teddy bucked to get free. But he miscalculated his position and banged his head on the bed's iron frame. A blinding rage shot through him. Adrenaline pulsed. With a sudden maneuver, he was able to pull an unprecedented reverse on Joel, winding up on top of him. The pain continued to shoot through his skull, dizzying and infuriating him. Joel was laughing now – he didn't know Teddy was hurt. This made Teddy madder. He put a hand on Joel's throat. He could feel the muscle and bone and the beginnings of sweat. He pressed hard, harder than play.

'Say, "I'm a dirty nigger," ' he said.

Joel stopped laughing.

'Hey, fuck you, man.'

'Say it.'

Joel began to buck and squirm. But Teddy's hold on him was good, his best ever.

'Say, "I'm a dirty black watermelon-sucking nigger." '

Realizing there was no escape, Joel instead reached up and grabbed Teddy by the throat. His grip was strong. There was nothing careful in their ferocity now. Teddy responded by tightening his own hold. Their eyes had locked. They were fighting.

And then, as quickly as it had arrived, Teddy's anger was gone. All of a sudden he didn't want to be doing this anymore. He wanted to tell Joel it was over. Cry uncle. Whatever. But he couldn't speak. There was no air for speaking. He pressed down harder, trying to make his friend stop. But Joel only tightened his grip.

It ended unexpectedly, when the strongest hand Teddy had ever felt, a million times stronger than Joel's, clamped down on the back of his neck. And then Teddy felt himself rising miraculously upward, straight out of this fight he didn't want. There was no anger in this hand, no hurt. Just complete authority. Before he could think what was happening he was on his feet. He turned. Joel's dad stood behind him, his big yellowy eyes clotted with confusion. He looked at Teddy and then at his son.

'Get up,' he said, his usually booming voice hushed.

Joel stood, looking shaky. Teddy began to feel sick to his stomach.

'What the hell are you boys doing?'

Neither spoke. Teddy continued to look at Joel. With a word he could betray him, tell his father what Teddy had called him. He'd be in deep shit then. Nigger was one word you just didn't say. Not here. Not in Newton. But Joel didn't betray him. His eyes remained fixed on a point between his dad's size thirteens.

'We were wrestling,' he said quietly.

'Wrestling? Last time I saw wrestling like that a man like to got killed behind it.'

'It got out of hand, Mr Wooten,' Teddy added. 'I lost my temper.'

Wooten's eyes traveled between the two boys. He knew he wasn't getting the whole story but was wise enough to let it rest.

'Well, shake on it, then.'

They performed a soul shake right out of *Room 222*. Joel's father frowned – he didn't approve of the soul shake. But he let it pass. The incident was never mentioned again. For a few weeks after that Joel was frosty toward Teddy, but that soon faded. And yet a boundary had been defined, one it was up to Teddy to guard. He'd been careful since then. Never admonishing his friend for nigger-lipping joints. Refraining from taking sides in the teen center dispute. Keeping quiet when those nitwits raised their gloves in Mexico City. Race became a narrow but deep chasm that could swallow their friendship whole. It was up to Teddy to steer clear of it. That was why this past year, when Joel started making friends with other blacks, not the animals from the projects but decent guys like Alvin Matters and Lavelle Young, Teddy knew better than to hone in on them when they were hanging around the lockers, slapping hands and laughing a bit too loud. There was a part of Joel that it was better just to leave

105

alone. If he wanted to wear that ridiculous dashiki shirt his uncle had brought back from Zaire or listen to Stevie, that was cool. These were just minor things. Sideshows to the main attraction of their friendship. So it was stupid, saying that about Joel getting lynched. Especially now, when the guy was under so much pressure about being with Susan. It was just that the thought of the two of them running off made Teddy lose it for a minute. He couldn't bear the prospect of being on his own out here.

They reached Susan's house, one of hundreds of aluminum boxes in the flatlands east of the city center. It ws nothing like Mystic Hills, where Teddy and Joel lived. No big trees or rolling hills or sprawling homes on three-acre lots. This was where the GS-12's and retired soldiers lived. Teddy knew from his father that neighborhoods like this were the backbone of the city. The village centers, the bike paths, the whimsical street names, the open-plan schools and government projects – none of those could exist without these houses, built cheap and sold at a premium. Without them, the other stuff was just utopian window dressing.

He turned in his seat.

'Later, Susan,' he said, making his voice as friendly as he could.

She looked at him quizzically for a moment, as if she wanted to ask him a question that had been on her mind for years. Instead, she simply smiled and slipped out of the car. Joel followed her. On the front porch, beneath the wrought-iron eagle and the American flag twisted as tight as a tampon, they seemed to have a brief argument. At one point Susan gestured back to Teddy's car and shook her head angrily. But then Joel said something soothing and decisive. She smiled in surrender. He kissed her gently, almost chastely, and strolled back to the Firebird. There was some movement in an upstairs window. Susan's mother, watching Joel. There was a highball glass in her right hand.

Joel slid back into the front seat.

'You've got an audience, dude,' Teddy said, nodding up at Irma, who continued to stare down stonily, her mouth moving now. It reminded Teddy of the scene at the end of *The Graduate*, when everybody was cussing out Dustin Hoffman. Joel didn't look. Teddy dropped the car in gear and took off.

'That woman has it in for my ass.'

'You think she's going to do anything?'

'Nothing she can do,' Joel said. 'Not unless Sergeant Slaughter backs her up.'

'Any movement on that front?'

'Nah. Susan says he's too afraid of pissing off the Earl.'

'So there you go. In like Flynn.'

'As long as I don't get too blatant about shit.'

Teddy made a corner fast, his brand-new radials squealing.

'Joel, man, I didn't mean anything back there at the pool.'

'Nah. Forget about it.'

They drove in silence for a while, leaving Fogwood's prefab spread for the wooded, winding streets of Mystic Hills. Teddy was tempted to tell Joel about the latest chapter of his novel but somehow the silence was hard to break. There had been a lot of silences recently. Too many. They seemed to last longer, often right up to the time they said good-bye for the day. It was never like that before Susan.

They arrived at the Wootens' massive Federal. Joel's twin sisters were in the front yard, concocting some elaborate scenario with a dozen dolls and the family's woebegone cat.

'What you gonna do now?'

'Go see if I can find a present for my dad. So, you comin' to the party?'

'I think we might just hang at Susan's.' Joel paused. 'You want to come over, it's cool.'

'Yeah?'

'We're just going to be listening to music and shit.'

'This all right with Susan?'

Joel shrugged.

'Susan who.'

'I just might do that, then.'

'You can purloin some libations from the banquet.'

'Ever the jester, so I shall.'

Joel smiled. Teddy smiled. Susan who. This was better. This was good.

7

'The panther is on the prowl.'

Truax looked up from his bandaging. His wife stood at the bedroom window, idly licking the sweet scum from the rim of her glass. It was her second whisky sour. He'd have to stop her from having a third. He didn't want her drunk. Not tonight. Not at Swope's house.

'What are they doing?'

'Nothing. Talking. Teddy drove them home.' She squinted. 'He's a nice boy, I think.'

'Do you?'

She turned languidly toward him, her robe falling open to reveal a pearl-white slip. A patch of moisture ran across her abdomen from where she'd leaned against the bathroom's counter to get her face close to the mirror.

'Why?' she asked. 'Don't you?'

'I'm not too happy about that fatigue jacket he wears.'

'You and your uniforms. Who gives a damn.' She looked back at the window. 'Though I don't know how he can stand it, being around those two all the time.'

Truax resumed wrapping the Ace bandage, working his way up from the wrist.

'I think he loves her,' Irma mused.

'Who?'

'John, please. Either pay attention or don't be stupid. Susan? Teddy? I think he loves her.' She licked the last of the scum from the glass's rim. 'They say that about Nixon, you know. That he loved Pat so much he used to drive her on dates with other boys. Until she finally realized he was the one.'

Truax fastened the first of the three cleats he used.

'That's sick,' he muttered.

'Really? So now he's president and she's first lady. Real sick.'

'Not for long they aren't.'

Irma's attention was back out the window.

'Ah, here comes the kiss. That's right, nigger. Slobber all over her.'

'Irma . . .'

'Would you have done that for me, John?' she asked, her eyes still out the window 'Driven me on dates with other boys, just to be near me?'

The front door slammed. Susan was home.

'I think I'd have just killed the other boys,' Truax said, attempting levity.

Irma walked over to him, rubbing her hand through his hair. Smiling cruelly now. The knife-sharp odor of the Noxzema she'd used to obliterate the first, unsatisfactory application of Max Factor filled his nostrils.

'But you did, John,' she said sweetly. 'You killed them all. Twenty-three from my town alone.'

'Before my time, Irma.'

'But if you'd been there in forty-four you would have.'

The thought seemed to thrill her. Sometimes she scared him.

'Yes,' he said after a moment. 'I suppose I would.'

Susan was passing by their door.

'Susan?' Irma called out. 'Come in here, please.'

She pushed open the door but didn't cross the threshold. There were wet patches on her clothes. Just like her mother.

'Did you have a nice time at the pool?'

She shrugged.

'It was all right, I guess.'

'Do you want me to make you some dinner?'

Irma's voice was as cloyingly sweet as the drinks she favored.

'I'll get something later.'

'So what are you doing tonight?'

Susan performed a put-upon little shrug.

'I think I'll just watch some TV.'

'With Joel?'

Here we go, Truax thought.

'No,' Susan said, getting mad. 'Not with Joel.'

'I don't want him over here unless we're home.'

'How many ways do you want me to say no, Mother?'

'Just the one where you mean it, darling.'

They stared at each other for a long, spiteful moment.

'Anything else?' Susan asked sarcastically.

'No, dear,' Irma said. 'That's all.'

Susan retreated to her bedroom. Irma stared after her for a moment before returning to the bathroom and its big mirror. Truax watched as she popped her lips a few times, tilted her head this way and that, then began applying thick mascara to her strawberry-blond eyelashes.

The whining voice of some heart-struck singer began to drift out of Susan's room just as Truax finished cleating the bandage. He stood, examining himself in the dressing mirror beside the roller desk. He looked ridiculous in the clothes she'd chosen for him. Red-and-white-checked sports coat, a white polo neck and red trousers. Gleaming white loafers. But Irma said it was what men wore to parties these days. He stole a glance at his wife's reflected face, frozen in a cosmetic grimace. Her hand seemed steady enough as she swabbed the viscid gunk around her eyes. But it wasn't the hand that worried him. It was the tongue.

He headed downstairs, turning on the TV in the den to kill the minutes before it was time to go. Saturday evening, which meant his two favorite shows – *Mutual of Omaha's Wild Kingdom* and *Hee Haw*. He settled into the sofa, forgoing the beer he usually drank as Marlin Perkins ushered him into a world of savagery, violence and cunning. He would have to keep his wits about him at the party. Especially since Irma seemed so intent on losing hers. Still, he couldn't be too hard on her. She was the one who got them invited. Over the last few months she'd managed to become close to Sally Swope, using her card-playing skill to claw her way to the top of the Newton bridge circle's round-robin, where evidently winning was everything. She and Sally were partners now, queens of the hill. His wife had earned the priceless invitation after they'd consolidated their domination in a long session that left Irma so wired on caffeine and nicotine that she'd been up until nearly 5 A.M., rereading *The Carpetbaggers* from cover to cover.

The upshot of which was that Truax was going to Swope's house. Maybe there the lawyer would realize that he could be part of the team just as surely as any of those college kids. He double-checked the bandages. The last thing he wanted was for his hand to act up tonight. He wished there was some way he could get through the party without the dressing and the glove. Three months ago he could have swung it. The infection seemed to be in remission then, its only symptoms a slight swelling and a few patches of mottled skin. He was able to get by with nothing more than a Band-Aid. For a few weeks it began to look like the worst was over. But then the rot returned, starting with a long night of malarial sweats, followed by the swelling and the stink and the festering blisters.

It had been his only wound. That was what made it so hard. Three tours, and this was all that happened to him. Nothing in the delta in the bad days just after Tet, when it was patrolling and ambushing night after night in nipa palms so thick with booby traps that they seemed to be the very fruit of the land. Nothing during the thirteen months spent as a lane grader at brigade main base outside Saigon, using his delta know-how to teach boots the fundamentals of keeping their asses from getting blown off. Mortar and sniper fire were frequent there – of the ten master sergeants in his original instruction detail, four were wounded, one fatally, over the course of the year. And nothing, almost, during the ten sleepless months he spent in a highlands area of operations as hot as they came. He'd seen other men blown into so many pieces that they had to be shoveled into body bags. He'd seen soldiers die from spilled guts or sucking chests and he'd seen men killed by wounds so discreet that it took medics several full-body searches to find the hole. A corporal named Dalgetty had been shipped home a quadriplegic after a crunching tackle in a rugby game against some

Australians, and a black nurse whose name he didn't know had been crushed by a shard of stratospheric ice that fell off a B-52. He'd seen countless booby-trap wounds – pierced heels and scrambled gonads and dangling limbs. But this was all that happened to him. So small. And yet it persisted. While men he didn't think would live another hour were now healthy and whole.

It happened just outside My Song, the strategic hamlet in the middle of bullshit where he was posted during his final tour. By the time Truax got there in 1971, all pretense of pacification had been abandoned. The villagers knew the score – anyone who approached the wire would be greased. Grandmas, pregnant women, monks. Kids. It didn't matter. The platoon's sporadic patrols had nothing to do with protecting the locals or defeating the enemy. They were simply intended to make sure the NVA couldn't establish mortar or sniping positions within range of the camp. The war was over. The men at My Song were simply watching their asses until the last dust-off came.

It happened in April, just before monsoon. A staff sergeant had been shot in the elbow by a sniper and so Truax had to take his squad out on morning patrol. The heat was intense, so he decided to limit the circuit to two kilometers, through a small, steep valley the men usually avoided for fear of ambush. But Truax knew better than to leave a sector unpatrolled for long. The men grumbled but fell into line. The veteran sergeant was too well respected to suffer the petty insubordinations that plagued younger noncoms. Besides, he'd developed a reputation for luck among the superstitious grunts. When he was on patrol or watching the wire, they vied to be near him. So even when he announced they were going cross-compartment, avoiding the trails to hack their way through the prehistoric growth, the men simply tied down what was loose and waited for him to point the way.

The going was slow but relatively safe. The enemy was far less likely to plant booby traps here than on the well-beaten pathways. Truax had taken point – he didn't want some cherry leading them into a swamp. For two hours they cut through the jungle, encountering nothing more ferocious than leeches and jabbering monkeys. He was just about to join the trail back to My Song when he saw what looked like the entrance to a cave. He raised a hand, the squad halted. Caves were breeding grounds for the enemy. They had to be checked out and neutralized whenever encountered. Truax made everyone aware of what he'd seen, then crept forward, pushing aside the hanging fronds with his rifle barrel. As he drew close he could see the grin-shaped slit in a wall of mossy rock. It was about three feet tall at its center. Big enough to check out for himself. He handed back the rifle and took his .45 from its holster, then squatted perfectly still at the grinning mouth, waiting for movement. Everything seemed quiet. He considered shaking and baking the place with Fu Gas or maybe some C-4 but decided the resulting noise wouldn't be worth the trouble. So he switched on his shoulder lamp and went to look.

The cave's first ten yards were covered by a looming slab of rock suspended three feet off the ground. Truax duck-walked beneath it, his .45 leveled in front of him. The revolver had always been his weapon of choice. He paused at the end of the passage, hand-holding the lamp to illuminate the rest of the cave. It was a single rectangular chamber, no bigger than a two-car garage, its roof a good ten feet high. It was empty. There was no enemy here. Truax holstered his weapon and stepped up into the chamber. The air was damp and thick with mossy odors. In the lamp's pale glow he began to detect something on the walls. Whiteness. Motion. At first he thought it was simply a trick of his eyes, though he quickly realized that it was something living. He went to the nearest wall to check it out, scraping on his Zippo to supplement the lamp. It wasn't until he was inches away that he could see them. Big, colorless centipedes, clinging to the rocks. Thousands of them. So white they seemed to have never seen light. Some dangled from the cave's small abutments like highwire artists. They were a couple inches long and as thick as pistol barrels. In the weak glow they looked like so many wriggling fingers. Truax held the Zippo close to one – it writhed manically, as if the light caused it untold agony.

'Sarge?' an SP4 named Diaz called from the cave's mouth.

He'd forgotten his men out there.

'Secure,' he answered.

He let the Zippo flare out. A few seconds later the flashlight went dead. Just like that, pitching him into absolute darkness. Suddenly, unexpectedly, Truax felt something he rarely experienced. Panic. The chamber's liquid black and the after-image of those thousands of writhing fingers caused him to lose it for a moment. His heart began to pound; a fresh wave of sweat poured into his grubby undershirt. There was no air. This was what it was like to be buried alive. Everything he'd told himself not to feel these past three years suddenly poured into him and then threatened to burst out. He had to get out of here. He tried to scrape on the lighter but his hand was shaking so badly that he dropped it into the void. Enough was enough. It was time to go. He scrambled back toward the mouth of the cave in utter darkness, his equipment rattling against his body. He stumbled just as he reached that shelf of rock and blindly put out a hand to keep himself from slamming against the puddled floor. He felt something gelatinous as his right hand touched the wall, followed by a slight prick. He crouched and scrambled back out of the cave. The men stared blankly at him as he made it into the light. The idea that Sergeant Truax had lost it was so far from their minds that none of them noticed the telltale signs of panic. He quickly regained his composure.

'Anything?' Diaz asked.

Truax shook his head. As the squad formed up he took a quick look at his hand. There was a small emergent dome of blood just beneath the pinkie. He sucked at it for a moment. One of those centipedes had got him, most likely. He wondered if it was a bite or a sting. If maybe he should tell somebody about it. But then his men were ready to move out. The enemy was out there. By the time they hit the trail back to My Song, the panic he'd felt in the cave was completely gone.

The pain started an hour after he got back to camp. A sharp, insistent ache near the puncture. It reminded him of the time he'd splashed battery acid on his wrist while working on a jeep back in Frankfurt. During watch that night the pain seemed to increase with every beat of his heart. By dawn he could barely move his fingers. The skin on his palm was bright pink, swollen so tight he could count the pores.

The fever set in over the course of that day, worse than a spell of malaria. It spiked for the next forty-eight hours. Nothing seemed to help. Aspirin, salt tabs. At one moment he'd feel calm, the next delirious. He quickly dehydrated. They called in a medic from battalion but he was useless. The young platoon leader, usually in awe of his aging master sergeant, eventually countermanded his refusal to be transported. Seventy-one days before his time, Truax was dusted off.

He spent the next month in a Saigon hospital, running fevers and watching his hand grow gradually worse. The doctors tried a dozen different courses of antibiotics, none of which did any good. Truax tried describing the insect to them but nobody had heard of such a creature. One thing was clear – with a hand like that, Truax's war was over. He was eventually manifested on a Braniff back to San Francisco. He spent a month at the VA before returning to his family at Meade. When Irma saw his hand she didn't say a word. Truax's chances of making officer were over.

Soon after, the army hooked him up with a woman from EarthWorks, who told him about a job in the new city they were building. The company had a policy of recruiting NCO's who'd seen active service, especially those with manageable disabilities. They could offer him job training and a subsidized mortgage. Truax, it seemed, was just the sort of man they needed.

'Hi, Daddy.'

It was Darryl. Her lumpy fourteen-year-old frame was encased in painter's pants and a sweatshirt emblazoned with a vertical *JOY*, each letter beginning a different word. *Jesus. Others. Yourself.* She dropped heavily onto the sofa next to him, her mouth puffy with eight hundred dollars of metal, her headgear pulling her lips into a mirthless grin. If Susan had inherited Irma's Teutonic beauty, then poor Darryl was heir to Truax's lumpen Saxon stock, right down to her short limbs and limp, bark-colored hair.

115

'So what are your plans this evening, young lady?' he asked gently.

'Young Life. It's the whole county at the Interfaith Center. Some of the guys from Up With People are going to be there.'

'Sounds great.'

'They do these cheers?'

'I saw them on the Super Bowl.'

'Weren't they great?'

'Yes, they were.'

'So you and Mom got a party?'

'At the Swopes'.'

'And I guess Mom's going to get drunk,' she said matter-of-factly.

'Don't say that, Darryl.'

'Why not? It's true.'

Her voice was eerily matter-of-fact. As if she were talking about some wayward pet.

'Sometimes I guess it's not a great idea to say things even if they are true,' he offered.

'That's not what David says,' she claimed, referring to Truax's turtlenecked nemesis, the Reverend Abernathy. 'He says you should speak the truth loudly and whenever you can.'

Well, he's not married to a drunk, Truax thought. He didn't spend ten months sitting in shit outside My Song. And there's no extremity rotting on him.

'There are different kinds of truth, I guess.'

Darryl flashed him an incredulous smile.

'There's just one truth, Dad. Jesus.'

Truax turned back to the TV. Jackals were feasting on a slaughtered gazelle.

'Well,' Darryl said brightly. 'Gotta bee-bop-de-boo.'

And then she was gone, thudding out of the room and through the front door. Truax didn't bother to tell her to be home on time or be careful. He didn't have to.

Susan was next, appearing silently in the den's archway. Unlike her sister, she moved around the house noiselessly, hardly disturbing its regulated air. She had changed into her usual costume – hip-hugging jeans and a navy blue halter top.

116

No shoes. Her hair combed out, long and fine. She slid onto the sofa before the Naugahyde cushion had time to resume its original shape. She put her head on his shoulder, just like she used to when she was a little girl. She smelled of strawberries and Ivory.

'What are you watching?' she asked.

'*Mutual of Omaha.*'

She wrinkled her nose.

'Yuk.'

Truax wanted to stroke her hair – it looked so soft. But his good, left hand was pinned between them and he would not touch her with the glove.

'So you're planning to stay in tonight?' he asked gently.

'I guess.'

'And you understand what your mother said about no visitors.'

'Of course I understood. I'm not dense.'

'Susan . . .'

She pulled her head from his shoulder and looked at him, her expression more troubled than angry.

'I wish you two wouldn't fight so much,' Truax said with gentle exasperation.

'She starts it.'

'She's just worried about you.'

Susan shrugged.

'Nobody has to worry about me.'

'We just want you to be happy, Susan.'

The words set her off.

'But that's the thing, Daddy. I *am* happy. Right now. I wasn't happy when I was a little girl because we moved around so much. I wasn't happy after that because you were off in that dumb war. And her royal highness didn't seem to give a damn that I wasn't. But now that I am happy, it drives her nuts.'

She stood up.

'Susan . . .'

'You want me to be happy? Just tell her to leave me alone.'

Before he could think of a response, she was heading back upstairs to listen to those singers of hers, women whose voices

117

were far too sad for whatever paltry pain they might have suffered. At the doorway she passed Irma, now wearing the voluminous chiffon dress she'd bought for the party. Susan ignored her mother, who cast a quick, quizzical glance after her before turning her attention to Truax. Her sway was so slight that it was visible only to a husband's eyes.

'Ready,' she announced.

8

Wooten had counted on a leisurely Saturday before going to Swope's party. The plan was to sleep late, then call Sally to make sure the bakery had delivered the cake. Once that was set, he'd take the girls for lunch at Swensen's, where he would bribe them with banana splits to keep quiet about the meat loaf he'd consume away from Ardelia's systolic glare. Then, a couple hours watching his beloved Cards take on the despised Pirates, followed by a three-beer nap. After that would come a long, muscle-forgiving shower and, finally, the twilight stroll to Swope's. The one thing his day off would definitely not include was a visit to unit 27. There would be no trumped-up work to get him out of the house, no phantom runs to the hardware store. He was through with that. For good.

But his plans were shot to hell almost right away. The phone rang just as he was walking out the door. He froze, wondering why it never rang as he embarked on unpleasant tasks. They could be carting him off to his execution and the damn thing would stay tomb silent. But just let him try to grab a few minutes of family time and it would yowl like a trapped cat. Ardelia had shouted from the laundry room for him just to leave it. But he couldn't. It had been twenty years since he just left it.

It was Vince D'Armi, the weekend duty engineer at Newton Plaza. The news was bad – there had been another gaslight explosion. This one in Juniper Bend. Worse still, the homeowner had already called 911. Wooten cursed. Savage wanted the problem dealt with internally. There would be hell to pay if this made the papers. After a quick explanation to Ardelia, he jumped in the Ranchero and headed over to the site, hoping like hell he'd beat the Cannon County VFD.

The explosions had started two months earlier. Before that, there had been no hint of trouble from the gaslights, planted in every yard in the city, five-foot-high cast-iron stems housing a constant natural-gas flame. They were cheaper to run than conventional streetlights and, what's more, Barnaby liked them. They reminded him of simpler days, he'd once explained, when he was a boy growing up in small-town Kansas or a young architecture student in Chicago and the nights seemed to be suffused with warm, quavering gaslight. When the first one erupted everybody thought it was a fluke. Without warning, jets of flame burst through the four glass panels, making the lamp look like a rocket that had nosedived into the earth. The local fire department compounded the trouble by turning a hose on the damned thing. It wasn't until Wooten arrived that the situation was brought under control. Using nothing more than a screwdriver, he simply opened the panel at the lamp's base and worked the stopcock. The flame vanished immediately, leaving no more damage than a few bits of blackened glass.

Company engineers could come up with no cause. Wooten's guess – that there was a flaw in the surge suppressor located a few feet below ground – proved uncharacteristically mistaken when it was found to have been knocked out wholly intact. The problem had to be deeper. As a precaution, he flooded the pipes around the blown lamp with polybenzenoid swellants, figuring that would effectively seal any leaking jute-and-rubber gaskets. Everyone thought that was that until, two weeks later, there was a second explosion, this one over a mile from the first. It was bad, sending a shard of glass inches past the face of a passing jogger. Once again, it was Wooten who put out the fire. And once again, the post-mortem found nothing wrong, even after they dug up the light with a backhoe and shipped it to the forger.

Wooten began to suspect that the whole story wasn't being told. Having worked around natural gas since he was fifteen, he knew there was no way those lamps would blow unless there was a structural problem. His suspicions had been reinforced by the next two explosions. Still no injuries or property damage, though he knew that was just a matter of time. The experts continued to profess mystification at the cause. The latest theory had come from some egghead in Chicago who claimed that the explosions resulted not from any technical defect but rather from a flaw in the system's overall design, a theoretical anomaly in the distribution of pressure that caused random, unpredictable surges which no suppressor could control. The upshot being there was nothing to do but close down the whole damned deal. For good. But this would have left the city's streets in darkness, an unacceptable situation, especially given the recent trouble. Besides, nobody wanted to admit there was a flaw in Barnaby's design. So Savage had simply decided on a strategy of containment, hoping the thing would sort itself out.

Wooten remained skeptical. All this systems analysis seemed like so much hot air to him. If there was an anomaly it was in the lamp's construction. Or maybe the piping. The thing to do was roll up your sleeves and put some tools on the problem. When he mentioned his suspicions to Austin he'd been told that there was no way the company was going to dig up six thousand lamps without hard proof. For now, the main thing was to keep it out of the press. Wooten was to handle all flame-outs personally. The fire department would be contacted only as a last resort. After all, Earth-Works still had Phases III and IV to complete. Nobody wanted potential buyers to think they were relocating to some latter-day Vesuvius.

Today's fire proved identical to the others. That wagging tail of flame, the loose circle of citizens. Wooten grabbed the screwdriver he now kept on his dash. People made way for him with satisfied murmurs. This was the man. As he opened the hatch he could feel the erratic flow through the stem, two-second pulses that rattled the iron. Waves of heat washed over him, raising a sudden sweat on his back. He finally levered off the panel and worked the stopcock. The flame vanished with a gasp. After double-checking that there were no leaks, he stood and looked for a homeowner to reassure.

His eyes fell instead on the unwelcome sight of Sheriff Ralph Chones trudging up the lawn. He walked in his usual hunched manner, as if his sizeable gut were slowly pulling him over. He wore a bright orange hunting vest over his uniform. A plastic coffee stirrer dangled from his mouth. He stared at the smoldering gaslight for a long moment before turning to Wooten.

'What's that now, six?' he asked without preamble.

The lamp's frame was ticking with the settling heat.

'Five.'

Chones shot Wooten a quick look, as if he wasn't altogether convinced the foreman had his facts right. Wooten felt a quick pulse of annoyance. Though his relations with Chones were cordial, the sheriff always managed to let Wooten know that he didn't necessarily take him all that seriously. There was a moment's interlude that neither man seemed willing to break. The sound of an approaching siren finally did it for them.

'That'll be the water truck,' Chones said, moving the stirrer through his mouth.

'Are they really necessary? It's under control.'

'They were called,' Chones said, his voice flat.

Wooten stared at the sheriff, who wouldn't meet his eye. The first shoots of gin blossoms colored his nose.

'But there's no need for them now. Wouldn't they be better off back at the station in case there's a real emergency?'

Chones shot him another of those quick looks, this one suggesting impertinence. Wooten's annoyance now verged on anger. This was ridiculous. If the fire department came then there would be a report. The press would hear.

'Come on, Sheriff,' Wooten said. 'Give me a break.'

Chones raised his eyebrows, an inscrutable gesture he seemed happy to let stand. The siren drew closer. Homeowners watched. Wooten realized he couldn't stop this on his own. There was only one thing to do, much as he hated to do it.

'Look, you want me to call Austin so you guys can sort this out?'

The triumphant expression on Chones's face collapsed. He

looked down at his feet, where the toe of his polished shoe began to worry the edge of a sod square.

'Nah,' he said finally. 'Don't bother Swope. Not on his birthday.'

Wooten smiled obligingly at the remark, though Chones was already walking back toward his prowler. Wooten watched him make the call. Ten seconds later the siren stopped. Wooten raised his hand in thanks. But Chones never looked back. He just drove off, leaving Wooten standing there, his big hand poised in the air.

It was after four by the time he got home. No meat loaf, no game, no beer. And definitely no nap. He tried to call Austin but the line was busy. No matter – he'd tell him about the gaslight at the party. He took a long hot shower after that, letting the scalding water pound against the knotted muscles of his shoulders and neck. As he soaked he mulled over his discussion with Chones. Wooten knew the type only too well. Black man could tell them a lion was about to bite their ass and they'd look at him like he'd been at the Ripple. And then when they got bit they'd get mad at him for not telling them right. He'd hated invoking Swope's name, though he knew that Chones, set to be named the city's first public safety director come September, would do anything Swope asked. Besides, it wasn't Wooten's pride that was important. It was the company and the city.

A sudden, wicked thought came to Wooten. What if Holmes was right and Savage really did offer him the manager's job? That first meeting with Chones after the announcement sure would be nice. Oh, he'd still offer him the job in the end. When all was said and done Chones was an able lawman. But not until he made the man sweat a bit. Wooten savored the thought like he would a fine cigar, knowing that there was only a few minutes of sweetness in it. Still, it was nice to think.

A second thought hit him as he stepped out of the shower, something he hadn't considered up to now. Something that made that fleeting pipe dream of revenge seem a lot more real. What if they had unexpectedly big plans for Austin as well? What if they were moving him all the way up to headquarters, leapfrogging him into a vice-presidential slot? That would leave Newton manager wide open. Maybe the rumor had been right. That would be perfect. A fitting reward for them both. He was tempted to call his friend right now and share his happy suspicions. It was, after all, his birthday. But he knew that to defy Savage was wrong, especially at such a delicate time. It would be foolish to jeopardize things by running his mouth. The conversation with Austin would have to wait.

Ardelia was at the sink when he came out of the shower. She was dressed in a bra and half-slip, arranging her face in front of the big mirror. He hadn't told her about Savage's call, either. He'd been waiting for the right moment. Wooten rode a cloud of steam toward her, placing his hands around her waist and nestling into the side of her neck.

'Mmmm,' she sang, closing her eyes and moving back into him. 'You get your crisis sorted out?'

'Of course.'

'And how about the cake? Did you remember to call Sally?'

'Arrived in good shape.'

'You boys with your toys,' she said with mock disapproval.

'He'll love it.'

'Of course he will,' she said. 'It panders to his sense of grandiosity.'

'Not after I get through cutting it.'

'Joel's back,' she said more somberly.

Wooten pulled away. Their eyes met through the mirror's hazy mediation.

'Earl, you've been putting this off long enough.'

He turned and walked to the bed, where she'd laid out his clothes. After much discussion he'd decided on a navy blue blazer and gray slacks. White shirt, no tie. Ardelia would wear the sapphire dress she looked so fine in. Last year he'd felt so *loud* in his pea-green safari suit, even though the white men all dressed like Sonny Bono.

'Can't it wait?' he asked helplessly.

'Earl, that boy is going to be in college in two months. A good school where every mother's son is smart as a whip. And the last thing in the world I want him to be doing is sitting up there mooning over Susan Truax when he should be thinking E comp and trig.'

She turned, her dander up.

'I mean, do you think those professors aren't going to have their eyes on him? You think they're going to say, Oh, that's all right, son, we know you got a trashy—'

'Ardelia . . .'

'I'm sorry but yes, sweet as she is, trashy little honey back there in Maryland, so what we'll do is grade you on a curve, young Mr Wooten. Don't worry about getting a sixty on that quiz, we'll give you a *B* anyway, because we *always* make allowances for black boys coming in here dreaming about their blond girlfriends. Puh-leeze. And what if he meets some girl there who makes sounds a bit more sophisticated than popping gum? Black, white, whatever. What's he going to say? Sorry, but my heart belongs to the girl who works at A & P?'

Wooten walked slowly across the room and silenced her with a kiss.

'What?' she asked as he pulled away.

'You are without doubt the biggest snob I know. You make Sally Swope look like Minnie Pearl.'

'I just want the best for Joel. You know that.'

'Of course I know that.'

Ardelia was staring at him, her eyebrows aloft in expectation.

'All right,' he said in his most beleaguered voice. 'I'll talk to him.'

Wooten took his time getting dressed. He was none too happy about this talk with Joel, especially after the fight they'd had on Tuesday night. It had come after a long day, what with the fish kill and his confrontation with Vota. And then, as if to add insult to injury, Ardelia placed yet another no-fat dinner in front of him when he finally made it to the table. As he poked at the steamed broccoli and poached cod, Joel mentioned something about Muhammad Ali. Wooten, his temper as foul as the water in Lake Newton, spoke before thinking.

125

'You mean Cassius Clay?' he asked, a taunt in his voice.

'I mean Muhammad Ali,' Joel answered sharply, taking up the challenge.

'Muhammad Ali. Spare me.'

'Boys, please,' Ardelia said wearily. 'He's just a prize-fighter.'

'That's what you're supposed to call him,' Joel insisted.

'Says who? Not his mother and father.'

'Says the honorable Elijah Muhammad.'

'The honorable,' Wooten scoffed. 'Tell you what. I could call myself Ali Baba and I'd still be me. Give me the honorable Joe Frazier any day.'

'You can have him,' Joel said. 'Gorilla.'

Ardelia stiffened. The girls grew suddenly quiet.

'Young man,' Ardelia said, her voice vice-principal sharp.

Wooten put down his fork and pointed at his son.

'Let me tell you about Joe Frazier. The man *works*. He doesn't run his mouth and call himself fancy names. Doesn't hang around with a bunch of Chicago charlatans who think they're in OPEC.'

'Blood pressure, Earl . . .' Ardelia sang.

But he continued: 'Man does a job. Round one through fifteen. If he wins he takes his money. If he gets whupped he takes that money too. If that makes him a gorilla, well . . .'

Wooten caught himself when he saw the wounded look in Joel's eyes. He realized that he didn't want to fight with his son. Not about something as paltry as this.

'You've got to respect a man like that,' he said, his voice trailing off.

Since then, they hadn't said two words to each other. Which was wrong, especially since Joel would be leaving home in just a few months. He had no real quarrel with his son. Joel was a good kid. A great kid. Sure, he had his moments of rebellion and lip. They had their fights about clothes and hair and music and that motormouthed Clay. But deep down they had respect. When Wooten saw some of the children his friends and colleagues had been stuck with, he thanked his lucky stars. It was just that he knew there were things in boys you couldn't control. Invisible tides that swept

126

into them when you weren't looking out. Changing them. Making them do things that weren't in their character. Which was precisely why he was worried about this Truax girl. His reasons for wanting Joel to ease off the relationship cut much deeper than Ardelia's ambition. They didn't have anything to do with what grades he got or how trashy the girl was. No, it was the old, deadly formula. Black men with white women – it was bad medicine. A cruel magic that could bring out the worst in everybody, especially, as hard as this was to admit, the boy. Wooten had seen it too often to let the good intentions of a man like Barnaby or the faithful love of a mother like Ardelia convince him it wasn't so.

He finished dressing and walked down the long hall to Joel's room. He had to rap twice on the door to make himself heard over the music.

'Yeah?'

Wooten entered. Joel was sitting on his bed. He wore a lavender T-shirt and flared jeans. His hair was teased out into the medium-length natural he now wore. He was studying an album jacket decorated with a pastel painting of some black man looking out over a desert, a big beam of light shooting from his eyes.

livin' just enough

Wooten waited for a break in the song. Music was another sore spot between them. A few weeks earlier they'd been driving together when a song called 'Patches' came on the radio, a sentimental ballad about some down-home Negro whose momma tried to raise him up out of just the sort of hard times Wooten had known. It was sung in a quavering, mournful voice by a brother who knew the score. Suddenly, unexpectedly, Wooten's eyes misted over. Big mistake. Joel, who noticed everything when it came to his father's flaws, saw those clouded eyes. He said nothing at the time, though later Wooten heard him howling the song's refrain up in his room with Teddy, the two of them caterwauling like the spoiled children they could sometimes be.

'May I come in?'

Joel shrugged. Wooten snatched the desk chair and spun it around so he could rest his arms on its back.

'Mind if I turn this down a bit?'

Joel shrugged again. Wooten put the stereo down a few notches.

'So what you got on tonight?' he asked conversationally.

'Might hang out with Teddy.'

'You coming to the Swopes' party?'

'What, and watch a bunch of old people get drunk? No thank you.'

Wooten forced a smile.

'They don't all get drunk. Just most of them.'

Joel shrugged again. Wooten cast about for a way into this.

'We never really got a chance to talk about that fight over at the teen center,' he said finally.

'Some jerks.'

'You get into it?'

Joel screwed up his face.

'*Hell* no.'

'I heard it was outsiders.'

'Depends what you mean by outsiders.'

'I guess I mean people from outside the city.'

'There were some of them. Kids from the Heights, too.'

'Were you with Teddy?'

'Yeah. He didn't fight, either.'

'That doesn't surprise me. The idea of Teddy Swope throwing hands . . .'

Father and son shared a smile over this.

'Teddy's a negotiator,' Wooten said. 'Like his father.'

'Yeah. He negotiated his ass out the nearest exit.'

Wooten, happy to be bantering, let the curse go unchallenged.

skyscrapers and everything

'You going back if they open it?'

Joel shook his head.

'That's a shame. I know Mr Vine saw it as a place everybody can use.'

128

'Well, I guess *Mr* Vine was wrong.'
Wooten let that go as well.
'Susan there?'
Joel looked up sharply. Then nodded.
'Must have been scary for her.'
Joel nodded warily.
'So how is Susan? Haven't seen her around lately.'
'She's been around. You just been working.'

get in the cell nigger

Wooten looked at the nearest speaker.
'What is this?'
'Stevie.'
Wooten listened for a moment, then turned back to his son.
'Joel, we have to talk about Susan.'
Joel waited. Not nodding, not speaking. Just staring at his father.
'Your mother and I think maybe things are getting too serious between you.'
'What does that mean? Too serious?'
There was a defiant, almost contemptuous note in his son's voice. For a moment Wooten wondered if he might know something about the visits to 27. But he quickly dismissed the notion. Nobody knew about that.
'It means that you're focusing your energies exclusively on her and not on other things,' he continued patiently.
'What things?'
'Well, there's school . . .'
'It's summer.'
'But your last report card wasn't all that great. I mean, *B*'s are all right, but they aren't college.'
'I'll handle college.'
'No one's saying you won't. Look, son—'
'This is 'cause she's white, isn't it?'
'No, it isn't,' Wooten said, too quickly.
'It is, though.'

Wooten took a breath.

'We'd have the same position on this if she were colored or Chinese or—'

'You're scared.'

Wooten could feel the anger rising in him.

'Excuse me?'

'You're afraid of white women.'

'Where do you . . . that's not true.'

'What do you mean it isn't true? What would've happened if you'd stepped out with somebody like Susan back in the day?'

'This ain't then.'

'You think it is. You see me with her and you're all buggin' out.'

'That's not what it is at all.'

Joel looked away and shook his head.

'Well, I know what this is,' he said finally. 'Even if you don't.'

Wooten stood, swallowing his anger. He didn't want a fight with his boy. Once this week was enough.

'You're wrong, Joel. I don't mind that she's white. I mind that . . .'

'What?'

Wooten realized he didn't know what to say.

'So what's going to happen?' Joel asked.

'Happen?'

'Are you banning me from seeing her or what?'

'Look, I just wanted to talk. To ask you maybe to go a bit easy.'

Joel looked away, his jaw set.

'I can handle it.'

The song continued to play. The same line, over and over: *livin' just enough*. Wooten stared helplessly at his son for a few more bars, then stepped back out of the room.

The abortive discussion with Joel played through his mind as he waited for Ardelia in the front yard. The boy was wrong.

Dead wrong. He wasn't afraid of white women. He wasn't afraid of anyone. He just wanted Joel to know that the things he was feeling might not be as simple as he thought. But there was no telling him that. He had it bad for the girl.

Wooten stared up at his house, wishing he could make Joel see that all he wanted was what was best for him. All you had to do was look at this house to realize that. The sturdiest in the city. A no-frills Federal that Wooten had designed himself. Barnaby had offered to draw it for him but Wooten declined, indulging the dream that had buoyed him through three decades of overtime. His whole life he'd heard folks who couldn't even hold a hammer talk about how they'd built their house. Well, he'd *built* his own home, drawing up the blueprints on his nights off, overseeing its construction whenever he could grab a moment. Tearing down the first frame when he found it had been made of warped pine; sending back the roofing tiles when they turned out to be sub par. It felt good, allowing himself to be a pain-in-the-ass client rather than a put-upon contractor. And the result was fine. No gimmicks in the facade, nothing quaint in the yard. Twin gables. Hipped roof. Painted a green that blended perfectly with the surrounding foliage. There was nothing in it to suggest the life Wooten had left behind. No cracked bricks or broken-backed roofs or slamming screen doors. The large painted shutters would never have to close; the gently sloping lawn and circular drive opened wide to welcome visitors. Why was it so hard for Joel to understand that this was all for him?

He consoled himself with thoughts of the party to come. He couldn't wait until Austin saw his present. Each birthday, the two friends tried to outdo each other with gifts. It was a tradition that began during their first year of working together, when Swope had half jokingly given Wooten an elaborate dashboard compass for finding his way around the unmapped city. Wooten had responded two months later with the hand-tooled cherry-wood nameplate currently hanging on a hitching post beside Swope's front door. This April, Austin had summoned him to his office to give him a top-of-the-line Shakespeare rod – he knew how eager

Wooten was to take up fishing again once Lake Newton was stocked.

'Wouldn't mind trying this baby out now,' Wooten said, testing its heft in Swope's office.

'Why don't you?'

'In here?'

'No,' Swope answered. 'Out where it counts.'

Their eyes held for a moment. Both smiling. Realizing that this was their city. They could do anything they wanted.

'You know, I think I just might, counselor,' Wooten answered.

Swope commandeered a rowboat from the wizened old-timer who rented them on the first of the lake's three piers. A small crowd began to gather on the plaza as the two men stepped aboard. Wooten knew EarthWorkers would be watching from the opaque windows above them as well. But he didn't care. It was his birthday and he wanted to try out his new rod. He strung the line as Swope rowed them toward the middle of the lake. For a weight he used one of the keys from the fat ring he carried.

'Ready?' Swope asked when they were well free of the shore.

'Oh, yes,' Wooten answered.

He began to cast. It was hard at first – most of his fishing had been done when he was a Mississippi River rat, his poles custom-made from green branches that would snap back at him like a father's angry hand. The Shakespeare's fiberglass was infinitely more supple, bending toward the water like a divining rod and then switching unhurriedly back. His first few attempts were grossly overcast, the key slapping the water just a few feet from the aluminum hull.

'Ah, so the idea is to creep up on the fish and knock them unconscious,' a smiling Swope chided. He'd loosened his tie and was leaning back in the bow, enjoying the warm spring sun and the rare sight of an awkward Earl Wooten.

On shore, people continued to watch, astonished by the sight of the city's two most powerful men fishing an empty lake in the middle of a working day.

'Just give me a minute,' Wooten said.

And that's all he needed before he was sending his key soaring. It caught the sun as it arced, flashing for a moment and then landing gently on the tenantless water.

'Yessir,' Wooten said, reeling in. 'This is one fine rod.'

They spent the next half hour on the lake, talking business and then family as Wooten perfected his cast. It was one of those rare moments when Swope really opened up about his life, spending a good half hour describing his past disappointments and future hopes. The main topic was Teddy. Wooten always knew the man doted on his son, though it wasn't until that day that he fully understood how important the boy was to him. Teddy's life was going to be the one Swope had been denied. He would never have to scrape and struggle, never have to be his own parent or best friend. No doors would ever be closed on him – even if Swope had to kick them in himself. Although Wooten knew that his partner had been brought up in an unhappy working-class home, he'd never known just how hungry that childhood had left him for security and success. It became even clearer when the subject turned to Sally. In a voice so hushed that Wooten had to lean forward to hear it, Swope explained how, in the early years of their marriage, he'd constantly felt like he was letting down the woman who'd rejected a life of monied comfort back in Grosse Pointe to be with him. For the better part of a decade she'd had to stand on the sidelines, watching the well-connected Ivy Leaguers snag the best jobs and club memberships while her husband broke his back in real estate. Only recently had he begun to think that he was providing her with the sort of life that was her due. Wooten listened without interruption, knowing that was all he had to do. He'd never seen this side of Swope before. The insecurity. The tenderness underlying that steely ambition. As he spoke, the crowd on the plaza eventually dispersed. By the time Swope gently rowed them back to shore there was nobody watching except the old man.

'Catch anything?' the geezer asked sarcastically as they stepped onto the pier.

'We threw it back,' Swope answered coolly, his level stare indicating that the boatman had overstepped.

After he scampered off, the two friends began to laugh, and their laughter carried them all the way back to their offices and their responsibilities and the city they had yet to finish building.

'So how'd it go?'

Ardelia stood in the doorway, looking as beautiful as ever in the twilight. Just the sort of woman who should be walking out of a house like this on a fine summer's night. Five-foot-nine, those olive eyes sparkling, her caramel skin glowing. Her long hair held aloft by a system of pins and clamps more ingenious than the Pavilion's roof; her body still shapely, the ten pounds she'd gained with the twins perfectly distributed.

'Oh, do you look fine.'

'You too,' she said. 'A little too Bing Crosby for my liking but there you are.'

'When in Rome.'

They began to head along Merlin's Way, the tree-shrouded, tightly winding road that connected their house to Swope's cul-de-sac, Prospero's Parade. Mystic Hills was never better than at this hour, when light and shadow mingled in the trees. This was the best bit of real estate in Newton, five hundred acres of forest to the southeast of the lake, its big wooded lots arranged discreetly over a system of small hills. The houses here had distinct styles, unlike the neat rows of aluminum-clad clones in the other villages. Cape Cods. Monticellos. Post-and-beams. Colonials. Cedar shakes and mansard roofs. Redwood decks overlooking clusters of oak. They were occupied by upper-echelon EarthWorkers and the handful of Washington lawyers Swope had lured out here. Vine had chafed at the neighborhood's unplanned inclination toward exclusivity but Swope and Wooten had quietly defied him. After all, this was *their* families they were talking about.

'Well?' Ardelia asked.

'He seems to think I'm afraid of white women.'

'Are you?'

Wooten scowled at her.

'I thought this whole conversation was your idea,' he said.

'That doesn't mean *you* might not have ulterior motives.'

134

'Ulterior . . . woman, I've never had an ulterior motive in my life.'

She hummed musically for a moment.

'I am aware of the difficulties a black boy may have stepping out with a white girl, yes,' he said. 'Even in these times and this place. But I would never tell Joel he couldn't see her because of that. Never.'

'*I* believe you, sugar.'

They walked for a moment.

'All right. I'll talk to him again.'

'Good,' she said, speaking as she might to a recalcitrant student.

Wooten decided that the time had come to tell her about the trip.

'I'm going to Chicago on Thursday,' he said as casually as possible. 'I think Savage is going to offer me a new job.'

The play went out of her eyes.

'Oh? Where?'

'Maybe here.'

'Doing what?'

'City manager.'

She stopped and looked him in the eye.

'So Holmes was right?'

'Looks that way.'

'But that's Austin's job. I mean, what does he say about this?'

'They asked me not to tell him about the trip.'

'Now let me get this straight. You're secretly traveling to Chicago to talk to them about taking Austin's job?'

'Don't put it like that.'

'Then how should I put it?'

'First of all, the secrecy isn't about Austin. It's just how they do things. And the only way they'd be offering me city manager is if they had something better for him.'

'You're sure about that?'

'Of course I'm sure. Come on, Ardelia. I'd never keep a secret from Austin unless it was for his good as well as mine. I'm not like that. You know me.'

The words sickened him even as he spoke them. Though

this was different. The other thing was what it was. Besides, that deception was over.

'Well, I still don't see why you can't tell Austin something is in the offing.'

'How would it look to Savage if I go disobeying his orders just as he's about to offer me a big new job?'

'It would probably look like you were the same as every other man they got over in that snake pit.'

'Well, I can't afford to be like every other man. You *know* that. It's all just . . . politics. You know how it works.'

They walked wordlessly for a while, their good shoes ringing on the fresh asphalt. As they moved through the wavering twilight Wooten could sense a change in his wife's attitude.

'City manager,' she said softly. 'It would be nice.'

'Wouldn't it?'

'We could stay here.'

They let themselves travel through the fantasy for a while.

'And you're sure Austin will be all right about this? He's been talking about that job for five years now.'

'Ardelia, once they offer him a choice job in Chicago, I guarantee you he'll forget about Newton. If this is what I think it is, Austin will come out best of all.'

As if on command, Swope's house came into view. Unlike Wooten, he had let Vine design it, and the result was stunning. Situated at the bottom of a short cul-de-sac, it looked, from the front, like it was only one story, though at the back it fanned out into three floors. There were two parallel sloping roofs, each interrupted by a half dozen dormer windows that lifted from the wood like the just-opened eyes of lazing reptiles. The front door was encased in a twenty-foot-high wall of glass. An acre of freshly cut lawn buffered the front of the house, tiered by railroad ties and wood-chip oases. Out back there was a two-level deck and a couple more acres of lawn, centered around a gazebo with a purple-ring bug zapper that crackled throughout the summer nights. The entire property was surrounded by box elders and thick oaks that had been there for generations, just waiting for so perfect a house to shade. Cars already lined

Prospero's Parade; music wafted from behind the house. Ardelia and Earl Wooten paused.

'You ready?' she asked.

Wooten nodded grimly.

'As I'll ever be.'

9

Swope surveyed his backyard from the deck's upper level, thinking how much it looked like some sort of medieval encampment. A large striped marquee had been erected near the vine-encrusted gazebo, its inverse crenellations fluttering in a negligible breeze. Twenty feet to the right of the tent a line of cooking drums smoldered, attended by two chefs whose knives flashed like swords as they sliced pork and beheaded shrimp. Torch poles were planted at regular intervals around the yard's perimeter, spewing noxious black smoke into the surrounding woods. The deck where he stood had been transformed as well, its furniture carted off to make room for the guests. A bartender from the Cross Keys Inn was laying out an array of maraschino cherries, miniature sabers, cocktail napkins and plastic cups on the banquet table catty-cornered to the sliding-glass doors. On the deck behind him stood a row of gallon plastic bottles of Gordon's and Smirnoff and Johnny Walker. There was wine, a case of Italian red and one of Spanish white, as well as a big steel tub of iced Löwenbräu. The bartender was the only black working tonight. A dozen of Swope's guests would be black and he'd seen how touchy that sort of thing could get, especially when something got spilled. So he'd asked around, eventually finding a caterer who employed Filipinos. Word was they could move through a crowd with the stealth of jungle guerrillas. And nobody seemed too exercised about the dignity of Filipinos.

Swope checked his watch. Almost seven. People would be arriving soon. He ran through a quick checklist to make sure

138

everything was ready. Food, drinks, help. Music – Teddy had positioned speakers around the deck that were connected to the Panasonic in the den, where he'd be playing records from the stack Swope edited. *Switched-on Bach. Hot August Night.* Herb Alpert. Dionne Warwick. Maybe some Ray Stevens if people wanted to rock. Just nothing too Teddy.

Teddy, though. That gift. What a kid. What a damned kid.

Satisfied that everything was ready, Swope lit a Tiparillo, flicking the spent match into the raked pebbles below. He was satisfied, though hardly excited. His birthday was turning into a truly lousy day, a series of annoyances leading up to that afternoon's bombshell. His annual session that morning at Bethesda Country Club – eighteen celebratory holes and a Bloody Mary brunch – had turned out to be torture. There were three foursomes in all, mostly his former partners at Barger, Green, Applemans and Webb. They'd teed off just after seven. The talk was all Nixon. The consensus was that the man was done. You could stick a fork in him. Six months was the smart money, a year at the outside. Swope listened in silence, thinking what a bunch of losers his former partners had become. Semi-insiders who'd never get the White House calls or the Congressional memberships. His contempt affected his game – he'd played like shit, carding a shameful ninety-six, the second-worst score of the whole bunch. The half-hearted roasts at brunch had a nasty edge to them, his former colleagues now jealous of Swope's decision to take the EarthWorks job.

He'd driven home in a foul mood, unable to conjure any of the usual commercials to bolster his fading disposition. The house was in chaos, Filipinos everywhere, Sally bossing them around like some suburban MacArthur. He gladly went to pick up the booze from Fogwood Village Center. It was there that the day took its second nasty turn when he came back to his Town Car to find that its side mirror had been busted, dangling like the wing of a poorly carved chicken. Yet another instance of the vandalism that was becoming the norm in a city where such things were supposedly unthinkable.

The day had brightened considerably when Teddy ambled

into his office an hour later to give him his gift. And it was perfect. A Newton's cradle. They set it going straight away. Father and son sat there in companionable silence, their eyes following the clicking steel balls as they proved, time and again, the immutable laws of motion. Three to the left, three to the right. Four to the right, four to the left. Not many other kids would have put that much thought into their dad's gift. Swope knew he was a lucky man to have such a son.

But his high spirits weren't to last long. Soon after Teddy left the office, Swope had discovered something that threatened to ruin a lot more than his day. It happened by accident. He'd been playing phone tag for two days with Roger Tench, chief counsel at EarthWorks headquarters, about whether to sue the Pennsylvania hatchery. Late Friday, Tench had left a message instructing Swope to call him at home the following afternoon. Swope phoned from his study, eyes fixed on the five convex reflections of his face swaying at the edge of his blotter. A surly sounding kid answered. It took Tench a few minutes to come to the phone. He was out of breath.

'Just had the court rolled,' he explained.

They spoke for ten minutes. In the background Swope could hear the pock of struck balls. During the conversation he began to suspect that Tench had been drinking. Not much. A couple martinis. In the end they decided to give the hatchery two more weeks to come up with an offer before filing anything.

'Could you send me a copy of the initial agreement?' Tench asked.

'Sure.'

'No rush. Just have Earl bring it in on Friday.'

'Um, sure,' Swope said after a moment, hearing the surprise in his own voice.

Something changed in Tench's voice as well. The usually serene Midwesterner began to stutter and chortle.

'Wait a minute,' he said. 'I must be confused. Wooten's not coming this week. Is he?'

'Not that I know of.'

'I must be thinking . . . look, just mail it. That would probably be best.'

140

Swope sat in brooding silence for a few minutes after hanging up, unable to comprehend what he'd just heard. Roger Tench was the most highly organized lawyer he'd ever known. There was no way he'd think Earl Wooten was coming to Chicago if he weren't. A couple of drinks or not. And then there was that unconvincing attempt to cover up his mistake. But why would Wooten be traveling to EarthWorks headquarters? And why was Swope not supposed to know about it? He set Teddy's gift in motion, his eyes tracking the hypnotic action. This simply didn't compute. He and Wooten always kept each other fully informed about their dealings with headquarters. It was them against Chicago. That was understood. There was no conceivable reason for Wooten to go there secretly.

And then a connection was made deep in Swope's mind. Something terrifying and profound. He remembered Savage's threat about the manager's job. Suddenly, it didn't seem quite so hollow. Maybe there really were other candidates for the post.

Maybe Wooten was one of them.

But that couldn't be right. There was no way Earl would go after the job. He would never do that to Swope. They were friends. Their sons were practically brothers. They'd built a damned city together. Besides, the man had no interest in power or politics. And yet, no matter how hard Swope tried to dismiss the thought as the paranoid residue of a dismal day, it persisted. Bad facts began to accrue, easily dismissable on their own yet harder to discard when taken together. Those consecutive articles in *Look* and *Ebony*, for instance. Sure, they could simply be a happy coincidence. But they could also be the work of some publicity flak back at Earth-Works. Which would mean they were grooming Wooten for something. After all, there was a certain logic to the whole grisly idea. A popular black man appointed to help ease racial strife. The dark horse becomes a unity candidate.

This was crazy. There was no way Earl Wooten would stab him in the back. Not after everything they'd been through together. They were friends, even though Swope knew he wasn't the easiest man in the world to call a friend. There had

141

been too much silence and struggle in his life for him to possess the casual, locker-room conviviality of his former partners. Nothing had ever been easy for him. Not one single thing. Having to go to Michigan when they wouldn't take him at Harvard or Yale. Fighting like a cornered animal to keep his newborn son alive while other fathers strutted around with their healthy kids. Settling for the job doing property deals at Barger, Green when the white-shoe firms wouldn't hire him; then getting blackballed at Congressional because he was with the wrong outfit. Being treated like a stamp licker by the Montgomery County GOP when he approached them about a run for state assembly. All the while watching his wife stoically swallow back the disappointment when they didn't get the invites to the best parties and weekend retreats. And then, finally, John Mitchell shows some interest, only to turn out to be a crook. Swope knew none of this had anything to do with smarts or hard work. Those he had in abundance. He'd simply never got the knack of being on the inside. There had been too much solitude when he was a boy. He'd had to figure it all out for himself. No brothers or sisters to show him the way. Parents too old to pay attention. Local kids mocking him because his clothes and hair and slang were never quite right. There was a time to learn how to be one of the gang just as surely as there was a time to master reading and writing. And Swope had long understood that it was a lesson he'd missed.

And yet in spite of that – or maybe because of it – he and Wooten had become close. Somehow, it was this uneducated black builder who had come to understand him better than the golf buddies and conference room colleagues. Swope thought of the dozens of times Wooten had been there for him recently, ready to listen or help out. Like that day the previous autumn when he'd arrived for their weekly meeting to find Swope mired in the worst spell of his tenure atop Newton Plaza. It had been a real shit week, with problems piling up like cars on an icy highway. The first big fight had just happened at the high school. A lawsuit by a carpenter who'd lost a leg up in Juniper Bend was about to be lost. And Chicago was going nuts over cost overruns on the mall.

Worse still, Teddy's recent DWI scrape in Cannon City looked like it might have to be settled with a nolo contendere plea rather than a dismissal. By the time Wooten showed up, Swope was climbing his office's glass walls.

'Come on,' Wooten said after listening to his friend gripe for a few minutes. 'I know just what you need.'

They drove in silence to the southern edge of the city, Wooten's mischievous smile deflecting all questions about their destination. Though happy to be out of the office, Swope soon grew annoyed. He was too busy for games. Finally, they arrived at a former dairy farm Swope had prized away from a stubborn old coot named Atholton. A demolition crew was on the site, having already reduced the two barns to piles of dust-haloed rubble. The modest ranch house still stood, though it had been stripped of doors, fittings and roof. A Caterpillar tractor was parked in the front yard, its jagged scoop pointing at the facade like the crooked finger of a hanging judge.

The wrecking crew, a half dozen hard-eyed Viet vets Swope had hired to knock down the relics of old Cannon County, had gathered around someone's mud-splattered pickup for lunch. Wooten parked his Ranchero near the Cat and told Swope to stay put. The men watched him approach warily, though they relaxed after he began speaking. There were a few shrugs and nods. Whatever he had in mind was fine with them.

'Let's go,' Wooten said when he returned to the Ranchero, handing Swope a hard hat he snatched from the truck's bed.

Though he was nearing the end of his patience, Swope dutifully followed the builder across the pocked earth, careful not to soil his wing tips in the patches of sucking clay. Wooten stopped beside the Cat and smiled.

'You ready?'

'For what?'

Wooton chucked his chin up at the seat above them. It took Swope a few seconds to understand. When he did, an illicit, boyish thrill ran through him.

'Are you serious?'

'As a deacon, Mr Swope.'

Swope grabbed the roll cage and pulled himself up into the driver's seat. His leg brushed against the engine's greasy housing and for a moment he worried about soiling his suit's hundred-dollar-a-yard fabric. But once he was perched on the obdurate saddle, he wasn't thinking about any of that. There was just him and the tractor and Atholton's doomed ranch.

Wooten jumped up onto the running board to show him how it worked. Simple, really. Forward, stop, reverse. He then cranked on the engine to demonstrate the scoop's controls. He had to shout these final instructions over the diesel chug. Swope listened carefully, not wanting to make any mistakes, aware of the wrecking crew's stony stares.

And then there was nothing left to do but tear the place up. Wooten jumped off the tractor and spurred it on with a sharp slap to its splattered flank. Swope carefully slipped the gearstick forward and released the clutch. The tractor lurched, bouncing him painfully on the hard seat. He put some pressure on the clutch to regulate its momentum. By the time the scoop's teeth bit into the warped clapboards, he was traveling an unstoppable three miles per hour. The moist crack of old wood was almost inaudible beneath the motor's rumble. Swope let the scoop carry on deep into the house, stopping only when the roll cage reached the structure's edge. He continued to use the clutch instead of the brake, filling the yard with deep revs. He shot a quick glance at Wooten, who was smiling and nodding, like a proud father who'd just released his son's two-wheeler for the first time.

Swope went at it for twenty minutes. Of course, there was only so much damage he could do. Even as the machine gradually came under his control and he mastered the truculent scoop, certain walls and support beams remained beyond his reach. But still, by the time he'd called it a day, Atholton's house was in ruins. Drywall had splintered like frosting on a stale cake; beams were transformed into kindling. Arches of piping and fronds of electrical wire had been exposed. A blizzard of fine powder blew through it all, making the once-cozy house look like some blasted tundra hovel.

As Swope dropped the Cat into a final reverse, the day's

troubles suddenly seemed far, far away. The rack and moan of debris beneath the treads was one of the purest sounds he'd ever heard. The thick fumes tasted sweet in the back of his mouth. When he reached Wooten he cut the engine. It took a few seconds for the rattling to stop.

'Thanks, Earl,' Swope said, his voice muffled by gratitude.

'Sometimes,' Wooten replied, 'you just got to knock down somebody's house.'

Remembering this now, Swope realized how wrong he'd been to doubt Wooten. There was no way the man would betray him. When he saw him later he'd find out what was going on. He'd just have to be careful to weave the question into the conversation so Wooten wouldn't know he'd had these shameful suspicions. Either the builder had simply forgotten to mention it, or Tench was hitting the bottle harder than anyone suspected. One way or another, his distrust would be shown for the paranoid nonsense it was.

The doorbell rang. Somebody's eager, Swope thought. He stood his ground. Sally would greet them, attended by Evelyn, who'd volunteered to help with gatekeeping duties. He let his eyes travel back to those diminutive chefs, wielding their machetes with daunting aggression. After weeks of agonized soul-searching, Sally had finally decided upon shrimp and pork kebabs, wild rice and some sort of vegetable terrine. And of course the cake, organized under conditions of strictest secrecy and currently locked in the pantry.

Voices approached from inside the house. Swope stole a look at himself in the sliding-glass door to make sure all was in order. Tonight's costume comprised a vested azure suit from his namesake, Austin Reed, and a yellow silk tie. White-on-white shirt, its sleeves anchored by fourteen-carat cuff links depicting the city's tree-and-apple emblem, presented to him three years earlier by Barnaby Vine to mark the purchase of the last required acre of Maryland farmland. His black loafers radiated a deep obsidian luster.

Sally appeared, leading, of all people, John Truax and his wife. Swope felt a wave of annoyance at their presence. Sally, flush with some legendary victory at the Newton bridge round-robin, had invited them without clearing it with him.

The last person Swope wanted to deal with tonight was some salesman sniffing around for a job. Sally, to her credit, had a slightly peeved expression, as if she too were beginning to realize she'd blundered. And rightly so – the couple looked like audience members on *Duckpins for Dollars*. Truax was dressed in a checked sports coat and white shoes, that nasty-looking glove still on his right hand. The woman standing next to him seemed to have stepped fully faceted from a Brothers Grimm fairy tale. She had a fleshy, once-beautiful face dolloped with cheap makeup. Her pale blue eyes were rheumy and obscenely ardent; her ill-fitting chiffon dress looked like it had been tailored in a thresher.

'Ah, Mr and Mrs Truax,' he said. 'You're the first.'

They smiled dully. Without thinking, Swope extended his hand to Truax. After a moment the salesman took it with his inverted left hand. Even with the clumsy grip, Swope could feel his strength. He remembered some details from their interview. Master sergeant with nineteen years' service in the army. Three combat tours in Nam. The guy might not be able to sell houses, but he'd probably seen some stuff tonight's party people could only guess at.

'Mr Swope, this is my wife, Irma,' Truax said in a grim, clipped voice.

Swope offered her his hand. Her flesh was cool and damp. Her front teeth were streaked with lipstick.

'Happy birthday,' she said.

Swope smelled the liquor. Whisky sours, he guessed. Multiple, by the look of her. What a nightmare, he thought. And yet there was something about her that held his eye for a moment. A remnant of beauty, a last call for lust.

'Well, thank you, Irma,' he said.

She blinked several times, desperate to respond but unable to conjure the words. Sally hovered with a waxen smile. She looked tall and sleek in her lemon chiffon pants suit. Her Joy perfume sent the evening's other odors – the petroleum whiff of the bug lamps, the sharp tang of redwood stain, the woody rot from the surrounding forest – to flight.

Swope decided to put the couple out of their misery.

'So how are things down at the models?' he asked Truax.

'Good,' the sergeant lied. 'Fine. Excellent.'

Silence reclaimed them. Ring, doorbell, ring, Swope thought. He took a last drag on his Tiparillo, then dropped it onto the deck, where he quickly shepherded it into the crack between two planks with the toe of his loafer.

'So,' he said. 'I understand our children are friends.'

'Oh, yes,' Irma answered expansively. 'Teddy and Susan. He's so intelligent, your Teddy. You must be very proud.'

Swope met her eyes, which pulsed with coquettishness. Once again, he found himself momentarily unable to turn away. What was it about this woman?

The doorbell rang.

'I'll get it,' Sally said.

Irma continued to stare at Swope. Her eyelids slowly lowered into a squint.

'So,' Swope said. 'I understand your daughter's seeing Earl Wooten's son.'

The effect of his bland words on her was astonishing. The grinning flirtatious face in front of him changed immediately into a venomous mask.

'Not for long,' she said sullenly.

'Irma . . .' Truax warned.

'Really?' Swope said, suddenly interested in this. 'I'm sorry to hear that.'

'I'm not,' she said.

The others had arrived, a knot of couples who lingered at the edge of the deck, unwilling to interrupt. Music began to pour from the nearby speakers. 'Tijuana Taxi.' Good old Teddy.

'Problems?' Swope probed.

'It's not right,' Irma said.

'Not right as in . . .'

'It's wrong.'

'Ah.'

'The two of them,' she persisted. 'Together.'

Swope understood. The Truaxes hated Joel Wooten. For reasons that were none too hard to guess at. He looked at Truax, who suddenly found the cracks in the deck compelling.

147

'Well,' Swope said. 'I'd better . . .'

He nodded toward the other guests. Truax looked like he wanted to say something but thought better of it. Swope nodded a manly good-bye to him, then looked back at Irma. She was staring out at the dark woods, her eyes sharp with spite. She was truly a wreck. And yet, at the same time, there was something about her.

Truax watched Swope join the other couples, young Earth-Workers who knew what time to arrive. People who could talk to a man like Swope with confidence, instead of standing tongue-tied like some pathetic rube. People who knew how to ask for a job.

'I'm going for a drink.'

'Irma . . .'

But she was already gone, weaving across the deck to the bar. She was drunker than he'd thought. Somehow, she'd held it together until they arrived. Then the floodgates opened. Truax was tempted to plead illness and spirit her away. But Swope had already seen the state she was in. Leaving now would make it worse. There would certainly be a tussle. The only thing to do, he knew from long experience, was weather the storm.

His eyes followed the thick black smoke drifting from the torches into the woods, an image that unexpectedly brought back long-dormant memories of the shit fires at My Song, the conflagrations fueled by diesel oil poured into the halved fifty-five-gallon drums they used as latrines. New guys would cheer for the smoke to blow over the hamlet's hated citizenry, though old-timers like Truax knew it was better to have it waft into the treeline, where it would win them a couple hours of mercy from the mosquitoes. Something flashed in the corner of his eye – the chefs down by the marquee. Their knives, catching the light from the torches. He watched them work for a while, admiring their skill and focus. He could see by their faces they were Filipino. Cane cutters. He'd once served under a colonel who'd fought with MacArthur. That must have been something. A real war with a real commander.

Truax looked around the deck. It was filling fast with EarthWorks management types and their ostentatiously sober wives. Everybody on their best behavior – nursing watery drinks, speaking quietly, keeping an eye out for Swope. Irma's voice suddenly rang through them. She was talking to a couple of married engineers to whom Truax had recently sold a Ticonderoga. They stared at her with dread.

'. . . but it's just bullshit anyway . . .'

All right, Truax thought. Time to go. He made his way through the throng, careful not to jostle anyone.

'Irma.'

She almost stumbled as she turned. The engineers took the opportunity to vanish. Truax realized he had to be careful.

'I think we should get something to eat and then . . .'

But she wasn't listening to him. Her eyes had grown suddenly lucid as they focused over his shoulder.

'Oh,' she said, her voice low. 'Hello.'

Truax turned. Earl and Ardelia Wooten stood a few feet away, washed up by the human tide jamming the deck. They looked around uneasily.

'Good evening, Irma,' Ardelia answered, her voice friendly but precise. 'John.'

For people whose children had been dating for nearly a year, the two couples had almost no contact. Truax saw Wooten only occasionally around town. After one terse discussion affirming the fact that Joel and Susan were seeing each other, they'd never again mentioned the subject. The women spoke only when Irma was chasing down Susan by phone, their conversations cool and factual.

After five long seconds Wooten took the lead.

'John, how are you,' he said, offering his big hand.

Truax backhanded it.

'Irma . . .'

She nodded a grim hello. Her ten fingers remained on her highball glass, as if they were holding down the wildfowl pictured there. Someone jostled Truax from behind, moving him closer to the Wootens.

'Is Joel here?' Irma asked suddenly.

149

The question took everyone by surprise. Earl and Ardelia exchanged a glance.

'No,' Ardelia said after a moment, striving to be sociable. 'I think Joel believes we get up to too much hanky-panky here. It offends his sense of propriety.'

'Hanky-panky,' Irma said into her glass, an oblique smile parting her lips.

Wooten began to look around for an escape route. Ardelia's eyes remained fixed on Irma, waiting to see where that smile was going. Get her out of here, Truax thought. Now.

But before he could move Irma was speaking.

'Something must be done, you know.'

Her voice was cold and clear, her eyes fixed on Ardelia's expensive shoes.

'Excuse me?' Ardelia asked after a moment.

'Something must be done,' Irma said, raising her eyes with slow malevolence.

'About what?'

'About your son.'

'Our son.'

'Yes. Your son.'

'Ladies . . .' Wooten said.

'There is nothing wrong with my son,' Ardelia said coolly.

'Irma, please . . .' Truax tried.

'I did not say that there was something wrong with your son,' Irma said, enunciating every syllable, mocking the other woman's perfect English.

'Well, *vaht* are you saying?' Ardelia responded, taking the bait.

'Look, this isn't the time,' Wooten said.

'Then when is?' Irma asked, spitting out the words. 'When it's too late? When there's a little brown package on the way?'

Her words silenced everyone. A few nearby heads turned. That's it, Truax thought. He placed his good hand on her elbow. He could feel it stiffen in his grasp. He began to fear that he would have to frog-march her out of here.

'Now listen here, lady . . .'

Ardelia's words caught in her throat. She'd seen something behind Truax's back that checked her anger more certainly

150

than a choking hand. Wooten had seen it, too. As had Irma. Truax turned. It was Swope, standing just a few feet away, staring at Irma and then at the Wootens. His expression was agreeable but his eyes were sharp. He'd seen. Heard, probably. Truax felt something closing inside him.

Everyone waited for the birthday boy to speak.

'Dinner,' he said pleasantly.

They walked across the soggy lawn, surrounded by party-goers.

'Racist bitch.'

'Easy.'

'Don't easy me, Earl Wooten. Brown package. Who does she think she is? George Wallace without the wheelchair?'

'She keeps drinking and she's going to need one of them before too long,' Wooten joked.

Ardelia failed to see the humor. Wooten couldn't really blame her. He'd felt his own temper rise when Irma started talking about Joel. First Chones, now this. And that sorry husband of hers, just letting her go on. If Austin hadn't showed up when he did, Wooten was about to take the man aside and inform him he'd better control his woman if he wanted to have a future with EarthWorks.

'I'll have a word with Austin about it,' Wooten said.

'Well, all right,' Ardelia answered, only partially appeased.

They reached the marquee. Wooten looked around for the Truaxes, spotting them settling into a place at an empty table near the back of the enclosure. At least the man had enough sense to keep his drunken wife as far from things as possible. They seemed to be arguing intensely, with Irma doing most of the talking. Damn, would I hate to have to lie down next to that every night, Wooten thought. He felt a sudden wave of sympathy for Truax. Maybe he wouldn't be so hard on him. After all, you can't punish a man for family.

They found seats at the marquee's center table, the one reserved for Swope's inner circle. Wooten checked to make sure nothing was blocking the pathway leading down from the lawn – the cake would be coming later and he didn't want anything to impede its progress. He'd had it specially made in

Baltimore. Six feet by four, eight inches deep. Its surface re-creating the scale model in Swope's office, smaller and less detailed, but pretty fine nonetheless. Eighty-eight bucks, and worth every cent.

A minute after settling into his seat Wooten was up again, joining the food line before it grew too long. Tonight, he'd be able to eat as much as he wanted without enduring his wife's baleful stares. It was, after all, a party. He piled six kebab skewers on his plate, even though the normal allotment seemed to be two. It didn't matter. No one was about to question how much Earl Wooten was due.

Three young couples were at the center table when he returned, their reward for exemplary service during the year. Among them was Richard Holmes. They hadn't spoken since he'd tipped Wooten off about the manager rumor. When he saw Wooten he began to make his way around the table, eager to speak. Behind him, Swope had just burst through the crowd. He fell in behind Holmes, who stopped abruptly a few feet in front of Wooten, almost causing Swope to ram him.

Holmes plucked the unlit pipe from his lips.

'Any more good vibes on the grapevine?' Holmes asked.

'I think you're blocking the guest of honor's way,' Wooten interrupted.

Holmes turned and saw Swope, who smiled graciously.

'Richard, so glad to see you.'

'Mr Swope,' a flustered Holmes answered. 'Happy, well, birthday.'

Holmes moved aside to let Swope pass, then grimaced apologetically at Wooten. Everyone took their seats.

'So, Earl,' Swope asked. 'What was all that about?'

Wooten felt himself groping for the words. Just tell him, he thought. End this nonsense now.

'Up on the deck, I mean.'

Wooten's alarm vanished. Swope hadn't heard Holmes.

'I think Mrs Truax doesn't approve of my son.'

'Really?'

'*Somezing must be done.*'

'What's her beef?'

'What do you think?'

Swope leveled his gaze across the marquee at the Truaxes. They were still alone. Silent now. Truax's arms folded in front of his chest, Irma coaxing a recalcitrant ice cube from the bottom of her glass.

'Ah,' he said, his eyes on the Truaxes. 'Well, I'll have a word with the good sergeant about it. Let him know that's not how we do things in this man's army.'

Wooten nodded his head in gratitude.

'There was another gaslight fire this afternoon,' he said after a moment.

'Where?'

'Juniper Bend. Luckily, I was able to turn back the fire department. You know, Austin, I think it's high time we did something about this. Somebody's gonna get hurt behind one of these things.'

Swope looked for a moment like he was going to repeat the company line on containment. But then a better idea seemed to dawn on him.

'Maybe *you* should bring it up with Savage next time you two talk,' he mused. 'My star doesn't exactly seem to be ascendant in his firmament these days.'

Tell him, Wooten thought. Now. But he couldn't. He'd been ordered not to.

'Well, I don't have any plans to talk to Gus, but if I do, I will.'

Swope nodded once, then gestured toward the smoking drums on the lawn.

'I think I'll go get me some of this kebab everybody's talking about.'

The diced pork had a distinctly vaginal hue, a gristly pink tincture that foretold toilet-hugging bouts of food poisoning for those foolish enough to eat it. The shrimp was equally unpromising, grayish and speckled with bits of shattered shell. Swope had taken one skewer of each, but after examining them he made a mental note to stick with the charred bits of onion, green peppers and mushroom. The potato salad looked equally inedible, overcooked dices smothered in crusting mayonnaise.

He took his time returning to the table, stopping to say quick hellos to various minor guests. Though all he could think about was Wooten's denial that he had any plans to see Savage. The way he had to think for a moment before answering. The trapped look in his eyes. It just didn't seem right. And Holmes's question, followed by that shit-eating grin when he thought he'd been overheard. Something was going on. Swope's earlier confidence that this was all some foolish misunderstanding began to falter. Could it be that Wooten really was going to Chicago?

'Austin Swope.'

It was Ralph Chones, sitting at one of the outlying tables. He wore a dogtooth sports coat and a broad, shiny tie that was knotted noose-tight, pushing wattles of pale skin up under his chin. Beside him was his wife, a chunky woman with a tight do of steel-wool hair.

'Sheriff Chones,' Swope said, occupying the empty folding chair near them. 'I didn't see you arrive. Margaret.'

The woman nodded contentedly at him from above a pork kebab, which she nibbled like a cob of corn.

'I guess I owe you a happy birthday,' Chones said jovially.

'Well, thank you, Sheriff.' Swope leaned forward slightly. 'And I think I owe you an apology for my curt manner last Tuesday.'

'No hard feelings, Austin. It's a messy situation.'

'And your men handled it perfectly.'

'You wouldn't think so reading the papers.'

'Gettin's so you can't even arrest a colored anymore,' Margaret intoned over her stripped bone.

'Honey, please.'

'Well.'

Swope let the air clear of her statement before speaking.

'Ralph,' he said, 'you and I should get together soon and see if we can hammer out the specifics on your job. I'd like it to be my first announcement.'

Chones nodded, his eyes locking momentarily on Swope's before wandering up to the tent's stretched canvas.

'I'd like that Austin.' He smiled. His gray teeth were a boneyard of orthodontic neglect. 'I'd like that a lot.'

'I'll have Evelyn call you once I get the all-clear from Chicago.' He stood, picking up the plate of food he would never eat. 'Well, I better get back. I think somebody's going to give me a cake in a minute.'

Irma would not leave until they cut the cake. Not until the candles had been lit, the song sung and the big knife wielded. Even though Truax's instincts told him to get his wife the hell out of here before she could do any more damage, he knew that dragging her away now would cause a ruckus. If he waited until all attention was focused elsewhere then he might be able to make a clean getaway. So they sat in self-imposed exile at their mosquito-plagued table near the edge of the marquee, Truax stonily silent, Irma rapidly depleting the bottle of white wine that had been left in an ice bucket. She spoke occasional bitter words, most in German. Truax ignored her, contemplating instead his bleak future. Irma had finally done it. Mixed it up with the Wootens. On Swope's back porch. Truax might as well have kicked the foreman in the balls and spat on his wife. Just after taking his seat he stole a glance at the center table, where Swope and Wooten were conferring, a brief conversation that concluded with the lawyer casting a baleful glance at the Truaxes. So that was that. His career at EarthWorks was over. The week's accumulating hopes had been shot to hell. Truax ruefully considered what he might now do. He could drive. He'd liked driving back in his motor pool days. He'd been good, too. Never had an accident or a ticket or a reprimand. An unblemished record. He could drive a big rig. There were commercials on the TV about this outfit that qualified you. Maybe a Greyhound. That would be good. Decent money, long stretches away from home. Union. Pension. His dealings with people simple and anonymous. No boss looking over his shoulder. Next stop Kalamazoo.

But that couldn't happen unless his hand healed. How could he work the gears of an eighteen wheeler when he could barely hold a pen? Who would give him a chauffeur's license? No one. Which left – what? Clerking at a hardware store like his humpbacked father. That would be great. Maybe he could be the key grinder. Just like his dad. People would marvel at how skilled he was with only one good hand. Or maybe he could work as some sort of dispatcher, sitting in a crowded, humid room with a bunch of fat women as they popped gum and passed around photos of their grandkids. Or he could be a crossing guard. Wear a uniform again. He'd sit in his car when it was cold, drinking from the thermos that rested on his dashboard like a spent howitzer shell. Snapping back at the talk radio guys. Yes, there were all sorts of things John Truax could do now that his life was over.

He watched the smoke from the barbecues drifting into the trees for a while, then looked at Irma. She held her lipstick-stained glass to her lower lip. It was empty. Running on fumes, Truax thought. Her hair was losing its shape, a few brittle fronds sticking out crazily, others hanging limp. The mascara on her long lashes had clumped into oily orbs that reminded him of the warning bubbles they put on high tension wires around air bases.

There was a commotion at the far side of the marquee. Guests were standing, craning their necks to get a better view. Truax felt a swell of relief. The cake. Finally. Four Filipinos – the two chefs and the stoutest of the waitresses – carried it along a tarp runway. The candles were already lit. Moving through the dark yard, it reminded Truax of a burning sampan he'd seen one night as he flew in a transport above the Perfume River, a tablet of flame drifting through perfect blackness.

'Time to go, Irma,' he said. 'Get your things.'

Her head swiveled slowly toward him.

'What?'

'We're going home.'

'But I want to dance.'

Everyone was standing now, trying to get a better look at the cake.

'It's a city,' someone nearby whispered.

'There's not going to be any dancing, Irma.'

'What kind of a party is this, no dancing? I'm going to talk to Sally. She'll understand.'

'Irma, please. Let's just go. It's been a long night.'

Applause broke out. Irma looked around, gradually emerging from her stupor.

'What is happening?' she asked.

'They're bringing the cake.'

'The cake?' Her voice was that of a six-year-old.

She stood, teetering uneasily. Truax stood as well. The Filipinos were under the tent now, picking their way through the clutter of tenantless chairs. He could see the cake. It was huge, the length and breadth of a coffin. Its surface was decorated with small rectangular figures. It took Truax a moment to realize what it was. Newton. They'd made the cake into a city. He was so intent at staring at the decorations that he didn't realize Irma was heading toward the center table, hip checking guests out of the way.

They'd started to sing 'Happy Birthday' just as he set off after her, a few halting bars that quickly grew into a rousing chorus. Swope was on his feet, Wooten next to him, leading the singing like some black Sousa. Everybody was looking at the cake, which moved toward them with the brilliant inevitability of a comet.

Truax caught up with his wife two tables from Swope. He used his good hand to grab her by the elbow.

'Irma, please. Let's just go.'

She snorted and pulled away, taking a few more steps toward the center table. Candlelight rippled on the canvas roof. Singing people were watching the Truaxes now, their worried eyes at odds with their happy lips.

Happy Birthday dear Austin . . .

Truax caught her again, grabbing her upper arm. Hard. Her flesh was soft beneath his grip. This would leave a mark. His wife was a bruiser. She wheeled, her empurpled face bearing a look of naked hatred. Outstanding veins pulsed on her neck.

'Let go of me, you failing man,' she hissed.

The song was over. Her words rang through the tent. A stunned Truax did as he was told, releasing her arm just as she pulled violently away from him. The unexpected lack of

157

resistance caused her to pitch violently backward, her high-heeled foot catching on a chair leg. As she fell her eyes assumed a look of terror, as if she were plummeting from a tall building. Her shoulder struck the cake just after the front two bearers had placed their edge on the table. The other two, the chefs, had not yet begun to slide it forward. Irma hit the trampled grass with a grunt a split second before the dislodged edge of the tray landed next to her. The stunned chefs continued to hold onto their end, causing the cake to slide off its angled support and crumble into a sticky pile of sugar houses. A few of the candles still burned; the rest released wisps of smoke.

Everyone stared at the ruined cake. Then everyone stared at Irma. She sat in a strange position, the bottoms of her feet together, her legs splayed upward and outward, like butterfly wings. The gossamer fabric of her dress settled slowly over her knees. Her eyes were dreamy and unfocused.

And then Wooten was standing over her. He stared down at her for a moment, his expression almost sad. He offered her a big, open hand. Still dazed, she reached up and took it. He lifted her to her feet as if she were a child.

Truax finally moved forward. When Wooten saw him he released Irma's hand.

'Take her home, John,' he said gently.

Truax reached for his wife's arm but not before Sally Swope had intervened. Truax hazarded a look at Swope himself, who stood a few feet off, watching Irma with an intent expression.

'Irma?' Sally said. 'Let's get you inside and see if we can get you cleaned up a bit.'

Irma looked around, understanding suddenly where she was.

'No,' she said with surpassing dignity. 'We'll go now. Please continue. We will go.'

10

Teddy arrived at Susan's just after eight. He parked the Firebird around the corner to avoid prying eyes – his presence would imply Joel's, which would mean big trouble with Irma. These were the sorts of things Teddy thought about. Joel and Susan would have never been this careful. So often, it was up to him to do their thinking for them. They really were lucky to have him as a friend. He shuddered to think what they would do without him. He really did.

He'd hurried over right after seeing the showdown. Fuck the tunes – this was big. He'd watched it from his usual spot in the den, where he was spinning his dad's feeble, Bacharachian disks, dropping the needle squarely into the smooth, intersong valley every time, as slow and silent as the *Eagle* landing, with not so much as a whisper leaking from the speakers. The party was lame – ass-kissing guests crammed on the redwood deck, their conversations melding into a single upbeat chorus punctuated by arpeggios of soft laughter. Heads perpetually nodding, as if they were a field of poppies set swaying by a gentle breeze. Teddy had been about to call it a night when he saw something that caused him to drop the needle a good ten seconds into 'Son of a Preacher Man.' The Wootens and the Truaxes, facing off like football captains before a grudge match. The tension was obvious. The Earl stood as tall as Mean Joe Greene, his big head drawn back slightly, as if he'd just whiffed something unpleasant. Ardelia had her head cocked to the right, her eyes screwed up suspiciously, the same expression she used when dealing out detentions. It was hard to see Truax's face, though

Teddy could tell by the rigid set of his shoulders that this wasn't his idea of a good time. But it was Susan's mom who was clearly out of control. Her face was screwed up into a knot of anger and hate, her skin flushed a vivid pink. The highball glass teetered precariously in her hand.

Although Teddy couldn't hear what was being said, he knew this was about Susan and Joel. And then he noticed the Swope, staring coolly at the warring couples from ten feet off. Teddy wondered what he was thinking. Probably that he was going to can Truax. You do not, after all, fuck with the Earl. Finally, he stepped up to the foursome and said something that caused them all to look like they'd been caught circle jerking. Teddy decided it was time to boogie and tell Joel about this.

He stepped up onto the Truaxes' front porch and hit the button. At first he thought no one was home The lights were all out and the doorbell echoed emptily through the house. He glimpsed his T-shirt in the storm door. *I'm not as think as you stoned I am.* Written in hazy letters, like they were under water. Fairly fucking funny. As he waited he noticed the strange silence that gripped the street. It took him a minute to realize what was missing. Wind in the trees. The just-planted saplings that lined the road were still too small to catch much breeze. The only sound was the hiss of the Truaxes' gaslight. Various insects circled it, as if waiting clearance from some unseen controller to throw themselves into the flame.

He rang again. Still no answer. He began to wonder if Joel and Susan had made other plans and simply neglected to tell him. Anger began to rise in him, the kind of rage he used to feel back in Potomac, when the other boys would ditch him. It used to happen a lot. He'd see them whispering together, casting quick glances his way. And then they'd vanish, trailing a mist of mocking laughter. The first few times he just stood there, waiting for them to come back so they could all share a laugh. Because Teddy wasn't above a little joke at his own expense. Only they never did return. In the end he stopped hanging out with the Potomac boys. He didn't need those jerks. His dad was his friend. And then they left Potomac and he met Joel. The test results came in, the awards were awarded, the applications accepted. It had been a long time since anybody ditched Teddy.

Which was why he was getting so pissed standing here on the Truaxes' front porch. He'd reached out to ring for the third and last time when he heard bare feet hitting the hall's tiled floor. The door flew open and Joel was standing there, wearing jeans and a shirt that was too big for him. Something he'd stolen from his father, no doubt. It was unbuttoned, revealing the muscles of his chest and some recently sprung curls of hair. His eyes were hooded.

'Teddy, man,' he said. 'We crashed.'

Joel led him to the small den at the back of the house, trailing an odor of sweat and ammonia that cut through the house's usual cabbagey reek. One of his collar's wings stuck up, like an opened envelope. They arrived at the sliding-glass door at the back of the house. Joel worked the lock.

'Where's Susan?'

'Upstairs.'

'How about Saint Darryl?'

'Making the world safe for virgins.'

They stepped out onto the small deck overlooking the quarter-acre backyard. An unfurled hose snaked across the sod to a small island of wood chips. The sapling there didn't look like it was going to make it. Knee-high shrubs formed borders with the other yards. No fences in Newton, Teddy thought. Joel collapsed onto the weathered love seat; Teddy perched on a chair. The only other thing on the porch was a barbecue with a smoked-out window.

Teddy fired up a jay and handed it to Joel.

'So how was the party?'

'Bag of assholes.'

Teddy flicked burnt paper on the stained wood deck.

'Though your folks got into it with Susan's, I think.'

Joel looked up sharply.

'What do you mean?'

'I saw them all squared off.'

'Fuck. What were they saying?'

161

'Couldn't hear. But the knives were out, man. You shoulda seen Irma's face.'

Teddy imitated. Joel shook his head.

'Not good.'

There was a noise – Susan putting on a record in the den.

'Don't say anything to Susan about this,' Joel commanded.

Teddy mimed locking his mouth just as music began to waft through the open door. *Ram*. A choice that was no doubt intended as a deliberate slight. Susan knew he hated McCartney. In fact, he hated all the Beatles. They'd held back John's genius for years. Ringo, for instance, was clearly a knuckle-dragging cretin, while George had a terminal case of saffron on the brain. And Paul was a malignant little Muzak-meister whose sole purpose was to stand between John and his destiny. What was worthy in the band's output – 'Revolution' or 'Julia' or 'Come Together' – were basically solo efforts by John. The sublime genius of *Plastic Ono* or *Live Jam* only proved Teddy's point. It saddened him to think what would have happened if John had gone solo back in '64. He'd explained all this at length to Susan which was why her spinning McCartney's down-home horseshit was inexcusable. But Teddy decided to let it ride just as she emerged, wearing nothing more than a football jersey that hung to her knees.

'Hey, Teddy,' she said in the bored voice she used to greet him. 'How was the party?'

'Snoresville.'

She nestled close to Joel.

'You see my mom?'

'Yeah.'

'She sloshed?'

Teddy shrugged. He could feel Joel's eyes on him.

'She seemed all right.'

Teddy rolled another joint. Yet another skill of his. He was practiced in all the lesser hallucinogenic arts. Joint rolling and bong ventilation; shotgunning screwdrivered beers and seed separation in the crotch of a splayed record cover. He knew that the Rorer 714 was the only authentic 'lude and that black beauties made your sweat stink if you took them on an empty stomach. All that stuff. As he rolled, he told them about the

162

latest chapter of his novel, *The Widening Gyre*. He'd been working on the book since Christmas, writing nearly two hundred pages, roughly 10 percent of its prospective length. It was amazing, telling the story of Gideon Horniman, an American Everyman making his way through the just-concluded decade. Gid, as he's known, is the son of Orville Horniman, an Oppenheimeresque bigwig at the Manhattan Project, and his frail wife, Jenny, a former Hollywood B-movie actress. Born in 1944, Gid appears to be a genetic write-off, his father's irradiated gametes lumbering him with deformities so bad that Orville secretly abandons him at a Nevada test site after informing poor Jen that the infant succumbed to his defects. Unknown to Orville, the baby is discovered by Winston Hickey, a sort of latter-day shaman/scavenger who decides to raise him at his hidden ranch, the Bar None. Miraculously, under Hickey's herbalistic care, Gid outgrows his worst genetic taints, until the only remaining abnormalities are a gift for mind reading and a massive schlong. After the beloved Hickey is killed by a freak desert storm that impales him with two thousand windblown cactus needles, Gid sets out to discover the truth of his patrimony, a journey that takes him through the key events of the 1960s, including JFK's assassination, Vietnam, the Beatles at Shea (where he has a forty-one-page conversation with John), the DNC in Chicago and the march on Selma. His psychic abilities and gargantuan member get him out of all sorts of scrapes as he draws closer to Orville, who now runs a shadowy right-wing organization known as The Widening Gyre. Teddy wasn't sure how it would end, though he was planning to finish it by the time he graduated Harvard, so that it wouldn't interfere with law school.

Tonight, he was telling Joel and Susan about Chapter Eight, in which Gid stows away on a Mercury shot. Only, they seemed more intent on frenching than listening. Several times, Teddy had to pause for them to finish. When he finally got to chapter's end Joel was smiling. Teddy felt a sudden swell of pride. He liked it.

'Teddy, man – do us a favor.'

'Sure.'

'Could you keep an eye out for Susan's folks?'

Teddy's elation vanished.

'Why? Where are you guys going?'

Joel rolled his eyes. Susan shook her head and snorted quietly. Teddy got it.

'Oh. Yeah. All right. Cool.'

They were through the sliding-glass door in a heartbeat. He heard them laughing as they ran up the stairs. It was almost like they were laughing at him. But that couldn't be. Joel would never laugh at him. Still, this was most uncool. Inviting him over and then using him as some kind of early parental warning system while they played hide the salami. Teddy went back into the house and removed the stylus from *Ram*, replacing it with some Tull. He began to walk off his anger downstairs. The Truax house was dinky. A den that had one of those treasure maps you could buy at Pier 1. Living room decorated with a shelf full of Lladro sculptures – clowns and dancers and a girl holding a fawn. Cramped little dining room that could barely contain the six-seater table, its main decoration a display of ornamental spoons with German writing on them.

Pathetic.

The kitchen was clean but stank of sauerkraut, a smell so deeply pervasive that Teddy began to suspect Irma had hung cabbage wallpaper. The stuff certainly looked vegetative, with its pale green tint and bumpy texture. Teddy raided the fridge, downing a few slices of olive loaf. The pantry was a bummer – Irma's idea of munchies inclined heavily toward the pretzel. He finished off a bag of Rold Golds, chasing them with a drag of RC Cola. In the den, Aqualung was sitting like a dead duck. That old ditched feeling was coming back with a vengeance now. This sucked. He wasn't going to hang around for this. He thought about simply hopping in the Firebird and heading back to the party without so much as a by-your-leave. But that would be wrong. A Susan thing to do. Better to tell them he was going, so they could see just how bad they were doing him.

He killed the Tull and went to the bottom of the stairs.

'Joel?' he half called. 'Later, man.'

There was no response. He started to climb the steps. He'd never been upstairs at Susan's before. Even the time Joel showed him the picture of Irma with old Adolf he'd had to wait downstairs like some kind of fucking nimrod. But he knew the layout. These EarthWorks boxes were all alike. Bedrooms, bathrooms, walls. No surprises. The master bedroom was immediately to the left of the steps. He pushed the door open and turned on the light. There was a king-sized bed and a big dresser. A recliner and small roller desk. Closets. The bathroom off to one side. Something caught his attention – framed photographs arranged in a perfectly straight line above the desk. Teddy went for a closer look. All of them pictured an olive-fatigued John Truax at war. Seated at a card table outside a trailer. Standing next to a jeep. Crouching beside what looked to be the entrance of a small tunnel, a very large pistol in his hand. The last showed him squatting in front of a sandbagged bunker with a handwritten sign that read MY SONG MOTOR LODGE above the entrance. In each, he had that severe, lipless countenance that gave Teddy the willies. As if a single grim photo of Truax had been pasted on his body in each of the pictures.

Teddy squelched the lights and headed down the hall to Susan's room. He listened at her door for a moment. He could hear music. Across the hall was Darryl's room as tidy as her conscience. There was a movie poster on the wall, Pat Boone in *The Cross and the Switchblade*. Beside that was a watercolor of Christ holding a lamb. The single bed was piled with stuffed animals. He turned his attention back to Susan's door, unsure what to do. He didn't want to call out that would seem creepy, like he'd been spying on them. Just go, he thought. They don't care. They won't even notice you're gone. Then he saw that the door was off the latch. Inside, he could now hear urgent breathing and quick whispers. Before he could even think about what he was doing he'd given the door a tentative shove. It opened a few inches. He moved backward, waiting to be ordered away.

Nothing happened. He pushed the door open even farther. Susan's room was what he'd expected. Posters. A bulletin board ticketed with photos and concert stubs. A dresser cluttered with gels and potions. There was a big candle sputtering in the middle of it, encrusted by laval formations of multicolored wax. 'Killing Me Softly' warbled from the cheap cassette player on the floor. Just some girl's room. Except that Teddy's best friend was in it, lying naked on top of a girl whose bare legs were wrapped around his thighs. They were kissing deeply. Susan's eyes were closed, her brow furrowed, like she was trying to work out some deep puzzle. Teddy couldn't see Joel's face, just the back of his head and the stretched muscles of his neck. And then Joel began to move into her. Susan's head arched back, her upper lip sneering in pleasure. Teddy could see her breasts now, bigger than he thought they would be, their nipples dark and wide. Nothing like a girl's. He began to get hard. Joel rolled a bit to the side and Susan's hip rose up out of the turbulent blankets. There was a split Trojan packet on the pile carpeting.

Joel whispered something, breaking the spell, reminding Teddy where he was and what he was doing. He stepped back quickly, pulling the door as he moved. It remained an inch off the latch. He could feel his heart pounding like mad. His cock pushed against his Jockeys. Behind the door Susan cried out, a prolonged ululation that caused Teddy to retreat all the way into Darryl's room. Their bodies were in his mind, filling it up, pushing everything else out. He pictured himself sitting on the edge of that bed, running his hands over Joel's body and Susan's body, feeling the tip of her nipple against his palm, the soft kink of Joel's hair. He unbuttoned his jeans and freed his cock. It didn't take long. A few strokes. Susan's body and Joel's body. He remembered where he was just as he started to come. He reached out for the first thing he could get his hands on, a stuffed unicorn on Darryl's bed. He buried his cock in the fold betwen its head and body, pumping into it. Three times, four times. Feeling everything drain out of him. The pleasure. The excitement. The last thing to go was the image of Joel and Susan.

Desolation washed over him. You sick fucking fool, he thought. Look at yourself. If Susan saw you like this she'd laugh in your face. And Joel would simply shake his head. Susan loves Joel and Joel loves Susan and you're just in the way. The lookout. The one who gets ditched. He wiped the tip of his diminishing cock on the unicorn's smiling face and tossed it into a dark corner of the room. Figure that one out, Darryl. The holy spirit's crusty ectoplasm. He buttoned his fly. They were still making noises in Susan's room. The anger Teddy had been suppressing ever since his arrival finally boiled over. Who the fuck did they think they were dealing with, leaving him alone like this? The bitch Susan had stolen his one and only friend away. Turned Joel's mind inside out. And he fucking let her. Teddy had offered them his company and his wisdom and they'd spit in his face. He really would go now. Never speak to them again. It might take a few days but Joel would soon realize how badly they'd fucked up by doing him like this, how empty things were going to be.

But before he could move something froze him in the middle of the room like a jacklit deer. Headlights. They washed over Pat Boone and Jesus and then Teddy himself. They were gone as quickly as a pulse of lightning. And with the darkness came a faint tectonic rumble beneath his feet.

The garage door. Susan's folks were home.

Teddy looked at the digital clock next to Darryl's bed: 9:33. Way too early for anyone to be back. He moved to Darryl's doorway, listening to what was going on in Susan's room. The music continued to play. Laughter and sighs. A soft wet noise. They hadn't heard. Which meant he had to tell them. Quickly, so Joel could get dressed and they could hide while Susan dealt with the sarge. Or maybe they could just jump out the window like Butch and Sundance. Like the old days. Shouting *shi-i-it*, then laughing all the way to the getaway car.

Laughing. Susan had been laughing when they went up the steps. Joel too. Laughing just like the Potomac boys when they ditched him.

The kitchen door opened. Teddy leaned into the hall to better hear. There were footsteps downstairs now, Irma's heels clicking out a telegraphic warning across the linoleum. The sarge said something from the garage, three words that went unanswered. Soft, oblivious noises continued in Susan's room.

They had been laughing at him. They'd ditched him. And they would ditch him for good soon.

Teddy moved back into Darryl's room. He would say nothing. He would let this happen. His heart began to pound, even quicker than it had when he first saw their naked bodies. Irma's footsteps were at the bottom of the steps. On them. Teddy moved deeper into the room. Irma was on the second floor now. She switched on the hall light. Teddy moved all the way to the back corner of the room, slotting himself into shadow. There were two dull thuds as she kicked off her shoes, then the hushed sound of her nyloned feet coming down the hall. Teddy's heart was pounding so loud in his thin chest that he was sure she'd hear it. She stopped outside Darryl's bedroom. This is it, Teddy thought. Busted. But her attention was on Susan's door. She was about to knock when something stopped her. Her hand froze; her back stiffened.

There were more footsteps on the stairs. Heavier this time. Truax.

'We're almost out of pretzels,' he said.

Irma pushed her daughter's bedroom door wide open. From his vantage point, Teddy could see exactly what she saw. Joel, standing quickly, his semi-erect cock bobbing, the rubber making it paler than the rest of his skin. A creamy wattle shook from its tip like a miniature punching bag. Behind him Susan rose to an elbow before spinning quickly away, reaching futilely for covers that had been pushed into a single, insoluble knot at the foot of the bed.

Irma screamed. Teddy had never heard anything like the sound. It revved like an air-raid siren, starting as a low moan but quickly becoming a piercing shriek. She didn't move. There were no theatrical gestures, no grabbing of the head or flailing arms. Just the shrill, sourceless wail coming from her paralyzed body.

And then Truax was in the doorway. Joel had half turned by now and was desperately trying to get his foot into the twisted leg of his jeans. His sheathed cock continued to bobble. Truax pushed past his wife and moved toward Joel, who gave one last wild stab against his twisted jeans. He fell just as Truax swung his gloved fist. The blow skimmed off the top of Joel's head, doing little more than hastening his fall. He crashed through the open closet door, pulling several peasant dresses down on top of him. After that he lay perfectly still, his head and shoulders covered by the settling fabric, his naked legs sticking out into the room. Truax looked down at him. Irma continued to scream. Susan had yet to move.

'Go,' Truax said finally, his deep voice cutting through his wife's high-pitched screams.

Joel rose quickly, collecting what clothes he could, including that stupid fucking visor, which hung from a knob on the dresser. He left the shirt – Truax was standing on it. He covered his crotch with his balled pants and ran from the room in a half crouch. As he passed Irma she jumped out of his way, banging the door into the wall. Nothing happened in the room until Joel crashed through the front door downstairs. The sound seemed to release Irma, sending her racing across the room in her stockinged feet. She placed a knee on the bed and began to slap Susan's skinny back. After a half dozen furious blows Truax moved over to her, placing his big left arm between mother and daughter.

Teddy chose that moment to walk out of Darryl's room. quickly, quietly and totally unnoticed. He skipped down the steps and right out the still-open front door, leaving behind the sounds of Irma's shouts and Susan's sobs. He paused on the walkway, trying to see which way Joel had gone. The neighborhood was quiet. No lights flaring on. No gawking crowds. Just the night the lights went out in Georgia.

'Fuck.'

The voice came from the garage side of the house. Teddy hurried around the corner, finding Joel pulling on a shoe behind the big air-conditioning unit. He looked up, frightened, at Teddy's approach. His eyes quickly settled into anger.

'Where were you?' he hissed.

'I zoned.'

'Teddy, man . . .'

'Joel, I'm sorry. I didn't hear them.'

169

Joel looked up at the house.

'They caught us.'

'I know. I know.'

'I mean, Truax tried to kill me.' He looked back at Teddy. 'Where the fuck *were* you?'

Teddy didn't answer. Joel stood.

'I gotta go back to Susan.'

Teddy cast a baleful look at his friend.

'Bad idea.'

'I can't just leave her there, man. You should have seen them.'

Teddy could tell by Joel's eyes that he really was about to go.

'You go back up there and that crazy motherfucker *will* kill you.'

Joel sat down on the air conditioner and buried his head in his hands.

'What am I gonna do?'

At Joel's words, Teddy felt a wave of pleasure shoot through his body nearly as intense as the jolt he'd felt back in Darryl's room. For the first time in ages, Joel was asking him what to do.

'Look, I'll check on Susan.'

Joel waited. Listening. Needing Teddy now.

'Just let me get you out of here first. You can crash at my house.'

Joel looked uncertain. Though he was still paying attention.

'Then I'll come back here and make sure they haven't crucified her. I'll make like you didn't say what it's all about, just that you wanted me to see if everything was all right.'

Joel looked up at the night sky.

'I don't know, man.'

'Look, that way I'll be able to see what's what. Check how pissed her folks are. If they're going nuts on her I can stop them. They won't fuck with *me*.'

'I don't know.'

'Joel, look at me.'

170

He did.

'Let me handle this.'

Joel thought about it for a moment. Teddy could see he didn't want to go. But there was nothing left to do.

'Yeah,' he said. 'All right.'

Damn right it's all right, Teddy thought.

They didn't say anything on the drive back to Prospero's Parade. The enormity of what had happened hovered between them. Susan and Joel had been caught. Which meant they were finished. There was no denying it. They'd heard Irma's screams and seen the anger move through Truax's body like a shaken sheet. That sheathed boner, swinging out there for everyone to see. Jesus. Irma would chop her legs off before she let that thing near her daughter again.

And Teddy had let it happen. Not that he felt guilty. This was their fault. They shouldn't have treated him like they did. Besides, the more he thought about it, the more he realized he had just done his friend a big favor, painful as it might now seem. This Susan thing had gone way too far. Letting Joel get caught was like the removal of a tumor. It would be hard at first. There would be shock and pain. But Joel would eventually come around. Things would return to the way they were. Sure, he'd have his bimbos. Only now they wouldn't interfere with the friendship. There would be no more giggling in distant rooms, no more dirty looks from Susan. And there certainly wouldn't be any more ditching. It would just be the two of them. Teddy and Joel. As it should be.

It was after eleven by the time he'd settled Joel in the guest room and returned to the Truax house. He didn't bother to hide his car this time. The place was lit up like an ocean liner. Even Darryl's room glowed. Teddy thought about that unicorn and smiled, digging the humor of it now. Fairly fucking funny. Figure that one out, little sister. It took a long time for anyone to come to the door. It was Truax. The glove was off his right hand, revealing a bandage stained the color of a banana gone bad. His fierce expression wavered when he saw it was Austin Swope's son.

171

'Mr Truax, I hate to bother you at this time of night.'

Teddy could smell the hand now. It reminded him of the time he'd raked back a mound of rotted leaves to discover the maggot-riddled corpse of a squirrel.

'It's just . . . Joel came by my house and was pretty upset.'

Truax's small eyes darkened and his thin lips almost disappeared. But that single unassailable fact hung between them. This was Austin Swope's son.

'I think he and Susan must have had some sort of argument or something?'

Truax's expression clouded.

'Yes. There was trouble.'

'Well, this is awkward . . . but he just wanted me to come by and see if she was all right.'

'She's fine.'

'Which of course is exactly what I told him.' Teddy smiled. 'But you know Joel. He can be pretty . . . excitable.'

Truax nodded.

'Those two can get fairly intense at times, I guess,' Teddy continued.

'That's not going to be an issue anymore. And you can tell Joel that.'

Teddy held up his hands in mock surrender.

'Hey, I don't want to get involved here. I'm just doing the guy a favor. He wouldn't leave me alone until I promised. He's a good guy, Joel. Just sometimes he gets so . . . out of control.'

Truax nodded terse agreement.

'Well, I think I'll head on back. I'm really sorry to bother you . . .'

Susan suddenly appeared at the top of the stairs. Her swollen, teary eyes narrowed in confusion when she saw who it was. There was an angry red welt on her neck. Her hair was wild and she wore Paddington Bear pajamas.

'Teddy . . .' she said, bewilderment in her voice.

Before she could say another word her mother was beside her, hissing in German and pulling her back into the darkness.

'Good night, Teddy,' Truax said.

'Yeah. Cool. Good night.'

He smiled as he walked back to his car, the anger and shame he'd felt earlier gone completely. Nobody would be ditching him now. He drove home fast. His friend was waiting for him.

11

The phone cut into Wooten's hungover sleep like one of those machetes the Filipino chefs had wielded the night before. He checked the clock: 6:41. Which meant he'd only been asleep for a few hours. It had been very late by the time they finally made it out the Swopes' front door. Not that it mattered – the twins were sleeping at a neighbor's house and wouldn't have to be picked up until the afternoon. Wooten always shipped them out for Swope's party. It was the one night a year that he let himself stay out until all hours, knowing the next day he could sleep as late as he liked. So a crack-of-dawn phone call was the last thing he wanted. It took him three groggy attempts to pluck the receiver from its cradle. If this was about work, somebody was about to have a bad day.

'Hello?'

'Mr Wooten, this is John Truax.'

Last night swam into his mind. The angry confrontation on the porch. That cake, falling slowly, like a holed ship slipping into the cold sea.

'We've got a problem,' Truax said.

'A problem?'

'We have to talk.'

'Mr Truax, it's six in the—'

'Sergeant.'

'Excuse me.'

'It's Sergeant Truax.'

Wooten paused for a moment.

'It's six A.M. on a Sunday morning,' he said coolly.

'This concerns my daughter's honor.'

'Honor?'

Truax said nothing.

'Yes,' Wooten said eventually, understanding now that this was serious. 'All right.'

'You and your wife should come over here as soon as possible.'

'Now?'

'As soon as possible.'

Wooten hesitated. There was a stony silence on the other end of the line. He realized that there hadn't been much sleep at the Truaxes' last night.

'We'll be there by eight.'

'Fine.'

'Do you mind telling me what's going on?'

'Ask your son,' Truax said before hanging up.

Ardelia was sitting up in bed, staring at him wide-eyed.

'What?'

'It was John Truax. Says something happened between Joel and Susan last night. They want to talk to us right away.'

'What happened?'

'He wouldn't say.'

Wooten swung his big legs out of bed. There was an unsteady moment after he stood, his bloodhungry brain protesting at the early rise. But he quickly gathered his wits. There'd been trouble with his son. He hurried down the hall, tapping twice on Joel's door before pushing it open. It took him a moment to realize that he would have to wait a while longer for any answers – the bed was empty.

They left for the Truaxes' just before eight. It hadn't taken them long to track down Joel at the Swopes'. Wooten hated to call Austin so early, especially the day after the party. But they had to find Joel. Especially after that call.

Swope answered on the eighth ring.

'Austin, it's me.'

There was a pause.

'Earl? What is it?'

'I'm sorry to bother you but I'm trying to track Joel down. I just got a call from John Truax. Something seems to have happened between Joel and their Susan.'

He could hear another voice. Great. Now Sally was up as well.

'Hold on a sec . . .'

Swope and his wife spoke for a moment.

'No panic, Earl. Joel's in the guest room here. Sally said she saw him before she went to bed. She figured you knew.'

'Thank God.'

'You want me to wake him?'

'No, that's all right. Just send him home when he gets up. Hey, Austin – thanks. I'm really sorry about this.'

'Did Truax say what happened?'

'No,' Wooten said. 'But whatever it was he seemed pretty upset.'

'Let me know if you need any more help.'

'Thanks, Austin. I appreciate it.'

He hung up, glad to know that, whatever had happened in Fogwood, at least his son was in safe hands.

The Wootens arrived at the Truaxes at exactly one minute to eight. That was one thing about building a city – you knew how to get where you were going on time. Especially at this hour on a Sunday morning, when the only people on the streets were health nuts and the seriously religious.

Truax answered the door before the chiming had stopped.

'Come in,' he said grimly.

Wooten grasped his wife's elbow as they entered the house. A house Wooten had built, one of a hundred such models he'd raised in the past few years. Truax led them into the living room. Irma was sitting in a big brown chair against the far wall. She stood as they entered, wiping her hands on her skirt. For having been as drunk as she was ten hours earlier, she now looked as sober as a judge.

'Hello, Irma,' Ardelia said, not one to beat around the bush. 'What is this?'

'Is everything all right?' Wooten asked. 'Is Susan all right?'

Irma snorted.

176

'Won't you sit,' she said, her voice sarcastic, as if the idea of the Wootens sitting were laced with hidden implausibilities.

Wooten and Ardelia perched beside each other on the lumpy green couch beneath the front window. The shelving in front of them contained two dozen glossy sculpturines. Children and animals. Rustic scenes. A bird taking wing. Irma dropped back into her chair. Truax sat in its twin. Both now faced the couch at oblique angles.

And then Wooten noticed it. His shirt. Folded neatly on the coffee table in front of him, right next to a *National Geographic* with some African woman on the cover. She was right out of the Stone Age, this one – her neck stretched by some horrific metal collar, her nose and ears pierced by painted bone. Her hair was as nappy as a stray cat's. Breasts like spatulas. Wooten checked the date. Almost two years old. It was the only magazine in sight.

He looked back at his shirt. It was one of his favorites. Ardelia called it his Sammy Davis Special. Checkered, with twin breast pockets and squared tails that he could wear outside his belt without looking like a slob. He wondered for a moment what it was doing here. Then he rememebred that Joel had been wearing it yesterday. Now that he was filling out he could just about get by with wearing his father's things.

And now it was on the Truaxes' coffee table.

Wooten looked up. Irma stared at him, her pale blue eyes hateful and triumphant.

'We don't want Joel to see Susan anymore,' she said.

The Wootens sat through a silence.

'Why?' Ardelia finally asked.

Irma's gaze traveled from Wooten's face to hers.

'We caught them.'

'Caught them?' Ardelia asked.

Wooten understood immediately. Something moved inside him, a fear stronger than he'd felt in a long time. So now it's happened, he thought. He nodded once at Irma, letting her know that he got it, that nothing more needed to be said. She met his eyes and he could tell by her expression that she understood. The conversation could proceed. Arrangements could be hammered out, accommodations agreed upon. No details, no blame. Just four people making something wrong into something right.

And then she said it. The woman just went ahead and said it anyway. Maybe because she was German and didn't really know what the word would do. Or maybe simply because she was evil. Whatever the reason, she said it. Tossing it like a grenade into this bland suburban room.

'Fucking,' she said, those middle consonants sounding harder than Wooten ever thought they could. 'We caught your son fucking our girl.'

'Where?' Ardelia asked, the thinness of her voice making it clear this wasn't what she wanted to ask at all.

'In her room,' Irma said. 'In my daughter's room.'

Wooten looked back at Truax, his talk of honor suddenly making terrible sense. He wondered how that went. If Truax laid his rotten hand on his son. But if Joel were hurt Sally would have said something.

'And so I want them never to see each other again,' Irma said.

They were all looking at Wooten now. Even Ardelia. It was his move. He was the father of the boy who'd been caught. It was up to him and no one else to say that this thing would never be allowed to happen again. He hesitated, balking at the idea of doing what this woman asked of him. But that was just foolish pride. He knew there was only one thing to say.

'All right.'

'Earl . . .' Ardelia said.

He turned to his wife. He could see that she didn't want to agree to anything. Not yet. Not here. Not with these people.

'I mean, don't you think we should talk to Joel first?'

'What, and ask how it was for him?' Irma asked.

'Irma,' Ardelia said, drawing back, her mouth falling open.

Irma slapped her hand on the arm of the chair.

'Don't you look at me like that, Ardelia Wooten,' she hissed. 'Your son comes in here and makes this . . . ah, what's the word?'

She shook her hand. Her brow creased. She seemed to lose her train of thought for a moment.

178

'Miscegenation?' Ardelia asked finally.

Irma looked up, clearly not knowing what the word meant. Her eyes narrowed hatefully.

'Well, I don't know what other word you were going to use,' Ardelia continued. 'But whatever was going on last night, Joel wasn't doing it alone.'

Wooten gently put his hand on his wife's thigh. She shook it off.

'What is that supposed to mean?' Irma shot back.

'It means we have a problem, Irma. And we're not going to solve it if one of us starts blaming the other's child.'

'You think the boy is not responsible?'

'I think he shares responsibility, of course.'

'Shares? He comes in here with his big bright smile, and you think it's my daughter who's responsible?'

There was a moment's silence.

'Big bright smile,' Ardelia said, repeating each word slowly. 'And just what is that supposed to mean?'

'You know what it means.'

Here we go, Wooten thought.

'Yes, I think I do,' Ardelia said.

'Ladies,' Wooten said.

They both looked at him. Ready to pounce.

'I think we're getting off on a bit of a tangent here.'

'I think we're heading dead for center,' Ardelia said.

'My point is that there's no reason to argue about something that's already been decided.'

'Has it?' Ardelia asked. 'Been decided?'

'Well, yes.' Wooten noticed his shirt again. That African woman next to it. 'I mean, clearly things have gone too far.'

'Thank you,' Irma said curtly.

Wooten shot her a glance. Don't thank me, you bigoted bitch, he thought. Don't you dare thank me.

'I think what we have here are a couple of good kids who are in over their heads,' he said. 'That's the way I'd like to approach this. It would be the most productive route. John? Am I right?'

Everyone looked at Truax. Wooten realized he hadn't said a word since ushering them into the room. He also had the

179

strange feeling that the man hadn't taken his eyes off him once.

He nodded slowly.

'Okay, then. It's decided. Joel and Susan are not going to see each other for a while.'

'Ever,' Irma said.

'Well, ever's a long time. Especially when they'll both be eighteen soon.'

Irma looked disgusted by the fact.

'Irma?'

'Of course I agree,' she said.

'Fine, then. We'll speak to Joel and I imagine you'll have words with your . . . with Susan.'

'Words,' Irma muttered.

That's it, then, Wooten thought. Now we can go. Thank God. But before he could stand Truax finally spoke.

'How do we monitor this?' he asked.

'Monitor?'

'Shouldn't there be some sort of procedure for monitoring the situation?'

Wooten looked at him for a moment, then glanced at Ardelia for help.

'Well,' Ardelia said, using her teacher's voice. 'What we'll do is sit Joel down and have a talk with him. Explain the situation. And then he'll do as he's told.'

'But what if he doesn't?' Truax persisted.

'Well, I really don't think that's a problem . . .'

'He'll obey,' Wooten said.

Truax looked at him. Waiting for the rest of the sentence.

'You have my word of honor.'

Truax nodded. Once. That was what he needed.

'And how do you plan to, uh, monitor your daughter?' Ardelia asked.

'I've locked her in her room,' Truax said evenly.

'What, forever?'

'If that's necessary.'

His words cast a momentary hush over the room. Go, Wooten thought. Leave this place and never come back.

'Then it's decided,' Wooten said, standing. 'Ardelia?'

180

She stood as well.

'Don't forget the shirt,' Irma said.

Wooten had planned on leaving the damned thing there. But now he had to pick it up.

'If there's anything further you want to talk about,' Ardelia said calmly, 'please give us a call any time.'

'What, do you mean if she's pregnant?' Irma asked. 'Don't worry. He was wearing a rubber. I saw it.'

'Woman . . .'

Wooten grabbed his wife's arm.

'Come on, Ardelia. Let's go.'

But before they could move there were footsteps on the stairs. For a moment Wooten thought it might be Susan, wandering down to beg for mercy or curse them all. He wasn't sure he could handle that. He felt bad enough deciding the fate of two kids who were clearly in love without having to face one of them. But it wasn't Susan. It was her sister, a lumpy, slack-jawed girl who'd inherited her father's grim looks. She was holding a stuffed animal in her hand. A unicorn, its horn spiraled purple and yellow. She held it aloft in disgust. Something was clearly wrong with it.

'Mom . . .'

12

She watched from Darryl's window as the Le Sabre sped away, running right through the stop sign at the end of the street. Any hope that the early-morning summit had reached a peaceful resolution vanished as quickly as the car. She'd heard the muted hateful voices and seen the Wootens' faces as they left. It was official now. They'd been split up.

Susan looked helplessly around at Darryl's room, the para- phernalia of goodness filling every inch of it. She'd escaped her own locked room moments earlier, after her sister left the door unlocked when she'd come in to ask what had happened to her unicorn. There was some sort of crusty patch on its stomach. Susan said she didn't know and then, thinking fast, asked Darryl if she would take a letter to Joel for her.

'Don't you think it's time you stopped sinning?' Darryl asked in response.

No, Susan almost said. But didn't. She had enough enemies already. At least her sister had left the door open. Susan's first thought was to bolt down the steps and out the garage, cutting across lawns and bike paths to Mystic Hills. If she ran like crazy she could get to Joel's house before his folks. And then they could go, like they'd been talking about. Run away down to April's for a few days and then just vanish, leaving behind parents and locked doors and everything else in this city that seemed destined to keep them apart.

But she froze before she reached the top of the steps. There were voices down in the living room. Her parents. The Wootens. Locked in her room with Cat Stevens on loud she hadn't heard them arrive. She'd have to pass right by them.

Her father would stop her. Nobody could get away from him. Everybody knew that. She'd once met a scary man at Fort Meade who'd served with him over in that awful place, a dead-eyed soldier who'd come to visit unannounced one afternoon soon after her dad came home. He'd spent the whole time staring at the floor, a cruel smile on his face, saying things Susan didn't want to hear. How her father never slept and how he hunted people down. How the enemy knew his name and had a bounty on him. Her dad had finally taken the man away to a local bar, coming home drunk for the only time Susan could ever remember. He didn't talk to anybody for a few days after that.

So running away was impossible. Instead, she went to Darryl's room to watch the Wootens go. The best thing for now was bide her time. Be smart, for once. Her chance would come. It had to. She could just imagine how it had gone between her mother and Ardelia. Susan had always tried to keep them apart. And it wasn't just Irma's hatred of blacks that was the problem. There was also Ardelia's feeling that Susan wasn't good enough for Joel. She tried to hide it behind polite smiles and kind words, but Susan could see in her green eyes that she thought her son could do better. Well, they should enjoy their little breakup while they could, because it wasn't going to last for long.

There were footsteps on the stairs. Susan hurried back to her own room, silently shutting the door behind her. She climbed into bed, her back still stinging where her mother had hit her. She still couldn't believe Irma had done that. She'd regret it. Ten months from now when Susan called from California or wherever and she was begging her to come home, she'd regret it for sure.

The doorknob rattled. She grabbed a tub of skin cream from her nightstand, ready to bean her mother if she dared step into her room. But it was her father who appeared in the doorway.

'I thought this was supposed to be locked,' he said, nodding toward the handle.

'Darryl left it open. She was in here asking about some stuffed animal.'

'Do you know anything about that?'

'I don't touch Darryl's stuff. It's too clean.'

He looked at the floor.

'Don't say that,' he said quietly.

'Why not? Isn't that what this is about? Susan the slut.'

'We don't think that.'

'Irmagard does.'

Her father sighed.

'Susan, I came up here to tell you that Joel's parents were just here and we've decided that you two kids shouldn't see each other anymore.'

Even though she knew this was what he would say, the words still felt like a death sentence being pronounced on her. Tears welled in her eyes; sobs began to explode in her chest.

'No, Daddy, please.'

He looked at her. Anybody else would have thought there was no expression on his face, though Susan could tell that he was upset as well.

'I'm sorry. After last night, it's the only way. You two are in over your heads.'

'You can't do this!' she shouted.

Her father didn't say anything. He clearly hated this as much as she did. For a moment she thought she might be about to win a last-minute reprieve. But then Irma shouldered her way into the room. Her big blue eyes were watery as well, her voice a near-screech.

'We *can* do this! You are still under this roof!'

'Fuck you!' Susan screamed.

'Susan . . .' her father said.

'Yes, now the sewage starts coming up from the mouth.'

Susan stared as hatefully as she could at her mother, who was only too happy to return her gaze. So after a moment she spun back into the bed, burying her face in the pillows. Where there wasn't even Joel's smell anymore – the last thing her mother had done before locking her in her room last night was change her sheets, ripping them from the bed and triumphantly carrying them down to the laundry room, like the looted uniform of a slain foe.

Her parents left. She wanted to cry for a long time, but the tears soon evaporated, leaving her sobs raspy and pointless. She looked up. Her dad had left the door open, but that was only because it was Sunday and he would be in all day. She went to the bathroom and took a long shower, draining the house of every last drop of hot water. She wiped a circle of steam from the mirror and stared at herself. Her face was puffy, her eyes shot through with red. She examined her back, where her mother's handprints were raised like something done in kindergarten. Her wet hair hung in a limp cord above her spine. There were some shears in the medicine chest and for a moment she thought about just cutting it all off. Shaving it right down to the skull like her mother's people did to those poor Jews. She could leave the pile on Irma's pillow. But that would be stupid. Because she would be with Joel soon. And he liked her hair.

She walked naked and dripping back to her room, hoping somebody would see her. If they wanted to be shocked, she'd give it to them. But her parents were in the kitchen and her sister at church. She looked at her closet, where the rail and dresses still lay on the floor. She decided not to wear any clothes today. She put on *Blue* and crawled back into bed, holding her white tiger to her chest. Strategies of escape flashed inconclusively through her mind. Setting a small fire and using the ensuing panic as a smoke screen. Feigning illness and then slipping out of the emergency room. Lowering herself out the window like some fairy tale princess. But every idea ran up against the image of her father, watching over her. And then she remembered something even more depressing, an unnoticed statement among the hundreds of screamed words the night before. Something about her father's job going away. Which meant he would be here all the time now. Watching. Guarding.

Fucking Teddy. He was supposed to have been looking out for them. He'd probably got too stoned. Or maybe just left. She wouldn't put that past him. When he'd come back last night after it was all over she thought maybe he'd come on a mission from Joel. But when she saw that shit-eating grin she realized he was going to be no help at all. Which meant she was on her own. She had to figure a way out of this. She had to get to Joel. He'd know what to do. Sensing that something like this was about to happen, he'd recently begun saying how they would run away the moment their folks tried anything. Start the life they'd planned a bit early. There were other colleges he could go to. And she could always get work. While Irma would freak out on a permanent basis, Joel was confident that his parents would come around once they realized that he and Susan were going to be together whether they liked it or not. They'd give them their blessing in the end. Pay for college. Help with rent. They had to. Earl and Ardelia were decent people.

All she had to do was find a way out of here.

Her mind drifted back to last night. It had been so awful. Especially because just seconds before her mom arrived everything had been so perfect. They'd already balled before Teddy arrived and so there was no urgency the second time around. Joel was so calm, so steady. It was Susan who was going crazy. She didn't come very much – they hadn't quite got the knack of that. When it did happen it was like a sudden storm. And last night's had been a hurricane. Which was why she hadn't known her folks were in the house. She was coming like mad when the door opened. That was the worst thing – the aftershocks still running through her body even as her dad went after Joel, even as her mom slapped her around. The two feelings mixed together, good and evil, all happening at once. She wondered if coming would ever feel the same again. Or if there would always be that specter of pain attached to it.

The door opened. Her mother frowned at her nakedness, then crossed the room and turned down the volume.

'You should wear some clothes.'

'You should choke on your own vomit.'

Irma pretended to ignore the remark.

'Would you like to eat something? You must be hungry.'

In response, Susan turned toward the wall, showing her mother those handprinted welts and her bare ass and, most important, the last part of her daughter she'd see once Susan figured a way out of here – her back.

Part Three

13

They sat politely in their folding chairs. There were over four hundred of them, so many that they threatened to spill out the fire exits. Most were young and white; all were well dressed and orderly. They watched the stage with expectant eyes. Swope stared back at them, greeting as many as he could with a tight smile and friendly nod. These were his people. The Newton Homeowners Association. Purchasers of townhouses and single-fams and condos. Citizens, with mortgages, and second cars, water bills and children with braces. If they had long hair it was neatly combed; if they wore jeans they were freshly washed. When they finished their coffee they disposed of the Styrofoam cups in an orderly manner.

Membership in this particular club was simple. All a person had to do was buy a home in Newton, whereupon he was saddled with a first lien in his deed obligating him to pay an annual assessment to the NHA of 35 cents per $100 value of property, money which would be used to fund the city's public works and recreation programs. In return, the member could face the NHA's executive committee in a monthly general meeting to make recommendations, air grievances and petition for changes. Although members had no actual power, the committee weighed their requests with the utmost gravity. It consisted of five directors, currently sitting at a long table on the stage of Newton High's gymnasium, surrounded by unstruck decorations from a year-end production of *The Petrified Forest*. As executive director, Swope sat at the table's center. To his right was Wooten, the committee's

189

other permanent member. To *his* right was Richard Holmes, serving a six-month term, as was Chad Sherman, the young EarthWorks PR man seated to Swope's left. Beyond Sherman sat the board's one at-large member, a shoeless Juniper Bend housewife named Ellen Felice, whose loopy eco-agenda was routinely, if politely, voted down by the other four.

The NHA was Vine's way of gradually introducing democracy into the city. Although responsive to public opinion, it remained an agent of corporate control. If push came to shove, the inbuilt EarthWorks majority could easily quell any citizen uprising. Come summer's end, however, all five directors would be elected by the homeowners. Although the company-appointed city manager would still have the final say in fiscal matters, corporate power would no longer be absolute. Three years on, in the year of the nation's bicentennial, the manager post would be abolished in favor of an elected mayor. Phase IV would have been completed. Newton would no longer be a profit point for EarthWorks. At that moment, all political links with the company would be severed. The city would be on its own.

For now, however, it was Swope's show. Wooten had little interest in the committee's affairs, simply adding his technical expertise to matters under consideration. And the other EarthWorks representatives behaved like what they were – employees. As for Ellen Felice, she was happy for a few minutes to lobby for natural foods in school lunches and free birth control at the city's clinics. The meetings were so well attended that many members found themselves leaning against tumbling mats at the back of the gym. Uplifted backboards and climbing ropes hung above them like jungle canopy. As the school's vice principal, Ardelia Wooten served as host, sending janitors out for extra folding chairs and gently remonstrating with the occasional transgressors of the no-smoking policy.

The first hour of tonight's meeting had passed with the usual well-oiled monotony. Complaints were heard, budgets discussed, news related. Swope finessed the teen center situation by simply announcing that the flood-damaged structure was closed for repairs until further notice. Thankfully, nobody mentioned the gaslights. Wooten made a short speech announcing that Phase III housing starts were ahead of schedule, glossing over the fact that Phase IV presales had slumped. Holmes nodded sagely throughout, chewing on the stem of his unlit ebony pipe. Ellen Felice brought a motion asking that the Ecology Flag be flown outside Newton Plaza. Swope promised to take her recommendation under advisement. Sherman said he thought going slow on these matters was a good idea.

It was only when he reached the last order of business that Swope's mind came to life. The fence. This would be a tough one. On the face of it, the motion was simple enough. The residents of Zeno's Way, a small Fogwood cul-de-sac, wanted permission to build a fence to keep the kids of Renaissance Heights from cutting through their yards. They had petitioned Swope in May, submitting a respectfully argued document backed up by Polaroids of damaged shrubbery and vandalized lawn furniture. Their representatives had come to Newton Plaza to make their case with sweet reasonableness. They knew all about the city's restrictive covenants and Barnaby Vine's vision of a fenceless metropolis. Swope had nodded sympathetically when they said they didn't want to cause trouble. In fact, they wanted to prevent it.

'Let me see what I can do,' he'd said. 'I'll try to have something for you come the next NHA meeting.'

They thanked him, these solemn representatives of a dozen Newton families, two of whom, he noted, were black. That was good – he'd hate for this to become racial. Ever since that meeting, Swope had pondered the problem. It was a real poser. Although he sympathized with the good folk of Zeno's Way, there was, on the face of it, nothing to be done. Vine's city plan could not be more clear. His streetscapes allowed for no fences on residential property. No chain links or split rails or brick walls. No stockades or cyclones. Period.

And yet it wasn't that simple. To refuse the people of Zeno's Way would entail serious consequences. Underlying their petition was an unspoken threat – if they didn't get their fence, they would move. The stampede of Heights

191

delinquents had become rampant. They completely ignored the nearby bike path, kicking through the well-kept yards at all hours. Compounding the problem was the nightly cacophony of thumping music and domestic beefs emanating from the projects. Worst of all, there had been a break-in at one of the Zeno's Way houses. A stereo and some prescription drugs were pilfered. Swope shuddered at the thought of a row of For Sale signs appearing in front of those brand-new houses. Newton was supposed to provide a remedy for white flight, not another instance of it. The press would be all over that one. He could just see the photos and the headlines. Chicago would go nuts. Like the teen center, this was exactly the sort of dilemma a troubleshooter was supposed to gun down. If he couldn't, then maybe someone else really should be city manager.

It wasn't until yesterday, as he lay in bed after being woken by Wooten's call, that he came up with a solution. It was inspired. King Solomon himself couldn't have done better. The principle was simplicity itself – reversion. If they couldn't build fences on Newton land, then Swope would have to make sure that the land was no longer Newton. He'd revert a three-foot-wide strip of property around the cul-de-sac to Cannon County, who would lease it back to the homeowners for a nominal fee. And then they could build their fence. There would be some tricky paperwork involved and maybe an eminent domain writ. But all that was merely a matter of course. Come next month the people of Zeno's Way would have their protection.

All he had to do was get the NHA executive to rubber-stamp it at tonight's meeting. He'd saved the motion until minds were already beginning to wander out the door, hoping to minimize debate. He read out the petition rapidly, his eyes flittering occasionally over the Zeno's Way crew, seated, at Swope's request, in the front now. Then he sternly reiterated the city's policy on residential fencing. Shoulders began to sag and heads shake among the petitioners.

'However . . .'

In his coolest and most authoritative voice, Swope announced his reversion plan. He was sure to emphasize that this was a unique situation and, as such, called for radical measures. In no way did this suggest a change of EarthWorks policy. As he finished he could see to his delight that the crowd seemed more intrigued than outraged. Swope opened things up to questions. There were a few hardballs about violating the covenant, which he fought off with vague promises of more bike paths and an increased minibus service. After five minutes he could tell that there would be no trouble from the NHA membership.

He'd done it.

'Well, then, if there's no further discussion I propose we—'

'Austin?'

Wooten's voice seemed to come from very far away. It took Swope a moment to realize why – he was speaking into his microphone, causing the word to echo through the vast gym. Swope turned to look at his cochairman. His yellowy eyes were averted. His expression seemed both puzzled and determined.

'Earl, sorry. You probably have something you want to add about the kind of fencing we can erect.'

'Well, yes, I could talk about that. But first, I mean, do you really think this is a good idea?'

Swope could hear the creak of folding chairs as people sat up to pay attention. It sounded like the slow shattering of an ancient glacier.

'I think, well, yes, given the circumstances, it's the best possible solution.'

Wooten nodded, smiled briefly, then took a deep breath.

'I just . . . I mean, wouldn't it seem contrary to what we've been doing these past five years to throw up a fence over there?'

'I think we've noted that, Earl. But situations change.'

'Yes, I know, but I still think that this is an . . . over-reaction.'

Swope felt something cold move through him. Earl Wooten had just criticized his judgment. *Challenged* it. Over a microphone. In front of several hundred people. Swope was so stunned that his usually agile tongue failed him. He continued to stare at Wooten. Yielding the floor with his silence.

'What I'm saying is that, if you look at how we've street-scaped these houses, there should be no call for fencing of any sort. And if we go putting it in now we'll be ruining the balance.'

'Things *are* out of balance,' someone in the front row said. 'That's the problem.'

There were murmurs of assent, and not just from the front row. Thank you, Swope almost shouted.

'I understand that,' Wooten persisted, his voice almost musical with reason. 'And I think your problem is one we should solve before we do anything else. It's just that . . . well, I've built a lot of fences in my day. And I've yet to see one that people can't get over if that's what they have a mind to do. I think Mr Vine knew that when he put in his protective covenants. That's all I'm saying here. We build this wall and we've got one more structure people can abuse.'

There were whispers from the crowd at this. And not all of them negative. The people in the front row suddenly had trumped looks on their faces. Their eyes all wandered toward Swope. He realized that there was only one thing to do – put this to an immediate vote. But before he could forward the motion he noticed something. Ellen Felice's nodding head. Agreeing with Wooten in that absurd theatrical style she had. Beside her Chad Sherman stared at Swope with the expression of an about-to-be-fed puppy.

Swope did the math. Two on two. Which left Richard Holmes, sitting on Wooten's far side, his lips bunched around his pipe stem, his eyes narrowed in a pantomime of judicious consideration. Although a Wooten crony, he was still an EarthWorks man. There was no way he would vote against Swope.

Unless he knew something.

Just call the vote, Swope thought. But he remembered Holmes's words from the party. *Any more good vibes on the grapevine . . .*

'Richard, you've been keeping pretty quiet over there,' he said jovially.

Holmes plucked the pipe from his mouth with a wet noise.
'I must say I think Mr Wooten has a point,' he said.

Swope nodded once, trying to mask his stupefaction.
Unbelievable. If he called a vote now he would lose. Earl
Wooten would defeat him in front of his own people. He
suddenly had a cold, cold thought.

The word was out. Wooten was going to be offered the
job.

Swope looked at the table in front of him. The petition,
covered with his scribbled amendments, rested there like
an algebra test some dunce kid had failed. Suddenly, an
unfamiliar commercial began to play through his mind. This
one was set in a hotel ballroom. Balloons are falling slowly to
earth. The band packs their instruments. A tightly smiling
Swope appears on stage, surrounded by tearstained aides
fingering cheap boaters. Sally, looking grim, shrugs at someone offscreen. After scattered applause Swope begins to
explain that he has just phoned his opponent to congratulate
him. A chorus of no's sounds, which he silences with a stoical
hand. Maybe next time out, he says. Maybe next time.

'Well,' he said finally, chuckling in a self-deprecating way.
'It would appear that our plan needs a bit of fine-tuning. So,
if it's all right with the board, I'd like to take it back into the
shop and do a bit more work under the hood.'

'Absolutely,' Wooten agreed heartily. 'I think that's a good
idea.'

Chairs began to scrape, voices murmur. The folks in the
front row remained where they were, staring at Swope in
angry confusion. He rapped the table with bare knuckles. But
the gesture was superfluous – Wooten's words had already
adjourned the meeting.

After a brief bit of consolation work with the Zeno's Way
contingent, Swope headed toward the exit.

'Austin?'

Swope turned. Wooten was pursuing him, a grave but
friendly look on his face. Swope waited beneath a row of
climbing pegs that seemed well beyond his reach.

'Hey, Austin, sorry about that.'

'Not at all. I appreciate your input.'

'I just wish you'd run it by me first . . .'

'That was my mistake.'

'Look, what do you say we get together and talk about this? I'm sure we can do something for those peopole. If not a fence then—'

'Absolutely. Later this week?'

Wooten grimaced.

'Early next might be better.'

'Next week it is,' Swope agreed.

Wooten headed back to the crowd, but turned after just a few steps.

'Austin, I really am sorry. That all . . . came out wrong.'

'There's democracy for you.'

The two men smiled at each other for a brief, uneasy moment before Wooten walked off. Swope remained beneath the climbing pegs, watching as Wooten joined Holmes, Ardelia and Felice by the stage. Holmes said something and then Wooten said something. Everybody laughed. Swope turned and walked quickly out the door.

He went to Newton Plaza directly from the meeting. He wasn't sure why. It would be empty at this hour. He just felt he had to be there. Decisions needed to be made. He could hardly comprehend what had just happened. Wooten had opposed him. *Crushed* him. There could be no doubting it now. His job was in deep jeopardy. Wooten would have never pulled a stunt like that if he didn't know something. And there was no way Holmes would have opposed Swope unless he was privy to the same knowledge. Swope began to fear that if he didn't act now then this whole thing would slip away. The past five years would slide down the tubes, all that backbreaking work good for squat.

The maddening thing was, he'd gone into the meeting convinced that there was no threat from Wooten. He'd spent the better part of the day trying to find out for sure if he was indeed going to Chicago, using subtle and indirect methods to question everybody from Wooten's secretary to the Earth-Works travel office. But no one knew anything. By the close of business Swope was telling himself that he'd got himself riled over nothing. But now he wondered if his ignorance only meant that Wooten was being cagier than he'd ever dreamed possible. And then there was the fact that he couldn't meet with Swope later that week. Wooten always had time to meet.

Provided he was in town.

Swope sped along Newton Pike, passing the occasional car. Businessmen coming home late from work; shoppers leaving the closed mall. What he needed was a way to be sure. If he knew for certain that Wooten was going to Chicago, then he could act. Stop this thing before it turned around and bit him on the ass. Because if it was true, then Swope realized he had been catastrophically wrong about Wooten all these years. The man was a schemer of the first order. Look at the way he'd continued to act as if they were the closest of friends even while packing his bags for Chicago. That cake, for instance. Presented with a brotherly flourish. Or that Sunday morning call. Like they were still just a couple of buddies who could help each other out when their teenagers got up to the usual nonsense.

As Swope approached the Plaza he started to dwell on that predawn call. How concerned Wooten had been. The way Joel had crept into the kitchen later that morning, his expression that of a Biafran refugee.

'Want some coffee?' Swope had asked the boy, deciding to put things on a manly footing.

'Um, no thanks. I better get home.'

'Rough night last night?'

Joel looked even more embarrassed.

'Uh, yeah.'

'How's that little friend of yours?' a curious Swope wondered. 'Susan, right?'

'She's . . . I really better go. Could you tell Teddy I'll call him?'

'Sure. Oh, and Joel – your dad phoned this morning. I think he's looking for you. Urgently.'

'Shit. Okay.'

After he was gone, Swope had decided it was time to talk

to Teddy. He climbed the carpeted stairs, steaming mug in hand. He tried to avoid his son's room as much as possible. It wasn't so much the mess as the downright funk of the place that kept him away. Incense and chewing gum and a dozen other fragrances that he saw no good reason to characterize. And then there was the undeniable fact – painful for a father but a fact nonetheless – that Teddy himself did not always smell altogether rosy. He knew it was just the usual pubescent secretions, something that would dry up once the kid's glands ratcheted down a gear. But still.

He stood in the doorway, staring down at Teddy for a moment. He slept on his back, his gasping mouth half open. Seen like this, there was something pupal and unformed about him. A constellation of acne spread across his hairless chest. His nipples were so small they might have been two additional zits; his pectorals were as thin as prime-cut veal. And then there was the deep concavity that had been there since birth, the malformed breastbone that had almost killed him as a newborn. It had pressed right against his heart, causing the doctors to give him scant odds of making it. Swope had spent four unbroken days beside that primitive incubator, his index finger extended through a tube hole in the clear plastic for his infant son to grasp. Sleeping in his chair. Ignoring the nurses as they tried to coax him away. Threatening to break the hand that attempted to pull the plug. Willing his son to live as Sally wept in another room and the doctors talked doomily about nature taking its course. He and he alone believed that the boy would make it, so much so that when the child seemed to give up the fight that second night, Swope had torn back the lid and shouted in his face, startling him back to life. And Teddy had survived. Because he was a Swope. Because his father would not allow his death. Would not allow defeat.

'Teddy.'

His eyes fluttered open.

'We have to talk.'

They'd gathered in Swope's office, Teddy sitting in an oxblood leather chair positioned in front of the inglenook fireplace, Swope taking up a position behind his desk. His study was done in the English baronial style, complete with floor-to-ceiling bookshelves and Hogarth illustrations. Swope nurtured his third cup of coffee. Teddy sipped a Yoo-Hoo, a bluejeaned leg slung over the chair's arm.

'Earl Wooten called this morning,' Swope started, idly setting the balls of the Newton's cradle in motion. 'Early. He said something about some trouble at the Truaxes'. Know anything about that?'

Teddy's eyes had flickered toward his father for a fraction of a second before resuming their casual focus on the fireplace. A thin chocolate mustache wreathed his upper lip.

'Don't know,' he'd mumbled.

'I think you do. Either you were there when it happened or Joel told you about it when he came here afterwards.'

Swope rarely used a strict tone with Teddy. When he did he expected him to understand the gravity of the situation and respond accordingly. To Teddy's credit he got the message straight away.

'All right,' he conceded. 'But you can't tell Joel I said anything.'

'Teddy, I have no intention of discussing this with Joel or his father or anyone else, for that matter. But Earl Wooten has involved me – at six o'clock on a Sunday morning – in a potential conflict between two of my employees. I need to know the facts before I can decide whether I should get involved.'

'Susan's folks caught her and Joel doing the dirty deed.'

Swope stared at his son evenly.

'You're joking.'

'I kid you not.'

'Where?'

'In Susan's room.'

'Irma and John walked in the door?'

'Yesireebob.'

'And just so we're clear – the dirty deed means?'

Teddy made a fist and punched it slowly forward.

'Joel told you this?'

'That's right.'

'And then what happened?'

'Much histrionics from the German contingent. Then Sergeant Truax launches a frontal assault.'

'Wait a minute. Are you telling me that John Truax physically attacked Joel Wooten last night?'

Teddy nodded.

'But I just saw Joel and he looked fine,' Swope said. 'I mean, John Truax seems like the type of guy, he hits you, you stay hit.'

Teddy's voice went Cosell-nasal.

'It was a glancing blow.'

'Ah. And then what happened?'

'Joel retrieved the majority of his threads and hot-footed it over here for some sanctuary.'

'Not wanting to be around his own parents when the feces hit the fan.'

'Bingo.'

Swope tried to picture the sight of a drunken Irma Truax discovering Joel humping her peaches-and-cream daughter just minutes after her very public fall from grace. That would certainly have been one for the books. He reached forward, grasping three of the cradle's balls. He pulled them to the right, then released them. Three balls, including one from the original group, swung out to the left. The procedure was repeated in the opposite direction. And again. And again.

'Dad?'

Swope snapped out of it.

'Thanks, Teddy. I appreciate your telling me this.'

'So what are you going to do?'

'Me? Nothing. I'm sure the parents will work it out.'

'Yeah, right. Then they'll get Nixon and Sam Ervin together for lunch.'

Swope made an open gesture with his hands. Teddy got up.

'Oh, and Teddy – keep me informed about things on your end.'

'Affirmative, Will Robinson.'

'I just don't want this to get out of hand.'

Teddy bobbed his head a few times, then sauntered out of the room, leaving his empty Yoo-Hoo behind.

Swope hadn't thought much more of the episode since then. But now that the prospect that Wooten was after his job had returned with a vengeance, he found that he couldn't stop thinking about the scene. John Truax had caught Joel Wooten fucking his daughter. And attacked him. The same man who'd been chasing Swope so desperately for a job.

By the time he pulled into his darkened parking place he knew what he was going to do. Even though the plan was still in its infancy, he knew that it was his only way to be sure if his job was in trouble. It was full of risks, but so was everything else worth having on this wretched planet. He piled out of the Town Car and headed toward the lobby. He could see through the glass that the night watchman wasn't at his desk. Probably on his rounds. No matter – Swope had keys.

Twenty feet from the door he heard the scuffle of feet behind him. There was a voice, not quite making words. He turned, thinking it was the guard. But it wasn't the guard. It was kids. Four of them. Black. Sixteen. Maybe younger. Their hair had been teased into nimbuslike Afros. One of them, dressed in an Orioles T-shirt, stepped forward. A comb with a handle shaped like a fist rose from his head.

'Got a quarter?' the boy asked.

Swope stared incredulously at him for a moment, trying to register the menace level. The tasseled toothpick dangling from the boy's mouth didn't help clarify matters. He glanced into the lobby – the guard was still AWOL.

'Listen, fellas, you don't know who—'

'Chump, just give us a fucking quarter.'

Somewhere in the back of Swope's mind it occurred to him that he was about to be mugged. All those years working in the District and not once had he been shaken down. And yet now it was happening, in this clean, planned city.

'Sure,' he said. 'No sweat.'

He fished a coin from his pocket and flipped it toward the boy in the Orioles shirt, who snatched it from the air with a nifty backhanded grab.

Swope turned and walked away.

'Chump,' a voice called after him.

Not yet I'm not, Swope thought.

The bird hit the window with a hollow, leathery thud that sounded like a football being punted. Swope was lost in thought when it happened, hammering out his plan's details. He swiveled in his chair to look. It had struck directly behind his head, almost as if it were coming straight for him. Some sort of gull, white-headed with chrome-colored wings. Heading for the late-night light of his office. Though it died on impact, a strong biological glue – some adhesive blend of histamines and corpuscles – caused it to stick to the glass. Swope rose from his desk to examine the creature. Every few seconds it would slip down a fraction of an inch, laying a vertical highway of muck on the window. But it showed no sign of falling. He wondered if it would continue like this all the way to the ground, passing level after level before settling gently into the shrubbery. Swope leaned forward, his nose almost touching the Thermopane. The bird's head had been twisted by the impact, allowing a clear view of its dead eye. Jelly pasted it to the window. As the bird moved downward the ball was slowly rolling up into the socket, exposing black veins. A few more earthward pulses and it would pop right out of the head.

Suddenly repulsed by the vision, Swope turned his attention to the Plaza. It was empty. The muggers were gone. A couple of human figures were perched on the edge of the ruined pier, their silhouettes framed by the lucent water. In the darkness it was impossible to see who they were or what they were doing. Swope would have to do something about that damned thing. All he needed was a lawsuit after somebody slid off. Dead fish flashed in the water beyond. Not many – only a couple dozen had surfaced since the cleaning crew had knocked off that afternoon, leaving a big pile by the edge of the boardwalk. Rotting and stinking to high heaven, no doubt.

He checked his watch. It had been a half hour since his call. He strolled across the office to the model city, squatting so he could place his eyes just inches from a little plastic woman playing tennis. She was tiny, no bigger than a pencil's eraser. But well made. The sweep of her arm as she prepared to meet the ball, her shiny helmet of hair, the twist of her legs. He reached out, pinching her between his thumb and forefinger. Testing how firmly she was grounded.

'Mr Swope?'

The voice startled him, causing him to yank the figure from its setting. There was a muted Styrofoam shriek. He closed his fist around it as he casually turned. John Truax stood in the doorway. Jesus, Swope thought. How the hell did he get in here so quietly? His eyes were just coming off the sight of the dead bird. As far as Swope could tell the man had no reaction at all to the gruesome tableau.

'John, come in.'

Truax wore his company blazer, kelly green, the tree-and-apple emblem stitched onto its breast pocket. Sears action slacks and some sort of regimental tie.

'The guard let me in.'

'Glad you could make it,' Swope said as he strode across the room. He held out his hand. Just as at the party, Truax was forced to grasp it with his left hand, palm cupped downward, like he was steadying himself on a rail. The difference being that this time Swope knew that was what the man would have to do.

'Please. Sit.'

Swope gestured to one of the seats facing the desk, then dropped into his swivel chair. As he sat he noticed that the bird was still clinging on behind him.

'Some party the other night.'

'Mr Swope, I'd like to apologize for Irma . . .'

Swope waved away the man's apology.

'Forget it, John. Really. It's a party. People are supposed to let their hair down. And if one or two cakes get smashed in the process, so be it.'

Truax nodded once. He was confused now, clearly wondering what Swope was driving at.

'Well, I guess you're wondering why I called you here at this ungodly hour.'

203

Truax nodded. Swope brought his hands down on the blotter.

'John – I'm afraid we're going to have to let you go.'

Truax drew back his head and started to blink. Swope kept on talking.

'I've put a lot of thought into your situation and I just don't think there's room for you anymore at EarthWorks. I know it's tough, but it's only fair to let you know as soon as possible so you can start looking at other options.'

Truax nodded for a moment, then began to stand.

'Whoa,' Swope said, his voice friendly. 'Sit down. We're not quite finished.'

If he storms out now, Swope thought, this won't work. But Truax obeyed. Good soldier that he was, he sat back down.

'So, John,' Swope asked. 'Have you given much thought to your future?'

'My future?'

'That's right. Two kids, a wife – you must have some concerns in that department.'

'Well, yes.'

Swope waited. Truax said nothing. The man clearly didn't have a clue what was going on.

'I was thinking in terms of what sort of job you'd be looking for now that your sales days are over.'

Truax continued to flounder, his mouth opening and then snapping shut without making a sound.

'Don't worry about titles,' Swope said, his voice softening. 'Feel free to speak in general terms.'

Words finally completed the tortuous journey to the tip of Truax's tongue.

'It's confusing.'

'There are no wrong answers here, John. Only honest ones.'

'I work harder than any of those . . . others. But I can't seem to get ahead.' He was shaking his head doggedly. 'I feel like a fullback who's been sent into the game without having read the playbook. No matter how much I outhit or outhustle the other guy I can't seem to . . .'

'Avoid penalties,' Swope finished for him.

Truax nodded.

'I think I know what you need.'

Truax looked up.

'You want somebody to tell you what to do.'

'Yes,' Truax said, without hesitation.

Swope uncoupled his hands, making a rounded gesture, as if he were showing Truax the circumference of a prize melon.

'You want someone to tell you what to do and when to do it. You're thinking, If only I could be given a task every morning – not some vague job description but a nuts-and-bolts mission – then I could outwork any man in this city. Is that right?'

Truax nodded. Beyond words now.

'That was the problem down at the model village,' Swope continued. 'You had to invent the wheel every time someone walked in the door.'

Truax wasn't even bothering to nod anymore. Swope let a few seconds of silence pass.

'John, here's the thing – I want you to come work for me. *Me* as in me. Not EarthWorks.'

Truax stared. If he asks me what I want him to do, Swope thought, then the deal will be off. But he did not ask.

'Yes,' he said.

So there it was. The last hurdle cleared.

'Excellent. Here's the deal – I will pay you five hundred dollars a week. Cash. Which comes to, what, twenty-six grand a year. What you do about taxes is your business. In exchange for that fee you will make yourself available to me as a confidential security consultant on a twenty-four-hour basis. Seven days a week. To do whatever I deem necessary to safeguard the integrity of this office. Without question or delay. And you will tell no one about our arrangement. Does this sound acceptable to you?'

'Yes, sir.'

As Swope leaned back in his chair he noticed that the bird had come loose sometime during their talk, leaving behind a two-foot streak of erratic gore that looked like a child's finger painting. It occurred to him that Truax had not once looked at the grisly sight during their conversation, even though it had been directly in his line of vision. Even as it fell, his unblinking attention remained on Swope.

'Any questions?'

'When do you want me to start?' came the immediate reply.

Swope smiled. This was most certainly his man. If, as he hoped, his suspicions of Wooten turned out to be a simple misunderstanding, then Truax could be counted on to keep his mouth shut, especially when Swope used his city manager power to find him a new posting somewhere in the city. The whole sorry episode could be buried without a trace. Nothing unpleasant would have to be done. Everyone would wind up exactly where they belonged.

He looked back at the sergeant, patiently awaiting instruction. A public service announcement began to play through his mind. You couldn't watch five minutes of TV nowadays without hearing it.

Don't forget – hire the vet.

'How about right now?'

14

The waterfront plaza was empty. Some car had arrived in the parking lot a few minutes ago, though it was impossible for them to see down to the pier because of that stupid Gravity Tree. And there was no way the security guard was going to come all the way down here for a look. Not when he had doughnuts and a portable Zenith. Teddy and Joel could be conducting human sacrifices and nobody would bother them. They were safe.

They'd come here after leaving the mall. It closed at nine, Muzak choking off, security gates rattling shut. They'd talked about maybe going over to Joel's but things were still too heavy there between him and his folks. Teddy's place was equally uncool – for some reason his dad had taken a deep interest in Saturday night's proceedings. The less said about *that*, the better. And of course the teen center was out. Which left the slanting pier. They hadn't been here in a while because Susan thought it was creepy, the way you had to keep your balance at the end, where it sloped down toward the water. But now that she was history it looked set to become their primo summer retreat. All they had to do was hop the chain-link fence, a feat Joel accomplished in two abrupt moves, though it took Teddy the better part of a minute to summon the courage to make that final drop. Wishing as he balanced there that Joel would wait up. They sat at the downside, feet dangling over the murky water, as isolated as if they'd been out in the middle of the Atlantic. A few dead fish floated near the boat platform below, their silvery gills catching odd moonbeams. Word was that they'd continue to die for another week or so. Not that Teddy cared. Fishing was for idiots. You sat there for hours, only to end up with something you could buy at A & P. Wonderful.

Joel's sulky mood continued to dominate the evening. Although Teddy's verbal quiver was bursting with barbed stories and jokes, he'd decided to let his friend wallow in his sour disposition. They sat in silence, studying the lake's shoreline. Most of it was taken up by townhouses strung together by a waterside bike path. There was the Pavilion to the north and, directly across from them, the Cross Keys Inn. The candles and bug torches on the hotel's dining deck shimmered across the water, accompanied by random sounds – a spoon on a glass, a cough, the unanswered ring of a phone. Though Teddy knew from the times he'd eaten there that diners couldn't see the darkened pier. Traffic noise from Newton Pike washed down from the other direction. Moored paddleboats and Sunfishes scraped against the wood on the nearby piers with occasionally musical creaks, backed up by the arrhythmic pock of small waves trapped by the beams.

Teddy scraped on his Cricket to refire his extinguished joint.

'Fresh from our factory to you,' he said, passing it over.

But Joel waved it away impatiently. Teddy shrugged, took one more toke and then ground the doobie out into the deck. He stowed it back in the resinous pocket of his jacket, wondering how long this bad mood thing was going to last. Joel'd been sulking ever since Saturday night's meltdown. His voice taking on a whiny timbre, his broad shoulders sagging. That stupid leather visor looking even more ridiculous, like some kind of modified dunce cap. Not that Teddy was necessarily worried by all this childish emotion. It was nothing a few sessions with the doctor couldn't cure. But after forty-eight hours the patient still showed little sign of recovery. If anything, his condition was worsening. Teddy had tried to josh and cajole him out of his funk; he'd administered various pharmaceuticals. All, so far, to no avail. Worse still, there had even been some harsh words for Teddy himself, accusing him of being the cause of this whole fiasco. Words that continued to hang in the air, like a cloud of summer gnats that followed you no matter how fast you walked.

'You know what we should do,' Teddy said finally.

'What's that,' Joel answered, his voice free of curiosity.

'Hit the beach. Ocean City, man. Get the Swope to comp us one of those EarthWorks condos? Now that you're eighteen we can imbibe copiously. Much beer can be had. En route I can pay a visit to my herbalist to refill nature's prescription.'

Joel shrugged.

'Susan and I were thinking of going there,' he said in a voice that Teddy could only describe as wistful.

Jesus Jones.

'Well, you'd better cast such notions from your mind. Conditions are strictly Stalag Seventeen *chez* Truax.'

Joel looked over at Teddy. In the wan light it was difficult to read his expression.

'You shouldn't sound so happy about it.'

'I'm not happy about it Joel. It sucks.'

Joel said nothing.

'Look, man – alls I'm trying to do here is make it up to you. Get your mind off it.'

'You'd be better off using that big brain of yours to figure out a way to get me and Susan back together.'

Teddy sucked air between his teeth.

'A quandary. I mean, I wouldn't recommend any trellis climbing. The sarge just spent three years making sure he wasn't infiltrated by Charley.'

'Fuck,' Joel said.

Teddy glanced at his friend. He really did look awful. Almost as if he was in mourning. For a moment, Teddy feared that he'd made a terrible mistake by letting them get caught. Maybe Joel wouldn't snap out of it. Maybe he'd spend the rest of the summer walking around with this stricken look on his face, pissed off at the world in general and Teddy in particular.

'But I'll certainly give it some thought,' he added bogusly.

Joel looked at him.

'All right?'

'All right,' Joel said, managing a weak smile.

Teddy spent the next half hour graciously listening to Joel talk about Susan, figuring it was the quickest way to let him get her off his chest. By the time he was done the Cross Keys Inn had grown quiet, the traffic on Newton Pike had almost stopped.

'You want to sally forth and check out some tunes at Rancho Swope?'

'Yeah,' Joel said quietly. 'No Lennon, though.'

Teddy accepted this onerous condition with a gracious spread of his hands.

'You make the call. You can crash there if you so desire.'

As he stood Teddy noticed the light was on in his dad's office. Not surprisingly. The guy worked constantly. They walked back to the end of the pier, weaving through the fifty-five gallon drums that blocked off its entrance and once again scaling that nettlesome fence. They held their breath as they passed the big pile of stinking, rotting fish somebody had left there. As they mounted the long concrete steps he noticed the Town Car in the usual spot. And right beside it was Truax's Cutlass. Now, that was weird. Maybe the sarge was getting canned for taking a poke at Joel. He considered pointing this out to his friend but decided against it. He'd probably start thinking it meant he'd be getting back with Susan.

They passed the Gravity Tree, with its hammered steel trunk and that dangling brass apple. The city's logo, a dumb, optimistic visual pun that represented everything Teddy hated about EarthWorks. Though he knew his father could be allied with far worse outfits, especially the bozos currently running the Western world a few miles to the south, the happy clams from EarthWorks still gave him the willies. It was amazing how a select group of highly educated people could so blatantly miss the fundamental truth of the matter. Humans were *not* good. Progress was *not* possible. The future was *not* rosy. In fact, it was a wasteland, filled with mushroom clouds, rampant overpopulation, famine and plagues. Just read Nietzsche, sports fans. The Last Man had arrived. Evolution was over. The human mind was being softened into pablum by a constant bombardment of TV, bad music and illogicality. All you had to do was read a few pages of *The Widening Gyre* to see this. Or Teddy's honors paper on *Twilight of the Idols*, the one he'd stapled so propitiously to his Harvard application. The only hope for the planet was that people like the Swope clan be given the reins. Otherwise, they'd all be in caves by the millennium, eating bugs and berries, puzzling over the hieroglyphical scribbles of billboards and the books they used to fuel their paltry campfires.

'Quiet night,' Joel said.

'Yeah.'

'I wonder what Susan's doing.'

Choking on Fruit Loops, Teddy didn't say.

As usual, the Firebird was discreetly parked in a shadowy end of the lot. They were halfway to it when Teddy saw the figures coming toward them. There were four of them, moving with the speed of high-plains hunters. Joel saw them, too.

'Let's bolt,' Teddy said.

'Too late.'

He was right. The Firebird suddenly seemed miles away. And the lobby's guard station was empty. Teddy and Joel froze, both knowing from freshman experience how flight worsened these matters. It took the charging boys just a few seconds to surround them. They had it down to a science. Two in front, one on either side. Teddy recognized them from the teen center. Their leader was the one who'd fronted the charge on the Edgar Winter brigade. Tonight he wore an Orioles shirt, white with orange sleeves. There was a pick planted in his hair – its fisted handle emerged from his head at a sharp angle.

He moved directly in front of Joel.

'Gimme a quarter, man.'

Teddy looked at Joel. He was scared. More scared even than when Truax came into Susan's room.

'Mother-fucking, titty-sucking, two-balled bitch,' the one directly to Teddy's right said.

'Gimme a quarter, bwoy,' Fist Head repeated, apparently downgrading his assessment of Joel's age.

211

Teddy didn't have any change. His wallet was hidden beneath the Firebird's front seat. And Joel never had money. A long time seemed to pass. A bronchial whistle issued from the boy at Teddy's right side.

'Look,' Joel said. 'Just leave us alone.'

Fist Head stepped forward. Teddy noticed that the laces of his Chucks were untied.

'You say, nigger?'

'We don't have any money. We just want to go home.'

'Toms like you always got money,' Fist Head said.

The others laughed. Joel stiffened.

'Don't call me that.'

His voice blended fear with defiance.

'Man, what, you a Tom. I seen you with that white bitch and this faggot here. You think these people be with you, man? You think this bwoy is your *brother* or something? He fuck you up first chance he get.'

'*First* chance,' someone affirmed.

Untrue, Teddy thought.

'Come on, Joel,' he said instead. 'Let's just go.'

'Girl, you aren't going anywhere,' the boy with the cold said into Teddy's ear, projecting a mist of bacterial spittle onto his cheek.

Boy, how he wished his dad would come out of the building now.

Fist Head moved forward and put his face just inches from Joel's. Teddy could now see that he had a decorative toothpick between his lips.

'Say you a Tom,' he commanded.

Joel shook his head.

'Say it, bwoy.'

Teddy could feel the violence coming. Just like at the teen center. He shot one last despairing glance toward Newton Plaza. The lobby was still empty. Their only hope was that his dad was looking down. Seeing this. Calling the cops.

'No,' Joel said.

Teddy looked back at his friend's face, which had taken on the mulish cast he knew only too well. These guys were going to stomp them into grease stains and Joel was going all proud.

212

And then, in grim confirmation of Teddy's worst fears, Fist Head grabbed Joel's throat with his left hand. The boy with the cold took this as a cue to seize the back of Teddy's neck. Like anybody was going anywhere. His hand was wet and hot. Fist Head used his free right hand to yank Joel's visor from his head and Frisbee it toward some bushes. Then he put a finger right between Joel's eyes.

'Say it, bwoy.'

Joel tried to shake his head but could only move it once before Fist Head punched him in the face. It didn't look like a very hard blow to Teddy. But then Joel's nose was bleeding.

'Just say it, Joel,' Teddy pleaded.

'No,' Joel croaked.

Fist Head looked like he was going to punch Joel again but then, almost as an afterthought, registered Teddy's words. Still holding Joel's throat, he turned his attention to Teddy.

'Ass right. *You* say it. Show this nigger where it's at.'

The boy with the cold smacked Teddy on the top of the head, causing his glasses to slide forward to the end of his nose.

'Say what?'

'Tell this motherfucker he a Tom.'

Joel's eyes slid over to Teddy.

'Don't,' he croaked.

Fist Head punched Joel again, a crooked blow against his ear. It made a sound like fingers snapping.

'Shut up, bwoy.' He turned back to Teddy. 'Say it.'

Another slap landed on the back of Teddy's head. His glasses fell to the concrete. This is ridiculous, he thought. These were words they were talking about here. Meaningless epithets.

'He's a Tom,' he said. 'All right?'

'Tell *him*.'

Teddy looked at Joel, telling him with his eyes that this was nothing. Joel shook his head. But he was just being stubborn. He'd realize later how little this all meant.

'You're a Tom,' Teddy said.

The boy with the cold laughed for a few seconds. He was the only one. Joel was looking at the ground now. Fist Head continued to hold him by the throat. Teddy had hoped the words would serve as their abracadabra to freedom. But he was beginning to sense that maybe it wasn't going to end quite so easily.

And then a voice both familiar and strange was speaking.

'Let him go.'

Everyone turned to see John Truax standing a few feet away, looking very large among the long shadows. No one seemed to know what to make of his presence. He'd arrived so quietly. And there was an authority in his voice that made the snarled threats and curses of the last few minutes seem like nursery chatter.

Finally, Fist Head released Joel and started moving toward Truax, though the jaunt had left his stride, replaced by an ill-concealed wariness. Teddy was struck by the feeling that he was making a fundamental mistake.

'The fuck you?'

Truax ignored him. His eyes were instead on the boy with the cold, who continued to grip Teddy's neck.

'Let him go,' Truax repeated.

Fist Head stepped in front of Truax, blocking his view of Teddy.

'Man, you must want to get your ass—'

There was a sourceless gasping sound and then Fist Head was lying on the ground. His long arms cradled his stomach. His eyes were closed in a look of intense concentration. Teddy couldn't remember the part about him getting hit. It was as if someone had snapped those few frames from the film. After a few long seconds a sound like a dentist's suction emanated from his thoracic cavity. Everybody was looking at the downed boy except Truax, who had taken a step toward Teddy and the boy holding him.

'Let him . . .'

There was no need for him to finish the command. The hand released Teddy's neck. Its owner and his two friends bolted, running as fast as they could toward Newton Pike. Fist Head continued to lie on the ground.

'Are you all right?' Truax asked.

'Uh, yeah,' Teddy said.

214

Fist Head was on his knees now, moving as slowly as something on the ocean floor. Teddy pointed at the fallen boy.

'Jesus, what did you do to him?' Teddy asked.

Truax looked down at the boy, his face bereft of emotion. After a moment he reached down with his ungloved hand and grabbed the scruff of his neck, pulling the boy to his feet. He might have been lifting a sack of laundry. Fist Head shot Truax a quizzical look, then fled after his friends in a hunchbacked gallop. Truax didn't watch him. He'd already turned his attention back to Teddy, ignoring Joel, who was dabbing at his bloodied nose with the end of his shirt.

'You should get home.'

'Don't sweat it.'

Satisfied, Truax turned and began to walk toward his car. Teddy watched him for a moment, then picked up his glasses. They weren't broken. He put them on and looked at Joel, who continued to stand perfectly still, his eyes on the ground. He'd stopped dabbing at his nose even though there was still blood coming from it, a thin trickle that smeared his upper lip.

'You believe that guy?'

Joel, eyes downcast, said nothing.

'Hey, Joel? You all right?'

He finally looked at Teddy through narrowed eyes.

'You shouldn't have said that.'

'What? Oh, come on. They were about to kick our asses.'

'You shouldn't have, man.'

'It's just a word.'

Joel looked away. He seemed to remember that he was bleeding. He dabbed at his nose with his sleeve's end.

'Look,' Teddy said. 'This is ridiculous. Did you really expect me to stand here and let us get our butts whipped?'

The headlights from Truax's Cutlass washed over them.

'I don't expect anything from you anymore,' Joel said quietly.

With this, he turned and walked away, heading toward the bike path at the bottom of the plaza. The shortcut back to Mystic Hills. Teddy watched him for a moment. This was so stupid. He'd just saved his friend from a bad beating and now he was supposed to have done something wrong? Forget it.

'Joel . . .'

He kept on walking. Teddy realized he planned to walk all the way home. He set off after him, catching him just before he started down the asphalt path.

'Wait,' he said as he stepped in front of him. 'Wait!'

Joel stopped, though he wouldn't meet Teddy's eye. His nose wasn't bleeding so bad now.

'I'm sorry,' Teddy said. 'All right? I saw that guy wailing on you and so I just—'

'That's not the problem,' Joel said.

'What is?'

'You wouldn't understand.'

'Joel . . .'

But he was already walking, weaving around Teddy and plunging into the darkness. Teddy thought about going after him but knew it would be useless. Joel could be fairly fucking stubborn about these things. As if anybody cared. Tom. Dick. Harry. Let's grow up a little bit here, boys and girls. He watched until Joel disappeared into a copse of trees, then headed back to Newton Plaza. Time to report the incident to his dad. This shit was getting ridiculous. They had to get some more pigs in this place. Pronto.

But just before he reached the lobby he remembered Joel's visor sailing into the bushes. For a moment, he was tempted to leave it where it was. Do Joel a favor. Though giving it back would be a good way to make up for what had just happened. And so, wishing that somebody could see him doing this, Teddy delayed his meeting with his father to tramp around in thornbushes while savages lurked nearby. Just to get some stupid leather hat.

Because that's the kind of friend he was.

Part Four

15

Earl Wooten slept late. Although his plane wasn't until four, he would not go to work today. He didn't want to get involved in any crises or impromptu meetings that would draw attention to his departure should he have to leave quickly. Besides, he had other business that needed to be taken care of before he headed off to Chicago. Something that had nothing to do with work.

It felt strange to slumber in his king-sized bed while the city he'd built carried on around him. He'd wanted to take the phone off the hook but Ardelia wouldn't allow it — she had a couple hundred kids in summer school as well as a handful of teaching posts to fill. So she was under careful instruction not to put anything through to him, even if the lake should burst its shores or Newton Plaza crumble to the ground. The story they were telling was that there was a family illness down in Atlanta requiring his presence. He wouldn't be back at work until Monday. He hated lying about kin being sick but he couldn't think of anything else that would explain his sudden absence from the city. Especially when Austin called.

As he drifted in and out of consciousness, Wooten realized that this was the first time he could remember taking a day off. Ever. Good God, had it really been thirty years since he'd simply taken a day? Thirty years. Which was how many hours? He'd need a computer to figure that one out. Three decades of solid work. He'd started before his voice even broke with the real backbreaking stuff. Digging and cutting. The sort of work you never saw anymore, what with unions and modern machinery. Twenty-seven cents an hour, twelve hours a day, six days a week – and you best believe one of those days was a Sunday. After that came the minor skills. Dropping plumb lines or pulling the ornery levers of some big Caterpillar. Hour after hour, day after day, until he finally realized that there was more to him than back muscle and hand callus. With his transformation from mule into driver, one sort of difficulty gave way to another. Ditch digging yielded to four-hour meetings with bankers to discuss the purchase of improvable basin land. Long days drywalling turned into sessions with accountants to structure payrolls, backhoeing to siteside huddles with engineers about drainage strategies. Things a man who'd only finished fifth grade was never supposed to be able to do. But he'd taught himself that kind of work, just as he'd schooled himself how to fix the pneumatic motor of a jackhammer when it went down in the middle of nowhere. Hour after hour, day upon day. All of it leading up to something, a prize even greater than the things he'd already won – the perfect wife and sturdy home and beautiful children, the money and respect. A prize wrapped up in a big box currently being held in Chicago. Waiting to be opened in a mere twenty-four hours.

One of the twins started to cry downstairs. There was exasperation in Ardelia's voice as she asked what was wrong. Time to get up. Though it was not yet nine, he felt like he'd slept 'til noon. Ardelia would soon be taking the girls to their nursery, leaving Joel alone in the house. He still knew nothing about Chicago – they'd agreed to tell him that his father was going to Atlanta on unspecified family business, just in case he talked to Teddy. Not that Joel would care what his father was up to. Since Sunday, when Wooten had told him that he would no longer be able to see Susan, Joel hadn't said word one to him. Not even Monday night, when he came through the front door with a bloody nose. Wooten and Ardelia had followed him up the stairs, asking him what had happened. He'd slammed the door in their faces. Fearing that there had been trouble with the Truaxes, Wooten spent a restless night waiting for the phone to ring. But then Tuesday morning Ardelia got him to admit that he and Teddy had

220

been in some sort of fight down by the lake. Evidently there was bad blood between the two friends because of it. He'd tried to talk to Joel about it Tuesday night but had been met by a stony, shrugging silence.

As he dressed, he knew that he would have to talk to his son once again. Sunday's discussion had been a disaster. Although Wooten had left the Truaxes steaming with anger, by the time he'd arrived home Ardelia had shown him how it was Irma he was really mad at. The boy hadn't done anything wrong but love the girl too much and too foolishly. To make their separation seem like punishment would further confuse his already baffled heart.

Wooten agreed. He'd gone lightly to the boy's room, patiently explaining that he would not be allowed to see Susan for the rest of the summer. He admitted that it sounded harsh but there was nothing else to be done. The girl's folks were adamant. The thing to do was tough it out until it was time for Bucknell. A stiffly chuckling Wooten guessed that once Joel got a look at those college girls, Susan would become little more than a memory. A fine memory, yes, but a memory nonetheless. It was for the best, he told his son. It really was.

There was only silence after Wooten spoke. Joel avoided his father's eye, staring instead at the ceiling. After a while he snorted and turned toward the wall. Wooten spoke his name a few times but there was no reply. He felt the anger rise briefly in him, though it vanished when he remembered Ardelia's words. The only thing the boy had done wrong was love too much.

So now, four days later, there was still a talk needed. Wooten walked down the hall and paused at his son's door. Music drifted through the composite wood. That blind Stevie Wonder again. Something about a golden lady. He knocked.

'What?'

Wooten knew that was as close to an invitation as he would get. He pushed the door open. Joel sat up on his bed, reading a page covered by a girl's florid handwriting. His face registered a shift of emotion when he saw that it was his father. Something hard entered it. Unforgiving, in the way only the young can be.

'Mind if I pull up a chair?'

Joel shrugged. Wooten twisted around the desk chair and positioned it a good five feet from the bed. As he sat he could see that Joel was reading an old letter. No doubt from Susan. There were dozens more surrounding him, most loosely packed into unstamped envelopes. Probably written in study hall and passed during lunch hour. Wooten was suddenly struck by the feeling that there were vast landscapes within his son he had no knowledge of at all. Maybe the boy was hurting worse than anyone knew. But there was nothing they could do. The girl's folks had decided.

'Joel, I don't know if your mother told you, but I have to go to Atlanta on family business for a couple days.'

Joel shrugged. He didn't care.

'So how are you doing?' Wooten asked after a few long seconds.

Joel looked at him incredulously.

'How do you *think*?'

'Well, I think you're probably still mad at the world. But like I said on Sunday, none of us have any choice here. Especially seeing as how the girl's a minor.'

Joel looked up, bitterness in his eyes.

'That isn't why you're saying I can't see her.'

'It isn't?'

'Nuh-uh.'

Foolishly, Wooten took the bait.

'Then maybe you can tell me why I am.'

'Because you're a Tom,' Joel said, his voice matter-of-fact.

The paternal smile dropped off Wooten's face like an icicle in the morning sun.

'What did you say?'

'You're a Tom,' Joel said calmly. 'Mr Pale says jump and you say how high. Been that way your whole life.'

Wooten told himself not to get angry. It was just the boy's sorrow talking. His shame at getting caught. That's all. Just sorrow and shame.

'That's not true, Joel.'

'No? Then what is it?'

'Those people caught you in their *house*. Do you honestly believe there wouldn't be any repercussions?'

Joel had no answer for this. Wooten took a deep breath. Tom. The boy had called him a Tom. Though he didn't mean it. He couldn't mean it.

'If you want to make out that I'm some sort of evil coward then go on and do it. I can ride with that. But the fact is that Susan Truax is a minor. Her parents don't want you to see her. We have no *choice* in this matter. Is that clear?'

Joel shrugged.

'Think that if you want,' he said.

Wooten stared at his son for a moment. He was getting so big. So close to being a man. But not yet. Some things still had to happen for that. Some things still had to be understood.

'Joel, believe it or not, I want you to be happy. But I also have to make sure you're safe. Sometimes the two things aren't the same. And when push comes to shove, I've got to choose safe.'

Joel didn't answer. Instead, he began to rummage through the letters on his bed, as if his father weren't sitting a body length away. Wooten stared at his son for a moment longer. Not angry now. Not frustrated. Just saddened. He stood and walked wearily from the room, closing the door tight behind him as that blind Wonder continued to sing about a golden lady.

The word echoed through his mind as he packed his suitbag for the trip. *Tom*. There was no way the boy could know what it meant, to call him that. All he knew was that it was a way to hurt him. But it had been a long time since anyone called him a Tom. In the old days he used to hear it often. Though it was painful at first, Wooten eventually realized that the only folks using the term were either shiftless bums or people so twisted with rage they didn't know what they were saying. Of the dozens of people who called him Tom, none had ever owned his love or respect. Until now. But Joel couldn't really mean it. He knew his father had never tried to curry favor or play a part. Never scuffled or sirred or went cap in hand to

223

Miss Anne's kitchen. Never let any cracker mouth him off or use his first name without being allowed. There were only two kinds of men in Earl Wooten's world – his equals, and those who'd let themselves become inferior to him. He would never concede that anyone was his better. Not Swope. Not Savage. Not even Barnaby Vine.

Joel couldn't believe what he said. He was just saying it because he knew it hurt.

He left the house an hour later, telling Ardelia that he'd arranged to meet with a Glen Burnie contractor at the airport before his flight. More lies. Lies within lies. He consoled himself with the thought that these would be the last he would tell. To Austin or to Joel or to Ardelia. Especially to her. Today it ended. For nearly a year this thing had been in his life, like some kind of malignancy. The time had come to cut it out. So he could fly to Chicago free and clean.

It was a fifteen-minute drive to Renaissance Heights. Wooten parked in his usual spot, just beyond the minibus stop on the pike. He locked the car and headed down the bike path, which snaked through landscaped woodland before joining the project. Thankfully, there was no one around, not even at the tot lot. At one point he thought he heard some big dog crashing around in the woods above the path, but when he looked there was nothing.

A hundred yards from the project's entrance he saw the backs of the houses of Zeno's Way. Graffiti and beer cans littered the common land bordering their yards; a condom dangled from a ruined sapling. The sight brought Monday night's meeting unhappily to mind. Although Austin claimed not to be upset by what happened, Wooten could tell that he'd been sorely aggrieved. But he also knew he was right. Even as he now looked at those people's damaged property, he knew that once they built the first fence there would be nothing stopping hundreds more from following. He just wished he'd been able to halt the motion in a more diplomatic way. He'd tried without luck to get hold of Austin since then to smooth things over. Though Evelyn always had plausible excuses for her boss's unavailability, Wooten knew that there was damaged pride involved. Squaring things with his friend would be the first order of business upon his return. All this cloak-and-dagger nonsense would be a thing of the past. As he passed through the colony of Dumpsters at the edge of the complex's parking lot, Wooten took comfort in the thought that in just a couple of days the misunderstanding with Austin would be water under the bridge.

The big black button emitted a harsh, industrial buzz, the sort of sound Wooten always thought should be accompanied by an electric shock. It took her an eternity to answer the door. The chain seemed an insoluble puzzle, rattling for a good ten seconds before coming free. She was dressed in the kimono she'd picked up at some secondhand shop, its decorative waterfalls shrouded in a gray detergent fog. Behind her the boy made the faint, plosive sounds that accompanied the endless battles he fought with those two limbless GI Joes. Though Wooten had given him newer, better toys, he still preferred the scarred dolls.

She looked bad, even while she looked so good. Her uncombed hair was matted; the bruise-colored crescents beneath her eyes were darker than ever. She moved with that liquid quality that usually struck him as graceful but today only seemed tired. And yet, bad as she looked, he felt his resolve starting to slip. Before he'd even crossed the threshold. Before a word had been said.

She moved aside to let him past. Wooten took a few steps into the room and stopped, uncertain what to do. Usually they went straight to the bedroom, crawling beneath the velveteen sheets that were her only luxury. But he would not be doing that today. It was what he'd decided. He could feel her staring at him. Waiting to follow wherever he went.

The boy was trapped by the catty-cornered coffee table, his attention focused on the two dolls he continued to butt into each other. A half-empty bottle dangled from his mouth, its nipple stretched by the weight of the Kool-Aid inside. Leaking juice gave his periodic noises a gurgling aspect. Small mounds of half-chewed food dotted the carpet around him, like scat.

'Hey, Mookie,' Wooten said.

The boy didn't look up. She moved next to him.

'He been like that. They got to change his medicines or something. I'm going back to the clinic Saturday morning.'

'Are you working tomorrow?'

'Uh huh.'

Wooten nodded. She worked in the cafeteria at Newton Plaza. They met when he started going there for the food he couldn't get at home. He'd see her a couple times a week, standing behind the chipped ice. They'd joke about him breaking his diet. She began preparing things especially for him, disappearing when he walked into the cafeteria, returning with a covered dish. And then she started cooking for him at her apartment. It was his idea. So nobody would go blabbing at Ardelia. Biscuits with gravy. Chicken-fried steak. Crab cakes. She was good, having studied it for a while before her trouble. Ardelia could never understand why he wasn't losing weight, why his blood pressure stayed high.

'I ain't got no food here,' she said.

He usually brought her a couple bags from A & P. For his meals but mostly for the two of them. The checkout ladies thought it was sweet that a man in his position found time to shop for the family. It wasn't where Ardelia shopped. She preferred the Giant down in Juniper Bend. The food there was better quality.

He looked around the room, telling himself that he was seeing it for the last time. The durable beige carpet. The walls painted a cracking eggshell white. The galley kitchen with its small inbuilt appliances. Outside light was nullified by a blanket draped over the back window. The furniture was minimal – a sprung sofa and that tipped coffee table. A bean bag chair that had begun to rupture tiny Styrofoam balls. The kitchen sink was clotted with dishes. There was a table that listed badly to port, surrounded by three chairs with splintered ribs. Small detonations of clothes covered everything.

'That's all right. I can't stay long.'

'How come.'

'I have to go to Chicago later.'

226

'Chicago?' she asked listlessly. 'What you gonna do there?'
'Work.'

She moved in front of him then, commanding his attention.

'So how come you ain't been by, baby?'
'Busy.'

In this light he could see her beauty. It hadn't been there when she opened the door but now it was. It wasn't like Ardelia's beauty. There was nothing in it you wanted to preserve. Just use up. She put her skinny hands on his chest. Their eyes held for a moment. The boy continued to make his sounds. It didn't matter what they did in front of him.

'Too busy for me?'
'I didn't come for this.'
'I know.'
'I came to tell you we have to stop.'
'I know.'

He felt her hands at his shirt's buttons. He closed his eyes. She hadn't been beautiful at the door and she hadn't been beautiful in his mind these last few days. But now she was. The last time, he thought. You'll do this and then you'll go to Chicago. Things will be different after that.

He must have slept because the song was almost done when he first heard it. 'Let's Get It On.' He knew it from his son's collection. It seeped through walls that were no thicker than HUD demanded. Four inches, the width of the support beams. Add to that a couple three-quarter-inch slabs of drywall. Five and a half inches, loosely packed with cut-rate fiberglass. Not much protection. The song stopped and then started again, those three slinky notes like a barker's obscene call.

She was staring at him, her head swallowed by a deflated pillow.

'You shouldn't let me sleep,' he said.
'You look so tired, Earl. Your eyes.'
'Work,' he said.
'You best take it slow or you're going to end up like my Andre.'

'You're not telling me that he worked too hard, I hope.'

'No. The police shot him at a CITGO station 'cause they thought he was some other nigger. What I meant is dead.'

Wooten looked up at the ceiling. The watermark was getting bigger. It was the size of his hand now. He'd asked her to call Building Services to check it out. He'd do it himself, though somebody might wonder what he was doing looking at this woman's ceiling. Wooten felt a short spell of disgust – the building was not even a year old. Far too young for structural problems. This was a man-made mess. He tried to imagine what the people in 3-E were up to. There had recently been reports of strange goings-on in these apartments. A fully operational bootlegger's still. A gaggle of abandoned kids, their mother tracked down three days later to an Anacostia shooting gallery. The first signs of systemic roach infestation.

The music stopped for good and was replaced by the rude music of daytime poverty. The tinny bleat of cheap TVs, the echo of slammed fire doors, arguments that flared up and died in a matter of seconds. When they'd first started moving people in, there was an eerie, daylong silence about the place. Now, the racket started in midafternoon and ran without interruption until nearly dawn. And it wasn't just the noise. Sharp odors of boiled vegetables and recent urine hung in concrete stairwells that were lit so murkily that the air looked like an unflushed toilet. The parking lot had filled with pickups carrying questionable cargoes and big sedans whose undercarriages rained rust. He thought for a moment about those people on Zeno's Way and their fence. Maybe Austin had been right. Maybe it had been a mistake to oppose him.

'You hungry?'

'No.'

' 'Cause I can make you some eggs. And I can get some Canadian bacon from that Russian lady downstairs long as you give me some money to pay her back.'

Wooten sat up. The boy was making falling noises now.

'No,' he said, his voice sharper than he intended. He smiled weakly at her. 'I got a plane to catch.'

She closed her eyes.

'I don't know why you come here if it pains you so much,' she said. 'I only like it. That's all I'm doin'. I ain't asking you to put me in a townhouse down at the lake or be nobody's mack daddy. I only like it.'

He reached down and touched her cheek.

'I know,' he said. 'I like it, too.'

She opened her eyes.

'There's money in my wallet,' he said softly. 'For the bacon.'

He took a quick shower, standing forlornly beneath the weak stream of slightly foul water, soaping his scrotum with particular care. The water was cold. Hot ran out by ten in the morning and didn't replenish itself until evening. The boilers were too weak for the amount these people wanted. They made instant coffee with it. So Wooten suffered a cold dousing, fancying it a kind of cheap penance.

Eleven months now. Things weren't supposed to have worked out this way. It was only supposed to be for food. It had been a joke, almost. A challenge. It was strangely thrilling at first, to do something innocent that looked so bad. By the time they started going to her room he was adept at deception. In fact, that initial fry had felt more dangerous than the first sweaty tussle on her creaking bed. None of this would have happened if the doctor hadn't ordered him to lose twenty pounds. One for every point his pressure was high. Telling Ardelia was his mistake. He should have just told her everything was fine. One little lie to avoid the bigger ones to come. She set about managing his diet like it was some kind of mission. Placing broiled fish, skinned chicken and butterless vegetables in front of him every night. No eggs or bacon or steak. Nothing fried and nothing with sauce on it. For years she had been after him about his weight and his appetite. Given license to stop him, she wasn't about to let the opportunity slide.

Only, there was one thing she didn't understand. Wooten could not go on a diet. Because he could not be hungry. Plain and simple. The mere thought of it drove him into a state of panic that made it impossible to think straight, much less work. It wasn't merely that he didn't like being hungry, just as another man might not like exercise or getting out of bed in the morning. He could not endure it. Hunger made him crazy and weak. It was like too much sun or extreme cold. The panic started with even the vaguest pangs.

The reason was simple. He had once been hungry. For two months, when he was seven. Truly, deeply famished. A hunger that almost killed him. This was just after his father died, struck by lightning while digging sand traps for a country club up near Chicago. The men had wanted to come in but the straw boss was behind schedule. Wooten knew exactly how that would have gone. The mutinous mutters, the eyes on a darkening horizon. Outright rebellion forestalled by thoughts of all those mouths to feed downstate. And then the sudden flash, followed by a crack of thunder too late for anybody to hear. Two men had died in that ditch, three more left drooling and worthless.

Wooten's mother had gone crazy for a time after that. Took to bed and wouldn't get out. Wooten and his four sisters had been shipped to whichever relatives would have them. He went down to stay with his great-aunt Mary in the Ozarks, a kindly if eccentric widow who lived in a rural isolation that suited her just fine. Only, bad luck seemed epidemic that summer – the day after he arrived she had a bad stroke. She'd been shopping for the two of them at the time, leaving him to rest at her isolated house after his long journey down on a series of shuddering buses. Speechless and paralyzed, she'd spent seven maddening weeks trying to make the nurses understand that there was a little one back at her place. Of the few people she'd told about her nephew's visit, none remembered that it was supposed to have started yet. And nobody seemed inclined to make the long trip up to check on the hermit lady's home. Times were hard. People had their own problems.

Wooten, meanwhile, found himself abandoned in a strange and terrifying place. Accustomed to the open fields of southern Illinois, he found the dense and mysterious Ozark woods unfathomable. His aunt had told him not to leave the property until she came back and so – taught duty by his father's flame birch wand – that's what he did. Even as the food began to run out. Cans wouldn't open; raw flour stuck to his tongue. He tried eating the berries and the long grass around the yard but they only made him sick. He grew so delirious that when an old man named Dacey took it upon himself to check on the place ten days after Mary was stricken, Wooten thought him some terrifying forest beast and hid under the house until he left.

The hunger grew so bad that he could hardly stand, his guts twisting into a tight ball of heat, the strength leaking from his legs. He would catch bugs and eat them alive, feeling them die beneath his small molars and then seeing bits of them emerge in his yellow acid shit. He ate paper from a catalog he found, some of the pages showing pictures of food that he pretended to taste. One day he bit the tip of his finger and drank the blood but that night he dreamt the devil came to get him and so he never did that again.

And then the hunger vanished. There was no longer any need for food. He began to float through the trees surrounding the house, flying all the way up into the clouds, looking for the angels who made the lightning that killed his father. More bad men came out of the woods but he was living beneath the house. It was easy to be quiet now that he was no longer hungry. He could lie still for hours. Flying.

Finally, blood returned to the speaking part of his aunt's brain. It took the deputies an hour to find the terrified boy. It was hard to get hold of him but once they did he was as light as a sack of dry leaves. They took him to the same hospital as his aunt, keeping him away from her for almost a week while they put food into his arm. Nobody wanted her to have another stroke at the sight of him. He caught glimpses of himself in a mirror above a sink, this charred doll they had stuck Earl Wooten's big eyes onto. Finally he was well enough to move in with his aunt. They kept him there for three more weeks, feeding him sweet potatoes and pork and corn bread. Sometimes he'd catch her looking at him, tears rolling from the outside corners of her eyes. She made him promise never to tell what happened and Wooten thought this was because he'd been bad. That fall, word came that his mother was out of bed. He went home, never telling anyone about the foolish boy who didn't have enough sense to walk down the road and get something to eat. His aunt died two years later, taking their secret to her grave.

Wooten had never been hungry again. There was no resolve involved, no conscious decision. Avoiding hunger simply became an instinct, like blinking or taking that next breath. In the early days of working he always remembered to take along some biscuits or bread, especially on the most remote and difficult jobs. Once he began to make money it was easy to ensure that the larder was always bursting and a replenishing break was just a few hours away. Men who worked for him were always sure to be spoiled by boxes of doughnuts and small mountains of sandwiches. Memories of those bad two months were gradually buried beneath a million calories.

Or so he thought. They returned with a vengeance when he woke up on the second night of his diet in a cold sweat, the pangs in his stomach like a stiletto's stabs. He sneaked down to the larder and ate the first thing he could get his hands on – a can of garbanzo beans. Just spooned them right down into his churning gut. He'd wanted to explain to Ardelia why he could not do this thing but he knew she would never understand. He had a wife and children and a city to build. To risk a heart attack for something long past would be seen as the worst sort of foolishness.

So he started to cheat. Biscuitville. Arby's. 7-Eleven. Mary's Bar BQ down in Powdertown. The dimpled metal lunch trucks. Trying to eat just enough to keep the hunger away. But it was hard. He actually began to *gain* weight on his diet. He was beginning to think that he would have to tell Ardelia that he could not do this. But then he had that first joking conversation with the frail cafeteria woman whose eyes said she knew all about hunger. She could cook something for him that would taste as good as it got without his putting on too much fat.

All he had to do was come by her place.

* * *

He cranked off the shower, letting the water run off him for a moment before stepping into the cramped bathroom. He wiped the mirror and stared hard at himself for a moment. She was right. He did look tired. When he came out she was in her uniform, everything except the paper hat. He wouldn't let her wear that around him. The smell of cooking filled the stale air. He went over to the boy. Inside the cage there were soldiers from the bucket Wooten had brought him. Pale bite marks covered their necks. The barrels of some of the guns had been chewed off.

'Hey, you aren't supposed to be eating these.'

The boy started banging the heads of the GI Joes together harder. Wooten stared at his lint-laced hair for a moment, then started to collect the little soldiers. Without looking, the boy began to moan, the first revving of something far worse.

'No, it's all right,' Wooten said quickly.

He dropped the toys. He didn't need to hear that screaming. Not today. Besides, a little plastic in the guts wouldn't harm this boy. Not any worse than he already was. He thought about his own son for a moment, sitting at home on his bed. Hating him. He wondered what Joel would think if he saw him here now. This was definitely the last time. For sure. Just one more meal and that was it.

He stood and walked into the galley kitchen. She was almost done. He put his hands around her skinny waist.

'Smells good.'

'You don't want to be eating that airplane stuff.'

He could feel his stomach rumbling. He'd tell her after he ate.

16

Truax stood perfectly still amid the Dumpsters, his gaze locked on the squat brown building. He had a good view across the parking lot. And the Dumpsters provided perfect cover. If anybody came with their trash, all he had to do was step back into the shadows. Others might not have been able to stand the stench of the rotting vegetables and curdled milk, the odors rising up from the stagnant multicolored puddles. But Truax had long since become accustomed to evil smells. First of a dying country and then his own putrid flesh. He could handle this.

He'd almost lost Wooten back on Newton Pike. He hadn't expected him to park where he did, right on the side of the road. Truax had to think fast, speeding past the Ranchero and then pulling into a side street. Luckily, there was an unloading Mayflower he could use to shelter his Cutlass from Wooten's view. For a moment he feared that Wooten had spotted him and was pulling some sort of diversionary tactic. When the builder got out of the car and headed down the tree-shrouded bike path, Truax set off warily after him. He plunged into the woods a hundred feet before the path's entrance, crouching behind the first big tree for a quick look. He relaxed when he saw Wooten walking obliviously on. If he intended to spring a trap he'd have done it by now. Truax set out through the gentle woods. It wasn't hard to track Wooten. The pine trees were widely spaced, the thickets sparse. Truax stayed on the ridge that ran parallel to the sunken path, Wooten's large head bobbing at ground level just ahead of him. Things went perfectly until he stumbled in a leaf-filled rut, causing Wooten to turn. Truax froze, not daring to beathe. But Wooten walked on after a short pause. The man had no idea he was being followed. A hundred yards later Truax saw a tot lot looming in his path. If challenged, his plan was to claim he was looking for a lost dog. But his luck held – there was no one around.

After a quarter mile of bends and switchbacks Wooten entered the vast Renaissance Heights complex. Truax was momentarily confused as to why Wooten would walk so far to a place easily reachable by car. But the question brought its own answer. Because he didn't want to be seen here. Truax's heart started to pound; his senses sharpened. His work was about to pay some dividends. Wooten walked quickly across the parking lot, disappearing into a dark stairwell. On the second floor he rang a buzzer. A black woman in a once-bright robe answered the door. Truax raised his nocs for a closer look. From a distance, she seemed both young and old. After waiting in the trees beyond the project's border for a few minutes, he headed toward the Dumpsters that were situated just inside the spot where the path joined the parking lot. Once established there he again used the nocs, though the sun on the window prevented him from seeing into the apartment. He could read the number on the door, however. 27.

This was Truax's third day on his job. His third day of rising before dawn and staying with Wooten until late at night. His mission was simple – to shadow the builder everywhere he went. He'd started late Monday night and would continue indefinitely, sticking with the builder and recording every action he took. Rising before he rose. Following him wherever he went. Not sleeping until he slept.

Until Swope could be sure.

Even now, as he stood among stinking Dumpsters, Truax could hardly believe his good fortune. When Swope had called him Monday evening he'd thought his working life was over. Menial jobs and government handouts littered an already dark horizon. Irma's behavior at the party and the Sunday morning confrontation with the Wootens had wrecked his chances at EarthWorks. Wooten had no doubt gone to Swope after leaving his house, concocting some cock-and-bull story that made it seem like Truax was a raging bigot, when all he was really doing was protecting his family's honor. So when Swope's call came he'd put on a coat and tie and gone to face the music. But then, the miracle happened. Swope offered him a job. And this was no cluster fuck in sales, either. Personal security element for the head man himself. Free to use all the know-how and initiative he'd picked up over the last two decades. He shouldn't have been surprised. Like any true leader, Austin Swope had the ability to cut through the bullshit. What he'd said about always getting penalized – the man was surely some kind of genius. After two years of dealing with civilians who simply did not understand, Truax had finally got through to one who did.

Swearing him to secrecy, Swope had laid it out for him, explaining how he had come to suspect that Wooten was systematically looting thousands of dollars of equipment from poorly guarded sites around the city, selling them to out-of-town cronies and using the proceeds to pad a Bahamian account. There was no use calling Chones – the sheriff and others in the Cannon County establishment were almost certainly in the builder's pocket. Everybody knew how corrupt Maryland could be. Swope needed to work this one on his own. The problem was who to use. Newton Plaza was even more riddled with Wooten supporters than Cannon County, not least of whom were the jokers in security, who'd clearly been turning a blind eye to whoever was pilfering the company's copper piping or thermal windows. And those rare employees in the rank and file who Swope could trust – Chad Sherman over in PR, for instance – lacked the skills for what had to be done. What Swope needed was somebody who was both out of the loop and yet absolutely loyal to his office. Somebody with the right sort of field experience for the job. Somebody he could be sure was no friend of Earl Wooten's.

He needed John Truax.

The plan was simple. Truax would follow Wooten, gathering evidence of his activities. Everything he did would be logged, no matter how trivial. Of special interest were any

236

out-of-town trips. Truax started work the moment after he saved Teddy's ass from those muggers. After fishing his pair of 10 × 42 nocs from the basement and buying a stack of notepads from 7-Eleven, he headed over to Mystic Hills, parking around the corner from Wooten's house. Dawn came eventually. The few people who passed didn't notice him. There were always workmen around in the morning, waiting for the boss to show. Wooten left his house just after seven, driving out to a site in Juniper Bend. After that he went to another site, then to his office in Newton Plaza. And so it went. Nothing much happened that first day. Truax was glad – it allowed him to learn the man's pace. He was pleased to discover that Wooten was a slow driver. That made things easier.

That night, Truax lucked out yet again, finding an observation post in a roomy tree house just beyond Wooten's back lawn. He'd brought along his poncho and some Off! in the belief that he would have to make his own shelter in the thick woods. But then he stumbled onto the gleaming plywood structure, built in the sturdy crotch of a big elm. It was the perfect lookout. Not only did it provide a panoramic view of the house, but the infinity of dewy webs and absence of toys made him suspect that the kids no longer had any interest in it. And even if someone did approach, Truax could pull back by the time they'd made it halfway across the lawn. It was sturdily built, resting a good eight feet off the ground. Treated plywood walls, two-by-four beams, particleboard floor. Tarred roof that hadn't let in a drop of rain since the day it was raised. Shuttered windows in every wall. Truax knew families back in My Song who would have killed for a place like this. He stayed until well after the Wootens turned in on Tuesday and returned before dawn the next morning, sitting perfectly still in its shelter as the night sounds turned slowly into morning sounds. It reminded him of some of the good dawns he'd passed in country.

This is better, he found himself thinking. This is work.

The second day proved as uneventful as the first. Wooten toured sites, made a quick trip to Arby's and then spent the rest of the day at Newton Plaza. He was home by six. By then, Truax had the knack of shadowing his man, having established a comfortable buffer between them. Not that there weren't some minor foul-ups. They'd bumped into each other at a Gulf station late Tuesday and Truax lost track of him for a half hour late Wednesday morning. But these were simply part of the process. By dawn Thursday, trailing him had become second nature.

The only truly difficult moment had nothing to do with Wooten. It came when he returned home late Tuesday night. Swope had sworn him to secrecy and he'd been able to stonewall Irma on Monday, saying that he'd merely been reprimanded about the party. It was a good lie – there was no way Irma was going to press him on the subject. But Tuesday was different. He arrived just before midnight to discover her on the warpath. She'd heard about him getting fired at her bridge circle. Knowing that keeping his assignment a secret would be more dangerous than simply telling her, Truax led his wife to the bedroom and locked the door. Irma perched on the edge of the bed, staring up at him with an expression that balanced anger and fear.

'Well?' she asked, her sharp stenciled eyebrows rising on her forehead. 'What do you have to say for yourself?'

'I'm working for Austin Swope.'

She stared at him for a long while.

'Swope?' There was still doubt in her voice. 'Doing what?'

'Security.'

She began to smile sarcastically, though she quickly remembered that her husband never lied. She nodded, a single terse dip of her strong chin. She wanted more.

'Mr Swope suspects that Earl Wooten has been stealing from EarthWorks. Evidently he has half the county working with him. My job is to help make the case against him.'

She pointed at him.

'I knew,' she said.

'You mustn't tell anyone, Irma. I mean it. If you talk about this even to Sally then I will lose the job.'

She stood and walked over to him.

'For Mr Swope? You are really working now for Mr Swope?'

He nodded. She stared at him for a moment, her eyes filling with tears.

'Don't worry, John,' she said, pulling open the buttons on his shirt. 'I will tell no one.'

A fat white woman wearing baggy jeans and a tentlike blouse emerged from the stairwell next to Wooten's, carrying soggy A & P bags in each hand. A cigarette dangled from the side of her mouth. Truax stepped as far back into the shadows as he could. The woman arrived, flinging the bags up into the middle Dumpster. The splotchy skin of her double chins waddled with the motion. Something fell out of the second bag as she threw it – a Hamm's bottle. It rolled to Truax's feet. He remained perfectly still. The woman stared after the bottle for a moment, as if she might come in after it. But then she turned and headed back to her building, the stretched fabric of her jeans making hushing sounds with every step she took.

Wooten remained in the apartment. Truax stood his ground. Heat pulsed from the sun-drenched Dumpsters; the stink became even greater. Sleep began to stalk him. It had been days since he'd rested properly. He hadn't slept at all Saturday night, with Susan and Irma both wailing until nearly dawn. He'd only managed a few fitful hours on Sunday, images of naked Joel Wooten and his falling wife waking him every time he drifted off. Excitement over his resurrection had kept him up Monday. And after that he was working. Sleep was no longer a priority.

Not that Truax cared. Compared with My Song this was nothing. In his ten months there he never had a single night's sleep. Not one. The week with Irma in Manila included – every time he was about to sink into that undulant Holiday Inn mattress he'd wake to find her straddling him, calling for him so loudly that the GI's in nearby rooms were soon mocking them, raising an echoing chorus of 'Fuck me, John's that drew the attention of first the assistant manager and finally two bemused MP's. So great was his ability to function without sleep that Truax soon became a legend in his platoon, then in the company and, finally, the whole battalion. The boots fresh out of Bien Hoa couldn't believe he did no drugs, not even the mild bennies the medics would pass out like Good 'N Plenty. Some of the bloods started calling him Dracula. But there was no malice in it. Just awe. And relief, because knowing Truax was on the wire meant they could sleep safely. Not that he *never* slept. He'd usually catch a few hours just after dawn, when it was clear that no attack was coming. Or in the afternoon, when Charley slept as well. But never at night. Even if some new lieutenant ordered him off the nocturnal security element, he would still be out there with his men, his eyes focused beyond the six-level concertina.

The strange thing was that even though he never slept on those nights, he was almost always dreaming. Maybe that's why he could go with so little sleep – the dreams were able to rest his weary mind without even overtaking it. He'd prop himself in a chair of sandbags he'd built in front of an M-60 or Claymore det cords, facing whatever direction needed checking out, a canteen and a ration can next to him, .45 on his hip. If it was monsoon season he'd make a tent out of his poncho. And then, once everything was secure, he'd begin to dream. Eyes wide open. The visions would come half willed and half random, quickly becoming as real as the jungle night. He could be making love with Irma back in Germany and before long her sharp odor would come to him, that heady mixture of talc and sweat and cheap PX perfume. He could feel her soft, goose-pimply flesh. Whole conversations with her would ring in his ears. It was as if she were superimposed on the hot Vietnamese night. Or suddenly his daughters would be in his arms, their soft insistent limbs entwining him. He could conjure the laugh of a Tu Do whore or the smell of a Frankfurt beer hall and in an instant he would be right there, transported by the warm jungle air and the incessant madrigal of insects. The dreams would sometimes run for hours, as fully faceted as Hollywood films. And yet they never affected his ability to guard his post. His reactions were still as sharp as the concertina around him. In the early days, when sappers would try to bust through, Truax would snap to so quickly that the invaders would be routed before the other

240

grunts could even get off a round. It wasn't long until the enemy ceded those My Song nights to Truax.

The dream he called upon most often was an almost forgotten memory from his days posted at Fort Bragg, in the quiet years between Germany and Vietnam. Susan was ten, Darryl seven and Irma happy to be finally stateside, not yet understanding how little of the country's bounty had been reserved for her. It was late January, the time of ice storms that would leave the Carolina countryside strewn with frosted branches. A rare blizzard had come the day before, dusting the central-state plains with four inches of wet snow that partially melted at dusk and then turned to ice overnight. The next morning, Susan reported excitedly that kids were sledding on a hill at the southern end of the base. She was desperate to join them. Because Irma was afraid it would be dangerous, Truax went with her. The problem was that he had no sled. They'd had a beautiful, hand-tooled toboggan in Germany but had been forced to give it to one of Irma's grasping cousins when the army put a weight restriction on their homebound consignment. Truax swung by the PX but the few measly aluminum saucers they had in stock were long gone. He went to the hill anyway, thinking that maybe they could borrow something there. But what few Flexible Flyers there were among the hundred-odd kids gathered at the top of the hill belonged to the children of officers, spoiled brats who'd been taught not to share with enlisted kids before they left their mother's tit.

Truax stood in the cold wind with a bunch of grunts and their fidgeting children, watching the sons and daughters of majors and bird colonels soar down the hill. He had to admit, it was one hell of a slope, reminding him of Killer Hill back in Johnstown, where he and his brother Luke used to spend long days plummeting at breakneck speeds. Five hundred yards long, easy. Fifteen-, maybe twenty-degreee gradient. No boulders or trees. Lots of braking room at the bottom. The kids lucky enough to own sleds were flying down the slope. Whooping and laughing. Having the time of their lives. Ashamed and freezing, Truax wanted nothing more than to get out of here. But the look on Susan's pink face bore

241

such pure desire that he realized he had to do something. Already beginning to suspect that her life would be full of big disappointments, he'd fallen into the habit of doing what he could to mollify the small ones.

Then he saw the empty storage shack, situated among some fir trees by the big perimeter fence, a hundred yards along the crest of the hill. It was one of the hundreds of meaningless structures dotting the base. Nobody in authority cared enough to order it demolished; nobody else wanted to catch shit for tearing it down. Truax told Susan to wait where she was. It didn't take him long to liberate a three-by-six-foot sheet from its rusted bolts. It was lighter than it looked and miraculously free of significant warps. Time had shaped one end into an aerodynamic curl. Yes, this would provide a ride of the first order. When he returned from the woods he could see the embarrassment on Susan's face. Truax smiled at her and told her that it would be all right. Because he was her father, she followed him to the edge of the hill.

Other kids and enlisted men gathered around as Truax dropped the metal sheet on the ground. He knelt beside it and scooped up a handful of pine needle-ridden snow, rubbing it hard along corrugations, cleaning and icing them at the same time. They would make perfect runners. Some of the officers' kids snickered. A corporal from supply jokingly asked if he had the right requisition forms for the equipment. Truax ignored them as he carefully slicked up every inch of metal that would touch the snow. When he was done he flipped the sheet over. Its warped end faced downhill. It would never bite. He could feel his sled strain for the bottom of the hill beneath his steadying boot. He turned to Susan. Dread gripped her frozen features. She looked like she wanted to be far, far away. Truax held out his hand. His still-good hand. And because she was his little girl, she took it, braving the ridicule that blew through the winter air more sharply than those freakish winds. He carefully situated her in the sled's exact middle, then settled in snugly behind her, pinning her in with his outstretched legs. That curled front rose a few inches higher.

'Ready?' he asked.

She nodded weakly. Two of the officers' boys rushed from the crowd and dropped their Flexible Flyers on either side of them, ready to race. There was laughter and a catcall. Somebody shouted *Go* and Truax pushed off with his gloved hands. His toboggan moved sluggishly. The sleds shot ahead of him. Derisive laughter spilled over them. Truax could feel his daughter's shoulders stiffen in shame.

But then they began to pick up speed as the corrugated runners found their depth in the snow. After twenty yards the Flexible Flyers were no longer pulling away from them. Twenty yards after that Truax was gaining on them. By the time they passed the officers' kids it looked like they were standing still. The shame left Susan's shoulders. Her small hands grabbed his shins for support. Their speed seemed to double by the second, the gaps beneath the sheets serving as aerodynamic foils. By the halfway point they were going so fast that Truax began to wonder if this was such a good idea after all. But there was no stopping. He did what he could with his body weight to keep them on an even keel, even though he knew they were at the hill's mercy. They must have been going forty by the time they reached the bottom. They raced across a short icy plain and then began to climb a mild incline. The sled was finally stopped by a bank of snow, not unlike the runoffs on highways for trucks with blown brakes. They rolled harmlessly through the soft snow, winding up lying next to each other. Cheers echoed down from the top of the hill. The Flexible Flyers were nowhere in sight. Truax looked for fear in his daughter's face. But she was smiling, her eyes as bright as the sun-soaked snow around them. And then she said the breathless words she used to say when he played with her as a toddler, words he hadn't heard in years and was never to hear again.

'Again, Daddy,' she said. 'Again.'

And so they did, time and time again, racing past the store-bought sleds like they were nothing more than parts of the landscape. They must have made thirty runs before she'd finally had enough. That night a warm front moved in and the snow melted. By the time another storm came Truax was half a world away from his daughter. And yet the memory lived on, almost as strong as the real thing, filling his tired mind as he waited out those long jungle nights at My Song, ready to kill anything that moved outside the concertina. Again and again, John Truax and his daughter would race faster than anyone else down that long slope.

Wooten finally emerged from the apartment. The woman, still dressed in her colored robe, stared after him from the doorway with eyes that told Truax everything he needed to know. He slid to the back of the Dumpsters, listening to the heavy scuffle of Wooten's steel-tipped boots as he passed no more than ten feet away. He gave him sixty seconds, then set out in pursuit, cutting back through the woods. It felt good to be moving with stealth through the cover. The city was finally beginning to make sense.

He raced ahead of Wooten, arriving back at his Cutlass thirty seconds before the builder reached the Ranchero. Truax watched as he pulled a U across Newton Pike. He was heading back to Mystic Hills. Truax fell way back, following him as far as Merlin's Way before turning off onto Rhiannon's Rest, the curving side street that ran into the undeveloped land behind Wooten's house. It was where Truax kept his Cutlass while he was in the treehouse. Building had yet to begin here – flagged lot markers, exposed fireplugs and the hieroglyphic scrawl of surveyors were the only signs of civilization. From here, it was just a few hundred feet to the treehouse. Truax pulled himself up the rope ladder in time to watch Wooten moving across his upstairs bedroom. He came down a few minutes later, dressed in a sports coat and carrying a suit bag. He was leaving town. Truax felt grim satisfaction as he raced back to his car. Today's report would be a full one. He picked Wooten up on Merlin's Way and followed him until he joined the interstate near Cannon City. He turned east, toward Baltimore. Truax wondered if they would wind up in a bad neighborhood. He suddenly regretted not getting his .45 out of the basement. He followed at a safe distance, letting cars intervene. They'd gone nearly twenty miles before Truax saw the sign for BWI and realized they weren't going to the city after all. Of course. The suitbag. The tie. Wooten was flying off.

Truax tightened up the tail when they reached the airport – he didn't want to lose Wooten in its labyrinth of lanes. After watching the Ranchero enter the long-term lot he sped back to short-term, driving so fast that he almost slammed into a Pinto. Careful, he thought. Steady gets you there quickest. And it gets you there alive. He picked up Wooten at the entrance to departures, hanging back behind a bank of pay phones as he checked in at the United desk. After that it was easy to follow him to the gate. Wooten was in a hurry – the plane was boarding. Truax waited until they pulled back the ramp, just to make sure. Then he went to inform his boss that Earl Wooten was on his way to Chicago.

17

Swope watched Truax walk quickly up the twilit cul-de-sac toward Merlin's Way. He'd parked his car somewhere out of sight, even though this was not part of Swope's instructions. The man was definitely showing some serious initiative. He had a strangely anonymous way of moving along the sidewalk, Swope noticed, deflecting attention from himself without making any real effort to hide. Something in his carriage, in the set of his shoulders, creating his own pocket of negative space. Swope doubted passersby would remember a man walking away from the big house at the bottom of the road. This guy was a gem, festering hand notwithstanding. Loyal. Discreet. Uncomplaining. And without doubt the most dogged human being Swope had ever met. He pitied the poor fucking VC who'd tangled with him back in that idiotic war. The gamble of hiring him was already paying off.

If only the information he'd brought wasn't so cataclysmic. Wooten was going to Chicago. No ifs, ands or buts. He was in the air that very moment. Flying the friendly skies. Which could mean only one thing – they were going to offer him the job. Maybe not today. But it was going to happen. There was no other reason he would be going out for a solo trip. Not in secret. Swope couldn't believe it. Earl Wooten had lied to him. After five years of partnership, he had planted a knife squarely between Swope's shoulder blades. Just like that. No qualms, no hesitation. Monday night had been nothing more than the first little twist. More painful thrusts were to come. You spend half a decade thinking you know a man and then this happens.

Well, it wouldn't stand. It would not stand.

Truax was gone, somehow vanishing before reaching the end of the road. Swope went back to his desk and stared at his blotter for a moment, where he'd jotted down the information he'd just been given: *Bldg 5. #27.* After a moment he picked up the phone and dialed the Wooten home. Ardelia answered on the second ring.

'Ardelia, Austin here.'

There was the slightest pause. Undetectable – unless you were listening for it.

'Oh, hello, Austin.'

'Earl isn't around, is he? I've been trying to chase him down all afternoon.'

Another pause. This one a nanosecond longer. An infinity in the chronology of deception.

'No, Earl had to fly off to Atlanta on short notice.'

'Atlanta?'

'His sister has taken ill. You know, the youngest one Dolly.'

'No. I'm sorry to hear that.'

'Oh, I don't think it's all that serious. But having Earl there makes her feel a lot better.'

'As it would anyone. The man is a walking, talking tonic to the ill and the downhearted.'

Ardelia laughed stiffly, the usual good cheer absent from her voice.

'I can have him call you from there . . .'

'No. It's nothing that can't wait. Let him look after his sister.'

'He should be back tomorrow night.'

'If you could have him call me that would be great.'

'As soon as he gets in.'

Swope hung up. Ardelia Wooten lying – it was as improbable as Teddy captaining the crew up at Harvard. But though that pause in her voice may have been subatomic in duration, it was as eloquent as a speech by Martin Luther King himself. Unbelievable. All that righteous, vice-principaled propriety chucked out the window as soon as it became an obstacle to climbing the greasy pole. Swope shook his head in astonishment. These people were supposed to be his friends. And now they were betraying him. He felt like such a fool, such an absolute fool. He'd *confided* in the man. Let him into his life. Given him gifts. Defended him against bigots and back stabbers every inch of the way. Believing that they were deep down the same. A couple of hardworking outsiders trying to grab a slice of this freshly baked pie. Two men who knew that if you were willing to sweat and sacrifice, you could build a life from the ground up. But all the while Wooten was just another jackal waiting for the right moment to pounce and take what wasn't his.

What a fool I've been, Swope thought.

He reached forward and set three of the cradle's balls in motion. It was a remarkable thing, this contraption. He didn't understand the science behind it – something about the conservation of energy. Or maybe inertia. Teddy had offered to explain it but Swope told him not to bother. Not that he didn't like listening to his son wax lyrical on the nature of reality. It was just that he liked some things to remain mysteries.

He looked up at the rows of law books lining the twelve-foot walls of his home study. His collection. His pride and joy. There were just under two thousand of them, worth at least fifty grand. Statutes and codes of the federal government, the District of Columbia and the State of Maryland. Case histories in property law that detailed disputes over boundaries and good title, inheritance and right-of-way. Judgments rendered, precedents established. An entire corpus of law and tradition bound in the best leather. It was easily the best law library in Cannon County, probably in all of central Maryland. Collecting legal books was Swope's hobby, started a decade ago when he'd nabbed some redundant copies about to be shitcanned by Barger, Green. More than once some local mouthpiece had asked to borrow something from the collection. Jill Van Riper in the county attorney's office always had something out. Swope was only too happy to oblige them. A favor, after all, was a favor. And these were no window dressing, either. Swope had read them all. Well, almost. Anybody off the street could come in here and randomly choose a case and the odds were good that Swope would be able to quote chapter and verse on it. Because that was what he did. He read, he learned and he remembered. In law school at Ann Arbor, as an associate, even as a partner, when he could have farmed out the work to paralegals – Swope hit the books. And when he became general counsel for Newton, his reading became even more exhaustive. Obsessive, if you listened to Sally. During these last five years he'd studied nearly every case that related to property law as it was practiced in Maryland. He became the master of his brief. Lawyers from Frederick and Aberdeen called him up at a hundred bucks a pop to ask him arcane questions about land clearance or zoning; the Cannon County magistrate, Lon Spivey, merely waved a weary assenting hand when Swope offered to quote precedent in the countless cases he'd brought before the local court. He had recently figured out that if he'd spent five hours a day dealing with the written law (a conservative estimate) during three hundred working days per year (archconservative), that meant in the twenty-two years since he'd matriculated at Michigan he'd devoted thirty-three thousand hours of his life to learning, interpreting and applying the law.

The killing irony, of course, was that he'd never really understood a word of it until five days ago, on the afternoon of his forty-fourth birthday, when Roger Tench had dropped his bombshell. That call had begun Swope's true legal training, a lesson that had concluded a half hour ago when John Truax sat at this very desk and informed him that Earl Wooten was flying secretly to Chicago to steal the job that was his and his alone. With that, Swope suddenly understood the fundamental principle supporting every edict, ordinance and statute he'd ever read. It was simply this – the law was a steaming load of crap. You could write it in the highest of the King's English and bind it in the finest Spanish leather, but it was still just so much gobbledegook. Big dogs kicking the shit out of little dogs. When all was said and done – the motions filed and precedents read and judgments rendered – that was all there was. Cunning backed by force. It was a principle Swope had unwittingly put into practice countless times these past five years while dealing with frightened and ignorant landowners. Hiding behind a scrim of legality when all he was really doing was pushing around people who knew in their bones that they were being wronged and couldn't do a damn thing about it; small-minded, weak-willed losers who didn't understand that the laws ruling their lives derived not from eternal principles of justice but rather from the simplest, oldest precept of them all – Fuck you. It was the men with the biggest balls and the steeliest vision who wrote the law, who wove its seemingly intractable principles to fit them like a silk suit. Always had been, always would be. Millennia ago this had meant clubbing some poor schmuck and taking what he thought was his. Centuries ago it meant using blue smoke and mirrors to hoodwink enough peasants into doing your bidding. Nowadays it meant being able to stir the sheriffs and the marshals away from their doughnuts long enough to kick ass and transfer titles. Same difference. It was the man with the money and the guile and the will to get the job done who determined what was held up by those fine spines staring down at Swope. Everybody else was just waiting for a knock on the door.

It was a good thing to have come to know. Especially now that he really needed it. Anybody could read the books. Christ, an infinite number of monkeys working an infinite number of typewriters could write the damned things. But only a few realized that there was, ultimately, nothing between the covers but sweat and will and blood. A great lawyer, Austin Swope now knew, was like a mathematician who spent a lifetime learning every theorem and axiom knowable to the human mind, only to discover in the end that the universe was nothing more than the random fancy of a capricious god. Two plus two equaled four on a strictly provisional basis. Once it benefited the big guy, it would add up to five. And pity the fool who complained. Law was simply the refined grammar of power, more efficient and less messy than its grunting, slobbering twin, violence. Savage knew this. The Kennedys. Dick Nixon, though he'd become sloppy. The humiliating thing was that Earl Wooten, who'd probably never read a book cover to cover in his entire life, seemed to have figured it out while Swope was poring over his useless tomes. The man must have taken a crash course in the Fundamentals of Applied Asskicking. He'd shown himself to be a master. So good that he was close to taking away Swope's job.

Close, but not quite there. The game wasn't over yet. The moment Truax had said he'd seen the foreman stepping on that Chicago plane, Swope realized that he'd have to act. Wooten's free ride was over. The question was where to start. Swope's eyes traveled to that scrawled address: *Bldg 5. #27.*

'Austin?'

Sally stood in the doorway, concern creasing her normally serene face.

'Is everything all right? I thought I heard voices.'

'Just me on the phone.'

'Oh.' She looked at him more closely. 'Why are you sitting here like this? Are you sure nothing's the matter?'

He met her eye. He'd have to tell her something. She'd seen him in too many battles not to sense that another was looming.

'There might be some sort of problem with the city manager job.'

Sally scowled dubiously.

'Really? What makes you think that?'

Swope hesitated, wondering if he should tell her about Wooten. But then she might start noticing the measures he was being forced to take. And she would never understand. As good a woman as she was, she couldn't fathom how bad things could get – or what had to be done to set them right. She may have defied her rich Grosse Pointe parents and prep school friends to marry him, but that didn't mean she would ever comprehend what it took to keep their heads above the deep, dark water. Swope had protected her from that reality ever since they met. He wasn't about to start letting her in on it now, when she was just beginning to get the life she deserved.

'Nothing specific,' he said. 'Just a feeling I've been getting from Chicago. They might be looking at someone else for the position.'

251

'Nonsense. Have you talked to Gus about it?'

'That's not how it works, Sal.'

She gave her head a brief, frustrated shake.

'Austin, come on. I thought we weren't going to do this anymore.'

'Do what?'

'Get all paranoid and defensive. Wasn't that the idea behind moving here – to get us away from all the brooding and distrust? Isn't that why we left that viper's nest in DC? So you wouldn't have to sleep with one eye open?'

'It's not that simple, Sal.'

'Only because you won't let it be.' She pointed a tapered finger at the desk. 'Pick up the phone and call Gus. Right now. Let him know what's on your mind and I guarantee you he'll tell you to stop being so silly.'

'I can't do that.'

'Why on earth not?'

'It would make me seem weak.'

'*Weak*? Austin, for heaven's sake . . . '

She walked across the room and perched on the edge of the desk. 'Listen to me. You are the strongest man I have ever known. That's what drew me to you in the first place. Forget those pampered little boys with their sports cars and Daddy's money – it was *you* I wanted. Don't you think I remember when Teddy was sick . . .'

Her voice caught. A bright mist coated her wide eyes.

'Any other man would have let him die. But you didn't. You wouldn't. You saved him with your strength. People *depend* on you, Austin. Not just me and Edward but everyone else in this town. Gus Savage knows that just as well as Barnaby. He's no more likely to think you're weak than that you're from Jupiter.'

Swope looked down at his desk, unable to bear the righteous intensity in her eyes. Maybe she was right. Maybe he was reading too much into the situation. They would never deny him the job. And Earl would never betray him. He'd come to his senses. They all would. Because they depended on him. They knew he was the one.

But then the facts that had been accumulating since his

birthday rushed back into his mind, obliterating the small particle of hope his wife's words had brought. Tench's call. The NHA meeting. Wooten's trip. That hitch in Ardelia's voice. There was simply too much to deny. Yes, it would be nice to think that the world was as Sally described, where promises were kept and friends did not betray each other. Where people played by the rules, whether it was at bridge or business. But such a world existed only for those who had others to fight for them.

'Austin?'

He met her eye.

'You're right,' he said. 'I should talk to Gus. Look, I have to go into the office for a little while. I'll call him from there.'

She leaned across the desk and kissed him. Her lips were so soft and sweet. He hated to lie to her, though there was no way she'd know about this. Ever. It was up to him to be the strong one. The fighter.

'Now this is the last time I want to find you sitting in the dark brooding,' she lovingly scolded as she pulled away.

He managed a smile.

'No more brooding. I promise.'

When she was gone Swope noticed that the balls had fallen still on the Newton's cradle. He reached forward and set them back in motion. Sally may not know much about how the world worked, but she was right about one thing. Sitting here worrying was futile. It was time to start taking action. He looked down at that address one last time, consigning it to memory before blotting it out with his pen. As he turned out the desk lamp a phrase began to echo through his mind. Something Wooten had said last fall on a remote site.

Sometimes, you just got to knock down somebody's house.

Part Five

18

The express elevator moved through the skyscraper with that strange combination of stillness and speed that always gave Wooten a boyish thrill. A dreamlike sensation, similar to yesterday's takeoff, though thankfully without the shrieking intimations of mortal splatter. The flight from BWI had been a bad one, jostled by turbulence that belied the clear blue skies over Pennsylvania and Ohio. It had almost spoiled the pampering they gave him in first class, the champagne and hot towels and coy smiles from the stewardess, who looked a whole lot like Pam Grier. Almost, but not quite.

He was finally in Chicago. City of his future. After nearly two weeks of constant anticipation and guesswork, he was at last making his way up to the place where the mystery would end. Wooten looked at the brass indicator panel above the door. The light hadn't even begun to register yet, wouldn't until they reached 38. Staggering elevators had been one of Barnaby's many innovative ideas, a way of keeping people who worked on the upper floors from suffering a second stop-and-go commute. Every time he came here, Wooten wondered what it must be like to build so tall, to cut right into the sky. The highest he'd ever got was co-contracting on a fourteen-story bank building in Clayton. And then of course Newton Plaza. Strange to think of Vine cutting his teeth in this vertical metropolis, building higher and higher while dreaming of a city where next to nothing rose above the trees. Wooten had once joked with him about designing his ground-hugging city in such a tall building.

'I like skyscrapers, Earl,' he'd answered in his reedy

Midwestern twang. 'I just happen to be of the opinion we've enough of them on this particular planet.'

As the floors began to tick by, Wooten wondered how the old man was doing. From what little he'd heard, the second stroke had been bad. Flying into O'Hare last night, it occurred to him that it had been almost a year since his last actual conversation with Vine, the day they'd opened the lake's sluiceway. Savage had hinted there might be a meeting with him later in the day, before Wooten caught his five o'clock back to BWI. He hoped so. He missed Barnaby.

The elevator reached the seventy-eighth floor, the executive level of EarthWorks World Headquarters. He announced himself at the big reception desk and then sat in a real leather chair beneath a photo of one of the massive digging machines EarthWorks had recently deployed in Saudi Arabia. The company was moving into the region in a big way, doing battle with archrivals Bechtel for some of those petrodollars bubbling up out of the sand. Desalination. Aqueducts. Air-conditioned shopping malls. Wooten suddenly worried that they might have something like that in mind for him. He hoped not. Ardelia would definitely not be up for wearing a veil. He looked into the aquarium on the small table next to him. Phlegmatic fish swam through a plastic shipwreck; strands of shit hovered like kites in the water's murk. Down the hall there was laughter, a ringing phone.

So here you are, he thought. Waiting to hear what they have in store for you. It was all happening so fast. Last night he'd been picked up by a limo at O'Hare and driven to the Hyatt. There was a fruit basket in his suite and an invitation from the manager to dine on the house. Before he'd even washed his hands a Miss Robert from Savage's office called to tell him the limo would return for him at nine the following morning. Wooten didn't remember her from his last visit. She sounded black. Just. He phoned Ardelia, who said that Swope had already called looking for him. Wooten fretted about that for a while after hanging up. He couldn't wait to get back home and square this thing away.

'Mr Wooten?'

A beautiful mocha-skinned woman had materialized in front of him. She was truly gorgeous, as fine as anything you'd see in a magazine. Definitely new. Wooten stood, straightening the lapels of his suit coat.

'I'm Cheryl Robert, Mr Savage's personal assistant.'

It took him a moment to realize she'd offered a thin hand. Wooten took it. Her tapered fingers were as cool as lettuce.

'Earl Wooten,' he said without thinking.

'Oh, yes, we know who you are,' she said slyly. 'Won't you come with me?'

For the next thirty seconds Wooten looked everywhere but at Miss Cheryl Robert's swaying behind as she led him through the maze of corridors. They passed dozens of big offices where men in shirtsleeves leaned back in recliner chairs like anglers reeling in a big one. Some talked on phones, other bullshitted with colleagues. After moving through a heavy oak door they entered a hallway where the walls changed from industrial white to burnished wood, the floor from scuffed tile to burgundy carpeting. The doors were more widely spaced. Secretarial anterooms guarded inner sanctums that were decorated with chandeliers, dark paneling and thick rugs. The voices echoing inside were quieter. Slower. Deeper.

Savage's lair was at the end of the hall, guarded by consecutive outer offices. The first had two secretaries furiously typing dictation from earphones. Neither looked up as Wooten passed. The second room, he supposed, belonged to Miss Robert. It smelled of lavender. She knocked twice on the final door, then nodded for Wooten to enter.

Savage's office had no desk. That was the first thing you noticed about it. He'd once explained that he considered them 'moribund barriers to interpersonal communication.' Wooten and Swope had laughed themselves silly over that one back at the Hyatt, Swope referring to the restaurant's table as a 'facilitator of strictly personal digestion.' In lieu of a desk, the room's half dozen black chairs formed a precise, dead-center rectangle. Each had a small stand for folders and drinks. Savage's seat – democratically identical to the rest – faced the door. The only concession to his status was a small phone on its stand. Directly behind Savage's chair were the office's two windows, thin vertical slits shrouded with louvered shutters. Light came from discreet conical lamps and muffled halogen bulbs. The walls were bare except for a series of Mondrians that Wooten knew to be real. There were no plants, no magazines or photos. No pictures of orthodontured children. No paper anywhere.

Savage was standing with his hands on the back of his chair. He leaned forward slightly – something about his posture suggested a tennis player about to serve.

'Earl.'

As Savage came around the chair Wooten recalled how short he was. Five-five on a good day. It was a quality you never seemed to remember unless looking right at the man. He wore a dark blue Italian suit with broad lapels. No tie, though the collar of his beige madras shirt was buttoned tightly beneath his prominent Adam's apple. His longish hair was brushed back behind small ears; broad sideburns covered his cheeks. His small brown eyes were set close together, giving his gaze an added intensity. The Fu Manchu mustache that had perched above his mouth like a sunning snake last time Wooten saw him was gone. Wooten knew that he was fifty-one, though he looked ten years younger. The company he ran was now the eleventh largest in the nation. And growing.

'Gus, good to see you.'

They shook hands and Savage gestured to the seat on his right. Wooten dropped into it. Pockets of air slowly escaped from the cushion beneath him. Savage sat slowly, almost reluctantly. Wooten noticed a stack of poster board leaning against his chair.

'Call Seven Oaks and see to it they're ready for us in two hours.'

For a moment Wooten thought Savage was speaking to him. He turned when he realized that Miss Robert was still in the room. He made sure not to watch her leave.

'Barnaby wants to see you,' Savage said.

'How is Barnaby?'

Savage grimaced.

'Not well, Earl. The last stroke . . . you should brace yourself.'

Wooten nodded gravely. He noticed something next to Savage's phone – a black bowl filled with small, fetal oblongs. Savage tracked his gaze. He picked up the bowl and offered it to Wooten.

'Garlic,' he explained. 'Thins the blood. Want one?'

'No. Thanks.'

Savage returned the bowl to the stand. He ran his fingers along its smooth rim for a moment before speaking.

'Well, I suppose you're anxious to hear why we dragged you all the way out here.'

'You could say that.'

'Earl, how are you set up for Phases III and IV?'

'Set up?'

'How essential are you to their completion?'

'Well, not very, I suppose. I'd like to see it through, but we've cracked all the big problems out there. Well, the gaslights. But basically those units are going to pretty much build themselves.'

'So I thought. In that case, we'd like to transfer you to another project that needs immediate attention.'

'I'm all ears.'

Savage lifted those poster boards from beside his chair and placed them on his lap. Wooten could see charcoal and crosshatching and bold letters.

'Earl, for the past year we've been secretly buying up tracts of land out on the Virginia-West Virginia border. Clarke County? Not far from Winchester, if that helps you. All very hush-hush. The process is ongoing, though we're just about there. The idea being to build . . . this.'

He handed Wooten the poster boards. The top card was a crowded sketch of what at first appeared to be a bustling urban community. It took Wooten several seconds to realize what he was seeing. He read the name at the top of the card at the same moment Savage spoke it.

'AmericaWorks.'

'An amusement park?'

'Theme park. Yes.'

Wooten looked back at the drawing, with its serpentine pathways and clustered buildings and happy families. He realized why it had taken him a minute to get it – the rides were all hidden inside replica monuments. A roller coaster snaked its way through various facial orifices on Mount Rushmore, some sort of water ramp sent little barges hurtling across the Mississippi River, and a Ferris wheel was enclosed in the familiar curve of the Gateway Arch. God knew what that thing wrapped around the Statue of Liberty was. Between the rides were various ersatz communities. An Indian encampment. A settler's fort. Something that looked like a turn-of-the-century tenement street. A rodeo.

'Our thinking is pretty obvious from the schematics. A combination of history lesson and the more visceral charms of a conventional park. We're going to clean up on the school-trip-slash-family-outing market. Just look at all that parking for buses.'

Wooten began to flip through the cards, each detailing a specific complex. A working prairie farm with a big picnic area. A Malibu beach complete with a pool that looked like it generated its own waves. In greater detail, he could see that they intended to wrap a winding slide down the folds of Liberty's gown. The penciled kids using it rode what looked like squares of carpeting. They were all laughing.

'The plan is this. We announce as soon as the land's all squared away. Should be a month or so. Break ground in the fall with an eye toward grand opening around Easter of seventy-five. We'll miss that, of course, which means Memorial Day. What we're offering you is a two-year contract as building director. The salary package is terrific but the real sweet thing about this deal is you get premium shares.'

Wooten looked up. Savage smiled.

'That's right. Premiums, Earl. Which means every time a ticket gets punched you get a hundredth of a hundredth of a penny. Or whatever. You're lying in bed on New Year's with a hangover, the meter's running.'

Shares, Wooten thought. Good God. He turned his attention back to the cards. The scope of the place was amazing. It must be twenty thousand acres. Two years would really be pressing it. He didn't dare ask how much they were spending on it. Not that it mattered. This place would be a license to print money.

'We'd also like to use you up front in our ads. You know. America *Works*. Really hit the sleeves-up end of this baby. As you'll see from the schematics we've got a lot of hands-on stuff. Smithies. Butter churns. Musket shooting – kids love that. There's a pretty nifty sweatshop somewhere in there. You know, just the way Grandma used to do it. Amazing stuff.'

'Sounds good.'

'The other thing we'd like to do is maybe get your family involved in the campaign. Ardelia and the kids. You know, from our family to yours. The guys down in PR have this whole spiel worked out. Like it's your backyard the people would be coming to. Don't worry – nothing too onerous. Just some photos and maybe a little copy. We just want to give it a homey feel.'

'Gus, I don't know what to say. That would be fine. We'd love to help.'

'Oh,' Savage said as Wooten continued to flip through the cards. 'We've also done a sweetheart deal with our friends in the Commonwealth of V-A to run a six-laner from the DC Beltway right to our front gate. A sixty-mile driveway. Think about it. It'll be easier to get to than Mount Vernon.'

Wooten flipped another card and froze. It took a moment for his conscious mind to catch up with the stomach-tightening feeling the image brought on. The Doric columns. The parasols. The low dark shacks.

'What you got there?' Savage asked, registering the change in Wooten's mood.

Wooten held up the card for him to see.

'Yeah. Magnolia Manor. We were gonna call it Tara but there was a copyright thing. Gotta have the Old South. Especially with I-Eighty-one so close.'

'Slaves, Gus?'

'Quarters, yes. But no slaves. We canned that idea.'

'But still.'

263

Savage's expression darkened slightly.

'We've focus-grouped the hell out of all this stuff, Earl. What's your point?'

Wooten realized he'd better zip it or else they'd find somebody else to give that hundredth of a hundredth.

'I just want to make sure we don't wind up with protesters blocking the entrance.'

Savage's expression relaxed. This was more like it. Just business.

'A little of that never hurt anybody. Besides, they'll get bored. This place is seriously out in the boonies.'

Wooten looked back at the card in front of him, his gaze momentarily pulled by one hastily drawn stick figure in the upper right corner, a tall shadow wielding a hoe that was poised in midswing over his shoulder. There were no shoes on his feet. Behind him loomed a kudzu-choked forest. Someone had drawn a circle around him and then crossed out the image within.

Wooten shuffled the cards back together and placed them on his lap before meeting Savage's coolly expectant gaze.

'Well?'

'I never knew Barnaby had anything like this in mind.'

Savage brushed nonexistent dust from his chair's arm.

'This is a post-Barnaby project.'

Wooten suddenly smiled, remembering his suspicions of the past few days.

'What?'

'No, it's just . . . never mind.'

'Earl – what's on your mind?'

'You'll think this is funny, but I came out here thinking that maybe you were considering me for Newton city manager.'

'Really? Whatever gave you that idea?'

'I heard a rumor.'

'From who?'

'Richard Holmes. Via Hollis Watson.'

Savage thought for a moment, then frowned.

'Yeah, I know where that came from. Hollis and some of the other guys at Afro-Am were after me a few weeks ago about not having any blacks in senior management positions. I told him to keep his powder dry, that the next big offer was going to go to a certain man from St Louis.'

'And so he assumed it was Newton manager.'

'Logical, as nobody knows about AmericaWorks but a chosen few.'

'But why is that?'

'Think about it. Word gets out and the people who own that land are suddenly sitting in the catbird seat.'

Which explained why Austin wasn't to know. This had nothing to do with Newton. It was about property prices in some godforsaken corner of Virginia.

'So manager's still Austin's job?'

'Of course. I mean, we've had to beat the jungle drums a bit to get him going these past few months, but sure. It's his job.'

'And what about construction for the rest of the new cities? Who's going to be handling that? Because I think Barnaby sort of had me in mind.'

Savage snatched a clove from the bowl and popped it in his mouth.

'There aren't going to be any more new cities.'

Wooten sat in shocked silence for a moment.

'Excuse me?'

'The decision was taken a few months ago.' He swallowed the garlic. 'Look, Earl – Newton isn't working.'

'Excuse me?'

'The city. It's failing.'

'Now, Gus, I've got to say, I don't see *that* at all.'

Savage waved a calming hand.

'Obviously, from a construction viewpoint, we couldn't be happier. Housing starts, infrastructure, the whole nine yards. We're happy as can be. Glitches like the lake and the gaslights notwithstanding. But there are other factors at work here that make the picture gloomy.'

'Such as?'

'There's been a sharp fall in home inquiries all spring. Sales are starting to slip as well. The summer picture is down. If the slide continues into the fall, forget about it. Seventy-four will be a nightmare.'

265

'I didn't . . . is this because of the fights and the bad press?'

'I'd be a liar if I said they weren't a major factor.'

'Come on, Gus. A couple kids go upside each other's heads, you get that anywhere.'

'Ah, but Newton isn't anywhere. Social harmony is our number-one selling point. Between you and me, I think Barnaby put too many eggs in *that* basket.'

Wooten remained quiet.

'This is an extremely delicate time for us right now, Earl. I won't go into the numbers, but the city's financial viability is in the balance. If we're going to attract the homeowners for the next phase of housing then changes will have to be made. The fights and the bad press must stop.'

'What changes?'

Savage stood and walked to one of his twin windows. He separated two of the louvered panels and peeked through, as if checking to see if Chicago was still there.

'Closing the HUD projects,' he said eventually.

'Closing them?'

Savage turned.

'Concurrent with the AmericaWorks announcement we'll let it be known that we're discontinuing Newton's HUD program. Renaissance Heights and Underhill will be converted into rental units. The other four complexes will be sold as condos. Current residents will be given first crack at re-renting once a competitive pricing structure is drawn up, though I'd imagine few of them will be able to afford it.'

'And so what will we do with them?'

'They'll be benignly relocated into EarthWorks reclamation schemes in deprived areas of Newark, Baltimore and Washington. We believe those HUD dollars can be better spent in existing ghetto neighborhoods than in our newer communities.'

Savage shook his head wistfully.

'Off the record, Earl? Barnaby blew it. He thought the city would change people. Make them behave differently. That's why we're so underpoliced out there. He didn't think cops would be necessary. The board went along because there was a niche for this kind of thinking five years ago. A certain sort

266

of homeowner who'd buy into the Newton ethos. You know the type. Young couples weaned on all that idealism, kids who thought the 'burbs were unfashionable. Black families with a little spare change. Newton people. The HUD projects were seen as a good part of the mix. Bait, if you will.'

'Bait? Barnaby saw them as bait?'

'Well, no, not Barnaby. He believed in them. Hook, line and sinker. No, I'm talking about the board and the banks. Dreamers need capital, right?' He shrugged. 'We always knew there was a risk, that this sort of backlash might happen. It was an eventuality we've been preparing for.'

Eventuality, Wooten thought.

'And there's another reason, Earl. One that cuts even more directly to the heart of the matter. We simply cannot afford the projects anymore.'

'But I thought the Title VII money . . .'

Wooten let the sentence die. Savage returned to his chair.

'Earl, I have three Nobel prize-winning economists at the University of Chicago on fat retainers and you know what they're telling me? That we're entering an inflationary cycle that is going to knock our socks off. My people out in the Middle East paint an even more dire picture. OPEC are just waiting for an excuse to jack up oil prices. Twofold, threefold. More. And that will mean one thing, Earl – hyperinflation. Right here in the heartland. Banana republic time. All that spare money Barnaby thought he could use to finance his dream is going to dry up quicker than a puddle of piss in August. Government funding will no longer cover the costs of places like the Heights. You think HUD is going to be pegging us inflation-indexed rises if the prime's at fifteen percent? Give me a break.'

Wooten nodded. He was beginning to get the picture.

'What's worse,' Savage continued, 'house prices are going to go through the roof. This at a time when savings are being squeezed. Nobody's gonna want to buy anything, much less an overpriced piece of aluminum. Idealism lives in the margin, Earl. When that vanishes, it's out on its ass. We're gonna need the cash those HUD units can generate as condos, especially when our first-time buyers realize their devalued dollar can't swing a house. More importantly, we've got to move the lion's share of the houses by the time the current selling cycle ends in November. Because unless Alfred Nobel is backing losers then this winter is going to see a big change in the whole shooting match. The last thing in the world we need are buyers holding back because of some adverse publicity. We got to close out Phases III and IV before the crude hits the fan.'

'But what about HUD? Won't they kick up a fuss?'

'That's where Swope comes in. He can hang those chumps out to dry. Besides, the federal government is in no position to give us any trouble. They owe us a lot more than we owe them. My people in the Mideast? They aren't all engineers. I won't bore you with the gory details, but trust me. And anyway, turn on the tube. Nixon's got bigger fish to fry than a bunch of dinky apartments.'

'Does Austin know about this?'

'The decision has just been made. I'll be talking to him about it next week.' He brushed the chair again. 'But we're getting way off track here, Earl. The question being – do you want to build AmericaWorks for us?'

Wooten stared at the naked cloves for a moment. They looked like a litter of something born too early to live. He thought about those shares. He thought about the fact that he'd be able to stay in Newton – Clarke County couldn't be more than an hour away. His picture would be everywhere. The man who built what had to be the world's largest theme park.

'You know, Gus, I think I would. But I'll have to talk to Ardelia about it.'

'Of course. Though I'd like your answer by Monday morning. We're really raring to go on this one.'

'I'll call you first thing.'

Savage smiled grimly.

'Excellent. Now, what do you say we go visit Barnaby? He's dying to see you.'

Seven Oaks was located on the shore of Lake Michigan, an hour north of downtown. Wooten had seen photographs of the house but had never visited. His meeting with Vine had always been at EarthWorks headquarters or the Newton site. And, of course, their first session, when Vine recruited him back in 1967, after Wooten had made the news by rehabilitating twelve blocks of St Louis brownstones into a community for working black families. Vine had come to Missouri himself, a tall, spry man on the cusp of old age. He had the impatient air of someone who'd been probing the world for seven decades and still found it wanting. He'd driven down from Chicago with his dog, Cicero, a remarkable animal who'd endured Joel's attention with the same stoic reserve with which his master weathered the follies of man. For three hours, Vine spoke to Earl and Ardelia at their kitchen table, his Midwestern voice as dry and rich as harvested wheat as he told them about the perfect city he wanted Earl Wooten to build. By the end of his un-interrupted speech they were hooked. Earl would start digging right away; Ardelia would have a job teaching at the first of the city's schools. The children would grow up on its safe streets, its tot lots and bike paths. The Wootens put their house on the market two days after watching Vine stride back to the limo. The chauffeur opened the door for the dog, who looked like he was as accustomed to the service as his master.

After that Wooten saw Vine regularly at the long, numbing strategy sessions in Chicago, where they tried to iron out every detail and anticipate every problem of the colossal building project they were undertaking. As they worked together, Wooten began to learn details of the man's life. The childhood in Nicodemus, Kansas, where he was the only son of a Methodist minister. His brilliant early career as a builder of high-rises; his wartime service designing army camps for Ike. The disillusionment with urban life that led to his formation of EarthWorks in the mid-fifties. The successes with shopping malls and subdivisions and revivified down-town markets. Newton was the culmination of his life's work.

Once the Wootens moved to the house Ardelia half wistfully dubbed Fort Apache, Vine visited his city on a near-monthly basis, quietly looking over Wooten's shoulder, occasionally uttering a word of advice. After the decade's end he came less often. Between visits he seemed to age years rather than months. In 1971 he came only four times for brief, distracted stopovers. And then, last summer, he'd had the first stroke. He was in the hospital for two months and spent the rest of the fall convalescing. Swope had seen him briefly just before Christmas. His condition hadn't seemed too serious – a slight facial sag, some abbreviation in the movement of his left hand. The seventy-one-year-old brain remained as supple as that of a man half his age. The second stroke happened in March. No one had seen Vine since. Rumors were rife. The best claimed that he found it impossible to speak and had gone nearly blind. The worst, that his mind was gone, blown away like a pile of dead leaves in a stiff autumn breeze.

Savage spoke nonstop on the drive up, detailing for Wooten the nuts and bolts of AmericaWorks, the acreage and budgets, the subcontractors and designers. The thing really had been worked out to the last detail. Building it would be hard, there was no doubting that. But it was doable. It was just before noon when they arrived at Vine's house, passing through a spiked gate manned by a dozing security guard. The long driveway disappeared into a copse of pine before making a sharp bend. Seven Oaks appeared, so low that in places it seemed to vanish right into the duned earth. Its roof was flat, its walls severe and unadorned. There was nothing around it that could be called a garden or even a yard. Just sawgrass and dunes. Beyond it the lake stretched to the horizon, interrupted by occasional pleasure craft and big, Canada-bound barges.

Savage's limo pulled up to the front door. Wooten stepped out. Chicago's heat had vanished up here, blown away by a steady lake breeze. To the south, the highest of the city's buildings, some designed by Vine, jutted from a collar of haze. The only sounds were seagulls and the breeze.

'Here we go,' Savage said.

They were met at the door by a maid with the high cheekbones and sad eyes of a Plains Indian. She wore a simple black dress. Her PF Flyers squeaked on the marble floor as she led them to the back of the house, which possessed the same aversion for walls Vine had displayed in his creation of Newton. They moved through a single large room, centered around a four-sided brick fireplace. Long rows of double steps broke up the space, creating a series of plateaus, none of which seemed higher than the others. The room reminded Wooten of the Escher drawing Joel had on his wall, the staircase that only went up. Or down, depending on which way you were headed. At the back of the big room there was a lone hallway that Wooten guessed led to the bedrooms and the kitchen. They never made it that far, steered instead toward a sliding-glass door that led to a lake-facing porch. The maid pulled it open and nodded to the men. Wooten took a deep breath and followed Savage through.

Vine sat at a card table, facing the water. He was in a wheelchair, a Navajo blanket folded over his lap. He sat bolt upright, his hands resting on the table, each of them holding something that looked like a cigar. His thin white hair fidgeted in the sea breeze. A young male nurse, Indian as well, sat nearby, his folding chair leaning against the redwood rails. He was reading *Mad* magazine. He looked up. Savage nodded once. The nurse disappeared silently back through the doors.

They took the chairs facing Vine. The old man was gone. That much was clear immediately. The mind-swept eyes, all color drained from their once violet pupils. The slackened folds of his throat, covered by a perma-stubble as white as dove feather's. Wooten could now see what Vine held in his hands. Lincoln Logs. There was a whole set of them on the table, spewed from their chewed cardboard container. A few had been slotted together to form a rickety house frame, though most remained helter-skelter where they had fallen. A brief, sickening waft of Ivory soap mixed with something else, a cloacal substratum of decay, seeped from him. Wooten's eyes traveled down to the chair, where the blanket had fallen back to reveal blue pajama bottoms covered with an archipelago of crusty stains. Above the pajama's elastic waist-band was a swatch of glossy diaper. A thin plastic tube ran over its safety pin and down to a thermos-sized container.

271

The tube was speckled with small droplets that shone brilliantly in the sun.

'Barnaby,' Savage was saying. 'Earl's here.'

Something seemed to move in the old man's eyes, though it might have simply been a trick of lake light. Not knowing what else to do, Wooten reached out to touch the back of his clammy hand. The veins were as hard as electrical wire.

'Hello, Mr Vine,' Wooten said.

They waited. Nothing.

'He brings good news, Barnaby. Everything is right on schedule. Everything is just fine in the city.'

Vine had begun to squint as Savage spoke, as if the light from the water was hurting him. Wooten watched sadly as Vine's eyelids finally came together and his mouth slowly opened, as if there were some great, creaking pulley system at work behind his face. His tongue looked like it had been coated with Elmer's glue; his gums were pocked with deep purple sockets.

'Nu . . .' he said, his voice surprisingly vigorous and loud.

Savage and Wooten exchanged a look.

'Mr Vine?' Wooten asked.

But nothing more was coming. Vine's mouth began to close; his eyes reopened simultaneously. And then he was silent.

'We're going now, Barnaby,' Savage announced.

Both men stood. Savage glanced at Wooten, who realized that he should say something.

'The city's almost done, Mr Vine.'

They headed back through the sliding-glass door, walking in silence until they reached the limo.

'Hey, where's the dog?' Wooten asked.

Savage drew his finger across his throat.

19

Irma was poised to take Africa. Two more victories and she would achieve her mission. It had been a long campaign, fraught with sacrifice and setback. From the first roll of the dice she'd shown herself to be an impetuous player, ignorant of risk and overeager to commit her troops to battle. Just a few moves ago she chanced annihilation by massing her battalions in East Africa for assaults on Madagascar and the Congo, thereby leaving her Egyptian and South African flanks vulnerable. Teddy had to forgo his assigned mission – the liquidation of Susan's red army – in order to cover her ass. It was a pity, because it would have been easy to maul Susan's troops, drawing them into the frozen tundra of Yakutsk, where he could have turned them into husky food with just a few rolls of the dice. Or, if he wanted to take his time about it, lure her forces down to the Indonesian bottleneck, where they could be systematically driven into the sea.

But Teddy wasn't playing to win. He wasn't even allowing himself the undeniable pleasure of smashing Susan. He was helping Irma. Secretly, of course. Technically, there was no way he should have known her goal. Mission cards were kept strictly under wraps. But Irma Truax wasn't exactly a closed book. Her goals were as apparent as the mascara fortifying her eyes. Asia had been the first continent he'd let her win, slyly setting up his infantry in Siam and the Ukraine to fend off the girls while their mother mopped up. There were some awkward statistical mathematics to get through at first as he tabulated the odds of five rolled dice, but after a while he got the hang of it. Luckily, Susan and Darryl played with neither aggression nor finesse. Whatever soldierly skill the sarge possessed had clearly been lost in the genetic shuffle. They were strictly cannon fodder.

Irma rolled the dice. Two fives and a four. Darryl, defending, responded. A three and a one.

'Ah,' Irma said, her eyes dilating with the thrill of international trespass. 'Madagascar.'

Yes, Teddy thought. And you've only lost eighteen battalions taking it.

'Looks like you're unstoppable now,' he sighed in a beleaguered sort of way.

'Whose turn is it?' Susan asked.

Teddy handed her the dice.

To be fair, Irma proved a more worthy opponent than he'd initially reckoned. Sally had mentioned how tenacious she was at bridge, an outsider who had clawed her way up through the ranks of the Newton round-robin with a doggedness that left the other women muttering. Though by no means gifted with much gray matter, she certainly kept the few cells she possessed working overtime. In Risk, this manifested itself in a refusal to retreat, no matter how many of her men got slaughtered. As they played, Teddy began to wonder if she'd had any relatives at Stalingrad.

This bullheadedness was a quality he'd come to cherish in her these past few days. A more passive mind would have been harder to bring along. But Irma, with her surging ambition and blatant prejudice, could be figured like a toy abacus. The trick was to make sure all the moves had been decided before too many drinks vanished down her gullet. Currently, she was on her third sachet of whisky sour mix. Still in the combat zone, though teetering on the edge of oblivion. One more highball and she'd be a goner. Her speech would slur, her expeditionary forces veer off course. Time to wrap this up, Teddy thought.

He rolled the dice.

This was the fourth day in a row he'd visited the Truax house. His first visit had been Tuesday afternoon, just a few hours after he'd unsuccessfully tried to patch things up with Joel. He'd driven over to his house that morning, carrying the salvaged visor as a peace offering. But there was no answer when he knocked at the big front door. Which was strange, since Joel never left the house before noon. He walked around back to peer through the sliding-glass door. Nothing. As he turned to go he glimpsed the treehouse where they'd spent so many hours together. The foliage was so thick now you could barely see it. Man, they'd had some serious times back there. Porno mags and Boone's Farm and Slim Jims. Hocking loogies into the surrounding trees, where they'd hang like larval sacs, sometimes for days. Teddy wondered if the graffiti he'd gouged in its soft wood was still there: 'Joels got a tweezer dick.' Fairly fucking funny.

This wasn't fair. It really wasn't.

He trooped back to the Firebird, visor in hand. Though he could have easily left it in the mailbox, he wanted to hand it over to Joel in person, so his friend could see how Teddy had gone back for his property at considerable personal peril. When he got to the car a stray bit of extrasensory intuition caused him to look back at the house. And there was Joel, barely visible behind half-drawn curtains. Teddy, figuring that his friend had been in the crapper or listening to some headphoned tunes, began to walk back toward the house. But the look on Joel's face froze him before he even made it to the gaslight. His eyes were as cold as a dead planet. He'd heard the knock. He knew who was there. Teddy spread his hands and gave what he thought to be an apologetic grimace. Joel vanished. Teddy stood his ground for what seemed like an hour, thinking that maybe he was coming down. But the front door remained firmly closed, the house quiet. In the end, there was nothing left for him to do but hop in his Firebird and split.

He couldn't believe his friend was doing him like this. He had to know that Teddy had called him a Tom only to get him out of a serious beating. They were friends. Teddy and Joel. Light-years beyond all that bullshit. How many times had he helped Joel out in the past? With homework. Getting him out of trouble with the Earl. Supplying him with gratis buds and copious brew. And then there were the thousand small slights he'd suffered without comment since the advent of Susan. There had to be something that would bring Joel around. A gesture to remind him that their friendship was indomitable.

Teddy spent the next few hours locked in his room, listening to *Plastic Ono* as he tried to figure out what to do. It ain't fair, John Sinclair, indeed. He ignored his mother's entreaties to come down for lunch. He'd stay in here all day and all night if he had to. This was important. There had to be something. But nothing he came up with seemed right. Dope, tickets, rides. That weekend in Ocean City. The usual things wouldn't work. He needed something special.

And then, halfway through 'I Found Out,' just as John was saying how he'd seen religion from Jesus to Paul, it came to him. Of course. The plan was so obvious he kicked himself for not coming up with it right there in the Wootens' front yard. There was indeed something he could give to Joel. A gift that would erase forever Monday night's betrayal. A nice blond package. About five-seven, a hundred and ten pounds. Scented with strawberry perfume and grape gum. Susan herself. Having taken her away, Teddy would now give her back to Joel, the forbidden fruit he thought he'd never be able to taste again. Better still, she would be the new, improved Susan. Gone would be the rebellious, gum-smacking, Teddy-hating bitch of old, replaced by an obedient, grateful and polite girl who would be utterly under his thumb. A demure young lady who would know the score. A gift to make Joel's life perfect. Teddy would arrange things so the two of them could get back together. Only this time there would be no ditching.

After the initial rush of inspiration he started hammering out the details. It would be a tough plan to execute. This was no dope run to College Park. The risks were substantial. But he was sure he could pull it off. And when he succeeded, he would have his best friend and his perfect summer back. And maybe, if he worked it just right, he'd be able to arrange some further glimpses of the sight that had lingered in his mind since Saturday and fueled a half dozen thundering jackoffs; a sight that had supplanted even his *Two Virgins* album cover as erotic inspiration – those two entwined bodies moving slowly through the candlelight.

By midafternoon Tuesday he was ready to get to work. First thing to do was breach the Truax bulwarks, no small task given the fact that Susan's father would be on the gate. But before he could even leave the house he was visited by an amazing stroke of luck. It happened when he found the Swope unexpectedly ensconced in his study, watching the Cradle's balls do their thing. Though in a hurry, Teddy decided to give the old man a few minutes. He looked like he could use some cheering up. He was glad he did. After the usual persiflage, his father swore Teddy to secrecy, then told him not to be surprised if he saw John Truax around the house over the next few weeks, as he was now working for the Swope in a hush-hush capacity. Teddy nodded soberly at the news, hardly able to keep from hollering in delight at this most excellent bit of serendipity. Not only did this mean that Truax would probably be out of the way for his incursions into Susanville – it also dealt Teddy a trump card to slap on the table if the sarge got frisky. After all, the man would have to think long and hard before crossing his new boss's son.

He set out for Fogwood in a buoyant mood. He decided to lay off the dope, knowing he'd need a clear head. His opponent would be formidable indeed. Not Susan, of course. Despite her pissing and pouting, she'd be so much putty. It was her mother who worried him. The redoubtable Irmagard Truax. He'd seen her at the party, seen her rage when she caught Joel. And he also knew that beneath the irrational histrionics lurked a calculating mind that would be able to sniff out what he was up to at the first slip-up. He would have to step lightly. One false move and she'd be on him like white on rice.

Sure enough, it was Irma who answered the door, her face a veritable mask of suspicion. She was dressed in a floral housecoat that exhausted all the available shades of yellow and green. He could smell the sweet booze on her breath.

'Hello, Mrs Truax. How are you?'

'Susan isn't seeing anyone today,' she said, her voice stern.

Teddy shook his head, as if he'd been misunderstood.

'Actually, it was you I wanted to talk to. Are you busy?'

This took her by surprise.

'No, I'm not busy.' She stared at him for a moment. 'Come in.'

She led him into their small living room, gesturing for him to sit in a chocolate brown chair beneath a small gallery of Lladro figurines. She perched on the edge of the sofa. Afternoon light poured through the picture window, forming a petrochemical nimbus around her Final Net-stiffened hair.

'Mrs Truax, I think I owe you an apology.'

There was another surprised pause. Teddy felt like Ali, softening her up with the left. Float like a butterfly, sting like a bee – Nazi can't hit what Nazi can't see.

'An apology?'

'I know about what happened with Susan and Joel.'

Irma's expression darkened. Careful, Teddy thought.

'And I feel sort of responsible for it.'

'Responsible?'

'A few weeks ago, well, I guess I began to wonder if something . . . inappropriate was going on between them.'

'Yes?'

'Joel, I mean, you know he and I used to be sorta close.'

'Used to . . .'

Teddy waved this detail off as something too painful to talk about right now.

'So a month ago he starts acting all weird. It's like he doesn't have time for me anymore. You couldn't *talk* to him. His eyes were all distant. It was like he was obsessed. Like some kind of . . . animal or something.'

He stopped, trying to gauge from her expression if he'd gone too far. But he could see that he'd have to travel many miles down this particular road to go too far. He relaxed into the chair's encompassing brownness. Round one to the challenger, Kid Teddy.

'And then, you know, he made it clear that he didn't want me around him and Susan. This was after those ni . . . after there was trouble at the teen center.'

'I heard about that.'

278

'It's a shame. Some people just don't know how to act, I guess.'

'No.'

'It was then that I heard something that bothered me.'

Irma was all ears.

'Joel was with some other guys at the mall, some blacks from Renaissance Heights. His new friends, I guess you'd call them. I went to say hello and just before I got there I heard him saying things.'

'Things?'

'About Susan. About what he was . . . doing with her.'

Irma looked at those glazed puppies and lambs. Her jaw working.

'Anyway, the point is, I've been thinking that maybe I should have said something to you. But it's just so . . . awkward. God, I don't know.'

They sat in silence for a moment.

'No,' Irma said eventually.

'No?'

'You must not blame yourself. It is only one boy's fault.'

Teddy nodded.

'Have you seen him since . . .' Irma wondered.

'I went by yesterday but he wouldn't even let me in. It's like everybody's to blame but him. I tried to tell him it was his own fault but he's practically slamming the door in my face. I guess ol' Joel's burning his bridges.'

Disgust clicked deep in Irma's mouth.

'He has a real bad temper, Joel does,' Teddy said wistfully.

'They all do.'

Teddy shrugged.

'Hence the teen center,' he reasoned.

'It's all this living so close together.'

Teddy decided to press home his advantage.

'What really gets me mad . . . I mean, I ran into these guys last night who saw Joel after, you know, Saturday happened. The way they put it – I mean this is gross – but they made it seem like he was *bragging* about getting caught by you. Like it was some kind of badge of honor or something.'

'Bragging,' Irma repeated darkly.

'When I heard that, I knew I'd better come over here and let you know that I'm not part of all this gossip about Susan. I mean, I really respect her. The thought of her name being besmirched galls me to no end.'

Teddy wondered about that 'besmirched.' It might not be in her vocabulary. But Irma didn't seem to be missing any of the essentials. Her creamy complexion had turned a just-slapped pink.

'Bragging,' she whispered.

'I just feel bad for Susan in all this.'

'That's nice of you,' she said, still distracted by her fury.

Teddy stood.

'Anyway. I just wanted to let you know that I feel bad. I mean . . .'

'Yes?'

'I know you're going to do what you have to in terms of Susan, but I just hope you keep in mind that, well, Joel can be pretty aggressive.' He shook his head. 'It's a shame. I really like her. It's just hard to . . . compete with a guy like that.'

Irma nodded, as if some deep truth had just been shared.

'Well, I better go.'

When they got to the door he seemed to have an idea.

'Can I ask you something? You can say no.'

'Ask.'

'Do you mind if I come by once in a while and see Susan? No big deal. Just watch TV. Go out for a walk or something. She's gonna get sort of lonely.' Teddy inserted a small choke in his voice. 'I know I am.'

Irma looked at him for a long moment. Teddy began to think he really had gone too far with that muffled sob. But then the faintest of smiles split her lipstick.

'That would be fine, Edward.'

He came by the following afternoon, once again making small talk with Irma in the living room. He could see right away that the idea he'd sown had taken root in her mind. Yesterday's wariness was gone. After a few minutes she called upstairs for Susan who descended with an aria of put-upon sighs. When she reached the bottom of the steps even Teddy was shocked. She looked like she'd been weeping for months. Her eyes were puffy and her hair wild. She wore a Fort Meade sweatshirt and a pair of khaki cutoffs. Teddy thought about those dark nipples and the way her body had woven with Joel's into a seamless knot of soft flesh. He felt himself start to get hard, so he thought of other things.

Susan gave Teddy a quizzical look.

'Hey, Susan.'

'Hey,' she said, her voice small and confused.

'How you been?'

She shrugged, then came into the living room and sat in the other brown chair, folding her long left leg beneath her. Irma continued to stand in the arched doorway.

'So what you been doing?' Teddy asked.

'Nothing. Listening to records.'

'You hear the new Zeppelin?'

Susan shook her head in confusion. She hated Led Zeppelin.

'I could tape it for you.'

She nodded slowly, her eyes narrowing. She might be stupid, but she'd also been around Teddy long enough to know that something was up.

'Sure.'

'Well, I'll leave you two alone,' Irma said. She pointed a stern finger at Susan. 'No going out.'

Irma walked off. Susan's expression grew serious, like she was about to say something. Teddy held a finger to his lips and cocked an ear toward the door. He could hear the consecutive thuds of Irma's tossed slippers on the kitchen floor, followed a few seconds later by the faint suck of her naked soles on the hall's tile. Teddy pointed a cautionary finger in her direction as he started to talk.

'I saw Drew Harvey this morning,' he said conversationally.

'Drew?' Susan asked.

No such person existed. Teddy opened his hands and mouth and eyes in a dumb show of exasperated encouragement.

'Oh,' Susan said. 'How's Drew?'

'He said Monica freaked out when she heard about him and Cindy.'

'Yeah,' Susan said, slowly getting into the flow. 'I guess she would.'

They spoke like this for nearly twenty minutes. Several times Teddy heard Irma retreat to the kitchen to rattle pots and fake phone calls, always creeping back to her hidden listening post just beyond the arched entrance. Occasionally Susan looked set to break the flow of their charade. Each time Teddy patted the air in front of him for silence. Finally, he announced that it was time for him to go. He heard Irma retreat quickly to the kitchen as Susan walked him to the front door.

' 'Bye, Mrs Truax,' he called.

She appeared in the kitchen door, wiping her dry hands on a paper towel.

'Good-bye, Edward. Come see us again.'

'I sure will.'

Teddy stepped through the door. Susan leaned out after him.

'Teddy,' she whispered. 'You got to tell Joel . . .'

Teddy held up his index finger.

'I'm going to tell you this once, Susan,' he hissed. 'Shut the fuck up.'

She screwed up her face.

'Do exactly what I say or you'll never see Joel again.'

'But . . .'

'Fine.'

He wheeled and began to walk away.

'Teddy . . .' she whispered.

He stopped and turned. Real slow. She looked at him for a moment, then dipped her head submissively.

'Okay.'

The door opened further, revealing Irma. She smiled at Teddy and began to stroke Susan's long hair.

'See you ladies later,' Teddy said before walking back to his Firebird.

*   *   *

282

He returned the next afternoon, wrangling a dinner invitation from Irma just moments after walking in the door. Truax was home, though he slept soundly upstairs, having already put in some long hours doing his hush-hush work for the Swope. Irma cooked corned beef hash and mashed potatoes, a coagulated mass of gristle and starch that Teddy knew would inhabit his gastric canals for days. He noticed that Susan ate practically nothing. Darryl, on the other hand, downed three helpings. Teddy decided to focus on the poor kid, regaling her with tales of the Dead Sea Scrolls, the Shroud of Turin and every other scientific proof of Christ's existence he could summon from his memory banks. Darryl listened in slack-jawed awe. She really was a fucking cow. If I looked like her and had Susan for a sister I'd be a Satanist, Teddy concluded. Out of the corner of his eye he noticed Irma's admiring gaze. Clearly, her Darryl was not usually afforded this kind of attention.

'All right,' he announced after dinner, clapping his hands once. 'I scream, you scream . . .'

And so they were off to Baskin-Robbins for Mocha Mocha and Rocky Road. Teddy drove. His car reeked faintly but he doubted Irma could detect the weed. As they stood in line she regaled him with some boring story about how the sarge first caught her attention back in Germany by bringing her an ice cream. Though he felt like sawing away at a notional violin, Teddy let her have her say. At home he simply dropped them off, not wanting to push too hard. He noticed that Truax's Cutlass was gone. The Swope must really be working the guy.

Susan was last out of the car.

'See you tomorrow,' he said, a wink in his voice.

She nodded and then slipped Teddy a folded piece of notebook paper. She meant to be sly about it but the gesture was awkward. If Irma had been looking she would have seen it for sure. Luckily, she was too busy finishing off Susan's unwanted sugar cone. Teddy jammed the paper under his thigh and smiled tightly at Susan.

'See ya,' she replied.

He stopped just after turning the corner, unable to believe Susan's stupidity. He looked at the paper. It was, surprise

surprise, a note to Joel. Teddy read it by the light of his Cricket. Susan's loopy scrawl was barely grammatical. 'I miss U so much.' 'I can't believe there doing this to us.' Nothing about Teddy, of course. Not a syllable of gratitude. He used the Cricket to set an edge of the paper alight dangling it out the window until it was fully involved. Unauthorized communications vill not be allowt, he told himself. He drove off, leaving her words smoldering on the asphalt.

Upon arriving Friday afternoon he asked Irma if she'd like to go for a walk with them around the block. She seemed tempted, but then thought the better of it. Teddy realized that she'd swallowed the second chunk of his bait. Having won her trust, he'd now convinced her that he had a crush on Susan. Once they were clear of the house, Teddy turned to Susan.

'If you ever pull another stunt like that note then we're done.'

'Did you give it to him, though?'

'Of course I did, Susan. What do you think I am?'

'Did he say anything?'

'He wanted me to give you a message.'

She nodded expectantly.

'He wants you to do whatever I ask.'

Her expression collapsed.

'Do you understand, Susan? Whatever I say. Otherwise this isn't gonna happen. All right?'

'All right,' she said with theatrical reluctance.

Teddy explained how it was going to work. She was going to start dating him. Slowly but surely, they were going to become embroiled in an all-American romance that would warm Irma's Teutonic heart. Meanwhile, Teddy and Joel were pretending to have a big fallout. Once everybody's parents were sufficiently bullshitted, Teddy would arrange it so Susan and Joel would be able to see each other.

'All right,' Susan said after a moment, making a big show out of hating the idea of dating Teddy. 'If that's the only way.'

'That's the only way.'

As they arrived back in front of the Truax house, Teddy

284

could see Irma's shadowy figure behind the living room's lace curtains.

'Smile,' he said.

Susan smiled.

'Laugh, like I said something warm and witty.'

She soundlessly tossed back her pretty head.

'Now say what a great guy you think I am.'

'You're an asshole, Teddy Swope.'

'Excellent. Now let's go play with your mom.'

The game ended with Irma taking the Congo. Her forces straddled the dark continent. Just as Teddy had planned. He stretched, then checked his watch.

'Well, I better get going.'

'No. Really? Not another game?'

Irma smiled demurely, a desirable fräulein once again. Flecks of whiskied froth clung to her lips like the remnants of an ocean wave.

'One drubbing per night's my limit,' Teddy said.

He hazarded a Euro-peck on her cheek. She accepted it with closed eyes and a smile. Darryl had to settle for a wave.

'See you tomorrow?' he asked Susan when they reached the front door.

She nodded. In the kitchen Irma was putting horses and men back in the box, watching them out of the corner of her eye. Teddy had an idea.

'Kiss,' he commanded.

Susan looked at him in astonishment. Teddy smiled in a way that let her know he wasn't kidding. So, after a brief sigh, she closed her eyes in reluctant assent. Teddy pressed his lips against hers. They tasted like cheap candy. He was surprised how cold they were. He would have thought they'd be warmer.

When they pulled apart he could see Irma still watching them out of the corner of her eye, a faint smile pouting her full lips.

Bingo, Teddy thought.

'Good night,' he said to Susan.

Petulant cunt didn't answer. Teddy slipped out the door

into the warm night, ambling triumphantly past the gaslight, whistling the bridge from 'Jealous Guy.' All he had to do now was organize an out-of-the-house date and he'd be able to give Joel the gift that would revivify their friendship. Thoughts of bong hits and wisecracks and that sortie to the seaboard put a little skip in his step. It wasn't until he'd made it all the way to the Firebird that a realization froze him in his tracks, further widening his smile and swelling his paltry chest.

He'd just had his first kiss.

20

His lips tasted like something that had leaked through slit cellophane onto the chipped ice in the A & P meat department. Cold and warm at the same time; wet and dry. That filmy root beer coating unable to mask their fundamental bitterness. God, she hated him. She couldn't wait until this was over. Her only regret about ditching him was that she wouldn't be able to see his eyes after she vanished with Joel. Because that's exactly what was going to happen as soon as Teddy got them together. They were going to be history.

After closing the door her first temptation was to bolt up to the bathroom and sop her mouth out with half a bottle of Listerine, then spend about twenty minutes brushing her teeth with those thermonuclear Pearl Drops her mother used. Instead, she walked back to the kitchen to help clean up. She had to be good now. No more defiance. No more fights. No more slammed doors. Any slips and her mother's slackening vigilance would tighten back up for good. And then she would never be able to leave. It would be Teddy and Newton forever.

Irma was still putting away the game, stacking the cards and slotting the little soldiers into their proper boxes. She'd freshened her drink, new froth mixing with old scum. Overlapping crescents of bloodred lipstick stained the tumbler's rim. Irma always refilled. Using new glasses would allow people to count her drinks. As if any fool couldn't see how many she'd had in her rheumy eyes and bright pink cheeks.

Susan collected dishes from the table and began to load them into the dishwasher.

'He is such a nice young man,' Irma said for the hundredth time.

'Yeah,' Susan tonelessly agreed. 'He's great.'

Irma smiled wistfully.

'I think maybe he let me win.'

No duh, Susan thought. Her mother was usually hard to bamboozle, though with Teddy she was as blind as a caveful of bats.

'I am thinking he very much likes you,' she continued.

Booze had the same effect on her sentences as the proverbial bull in a china shop.

'Really?'

'Don't you?'

Susan shut the dishwasher's door.

'Yeah. I guess.'

'Come.' The castered chair opposite Irma rolled backward a few inches, pushed by an invisible slippered foot. 'Sit here with me for a minute.'

Susan wanted nothing less than to spend more time with her mother, especially gossiping about the romantic possibilities of Edward Swope. But she couldn't afford to rouse suspicion. Not when she was getting so close. So she dropped into the offered seat, the bare backs of her thighs squeaking on the Naugahyde. The top of the Risk box rested in front of her. Susan studied it for a moment. Those white horses with their flared nostrils. The men with their furry hats and drawn swords. Her father had been a soldier. Though she knew his war was nothing like this.

Irma continued to put away the pieces.

'So. Susan. It is so good to see you happy like this.'

Susan smiled demurely as she fixed a stray frond of hair behind her ear.

'He's so different from the ones you've been with before.'

'How do you mean?'

'You know. More sensitive. Not such a . . . stallion.'

Christ. The words her mother came up with. Half the time she could hardly even speak English and then she hit you with these things nobody's even heard of.

'Believe me,' Irma continued. 'Those big manly aspects

don't count for as much as you think. Not when it is all said and it is all done. I'm speaking here of your father, darling, in case there is a confusion.'

Susan searched for an appropriate response, something that might possibly explain an attraction to Teddy.

'He's got nice eyes,' she said finally.

'And intelligent?' Irma answered her own question with a click of the tongue. 'That's what you want in a boy. I'll tell you, if I had been lucky to be born here like you it wouldn't be Sally Swope sitting over there in Mystic Hills.'

Which would mean you'd be wanting me to date my brother, Susan thought. Which would be just about typical.

'So. Tell me. After just a few days – do you think maybe there's something between you two?'

'Could be. It's hard to tell with Teddy. He's such a . . . gentleman.'

'There's nothing wrong with that.' Her eyes narrowed and she took another sip. 'Especially after our tree-swinging friend with his temper and his . . .'

Irma temporarily lost her train of thought. Susan bit her tongue.

'Let me give you some advice, young lady. Do what you have to do for this boy. You may be Miss America now but before long the blossoms are withering. What the Swopes have is what counts in this world. Get some of it now while you can afford it. Me, I had no chance when I was your age. All the boys.' She drew her finger across her throat and made a cranking sound. 'Either that or in the Russian camps. There were only Americans and who was to know about them? You find one who looks like maybe he can look after you and then you turn around and he's a Jew. So I went for the one with the broad shoulders and the gentle smile and look at me now. Living in this horrid little box in this ridiculous toy city while there are country clubs and senators out there.'

A bitter sheen now glazed Irma's face.

'I had *no choice*. This you must know, my Susan. I was *hungry*. You will never know hunger. But I did. The way your stomach closes like a fist and then starts hitting you from inside. I was a teenage girl. Do you think this is fair? And then your father comes along with an ice cream cone when there is no food. So suddenly I do have a choice. So I do the things a woman has to do to make sure there will always be one more ice cream, yes? I get away from the hungry place. We come here. And then the years pass and I find that I have made *the wrong choice.*'

'Mom . . .'

'No, I am not saying that John is a bad man. He is good. Better than anyone will ever know. The things he did for that rotten army . . . but he is not a vinner. All right? He is a loser. And nothing is hated more in this country than a loser.'

'I don't think Daddy's a loser.'

Irma shrugged.

'That's because you are a sweet girl.'

'But he fought in the war and . . .'

'Lost!'

'But that wasn't his fault. That was LBJ and Macna-whatever – all those awful old men. We read about it in history.'

'Tell that to the boys from my village they buried in a ditch out by the apple orchard. About losing not being the soldier's fault.'

She pointed at Susan over the glass she continued to grasp.

'That is why I won't let you see Joel Wooten. Not because of the fucking. The fucking is what we do to hold them. We wrap ourselves around those brainless things between their legs and hold on for dear life.'

Susan couldn't believe she was hearing this. Her mother must be more shitfaced than she looked. She had to say something. Even though she knew she should just nod and take it, she had to defend Joel.

'But Joel isn't a loser,' she said, trying to keep the anger out of her voice.

Irma's right eyebrow shot up at a scrutinizing angle. Susan realized she should be careful. Defending Joel risked blowing the whole charade. But this was the man she loved they were talking about.

'He's smart and he's from a nice family,' she continued, her voice matter-of-fact. 'He's going to college. And—'

'And he's a nigger.'

Susan stared incredulously at Irma.

'*Mother.*'

'Don't look at me like that, young lady. I am not blind. Twenty years I've been here and you don't think I see who the losers are in this fair country of ours? The niggers. I come from a tribe of losers, remember? You think I've traveled this far to see my daughter wind up joining another one?'

'That's just prejudice.'

'No. It is not. It is reality. I don't make the rules. I just keep my family from suffering under them.'

Susan took a deep breath. She wanted more than anything to fight her mother on this. But it had already gone too far. One more word and she'd lose her temper. And if she did then Irma would see what she was planning. Just play along, she told herself. In a few days you'll be back with him. And then you will surprise them all.

'Maybe you're right,' she said with a shrug.

It worked. That raised eyebrow on Irma's forehead dropped.

'Yes. I am.'

They sat in silence for a moment, Susan taking solace by picturing the moment when she and Joel would be able to see each other again. Although she hadn't been able to talk to him since Saturday, she was sure he knew exactly what they were going to do. They'd talked about it enough. They'd be at April's a few hours after they saw each other. As soon as the bus got them there. Then they'd get money, maybe even some wheels. By the time Irma thought to send her father after her they'd be long gone. So far that not even he would be able to find them. They'd never have to see this stupid city again.

She looked up to see her mother staring expectantly at her.

'So you think Teddy's cute, then?' Susan asked.

'Of course he is. Okay, there might be things about him that are not quite so . . . splendid at first. But he is very interested in you, my dear. Do not lose sight of that.'

Susan stood. She walked around the table and kissed her mother's soft cheek.

'No,' she said. 'I won't. I understand about the future, Mom. I really do.'

'That's my good girl.'

Something sharp adhered to Susan's bare foot as she started to go. She reached down to pluck it out. It was one of those little plastic soldiers from the game. Luckily, it hadn't broken the flesh.

Susan handed it to her mother.

'Ah,' Irma said, examining the piece closely, as if it had some hidden quality she was only now recognizing. 'There's always one that is left behind.'

21

Truax saw the words when he went to retrieve the thermos. He'd inadvertently knocked it over while stretching, sending it bumping across the treehouse floor's minor warps until it settled in a dark corner. That was where the writing was, scratched low on the plywood wall, behind a scrim of dead web. A damp stain had oblitered most of the sentence, leaving only its first and last words. *Joels. dick*. When Truax first saw them a pulse of fear ran through him. They knew he was out here. They'd come while he was away and done this to let him know. But he immediately realized that was absurd. This was written years ago. He was tempted to get his K-bar from the Cutlass's trunk and scrape away the remaining two words. But he decided to leave them be. As a reminder. To keep him sharp.

He checked his watch. After seven. It would be getting dark soon. The house remained quiet. It had been several hours since there had been any human movement behind its big windows. The only activity was the slow progress of shadows across the walls and the cat's languid relocations. An untrained eye would have thought the place empty. But Truax knew that there was someone inside.

It had been different that morning. He'd watched from his customary position behind the treehouse window, using his nocs to get a better view. The twins had come down first, clumsily assembling milk cartons and cereal boxes on the big kitchen table for breakfast. Though Ardelia usually accompanied them, today she was lagging behind. Which must mean she'd seen the letter as she came down the stairs.

293

Just as Truax had planned. Sure enough, she walked stiffly into the kitchen a good two minutes after the girls, her eyes fixed on the single sheet of notepaper. She ignored the milk her daughters had already managed to spill, letting the thin white waterfall plummet freely to the tiled floor. After a few seconds she half collapsed against the counter, her eyes fixed on the page, as if trying to memorize its contents. The twins could tell something was wrong – they had grown perfectly still, staring at their mother. Finally, Ardelia remembered where she was. She folded the letter back in the envelope and placed it on top of a row of cookbooks. Her actions were brusque and short-tempered as she cleaned up after the girls. A few minutes later a yawning, shrugging Joel came down. Ardelia spoke to her son as he stood scratching in front of the fridge. Judging by his astonished reaction, her words must have been unusually sharp. He watched her closely as she bustled the twins toward the front door, collecting the letter as she left the room. She said a few last impatient words to her son and then she was gone, driving down Merlin's Way with uncharacteristic speed. Joel remained behind, eating bowl after bowl of Kix before slouching back to his room. Truax felt the customary hate rise up in him as he watched the boy. It would be a long time before he got the image of that slick condom out of his mind. Those scratched words hovered at the edge of his field of vision. *Joels. dick.*

It was almost two hours before Ardelia returned alone. The letter was still in her hand. Once again, she placed it on top of the cookbooks, as if that was where it was now meant to be. If anything, this usually imperturbable woman looked more upset than when she'd left. She slammed around the kitchen for a while, at one point freezing in front of the sink, head bowed, her left hand pushing the hair from her forehead. Because she was facing away from Truax it was impossible to tell if she was crying. Joel, dressed now, appeared in the doorway a few minutes later. He tried to speak to her. Ardelia shook her head a few times without meeting his eye, then stormed past him, remembering at the last moment to snatch Swope's letter from on top of those books. Joel looked like he was considering going after her, though in the end he simply left the house. Some son, Truax thought. Ardelia soon appeared in the master bedroom's window, pacing the room for a few minutes before falling onto an unseen bed.

Since then, nothing. Ardelia rose once to go to the bathroom, but that was all. Joel stayed out. The twins were nowhere in sight. The afternoon passed. Heat gathered in the treehouse. Mosquitoes came but were repelled by the glistening layer of repellent Truax sprayed on his wrists and neck. He dreamed a few times, dissonant snatches of memory that came to nothing. Faint rumors of pain fluttered up from his infected hand, though he put this down to sleeplessness. He ate the lunch he'd packed, a Lebanon bologna sandwich and a couple of Ho Ho's. Chewing without relish. By five o'clock the big thermos of Gatorade was just about gone.

The letter had worked. Just like Swope said it would. Truax had planted it an hour before dawn. Swope explained that it was essential that it find its way into Ardelia's hands as soon as possible. Since there was no mail slot in the front door, Truax had to think of some other method of delivery. He'd considered folding it into the copy of the *Sun* that would be lying near the porch, though he immediately abandoned this plan when he saw that two previous papers remained uncollected. Other ideas kicked through his head. Putting it beneath the Le Sabre's wiper like a parking ticket. Getting some local kid to deliver it. In the end he decided there was no reason to be cute. He simply crept up to the front door and stuck it to one of its fan of windows. The envelope's sharp edge nestled snugly into the crack between the wood and glass. He made sure that Ardelia's boldly printed name faced inward. He worked without worry – there was no one around at 5 A.M.

They had come up with the plan the night before, after Swope's call woke Truax from the light sleep he'd fallen into after his airport mission. Swope had instructed him to stand down for a few hours, reasoning that Wooten wouldn't be back until the following evening at the earliest. So Truax took a quick shower and then changed his dressing, noticing a slight reddening in the deepest precincts of his wound. He didn't dwell on it. He had things to do. Downstairs, he found the house empty – Irma had left a note about going off for ice cream with Teddy and the girls.

And then Swope called with news that it was time to escalate.

He requested they meet at midnight in the empty parking lot of Newton High, explaining that two visits to Prospero's Parade in one night would have been unsafe. Truax joined him in the front seat of the Town Car. They spent nearly ten minutes talking as an infinity of bugs swarmed around the lot's sodium lights. Swope explained that he'd come to a decision. Wooten's trip to Chicago not only confirmed his thievery – it also suggested he might be getting ready to flee after making one last big score. It was time to start turning up the pressure on him. Simple surveillance would no longer suffice. They needed to start twisting some screws. Make him sweat. Force him to get sloppy and commit mistakes. Swope explained that not everything they had to do would be strictly legal. There might be some acts involved that naive people would construe as vandalism or petty burglary. But given the fact that Wooten had the local cops in his pocket, these moves were necessary. Swope had paused after mentioning this part of the plan, saying that if Truax had a problem with any of this he should speak up right now.

'No,' he answered immediately. 'I don't have any problems.'

It was then that Swope gave him the letter, describing it as their opening salvo. Truax had always liked that word. *Salvo.* That, and *enfilade.* He used them whenever he could back when he was an instructor. Of course he didn't ask what was inside the envelope and Swope didn't explain. He told Truax to get it anonymously into Ardelia's hands as soon as humanly possible and then provide him with a full account of the effect it had on the household. He was particularly interested in what happened after Wooten returned. Swope couldn't be sure when that would be, though he guessed it might be as early as Friday night.

'It doesn't matter when it is,' Truax said. 'I'll be there.'

Just before eight Joel returned, slouching up to his room. Truax was momentarily worried that the boy had somehow

296

managed to see Susan, though he quickly dismissed the thought. Irma was watching over the girl. There was no way Joel could get by her. Besides, Susan had other interests now. For the fourth night in a row Teddy was visiting. At first Truax had been suspicious that his interest was some sort of plot the two friends had dreamed up to allow Joel to get around Truax's ban. But Irma had then explained that Teddy and Joel had fallen out. In the three nights he'd sat watching the Wootens' house he'd seen no sign of Teddy. Irma's theory that he had only been hanging around Joel as a way of keeping close to Susan must have been right after all. Not that Truax was surprised. He may have been Susan's father but he was also a man. He knew how attractive she was. A boy would have to be crazy not to jump at the chance to be with her. According to Irma, Teddy was being the perfect gentleman about it. Not pressing. Including Irma and Darryl in things. Going slow. Acting like a Swope. If things kept up like this Truax might even consider letting his daughter out of the house again.

His thoughts were broken by the sight of the Ranchero racing into the circular drive. He glanced up at the master bedroom. The light remained off. Ardelia still hadn't moved. This was good. Whatever had been in that letter must have been a real bombshell. Truax knew it had something to do with what he'd seen at that apartment. The way that skinny woman had looked at Wooten.

Things were going to start changing now.

Lights flared on downstairs as Wooten entered his house. Truax used his nocs to watch. Wooten moved along the hallway and then stood staring into the dark kitchen for a long moment. Finally, he reached out and hit the switch. Fluorescent light flickered over him. He looked beat, that suit bag draped over his shoulder like captured prey. He hefted it, then turned and headed upstairs. The master bedroom's light came on five seconds later. Truax had to lean far to his left to see Wooten's face. He was staring down at the bed. He began to say something but then stopped. The beginnings of fear entering his eyes.

Now it starts, Truax thought.

22

The house was quiet. Which was strange – he'd expected to be greeted by the twins rushing him like blitzing linebackers, leaping up into his arms, writhing and giggling and craning their necks to see what he'd brought them. And Ardelia right behind them, wiping her hands on a dish towel, her head cocked, waiting to hear the news. There should have been tinny noise from the kitchen Zenith, the complicated smells of cooking. The upstairs thud of Joel's music and then his son himself, materializing at the top of the steps, looking non-chalant even though he really wanted to be in on this.

Instead, silence. And darkness as well. He hit some lights as he made his way down the long marble hall to the kitchen, his suit bag banging gently into the backs of his legs, hurrying him along. He didn't want to call out – the twins might be in bed, banished after some summer mischief. Besides, whoever was home would have heard him enter. Nobody had ever accused Earl Wooten of sneaking up on people.

The kitchen was empty. There were no signs of imminent dinner, no watery churn from the dishwasher. Dirty plates were stacked in the sink and there was a puddle of dried milk on the table. Wooten stood in confusion for a moment, trying to remember if he'd seen the Le Sabre in the garage as he parked his own car out front. Scenarios involving snapped bones and gashed flesh began to percolate though his mind. A mad dash to the hospital down in Cannon City. But then he remembered Ardelia mentioning she might take the kids to Western Sizzlin after picking them up from play school. That had to be it. He checked the refrigerator for a note.

There was nothing. Not that that meant much. They'd been married long enough where notes weren't always necessary.

Wooten relaxed, the worry that had begun to accumulate in him draining like unblocked water. He decided to head upstairs and grab a shower before they got back. Unpack the gifts he'd barely had time to buy at O'Hare. The Ernie Banks shirt for Joel. The wind-up tin birds for the twins. Ardelia's Pantou. Relax a bit before breaking out the best gift of all – the news of his job. Ardelia would say yes, there was no doubting that. First thing Monday, he'd call Savage. And then he could tell Austin. The time for secrets between them was almost over. Everything would finally be out in the open. Both men would have the best possible futures.

He passed the gallery of photoportraits lining the front hall. His ancestors, staring out from the dozen daguerreotypes Ardelia had hunted down and restored for his fortieth birthday. Closest to the kitchen was the photo of his mother and father, Hattie and Cyrus Wooten, captured on their wedding day in 1928. Cyrus just returned from his hell-raising days up in Chicago, his mother no older than Joel. Gazing boldly into a future that wasn't to be, denied them by something as improbable as a bolt of lightning. Next came the shredded picture of the Mound City house where Wooten was raised, its rickety beams and teetering chimney somehow surviving the storms that blew in off the plains. Wooten and his sisters, Jean and Dolly, were captured on the front porch, so blurred that they might have been anybody's kids. Wooten held a toy rifle his mother had been given by some white woman whose own boy didn't want it anymore. His sisters were dressed in the frilled frocks and bonnets that his mother always managed to keep clean. After that was the portrait of his father's folks, Daniel and Jessie, also on their wedding day, looking eerily similar to their son and daughter-in-law. And then came a half dozen more photos with less immediate connection to Wooten – a great-aunt posing in some St Louis studio, a parasol held jauntily above her head; a distant cousin in the stiff collar and leggings of the Expeditionary Force; a Mississippi work crew, most of them called Wooten, standing by some recently cut spillway.

Finally, just before the first baluster, was the photo that had sent a chill down his spine when he first saw it. Nobody had known it existed until Ardelia hunted it down in some archive of the Pulaski County library. Wooten remembered the look they'd exchanged when he opened it, the pride and the shame. The knowledge. It was the very first Earl Wooten. Big House himself. His great-great-great-grandfather. Taken in 1873, according to the scripted legend at the bottom. Ten years after the man had walked up to Illinois from Kimberly, Alabama, where he'd spent the previous fifty-odd years as another man's property.

Wooten paused in front of the photo for a moment, looking into those tractless eyes. The gaunt, opaque flesh of his sallow cheeks, the cordlike veins bulging from his scrawny neck. Those lips, cracked and dry. Hair as white as sugar. A hundred years. Four generations from this broken man to where Wooten now stood. He'd done it. Brought his blood-line from unspeakable indignity to the very brink of the inner circle. The place where there were no bossmen and no raging rivers to cross. Just a percentage that kept ticking, even if you paused to take yourself a breather. An image from Savage's sketches flashed through his mind. That shadowy figure by the fake kudzu, hoe held high. Wooten realized that he'd been wrong to criticize. With him building it, AmericaWorks would be a tribute to men like that.

He started the long climb up to his room, wishing Ardelia would hurry up and get back. There hadn't been time to call before he left Chicago – he'd had to rush down from Seven Oaks to catch his plane. She'd be thrilled, not just for the money and respect, but also because they wouldn't have to move. And the girls, able to tell their friends that their dad was building a place where every child would want to go. Even Joel would be proud. No, he wouldn't show it. Especially not with the past week between them. But Wooten knew that his son would come to see his father's triumph. See it and respect it.

He reached the top of the steps, momentarily surprised to see a light on in Joel's room. There was the faintest echo of music from behind the closed door. He must have decided to stay home. Too old and too cool to be seen with his mom and kid sisters at a restaurant. Wooten understood. He'd been there himself. He'd go see the boy after hanging up his things. Give him that Cubs shirt. Start to bury the hatchet.

He reached into his bedroom and turned on the light. He almost fell over when he saw Ardelia. She was lying perfectly still on top of the covers of their king-sized bed, stretched out like a corpse. Fully dressed. She even wore her shoes. Her eyes were closed but Wooten could tell that she was wide awake. Something in the room's atmosphere made him suspect she had been like this for a long, long time.

'Ardelia?'

Her eyes slowly opened. He could see now that she'd been crying. Her long face was drawn, her eyes puffy and distant. Wires of unruly hair shot out from her head. She held something in her hand. A handkerchief, it looked like.

Somebody's dead, Wooten thought.

'What is it?' he asked from the doorway. 'What's wrong?'

He could see now that it wasn't sorrow filling her green eyes. It was anger, so deep that it nearly drove him back into the hallway. She held up the handkerchief. He stepped forward, thinking she wanted him to help her to her feet. But when he reached for her she pulled back violently and shook the handkerchief at him. Only it wasn't a handkerchief. It was a piece of paper, moist and crumpled. She was telling him to read it. He took it from her and stretched it open. It was covered with crude and scratchy writing.

Mrs Earl Wooten,

You should know that your man has been stepping out with Alice Ivy down at apartment 27 of Renessence Hights. I know this because I am her friend unlike others. If you don't believe me then why does he drive a Ford Ranchero that he parks on the pike? I no you don't want to no about this but gwan over there and see if she isn't. I say this because I'm her friend and these mack daddy's have made her life HELL. Don't ask your lyin man just go see for yourself.

'A concerned citisen'

301

His heart was pounding. It was hard to get air into his lungs. Sweat erupted down the ridge of his spine. He continued to stare at the page. The words began to bleed into one another, as if the paper had been dipped in corrosive liquid.

'Lie now and we will never speak again,' his wife said in a voice as hushed as death.

Wooten looked up hopelessly.

'I went over there,' Ardelia said. 'She answered the door. We didn't have to say a word. She *recognized* me. And then she said that she was sorry. That she was *sorry*. That . . . child making noise behind her.'

She sat up so quickly that it seemed to be some sort of trick.

'Why is that, Earl? How come she recognized me so fast? Did you describe me to her? Or maybe you pointed me out? Where was it Earl? At the A & P?'

He'd never heard her shout before. It sounded like the words were ripping chunks out of her throat.

'Ardelia . . .'

'Get out of my house!'

'Wait. Let me . . .'

She was on her feet. She faced him, her chest heaving. A choking noise emerged from her mouth. For the first time in the twenty years they'd been together, words failed her. And then his ear was ringing and a constellation of pulsing stars filled his left eye. She'd hit him. Hard. And she looked like she was going to do it again. He fanned his hands out protectively, absorbing the twin blows she threw at his head. The suit bag swung around him like a third person in the room, banging into his wife's side, causing her to sit back down on the bed.

'Mom?'

Wooten turned. Joel stood in the doorway, his eyes fixed firmly on his mother. Who had just been knocked over. By his father.

'What's going on? Are you all right?'

'Joel . . .' Wooten's voice sounded like a stranger's.

His son looked at him. For that moment, Wooten was no longer his father. He was simply the man hurting his mother.

302

'What have you done?' he asked.

Wooten stared dumbly at his son. Nobody moved for a long time. It was Ardelia who finally broke the silence.

'Just get out,' she said quietly from the bed.

And that's exactly what Wooten did. Without another word or even so much as a glance at his wife, he walked out of the room and bolted down the stairs, his big body picking up momentum with every stride. It wasn't until he was out the front door and passing the hissing gaslight that he realized his suit bag was still on his shoulder, its bottom heavy with the gifts he'd brought his family.

23

Swope usually waited until morning to empty the traps, harvesting the night's slaughter by the light of a just-risen sun. There was something bracing about the routine, a sense that he had safeguarded his home before his first cup of coffee. But tonight he decided to make the collection by moonlight. There was no way he was going to be able to wait in his study – he simply had too much nervous energy. He was out of his chair every five seconds, wandering to the window, looking for Truax. Besides, if he had to watch the orbs of that Newton's cradle swing one more time, he was sure he'd enter a deep hypnagogic trance from which he'd never recover.

So he decided to burn some bugs. That would keep him busy. He went to tell Sally, finding her watching a sitcom in the den. He could tell by the way she looked up at him that she suspected nothing. She was very beautiful in the television light, her legs drawn up under her like a kid. The sight took him back to the first time he'd seen her back in Ann Arbor, sitting just like this on a lounge sofa in the library, where he stacked books, one of the countless jobs he'd taken to pay his way through law school. It took six months after that for him to break through the protective rings of sorority sisters and suitors and family to show her that he was the one. For a moment, he wanted nothing more than to spend the rest of the evening beside her. Watch nonsense on the television. Let her run her fingers through his hair. But it was too soon for that. Carefree nights would have to wait until he'd sorted out the mess Wooten had created.

'Want some ice cream?' she asked. 'I got mint chocolate chip.'

'In a while. I think I'm going to do some yard stuff. Could you give me a shout if the phone rings?'

She nodded.

'Did you ever get hold of Gus last night?' she asked before he could turn away.

'Yes,' he said after a moment.

'And?'

'You were right. I was just imagining things.'

She turned back to the TV.

'Of course you were.'

He went out to the garage, loading a big flashlight, some butane and a hand-sized spade into the wheelbarrow. He bumped it through the side door into the yard. It was a nice night, cool and slightly overcast. The real heat was still a few weeks away. He lit a Tiparillo, then pushed the barrow over to the closest of the traps. There were over two dozen of the contraptions spread throughout his property. Most dangled from the lower branches of the cherry trees he'd planted, though he'd recently hung a few from the poplars and beeches bordering the yard, even draping one from the gazebo's vine-covered trellises. Sometimes he thought they did no good – 10 percent of the yard's leaves had already been consumed. But he knew that was looking at things the wrong way. All he had to do was imagine how bad it would be if he hadn't put them up at all.

The first trap was nearly half full with lucent brown shells. Stray antennae poked through the cylinder's mesh casing. For some reason the Japanese beetles avoided the bug zapper that hummed and crackled out by the gazebo, preferring the toxic entrapment of the cages. He removed the trap and shook out the dead, using the spade to scrape the most tenacious from the wire. They made a hollow sound when they struck the barrow's aluminum bed. Some were still alive but too stuporous to move. Not that it mattered. The flames would take care of them.

Swope moved to the second trap, finding that it too was choked with dead and dying beetles. He started to wonder if a

305

city ordinance would be needed to deal with the problem, requiring all NHA members to maintain a certain number of traps per acre of property. Six seemed a judicious sum. Although the people of Mystic Hills were going after the pests aggressively, there had been reports of a slacking of vigilance in Fogwood and Juniper Bend. The situation was clearly worsening. The report Organic Services had issued looked ominous. The infestation was turning out to be far worse than anyone imagined. Entire trees were being denuded in a matter of days. The saplings EarthWorks planted gratis in every yard proved prime feeding ground. Maybe the company should provide traps. After all, it would be cheaper than the nursery restock bills they were incurring.

The wheelbarrow bumped benignly over the moist sod as Swope directed it toward the cherry tree just beyond the deck. Beetles notwithstanding, it had been a good spring for his trees, their ringed, reddish branches growing thicker than his fingers. Some had even flowered this year, though they had yet to bear any fruit. Swope felt his annoyance give way to anger as he marked the damage on this tree's brittle leaves, their edges serrated, as if someone had been at them with a hole punch. After emptying the trap he began to inspect the leaves more closely, finding a half dozen more bugs hidden on their moist underbellies. They barely reacted as Swope plucked them free and flicked them into the pile.

He wondered what was going on over at the Wootens. Ardelia must have seen the letter by now – it had been over twelve hours since it was delivered. The only question was if her husband was back yet to face the music. An unexpected wave of dread suddenly washed through Swope, carrying with it fleeting images of Truax being spotted by a restless Ardelia as he planted the letter. Or maybe the Wootens had recognized its author straight away and were even now laughing at this crude, desperate attempt to forestall the inevitable. But none of that would hapen. Truax would not be spotted. And the letter was too artfully done to be seen as a forgery. Once Ardelia went to unit 27 – as Swope knew she would – then nobody would be putting too much thought into who'd authored what.

He'd written it late Thursday, after his visit to Renaissance Heights, where it had taken all of two minutes to get the woman to admit what was up. His initial thought had been simply to offer Wooten a straight-up deal – silence in exchange for dropping his candidacy for the job. But he'd quickly abandoned the idea. It was too crude and obvious. Wooten could call his bluff in any number of ways, the most catastrophic of which would be to run to Savage. Swope knew that blackmailers often became even more compromised by a crime than its victims. Worst of all, it would mean he would have to look Wooten in the eye and admit the job was rightfully his. And that was wrong. It was Swope's.

That's when the idea of the letter came to him. Although Swope knew it was a merciless move to make, he realized that he had no choice. Wooten was in Chicago. The deal was about to be done. The woman was the only tool he had to slow this thing down. And the letter was bound to be a hundred times more effective than anything else he could dream up. Ardelia was a proud woman who would not suffer humiliation lightly. Word was certain to get out. Savage would be less than pleased to hear that his proposed manager had some ex-junkie lover down at the HUD projects. Those trial balloons they'd been floating in the press would come crashing to earth faster than the *Hindenburg*.

Composing the letter wasn't hard. He simply used his left hand, the natural hand that his parents had forced him to abandon as a child, their superstitious minds believing that southpaws were inferior creatures. As he worked Swope tried to keep at bay those unhappy memories of long Saturday mornings spent on a hard kitchen chair in the wet pajamas his mother refused to let him change, forming vowels and consonants with his clumsy right hand as his left gripped the table's cold iron leg. If he pulled it free she'd smack his palm with the spatula she was using for her weekly baking, leaving red welts that were dusted with bright white powder. It had taken him nearly a year to learn. Though he hadn't tried to write lefty since, the letters came with surprising ease, forming a plausible benefit-check scrawl. He had several dry runs before coming up with a paragraph that would include

307

enough detail to force Ardelia to pay that apartment a visit. After that things would start to happen fast and furious. He'd known the couple for five years now. Though Wooten might be able to deceive Swope, he'd never get away with lying to his wife. Not to her face.

But even as he consigned the block letters to the page, Swope began to worry that this might not be enough. Word might not get back to Savage quickly enough. As disagreeable as the thought might be, he would probably have to follow the letter up with some supplementary action, a series of small stunts that would make Wooten unacceptable as city manager. At least with Truax he'd have just the man to carry out such a campaign. Animated by hatred for Joel and possessing skills taught him at the taxpayers' expense, he would willingly go along. There was no shortage of things that could be done. Bills run up on company accounts. Meetings postponed. Graffiti daubed on walls smearing his name. A letter written to the *Baltimore Sun* signed by Wooten criticizing the Cannon County police for their heavy-handed actions at the teen center. All of it designed to create an ever-thickening cloud over the man. Casting doubts, raising suspicions. Nothing terminal. Just enough to finish him as a potential city manager.

And if this didn't work, Swope knew he would have to open up a second, more radical front. There was only one thing that was sure to be effective – the creation of a body of evidence suggesting that Earl Wooten had been secretly enriching himself by the systematic theft of EarthWorks property. It would be tricky. None of the accusations could be seen to come from Swope himself. In fact, he would have to maintain his position as confidant to the beleaguered builder right up to the end. Meanwhile, he could slowly leak the information to Chones and the county attorney's office, who would commence their own inquiry. A conviction wasn't necessary. Not even an indictment. After all, Swope didn't want to harm the man. Just stop him. Given Savage's hysterical fear of bad press, mere news that Wooten was under official investigation would be enough. The pall of suspicion would scotch his ascension.

As he worked Swope refused to indulge the occasional mutinous feelings of regret that drifted into his mind. There was no reason to feel guilty about any of this. It was Wooten who had betrayed their partnership. Sure, Swope's actions would cause him a few bad months. But Wooten could always go back to being a builder once the storm cleared. In fact, Swope would make sure that potential employers knew he'd been fully absolved. As for Ardelia, well, he'd seen marriages weather far worse. Swope would have actually done them a favor, nipping this insane adultery business in the bud before it grew into something unstoppable. The plain fact was that he was still willing to call this whole thing off at a moment's notice. All Wooten had to do was explain that he'd made a mistake. Understandable pride had gripped him. Swope was not vindictive. Even now, it wasn't too late. All Wooten had to do was make it right. A simple call. An apology. It could be over in five minutes.

Otherwise, he was going to have to be stopped.

Swope finished unloading the last beetle trap. As he pushed the wheelbarrow toward the back of the yard a light came on in the house, sending an amber wedge across the smooth sod. Teddy, arriving in his room. There weren't so many late nights for the kid now that the teen center was closed. And there seemed to be some sort of cooling of his friendship with Joel. That was good – the less time Teddy spent around the Wooten house the better. There would be fewer opportunities for breaches of security. Swope wondered if he'd visited Susan Truax tonight. According to Sally, he'd been spending every possible moment with her. It was good to see his hormones finally kicking in. And Swope had to hand it to the kid for his choice. The girl was gorgeous. A little raw, though he could make refinements in his taste up at Harvard. For now, she'd do. Though a late starter, he'd proven himself to be a Swope by jumping in right at the top.

He arrived at the rusty old bubble-top barbecue he used to immolate the bugs. Using the spade, he scooped them into the mound of charred husk and gray ash already filling the bottom of the hollow bowl, then soaked the beetles with lighter fluid. Those still alive writhed with renewed vigor. Swope took one last drag on his dwindling Tiparillo and tossed it into the pyre. There was a *woosh* and then the bugs were fully aflame. They crackled like kindling. After just a few seconds it was impossible to tell the living from the dead. Stray smoldering bits of them – legs and antennae – were vented upward by the gathering heat.

There was some movement in the corner of his eye. He turned to see John Truax standing a few feet away. He'd appeared so soundlessly that Swope didn't even have time to be startled. His square glasses reflected the flames. His bandaged hand glowed.

'He left home alone about an hour ago and checked into a motel down in Cannon City.'

'Hold on – she threw him *out*?'

'I saw them shouting. Then she hit him.'

'Hit him? My God.'

'He fled after Joel showed up in the room. He's checked into the Motel 6 in Cannon City. Room 112.'

'Do you need money for a room?'

'No. I'll use my car.'

'Good work, John.'

It was impossible to see Truax's eyes, hidden by the reflected flame. Swope turned back to the fire. The bugs were all dead now. The fire was beginning to settle.

'Call me here tomorrow evening,' he said. 'I should have the next step ready for you by then.'

Swope waited for an answer. When none came he looked up from the fire. Truax was gone.

Part Six

24

He picked Susan up at exactly eight. Which meant they had ninety long minutes to kill before meeting Joel. A lot of time, but Teddy figured they might need it, just in case Irma started running her mouth. He didn't want to seem to be in too much of a hurry. Not tonight, when all his work was finally coming to fruition. For the past week he'd played the woman like a grand piano. There was no reason to spoil the crescendo by being needlessly hasty. Besides, the idea of making Susan sweat a bit was definitely appealing. She'd been a real little bitch over the weekend, criticizing and sulking, forgetting just who was running things. Last night she'd said a few things that almost made Teddy call the whole thing off. The usual crap. Teasing him about his chest. Remarks about him not having a girl of his own. Snide offers to fix him up with one of her airhead friends. Teddy smiled along at first – he wasn't above a little teasing – but eventually told her to can it. Dumb as she was, Susan understood that she was pushing the envelope. She became all apologetic and submissive in that phony, slightly mocking way she had. Teddy decided to let it ride. Because that's the kind of guy he was. He just wished that she'd make an effort to appreciate the situation, to understand that the idea of Teddy running around with some cheerleader just so he could get his rocks off was too absurd even to contemplate. Joel might want that. It was cool. He could see the attraction. Just don't ask him to be the same way. He'd find his Yoko some day and when he did, it would be like nothing Susan or any of them could imagine.

At least Joel understood. He understood everything. After a bad week their friendship was back on track. Teddy had gone to see him Sunday afternoon, as soon as he was certain he'd be able to get Susan out of the house. He felt nervous as he approached the Wootens' big front door. If Joel rejected him now he didn't know what he was going to do. And the initial omens weren't good. Something bad had visited the Wooten household in his absence. Ardelia answered the door, looking like death warmed over. Usually totally composed, she now looked like she'd been up for weeks. She was still in her bathrobe, even though it was three in the afternoon. Her watery eyes didn't seem to recognize Teddy at first.

'Hey, Mrs Wooten – long time no see,' he tried.

She simply stared at him.

'I was wondering, is Joel around? There's a couple things I wanted to square with him.'

'Yes. Of course.' Her voice was distant. 'Come on in, Teddy.'

He stepped into the big front hall, with its wide staircase and marble floors. His eyes washed over the portraits of all those vanished Negroes, including Joel's something-or-other grandfather, who'd been an honest-to-God slave. Fairly fucking intense. The twins emerged from the den, staring at him in a way that made it clear they expected someone else. He gave them a jaunty little wave. They disappeared.

Ardelia had moved to the bottom of the steps.

'Joel?' she called out in a voice that wouldn't make it past the fourth baluster. 'Hon?'

'Mrs Wooten?'

She turned.

'Why don't I just go up?'

'Oh. Yes. I suppose that would be best.'

He could hear music as he reached the top of the steps. He took a deep breath, running over what he was going to say before heading down the carpeted hall, past neatly framed Jacob Lawrence prints. Joel's door was off the latch. Teddy knocked. He could hear the bed creak. A few seconds later the door came open. Joel's face creased in surprise, then took

314

on that same stony expression he'd had a week ago, when he'd stared down at Teddy from his window.

'How'd you get in?' he asked.

Not the greatest of openings. But.

'Explosives to break the perimeter fence. Then drugs to bribe the guards.'

Joel failed to see the humor.

'Come on, man. Your mom. What do you think?'

They stood there for a moment. Music seeped past Joel. The Stylistics. Just a few days away from Teddy's stern tutelage and the guy's tastes had already gone AM.

'Look, man, it's not going to work out,' Joel said finally.

'What?'

'You and me. When we were kids, it was cool. But now, I don't know. There's just too much bad shit out there for us to make it. Maybe we should just, you know, shake hands and call it a day. Go our separate ways. Or whatever.'

Teddy felt a brief moment of panic that he quickly reasoned away. This was just Joel's anger talking. An anger he was about to transmogrify.

'I just saw Susan.'

Joel stared at him for a moment. Curious now.

'Say?'

'In fact, I've seen her every day for the past week.'

'Bullshit,' Joel said. 'Where?'

'Her house.'

'Really?'

'You gonna ask me in or am I gonna have to stand out here like some sort of fucking doofus as I explain to you how I've saved your heinie? Just a question.'

Joel let him in. Teddy collapsed in the chair by the window. He paused for a dramatic moment, then let him have it. The whole shooting match. As he spoke he could see the hostility vanish from Joel's face. The old emotions returned. Respect. Admiration. Awe.

Friendship.

'What about the sarge? He must have something to say about all this.'

'He's got this new job. He's totally out of the picture.'

'Doing what?'

'Shoveling shit in Louisiana. Who cares?'

'So what's the plan?' Joel asked after a moment.

This is more like it, Teddy thought.

'Can you get out of the house?'

'Hell, yeah. They never grounded me. Just said I couldn't see Susan.' His voice dropped slightly. 'Besides, my folks had this big fight yesterday. Dad's in deep shit.'

'In that case, my swain, what do you say we gather at the broken pier come Tuesday night, me, you, and the nymph, to continue the summer's festivities?'

Joel's eyes filled with gratitude.

'That would be great, man.'

'Great's my middle name. Meet me at nine-thirty sharp. If I'm not there by, like, ten, there's been some problem getting her past Colonel Klink. Hasten back here and I'll come with alternative arrangements. Contingencies will be hammered out. Whatever you do, despair not. El Ted is in the driver's seat.'

Joel nodded.

'Well, I better go.'

'You want to hang for a while and doobify?' Joel asked.

Teddy was sorely tempted, though he knew that the less he was around Joel, the less anyone would suspect what they were planning.

'It'd be better if we pretended like we were still pissed at each other.'

'Yeah. You're right.'

'Not that we are or anything.'

Joel scowled.

'Hell, no. That was just . . . no, man, we're cool.'

Teddy smiled and rose.

'Tuesday night it is.'

He started to go.

'Teddy, man – thanks.'

'Hey, no sweat. After all, what are friends for?'

After arriving at the Truaxes, Teddy chatted with Irma, waiting for Susan to descend from her bedroom. The sarge was nowhere in sight. As usual. Irma was all dressed up

316

tonight, as if she were the one going on the dream date. Mauve slacks. Cork heels. A flowery satin blouse. Perfume, lipstick. They waited in the living room, talking about the new Bond film Teddy was allegedly taking Susan to see. Irma complained how all the stars these days seemed to be hairy, mumbling Italians. Teddy nodded heartily. Absolutely, he thought. Warner Bros über alles. In the past few days he'd realized that there was nothing this fucking woman would not say after knocking back a couple whisky sours.

Susan finally emerged, meandering down the steps in that slinky style of hers. Venus on the half shell, Teddy thought. She, too, had primped, wearing her best peasant blouse and those hip huggers whose knees were freshly patched with squares of paisley cloth. Silvery bracelets dangled from her wrists. Her blow-dried hair floated vaporously around her head.

Teddy stood upon her entry. Ever the gentleman.

'You look great,' he said.

'So do you,' she answered, the note of sarcasm in her voice detectable only to him.

'This is so nice,' Irma intoned.

She walked them to the door.

'We won't be too late,' Teddy said.

'Don't worry.'

They turned to go.

'Susan?'

She kissed her dutifully. Irma started to fuss with something in her hair, a tangled imperfection visible only to a mother's eye. Susan pulled away with a grimace. Irma clicked her moist tongue and looked at her daughter with frustrated affection. Susan rolled her eyes and turned to Teddy.

'Let's go,' she mouthed.

Teddy nodded good-bye to Irma.

'Have fun, you two,' she said, her words muffled by the closing door.

25

Wooten wondered if he should knock. Part of him knew the idea was absurb. This was his house, after all, built with his own hands. But he also knew that Friday's revelation had changed all of that. It would be a mistake to make too much of the fact that his name was on the deed. He looked around at the night-quiet yard and realized that he'd made himself a stranger here. And strangers knocked. Knocked and waited to see if they would be welcome, or have the door slammed in their face.

He was coming home. Finally. He'd had enough. It was time to set things right with Ardelia. He had to snap the bizarre string of calamity that had entangled him these past few days. Nothing had been right since Friday. Night, day. Work. Sleep. The simplest of conversations. Eating – Christ, he hadn't been able to swallow more than a few bites at a time since the flight back from Chicago. His head ached and his clothes stank and his guts were twisted by a hunger more profound than he'd felt in years.

He couldn't keep on like this. He had to be home.

It had been the worst four days of his adult life. The bad luck seemed to follow him out the door after his bedroom confrontation with Ardelia. Following that first sleepless night on strange sheets he'd emerged from his dank motel room Saturday morning to find a flat tire on his Ranchero. He'd called Ardelia from the piss-stained phone booth of a Phillips 66 after changing it, only to have her hang up on him before he could even tell her where he was staying. He'd spent the afternoon in Newton, going everywhere but home – or unit 27. Several times he thought about simply showing up on Merlin's Way, acting as if she had never thrown him out. But the prospect of enduring another dose of her anger made him keep his distance. So he spent the day visiting sites, pestering his men and lending a hand, before returning to the motel, whose plastic and mold he'd already begun to dread.

That night he went for a solitary dinner at Mary's Bar BQ down in Powdertown. It had been a long time since he'd been to the county's only soul food restaurant – Ardelia hated the place, with its fatty food and raucous atmosphere, its card-playing men and women who pulled up chairs at your table without an invitation. Children running riot. There was no Mary as far as Wooten could tell, just a big-bellied cook named JD Stacey, who wore his blood-splattered apron like a preacher's smock. He could be seen through the serving hatch, talking nonstop to no one in particular as tongues of grease flame licked the smoky air around him.

Wooten figured that if he had to eat alone he should at least eat well. There would be plenty of other ways to punish himself. He chose a corner table and sat facing away from the other diners. He'd brought along the thick binder of preliminary AmericaWorks specs that Savage had given him, though as he flipped numbly through the blueprints and costings and flow charts he found his mind too full of Ardelia's choking voice to concentrate.

'Know what you want?'

The waitress was young. High school. Already starting to go to fat.

'Ribs and tea,' said without consulting the menu.

It took her a long time to get this on her pad.

'You want somethin' else with that?'

'More ribs.'

She shot him a quick look, then lifted the menu from his table, her eyes scanning the wall above.

'Uh huh,' she said listlessly before retreating back toward the hissing grill.

Wooten continued to leaf aimlessly through the specs. But the sight of all that promise only served to sour his mood further. Twenty-four hours since he'd been offered the best

319

job in American construction and his wife still didn't even know about it. Nor would she any time soon, if her attitude this morning was anything to go by. Which meant that there was no way he'd be able to give Savage his answer on Monday morning, as promised. Now that the shock of discovery was wearing off, Wooten was beginning to fear that he'd done some permanent damage to his marriage. On the rare occasions he'd contemplated detection in the past, he'd somehow managed to convince himself that beneath Ardelia's anger would lie a substratum of understanding. She was bound to know how little the whole sordid mess meant to him. She was Ardelia, after all. She understood everything. There was no way she could fail to see this for the nonsense it was. But he now understood that this mythical forgiveness was nowhere in sight. The woman he'd left in the bedroom was hurt and confused and angry. What he'd torn into with his infidelity was the very part of her that was strong and placid. He hadn't counted on her emotions running away with her like this. It scared him.

The food arrived. Two thick racks of pork ribs, a mound of greens, half a corn cob. There was a baked potato, too, a rapidly diminishing ball of chive-studded sour cream sinking into its split opening. The ribs were covered by a sheer membrane of glistening fat. Subterranean crackles sounded from within them. Steam swirled from the vegetables and the sauce in its stainless-steel sidecar. Wooten realized that he was looking at the perfect meal. The sort of thing he'd ask for as a last supper. What he always hoped would be in the fridge instead of the neatly stacked Tupperware and anonymous packets of dimpled aluminum foil.

Problem was, he couldn't eat it. The intricate odor rising from the steaming plate hit him with the stomach-churning force of a ruptured sewer pipe. Suddenly, the food looked withered and putrid. Even the large mug of iced tea seemed stagnant, the wedge of lemon floating on its surface reminding him of Lake Newton's fish. He couldn't eat this. The thought of placing even a morsel of it in his mouth was abhorrent.

He summoned the girl.

'I'll just have the check now.'

Confusion spread across her broad face. She pointed at the food with her gnawed Bic.

'You ain't gonna eat that?'

Wooten slowly shook his head.

'Why, something wrong?'

'Not with the food.'

She waddled off to the kitchen to explain the situation to JD Stacey, who stooped to get a better look at the dissatisfied customer through the revolving metal ticket wheel in his hatch. Not wanting to get into it with the cook, Wooten pointed a dyspeptic finger at his stomach. Stacey rolled the toothpick from one side of his mouth to another, shrugged his commiseration, then returned to his spitting flames. The waitress returned to say Mr Stacey didn't want him to pay. Wooten slipped her a five-dollar tip for her trouble. She grunted and disappeared. He closed the EarthWorks binder and walked quickly toward the exit, careful to avoid eye contact. He'd almost made it when he heard a familiar voice.

'Lookeehere. Earl Wooten.'

It was Raymond McNutt, sitting with his family in the last booth before the door. His wife, Vonda, sat opposite him, her hair twisted into a beehive that made her look like a back-up singer for some long-ago girl group. She flashed Wooten a smile as phoney as a three-dollar bill. McNutt's two sullen teenage sons sat against the window, lost in the crevices of their sundaes.

'What you doin' here, man? I thought you never came down to Powdertown.'

Though McNutt's question came as a jolly shout, there was a barb in it. As the only black lawyer in Cannon City, he'd tried for years to get Wooten to join the various organizations he ran, most notably the venerable Colored Chamber of Commerce. Unspoken in all these invitations was a desire that Wooten become a client, even though he'd explained that he used Austin for all his legal needs. Some time last year the invitations had stopped coming, as they had from all quarters of Powdertown. Wooten knew that after a spell of intense but unrequited goodwill the local blacks now regarded him and Ardelia as being too high and mighty for their churches and clubs. Their resentment was an unfortunate fact of life for the Wootens. After all, they were Newton people. Its location in Cannon County was merely an accident of geography.

'Busy,' Wooten said. 'You know.'

McNutt nodded at him for a moment. He was a short, dapper man given to jaunty hats and the occasional cape. His ironed hair glistened with pomade that had the same insistent sheen as the ribs in front of him. There was a keloid scar on his neck, as big as a silver dollar. Ardelia found him unbearably crass. Wooten had to agree. The man was *loud*. That marcelled hair and the gold incisor and the overpolished Florsheims made him seem a bit too much like a hustler for Wooten's taste.

'Ardelia here?' McNutt asked, looking around.

'No, she's a . . . she's back in St Louis. Family.'

McNutt's gold tooth actually flashed as he shot Wooten a sly, complicit smile.

'While the cat's away, right?'

Wooten smiled tightly in return. The boys were nearing the end of their desserts, long spoons chiming against the bottoms of their fluted glasses.

'In that case you ought to pull up a chair and visit, Earl,' Vonda said. 'Have some coffee with us.'

Wooten flapped the binder in his right hand.

'Better run. Got all this work to catch up on.'

The smile dropped from Vonda's face like an overripe fruit. McNutt's eyes narrowed. The gold tooth was back under wraps.

'Man work as much as you, hard to see how he can ever get behind,' he said, the friendly bluster gone from his voice.

'Well, I'll be seeing you folks around,' Wooten said.

McNutt said nothing, his eyes still locked on Wooten. Vonda had begun to organize the crumbs on the table. The boys continued to peer into their desserts, trying to salvage one last remnant of sweetness.

'All right, then,' Wooten said with false cheer.

He'd almost made it to the door when one of the boys spoke.

'Stay black, bro.'

He turned in time to see McNutt going upside his son's grinning head. But, even from this distance, Wooten could tell that there was more affection than anger in the blow.

Back at the motel he started to call home, but never made it past the fifth digit. Phoning now would needlessly inflame matters. If Ardelia hung up on him in the morning, she was hardly likely to hear him out at night. Better to leave it until a new dawn. He propped himself in bed, chewing ice he'd harvested from the hall machine as he watched the Orioles. Sleep was a long time coming. And then, just as he finally drifted off, some joker pulled the fire alarm. By the time they let everybody back in their rooms it was almost three. Wooten knew there would be no more sleeping that night.

Sunday passed in a sluggish, half-conscious haze. He called home in the late morning. Once again, Ardelia didn't want to have anything to do with him, though this time she gave him a few seconds before consigning him to staticky oblivion. He took the opportunity to weakly threaten to come home anyway. She said that if he did she would call Austin and have him write her up an injunction barring him from the house. Wooten knew she was serious. Ardelia Wilson did not make idle threats.

So he spent another day driving aimlessly around the city. Since it was Sunday there was nothing for him to do. He bought a three-pack of Hanes underpants, a cheap shirt and some stuff for the bathroom. God knew how long it would be until he'd be able to get at his own stuff. At the lake he noticed that the cleanup crew had left yet another flyblown pile of dead fish by the damaged pier. He clocked nearly a hundred miles that day, stopping occasionally for a Coke or a hamburger he could barely swallow. As he drove his anger at himself increased, an inner odometer ticking over mile after mile of stinging guilt and futile contrition. He didn't know which was worse, the sin itself or the pride in believing that forgiveness would follow inevitably upon being caught. Only now did he begin to understand what joyless things his visits to 27 had been. Thinking back, all he could remember was the pungent smell of food, those velveteen sheets and the slack-jawed expression on that child's face.

Of course, Alice had written the note. He'd seen through her futile attempt at subterfuge the moment Ardelia handed it to him. She had no friends, at least none who would go to the trouble of sending a letter. She had panicked when he said that it would have to end. Somewhere in her addled brain she'd thought that precipitating a crisis would drive him to her. Several times during that long Sunday he found himself tempted to swing by and let her know exactly what she'd done to him. The pain she'd caused his family. But he knew he would not go. And it wasn't only because the situation had been caused by his own weakness and arrogance. Beneath that was the truly frightening suspicion that once he crossed her threshold it might not be all that easy to walk back out again.

His bad luck continued Monday morning, when he arrived at Newton Plaza to find his offices flooded. Not just his own personal suite, but the whole fifth floor. Barnaby's supposedly fail-safe sprinkler system had managed to go off sometime in the early morning, leaving the carpets waterlogged and the desks covered with useless wads of blueprint. So the better part of Wooten's day was spent in the maddening pursuit of alternative space for his people and efforts to salvage what he could from the mess. At least now he had an excuse for not calling Savage. What, after all, was he supposed to say to the man? That he had no answer yet because his wife had thrown him out of the house? It was hardly the start to a new job in which the happy Wooten family was supposed to figure prominently.

Austin came down in late morning to survey the damage. Wooten must have been showing the stress because Swope took him aside and asked if he was all right. He was tempted to blurt out the whole sad story of his infidelity right there. But the thought of shaming himself in front of Austin stilled his tongue. Instead, he mumbled something about it having been a long day. He tried to call Ardelia after that, finally

324

getting her in the early evening. Although she once again refused to see him, Wooten thought he could detect a softening in her tone.

Maybe tomorrow, he thought.

He arrived back at Motel 6 dead on his feet, barely having the energy to remove his steel-tipped boots before collapsing onto the sagging mattress. Not even the hunger gnawing at his guts could keep him awake. He felt like he'd been asleep for days when the phone woke him, though a quick glance at his watch told him it had been less than half an hour. He yanked the receiver from its nest, thinking it might be Ardelia. But whoever was on the other end of the line refused to talk, maintaining a stony silence that sounded more profound than a simple prank. For some reason Wooten had the impression the caller was close by. Sleep was hard to achieve after that. He finally drifted off around two. Once again, the phone woke him. The same silent caller. Wooten threw on his clothes and stormed to the front desk. The woman's shrug asked what he expected for $9.99 a night. Wooten told her not to put through any more calls unless the party identified herself as Ardelia Wooten. Back in his room he began to wonder if these events might be something other than bad luck. It was all becoming too much of a coincidence. Maybe it was the work of someone out to get back at him. For a while he tried to compose a list of suspects. Men he'd fired. Vota. Alice herself. But that couldn't be. No one knew he was out here except his wife. And she would never torment him. Not anonymously.

So it was on the back of four nearly sleepless nights that he arrived at his temporary basement office on Tuesday morning to find a stack of urgent messages. Half were from Savage, the rest from Joe Vota. Knowing he still had no answer for the EarthWorks CEO, Wooten concentrated on the site foreman. By the look of it, there was something seriously wrong at the Underhill HUD. He drove up there straight away, wondering why the hell Vota was still on the job. Swope was supposed to have fired him ten days ago. He arrived to find the entire crew gathered around the just-poured basketball court. The workers watched him approach with the bland, assessing eyes of union men. A few whispered among themselves. Vota stepped forward, his face creased with false concern. He spread his hands and gestured with his gristled chin toward the cement before Wooten could ask what was going on.

Two words had been written in the dried blond stone. The width and texture of the lines suggested they had been made with the bit of cracked cinder-block sticking up from the far edge of the court like a shark's fin. There were no footprints around – whoever had written this had been careful to obliterate them. The letters were neat and perfectly squared. Four feet tall. Visible from a good distance.

WOOTEN NIGGER

The faces of the men were stonily unreadable. Wooten looked back at Vota, who watched him with a guarded expression. Maybe it *was* him who'd been dogging Wooten these past few days.

'Who did this?' Wooten asked.

He immediately regretted the question, knowing it gave Vota the upper hand.

'Jeez, Earl, I don't know. We just showed up and here it was.'

'Just like that, huh?'

'You think *we* did it?' Vota asked, a trace of outrage now in his voice.

'Did you?'

Something changed in Vota's expression. That pretense of friendliness vanished.

'What, you think I'd pull a stunt like this?'

'Sounds about your speed, Joe. Yeah.'

Vota snorted.

'Come on, Earl. I wouldn't call anyone a nigger.'

The way he said the word was what did it. Speaking it while pretending not to. Wooten lost it. After four sleepless nights and four long days carrying around his guilt and shame like a bad fever, he snapped. Before he understood what was happening his hands were on Vota's weathered denim lapels. The wattled fat of the man's throat brushed against his knuckles.

'Who you calling nigger?' Wooten asked, his voice quietly furious.

When Vota didn't answer he jerked up on those collars, lifting the man right off the ground. The workers moved in and pulled at Wooten's arms and shoulders. Vota's eyes had begun to bulge. Sputtering noises rattled at the bottom of his throat. The men began pulling harder.

Suddenly, as thoughtlessly as he'd grabbed him, Wooten let the man go. The anger had passed. Vota's feet dropped to the ground. He staggered backward a few steps. There was a shift in his expression. Contempt replaced the fear.

The men released Wooten. Everybody waited.

'You saw that,' Vota said, his eyes firmly fixed on Wooten. 'Man put his hands on me. I didn't call him shit. You guys are my witnesses. All of you.'

'Look, Joe,' Wooten said.

Everyone waited out the ten long seconds it took Wooten to realize there was nothing to say. After one last look at the graffiti, he turned and strode back to his Ranchero.

'People gonna hear about this,' Vota called after him. 'Don't think they won't.'

After that, Wooten knew he had to go home. One more night away from home and he'd be lost. He delayed his return as long as he could, finding work to do until nearly dusk. There was plenty. Another gaslight had exploded, this one way out in Thunder Hill, in a yet-to-be-occupied Gettysburg. The electrician who discovered it knew the drill – no authorities had been called. Wooten got there in fifteen minutes. As he worked the stopcock he knew there was nothing left to do but drive up to Mystic Hills. He didn't call – that would only give Ardelia the chance to say no. If she wanted to summon the sheriff when he got there, fine. If he kept on going like this he'd probably end up in their hands anyway. He had to act to stop this free fall. The things happening to him were more than luck or coincidence. He'd brought this down on himself. Although not normally a superstitious man, Wooten knew there was a point beyond which you transgressed only at your own peril. And he'd crossed that line. He had to get back over on the right side of it before something seriously bad happened.

He decided to walk in without knocking. Enough was enough. He turned the knob and stepped into the front hall, avoiding Big House's permanent, searching stare.

'Hello?' he called out, his usually percussive voice sounding small and timid.

He waited for the twins to come charging out of the den or Joel to slouch down the steps. But there was only silence. She's left you, he thought. Packed up the kids and gone back to St Louis. He walked toward the lit kitchen, stopping dead in his tracks when he saw Ardelia seated at the head of the big table. She stared evenly at him. He'd worried she might be as much of a wreck as him, but here she was dressed up in her vice principal's finest, a tan pants suit with the Liberty scarf her brother had brought back from London. She wore makeup and her hair was perfect. A cup of herbal tea rested on the table, wisps of steam curving through the air in front of her. He could see the coldness in her eyes.

'Where is everybody?' he asked, his voice sounding bereft as it echoed through the copper pots and exhaust hoods.

'I just put the twins to bed. Joel is in his room cutting a tragic figure. Lucky me – I get Hamlet and Lothario under one roof. Maybe I should go back to teaching English.'

The remark stung all the deeper because he knew it would be the first of many. He took a deep breath and perched on a stool at the island, leaving a good ten feet of tile between them.

'Ardelia . . .'

'Have you seen her?'

'No,' he said. 'I swear to you.'

She knew he was telling the truth. Just as she would have known on Friday if he'd tried to lie. She waited. He realized he didn't know what he wanted to say. Four days on his own and he'd come up with precisely nothing.

'It's been a bad few days,' he said.

There was no forgiveness in her eyes, no effort to understand. He'd betrayed her. She didn't want to hear about the quality of his days.

'I'm sorry, Ardelia,' he continued.

She nodded once. Accepting the statement as fact and nothing more.

'So what do you want to do?' she asked.

'I think I should move back in here.'

'Why?'

'I don't think it's good, my being away. For Joel and the girls.'

She looked down at the steaming cup, considering this.

'If that's your reason, then yes, you may move back in.'

'I don't know what else to say,' he said after a long moment.

'Well, I suggest you think of something, Earl. Because until you do, this is going to be between us.'

He looked helplessly around the kitchen.

'I just . . . when I was there it was like I forgot who I was.'

'Who you were,' she echoed.

'Who I'd made myself into. It's hard to . . . I just needed a place where there wasn't all this pressure.'

She took in their house, their entire life, with a taut gesture of her left hand.

'Is that what this is for you? Pressure? Is that what *I* am?'

'Yes,' he said after a while. 'Not only, but yes.'

He thought his answer might send her into further fury. But it seemed to have the opposite effect, calming the growing storm that threatened to drive him back to that wretched motel.

'We all put pressure on each other,' she said. 'That's the only way we can make it in this world.'

'I know,' he said.

'It would be the easiest thing in the world for us not to put pressure on each other. To stay back in St Louis or move down to Powdertown. We could live that life in our sleep, Earl. But that wasn't the path we chose. We decided to do *this*.'

'I know.'

'Don't sell yourself short. Don't you dare. Because when you sell yourself short you sell me short as well. All of us. I don't know what you got up to down there and I don't want to know. That woman . . .'

She took a deep, controlling breath.

'I'm sure she has a story and I suppose in different circumstances my heart might even bleed a bit if I heard it. But when I looked into her eyes I could only see one thing. You, selling yourself short. And taking us down with you.'

She stood. She looked very beautiful to him now. He wanted to hold her, and by holding her to put all this far away from them. But he knew that it was too early for that. Way too early.

'You are welcome to stay in the guest room for the time being. If you feel you have to explain this to the children, you can tell them you have an *infection* you don't want me to catch.'

Wooten winced at her words. Any sense that this situation might be reaching a rapid conclusion vanished.

'I don't know where we're going to end up with this, Earl. I really don't. I'll keep up appearances for the children's sake but I refuse to deny my feelings.'

'No one's asking you to do that.'

She stared at him for a moment.

'Are you hungry?' she asked.

'Well, yes,' he said.

'Good.'

She left the kitchen without another word.

He sat on the stool for a while, feeling a sudden release of deep relief. The worst of it was over. Yes, there would be hard times ahead. Ardelia was a proud woman. There would be no rush to forgiveness on her part. That infection remark proved that. But still, he was back in the house. That was the main thing.

After a few minutes he followed her upstairs. The door to his room was shut. He knew better than to try to open it. Instead, he went down to see the whispering twins, whose joy at the sight of him proved a tonic for everything bad that had happened since Friday night. He read them six Dr Seuss books to make up for the nights he'd missed. After they finally nodded off he came back into the hall, pausing at Joel's door. A bass line thudded too loud within. Normally, Wooten would have told him to turn it down, but tonight he let the music play. He didn't want to have to face Joel tonight. At the end of the hall his pajamas and toothbrush rested in a neat pile outside his bedroom door. Wooten picked them up, then checked his watch. Eight-thirty. Fair's fair, he thought. He called good night through the door. There was no answer.

Downstairs, he made himself two ham sandwiches, eating them at the sink so he wouldn't have to clean up. At least his appetite was returning. After he was done he locked up the house, starting in the dining room, then moving through to the sunken den and the study, finally checking on the French doors in the living room and the kitchen's sliding-glass door. He wound up in the guest room, his quarters for the foreseeable future if Ardelia's attitude was anything to go by. It was at the back of the house, between the kitchen and the laundry room. Wooten had jokingly located it here so Ardelia's relatives would be as far away as possible while staying under the same roof. He slipped into his pajamas and switched on the old black-and-white they kept down here, then established himself on the unstatisfactory mattress of the hideaway bed to watch a movie about white boys who were drafted to go to Vietnam. It was set in boot camp, where they had all sorts of trouble with their drill sergeants. The movie made him think about John Truax. Whatever anger he still held toward the man from last Sunday's confrontation vanished altogether with the thought about him fighting in that ridiculous war. It was a shame, Austin firing him like that. Especially since he seemed to have given Vota a second chance. Maybe once things settled down he'd have a word with his friend. See if they might not be able to extend the poor guy a helping hand.

During a commercial break, Wooten thought he heard a noise near the front of the house. A footfall, a softly closed door. But when he went to check there was nothing. He crept to the top of the steps. Light seeped from beneath Joel's door. He was tempted to go see his son and try to explain to him what was going on. But memories of their last disastrous conversation dissuaded him. First things first. Make it up with Ardelia, then start working on Joel. He headed back downstairs, once again avoiding Big House's gaze as he passed his portrait.

The news was on when he got back to the guest room. Senator Sam banging his gavel, his eyebrows wriggling like angry caterpillars stapled to his forehead. The weatherman announced that tomorrow would be another fine day. The Orioles won again, Cuellar this time. Commercials came on. Wooten knew he should go to sleep now but was too keyed up to close his eyes. Besides, Richard Pryor was guesting on *Carson*. He decided to take advantage of this opportunity – Ardelia couldn't stand the man. One last guilty pleasure. As he waited for the show to begin he thought about the family sleeping soundly above him. It was going to be all right now. Everything would sort itself out. Ardelia and Joel, they'd come around. It was just a question of time. Tomorrow he'd tell his wife about the job. She might give him some grief, though in the end she'd see it was the right thing to do. And then he could finally make that long-delayed call to Savage. But that was for tomorrow. For now, the main thing was that he was home.

26

The room where Wooten lay was bathed in drab television light. The only movement for the last hour had been the occasional shift of his big feet beneath the blanket. There was no longer any doubting it. After four nights away, he was back home. An hour earlier, when Truax had watched the Wootens arguing in the kitchen, he'd thought that Ardelia was once again giving the man his marching orders. This time, maybe, for good. Truax prepared himself for another night in his car, parked in the darkness beyond the motel's Dumpsters. But Wooten had stayed put. Ardelia must have forgiven him. Swope would be disappointed, Truax's nightly reports of a worsening situation had clearly thrilled the lawyer, bolstering his decisions to turn up the heat on Wooten. Truax wondered what this homecoming might mean to the operation. Further escalation, he hoped. He was beginning to get the hang of this job.

This morning's writing in the cement had been their most audacious move yet. It had taken Truax nearly twenty minutes to scrawl the letters, working by the light of a waning moon. He'd had to bear down hard – the concrete was almost dry by the time he got going. He worked slowly, wanting to get the letters just right. He wasn't worried about getting caught. The odds of being nailed by some half-assed Earth-Works security guard were slim to none. Truax knew how to listen for the approach of hostile feet. And even if the impossible did happen, Swope would take care of things. After all, he was the one who'd chosen the location for this particular mission, claiming that there had been some sort of trouble between Wooten and the site foreman. Once Wooten saw the words, anything could happen.

But as Truax worked something strange happened – he experienced an unexpected hesitation, his first since Swope had hired him seven days earlier. He'd always hated the word *nigger*. He'd seen firsthand in the army how much damage it could do, the hurt and violence its mere utterance caused. And he could tell that Swope had felt uneasy using it as well. They'd kicked around some alternatives for a while, but in the end they knew there was only one word that was sure to provoke a showdown between Wooten and the foreman. Harsh as it was, they had a job to do. They had to push Wooten to the edge.

As usual, Swope was proven right. Wooten had exploded when he saw the message, putting actual hands on an employee in full view of two dozen witnesses. After a quick call to Swope he stuck with his man for the remainder of the day, until Wooten finally returned to Mystic Hills and reestablished himself back in his household. Once he'd settled into the room beyond the kitchen Truax knew he had to call Swope again, no matter how much he hated the idea of reporting this. It seemed like a reversal of the last four days' hard work. But he had his job to do. Keeping Swope apprised of all developments was essential. So, once he was convinced that the Wooten house was bedded down, Truax abandoned his post to make the call.

It took him less than half an hour. He called Swope's home from one of the space-age phone booths they'd planted around the city, Plexiglas bubbles that could not be broken or marred by graffiti. As expected, Swope seemed deeply upset by the news that Wooten was back in his house, lapsing into a minute-long brooding silence. But he overcame his disappointment, ordering Truax back to his post while he figured out a new strategy for putting pressure on the builder. They'd speak again first thing in the morning. By then Swope promised to have come up with a new plan.

Truax grabbed a large coffee from the Fogwood 7-Eleven on his way back – for some reason he was finding sleeplessness harder to deal with than he'd anticipated. Getting old, he thought. Or maybe just out of practice. He drove quickly back to Rhiannon's Rest, parking in his usual spot and moving soundlessly through the woods to the treehouse. Wooten remained in the guest room, the twin mounds of his feet still lifting the covers. There were lights on upstairs as well, in Joel's room. Truax took comfort in that last bit of illumination. Although he doubted the boy would make any attempt to get near Susan, he was particularly glad to know his whereabouts tonight, the first time his daughter had been out of the house since last Saturday. Until yesterday, Truax had no intention of letting her go anywhere until the fall. But Irma had cornered him when he came home after putting Wooten to bed at the motel. As he wolfed down a plate of bratwurst, sauerkraut and onion rings, she explained how Teddy had politely asked if he could take Susan to see *Live and Let Die*. Evidently he was still being quite the gentleman – he'd even offered to take Darryl along, unaware that she didn't see films unless they had a Christian theme. Irma was clearly beside herself with joy at the prospect of her daughter dating Austin Swope's son just days after her husband began working for the man. For the first time in ages, Truax could see that she was starting to believe she'd finally arrived in the United States of America. He hesitated for a moment, but it was just for form's sake. After all, they were only talking about a movie.

'I don't have a problem with that,' he said. 'As long as she comes straight home afterwards.'

And so Susan was out with Teddy. A week earlier Truax would have been suspicious of the boy's motives, though he'd seen no sign of Teddy and Joel being together since the night he'd rescued them from that beating down at Newton Plaza. According to his wife, the two had subsequently fallen out over something. Maybe it was the fight itself. Whatever the cause, their friendship seemed a thing of the past. And even if it weren't, there was nothing to worry about. Joel was up in his room.

It was still strange to think that Susan and Teddy really were becoming involved. Although Truax could not bring himself to actually *like* the boy, the fact that Irma did was enough for him. Besides, it didn't matter what Truax thought. Any fool could have seen that Teddy was as good as you could expect. Smart and polite. A future crammed with promise. And from the best family in the whole city. He'd grow out of the other things. The years would fill in his frame and his personality. And then he'd become a man like his father. Which should be enough for anyone.

A pulse of pain rang through Truax's hand. He removed his glove and then turned on his flashlight to have a look. Fluid had begun to leak through the bandage that he'd changed just a few hours earlier. There was no doubting it. The infection was getting worse. All that sleeplessness and hard work. He knew that he should make an appointment at Fort Meade to have it looked at. The last time he'd let it go the bacteria had entered his bloodstream, sending him into a three-day spiral of fever and delirium. But there was no way he could take that sort of time off now, especially with the operation having suffered its first setback. Once Wooten was in the bag – that was when Truax would go to the doctor. Until then there was nothing to do but carry the wound. He put the glove back on and returned his attention to the house. Wooten was out of bed. The bathroom door was closed, framed by a line of white light. Upstairs, Joel was still awake. Wooten came out of the toilet, hitching up his pajama bottoms. He stared at the TV for a moment, then switched it off, casting the room into darkness.

Truax decided to head home and change his bandage. Grab dinner from the hot plate Irma would leave him. Maybe he could even afford himself the luxury of a shower. It had been three days since he'd had one and he could tell by the looks people shot him at the 7-Eleven that it was starting to become an issue. He took one last look at the quiet house. There was definitely time for a shower and a shave. Wooten wasn't going anywhere.

Before Truax could descend the ladder he heard the sound of running feet on Merlin's Way. At first he thought it might be some late-night jogger. But then the runner turned abruptly into the Wooten's circular driveway. Truax snatched the binoculars from the floor and raised them to his eyes just in time to see Joel Wooten passing through the gaslight's pale umbrella. Truax didn't understand. Joel was in his room. Unless he'd slipped out when Truax went to call Swope. An image flashed through his mind – Joel Wooten in his daughter's bedroom, that Trojan's slick pouch swinging like a miniature wrecking ball at the end of his cock.

Truax watched through the kitchen window as the boy unlocked the front door and eased it open. He shut it carefully, then stood perfectly still in the front hall, checking to see if anyone had heard him. The master and guest bedrooms remained dark. Truax focused the nocs to get a better look at Joel's face. He looked confused and worried. Truax's heart began to pump; his muscle and flesh flooded with adrenaline. If he's tried to see my daughter he will have to be punished, Truax thought. As will his father. Who gave me his word.

Realizing that he hadn't been heard, Joel crept up the stairs. Even though he knew he should probably give the boy a few minutes to settle, Truax scrambled down the ladder and headed back to his car. He wasn't so careful about silence this time. He had to get home to make sure that everything was all right.

27

Swope sat perfectly still behind the desk in his study, contemplating the meaningless figures he'd doodled on his blotter during the course of his conversation with Truax. He couldn't believe what he'd just heard. Wooten was back home. Truax had watched the man settle into the guest room for the night. This was not good. Not good at all. After four days of unbroken success, the campaign had finally experienced its first major glitch. Trouble in Wooten's marriage had become a cornerstone of Swope's strategy. If he wound up back in his house before the job decision had been made, then he would no longer be seen as a philandering tomcat unworthy of public service. The entire 27 affair could be dismissed as nobody's business, especially if Ardelia went to bat for him. Once that happened, Savage would be free to nominate Wooten city manager well before Swope finished concocting the fraud case against him. And that would be that. Swope would be out of the loop, no longer able to orchestrate events. A mere spectator to Wooten's irresistible rise.

Up until Truax's call, Swope's confidence that he would be able to stop Wooten's ascent had been growing by the hour. The plan was working with grim efficiency. Maybe *too* efficiently – Swope had found himself wondering several times during these past few days if they were taking matters too far. That hateful word in the concrete had been an especially tough choice. But necessary, absolutely necessary. Pressure had to be kept up on the man. It was Wooten who'd set this thing in motion. They would all have to ride it as far as it went.

Besides, it was too late to stop now, even if he wanted. The poison letter to Ardelia had already paid off. Although he'd figured word of Wooten's ejection from his home would take at least a week to filter back to Chicago through the Earth-Works grapevine, Gus Savage's unexpected call late Monday afternoon showed that things were happening faster than Swope could have hoped.

'Austin, do you have any idea where Earl Wooten is?' Savage asked, his voice even more impatient than usual.

'I don't know, Gus. I saw him around earlier in the day. Is there anything I can help you with?'

'No, it's just that we were supposed to have a conversation this morning and he never called.'

'Did you try him at home?' Swope asked, his voice even.

'Ardelia said she didn't know where he was. I'm just starting to get worried that something's wrong.'

'I don't think so. I mean, I'm sure I'd have heard.'

'Listen, do me a favor – see if you can track him down and tell him to get on the horn to me right away, would you?'

'Sure will.'

After hanging up Swope stared at the phone for a long while, wondering how he should play this. Clearly, Savage wanted to talk to Wooten about the manager job. Probably expecting an answer after a weekend's deliberation. That was usually how these things worked. Only, Wooten hadn't spent the weekend deliberating. He'd spent it cooling his heels in a cheap hotel. Although he knew this was too good an opportunity to squander, Swope also realized he'd have to tread carefully. If he seemed too eager to inform on Wooten, then the ever vigilant Savage might suspect he'd been tipped off and was acting as a rival. But if he was too subtle then the moment to sow doubt would be lost. In the end, he decided to play the reluctant friend who puts the good of the company first. Which, after all, was exactly who he was.

He waited until late Tuesday morning to call back.

'Did Earl ever call you?' he asked.

'No,' Savage replied, sounding furious. 'You talk to him?'

'I haven't had any luck either. I even tried calling him at home late last night but Ardelia said he wasn't there.'

'Did she say where he *was*?'

Swope hesitated for a beat.

'Well, that's the thing, Gus. I pressed her a bit, you know, made it seem like an emergency. And so she gave me the name of a motel down in Cannon City. Some dive.'

'Really? You call him there?'

'No answer. Though he was registered.'

'Christ. What the hell's going on, Austin?'

'That's all I know.'

'I mean, has he left home?'

'I really couldn't say.'

'Could you find out?'

Swope sucked air through his teeth.

'I gotta tell you, Gus, I wouldn't feel comfortable doing that. I mean, these are my friends. If they're having problems I'd rather not go prying into it.'

'No, you're right,' Savage said. 'But, listen – I *do* want you to find Earl. And when you do, tell him to call me right away.'

Swope looked out of his office's tinted window at the clear morning sky.

'That I can do.'

Just after hanging up he'd learned that his plan had progressed even further when Truax called to say that Wooten had actually assaulted Vota. Unbelievable. The outraged site boss had phoned a few minutes later, demanding action. Swope promised to deal with the matter and indeed he had, writing it up in a memo which he forwarded to Chicago. Nothing terminal in itself. Just another piece in the puzzle that showed Savage his intended city manager was becoming increasingly unreliable. But now, a few short hours later, everything looked set to change. Wooten was home. He'd somehow convinced Ardelia to take him back. True, she'd exiled him to the guest room. But still. He was home. A configuration that would make it harder for the campaign of a thousand small wounds to work. A man alone was much easier prey than one in the safety of his own home.

With Truax's call still echoing through his mind, Swope

pulled a legal pad and a fresh pen from his top right drawer, then set the balls of his cradle rocking. There was only one thing to do – speed up work on the bogus paper trail. Though he'd initially allowed himself at least four weeks to construct it, he now knew he'd have just a few days to compose the counterfeit orders, invoices and bills of laden that would make it appear Wooten had been fraudulently requesting funds to replace stolen building material. Once the paperwork had been submitted, Swope would get anonymous word to Chicago, who'd run an audit to make sure they were paying for the replacement of goods that had actually been stolen. Since there were no police reports on file, Wooten's goose would be at least temporarily cooked once the double billing came to light. By the time the mess was cleared up Swope would be in his sixth month as city manager.

Although it was a sound plan, Swope knew that it was fraught with difficulties. Which was why he'd given himself weeks to work it through. Forging documents was always a risky business. The boys in the EarthWorks legal department weren't Ardelia Wooten. Besides, Wooten had actually been guilty of adultery. This time he would no doubt kick and scream with righteous indignation. Unless Swope worked meticulously, he knew this thing could blow up in his face at any moment. But time was no longer a luxury he could afford. He had no choice but to proceed with unseemly haste. Unsatisfactory as it was, framing Wooten quickly was the only ammunition he had left now that the man was back home. Delay would mean that he might still get the offer. After that, knocking him off his pedestal would be impossible. Swope would be out of a job – there was no way a man as scheming as Wooten would keep him around after this sort of coup.

Out of a job. Jesus, what a nightmare that would be. He might as well be sixty-four and ready for the pasture. One of those sad sacks you saw hanging around Denny's at three-thirty in the afternoon. Banging away on the public links to kill time before happy hour, which seemed to grow earlier by the day, like the advent of a permanent winter. Xeroxing out-of-town want ads in the public library. Schmucks who'd gambled and failed. The boys down at Barger, Green would love this. Don't say we didn't tell you so. Swope's shortcut to the inner corridors would have turned out to be a one-way ticket to nowheresville. He'd have to sell the house – the ignominy of living in the city he'd lost would be crippling. Take work as a hired goon for slumlords or redneck developers. Florida swamp thief. Rent-control leg breaker. While Earl Wooten set himself up for that reconfigured congressional seat and slipped right into Austin Swope's future. That bad commercial he'd first seen on his birthday began to run through his mind, the one where he stands alone on a stage, conceding defeat to a dwindling crew of supporters.

He uncapped the pen and buried himself in work to chase the image away. It was nearly eleven by the time he'd finished sketching out the scheme's preliminary details on three tightly written sheets. Tomorrow he'd raid Accounts for blank invoices and then start forging. He unlocked the bottom left drawer of his desk to store the plan, noticing as he did the aging document he kept there as a reminder of how things could go ass-up if you didn't keep your eyes open. It had been ages since he last read it. He took out the weathered parchment and stared at it for a long time. It was his father's death certificate, drawn up just three years after the first Edward McDonald Swope had retired from forty-two years of busting his hump, day in and day out, as a plant electrician at River Rouge. Pouring out his vitality into those circuits and wires for an hourly wage. Even taking a bad beating when, as essential maintenance staff, he had to break a strike. At sixty-five they'd turfed him out. Just like that. The letter had been signed by McNamara himself. After that it had been a rapid decline into senility, his hard-earned pension frittered away on adult diapers and day nurses. That was the thing they didn't tell you when you started out, how you could work sixteen hours a day, six days a week, and still wind up flushed down the American crapper. You had to watch your ass. For his troubles, old Edward wound up in a low-rent nursing home paid for out of his youngest son's junior-partner pockets. When Swope finally buried the man, the undertaker handed him the death certificate he now studied. It listed the cause of death as 'pneumonia, arterial sclerosis, etc.' Swope would always remember that. More than the clichés scrawled on the tombstone or the immediately forgotten bromides of a minister who'd never met the man, that was his father's legacy.

Cause of death – etc.

There was no way that would happen to him.

Swope put the letter on top of his notes and locked the drawer. Too keyed up to go to bed, he poured himself a glass of leftover rye from the party and fired up another Tiparillo. He closesd his eyes and chased away the bad thoughts of his poor father, thinking instead about how good it would be when he finally got the job. No more calls to Chicago. No more need to solicit opinions from the likes of Ellen Felice and Richard Holmes. Three years of doing things his way. And then it would be '76 and he'd be ready. A phoenix rising from the ashes of the GOP. A new commercial began to run through his mind, nullifying the vile image that had haunted him a few hours earlier. The same stage, though this time the band played loudly and the balloons shot up from the crowd like popcorn. Some loyal friend shouted unheard words into a microphone and then it was Swope himself appearing before the crowd . . .

His reverie was interrupted by the sound of the front door opening. Teddy, back from another session with Susan Truax. Sally'd said something about them going out to see the new Bond film. He wondered if the kid had got lucky with the girl yet. He wouldn't be surprised. She had easy lay written all over her. He envied his son. The thought of putting the wood to Truax's daughter filled Swope's mind for a moment, a warm, carnal haze as pleasing as another hit of that rye. Although there'd probably be more mileage out of the mother. She looked like she could kick until the cows came home.

But after a few seconds his reverie was broken by the first intimation that something was wrong. Teddy was still standing there. Usually, he vaulted straight up the stairs to his room. Or he'd plunge into the kitchen to raid the refrigerator, leaving puddles of juice and dustings of crumbs for Sally to tut over come morning. But he wasn't doing any of this. He was simply waiting by the front door, panting fast, loud and shallow.

'Teddy?' Swope called softly.

His son's breathing caught for a few seconds. And then sneakered feet made their way across the hall. They squished wetly. What the hell, Swope thought. It isn't raining out. It hadn't rained in days.

Teddy appeared in the doorway. The sight of him sent a chill down Swope's spine. His flesh was bloodlessly pale, his hair flat and damp. His clothes were soaking wet. His chest rose and fell like a fire hose. But what really terrified Swope was the look in the boy's eyes. Usually so bright and aloof, they were now frozen by deep terror.

'Dad,' he said, his voice very small and very weak. 'You've got to help me.'

28

They still had over an hour before the rendezvous with Joel. Teddy decided to kill the time by driving aimlessly around the city, listening to tunes and regaling Susan with the latest scenes from his book. Newton seemed particularly dead tonight, the ever-burning gaslights shining on empty lawns and swept sidewalks. Televisions flickered behind living room windows like rapped lightning. What pathetic lives people lead, Teddy thought as he fired up a jay. Quiet desperation rules. Ticky-tacky houses, with everything tucked neatly in its place.

Instead of being grateful, Susan had hit the car with a seriously bad attitude, treating Teddy like he was some sort of chauffeur. Forgetting, it seemed, exactly who was running this show. She sighed audibly every few seconds, making it obvious to all and sundry that she was pissed off about not knowing where the meeting was taking place. She'd been after him to divulge the location ever since he told her about it last Friday. But there was no way Teddy was going to let that particular cat out of the bag until he had her strapped into the Firebird's passenger seat, just in case she got any ideas about trying to wing this thing on her own. Finally, after fifteen minutes of endless lamentation, he put her out of her misery, telling her that they were meeting at the closed pier. Only to have her start to bitch about his choice.

'I hate it down there,' she said. 'That place gives me the creeps.'

Teddy was tempted to tell her that he knew the place gave her the creeps. That was why he'd chosen it. But he didn't want to start a big fight. Not tonight. In fact, after letting her stew for a few minutes, he offered her a conciliatory toke on his doobie. She waved it away.

'I don't want to get stoned,' she said. 'I'm happy as I am. Unlike some.'

He shrugged. Her loss. Tired of silence, Teddy started to regale her with the latest chapter of *The Widening Gyre*, in which the luckless Horniman winds up mistakenly posted to Vietnam, where he is press-ganged into a special forces unit whose job it is to rescue the ambassador's beloved poodle, Humphrey, recently snatched from the embassy by an all-girl squad of VC . . .

'Don't talk about that,' Susan said sharply, before he'd even got to the part where Horniman uses his massive rod to subdue the guerrilla chicks.

'What?'

'The war. It's not funny.'

Teddy looked across at Susan. She really seemed to mean it, blue eyes boring right into him.

'And why not, pray tell?'

'You know.'

Teddy got it. Of course. The sarge. He hadn't thought. Although she had no business forbidding him from exercising his right to free speech, he could see how this might be a sensitive area. Ever the peacemaker, he decided to honor her request.

'Sorry,' he said.

'You know,' she continued, as if he hadn't just graciously relented. 'Not everything is part of your stupid story.'

Teddy stared at her in amazement. He couldn't believe she'd just called *The Widening Gyre* stupid. This girl who probably couldn't even lip-read her way through Nancy Drew. And now she was calling his work stupid, after he'd just agreed to change the subject in deference to her sad-sack father.

'Be cool, Susan,' he said. 'Or it's back home to Mommy.'

She shot him a murderous glance, though proved wise enough to keep it zipped. They traveled in their respective silences for the next few minutes. Susan applied some lip gloss, scooping it with her pinkie from a little black tub and rubbing it into her lips. Teddy punched in *Some Time in New York City*. 'Woman Is the Nigger of the World' came on. Susan turned down the volume after three bars. Without even asking. Getting some of that lip shit on his knob in the process.

'I hate that word,' she said.

'What, *woman*?' Teddy quipped.

'No, Teddy, you're the one who hates *that* word.'

'Stifle yourself, Edith.'

He turned the volume back up. They drove for a while.

'What time is it?' she half shouted.

'Eight-forty.'

'Why did you have to make it so long before we get to see him?' she asked impatiently.

'I'm sorry – do you have a problem with the way I'm handling this?'

She simply stared at him.

'Maybe you'd like me to drop you off at Joel's house? Or perhaps I can give him a lift to yours?'

The song ended.

'Don't fuck with me, Susan. Or you're going to spend the rest of the summer playing with those stuffed animals of yours.'

She looked sharply at him.

'How do you know about them?'

Teddy felt a quick spell of panic. Careful, he told himself.

'About what?' he asked innocently.

'The animals my dad gave me. You've never even been up in my room.'

Teddy stared at her for a moment, then smiled.

'Joel told me about them,' he said. 'He tells me everything.'

Susan looked back out the window, her expression suddenly smug.

'Not *every*thing,' she muttered.

Teddy finally pulled into Newton Plaza at five past nine. It was earlier than he'd planned, but Susan was really starting to get on his nerves. He parked in a corner of the lot hidden from the building, just in case one of those lame-ass security guards decided to get motivated. Though after their performance during last Monday's mugging he doubted he had anything to worry about from that quarter. They piled out of the car to absolute stillness. There was just one other person in sight, some dog walker heading toward Mystic Hills. The only sounds were traffic noise washing down from the pike and water lapping gently against the empty piers. The building's glass cliff face was dark. Perfect, Teddy thought.

Susan started to head down toward the lake.

'Hold your horses,' Teddy said.

He reached into his cluttered backseat, rummaging through the books and clothes and wrappers on the floor for the flashlight, a six-battery monstrosity capable of casting a beam nearly as strong as a headlight. He shined it in Susan's face.

'Let there be light,' he said.

She waved the light away, as she would a swarm of gnats.

'Don't be a jerk, Teddy.'

He switched it off and led her under the Gravity Tree, giving the apple a little rub for luck as he passed. They moved across the vast concrete steps to the boardwalk. Teddy made her jump the fence first so she wouldn't see how awkwardly he climbed. The Pavilion's geodesic dome came into view as he balanced on top, lit up like the launchpad at Canaveral. The sound of a circular saw wafted across the water from somewhere beneath it, though the workers remained hidden by a row of lakefront trees. He lowered himself to the ground, knocking his glasses askew and half tearing the Union Jack patch off his jacket. Susan watched his struggles with a mocking smile.

'Come on,' he said.

She screwed up her nose as they passed a big pile of stinking fish somebody had left on the boardwalk. They wove through the fifty-five-gallon drums blocking off the pier's entrance and then walked the length of the redwood planks. Near the end, where the wood began its gradual lateral slope, Teddy had to help her along, even though it wasn't that hard to negotiate the gentle pitch. She wouldn't touch his extended hand, grabbing his jacket cuff instead. The saw's wailing stopped just as they reached the end. Teddy shot a quick look at the Cross Keys Inn. The tables were empty, the candles dark. They must have closed the dining pier early tonight. This was getting better and better. There was no way anyone would see them down here. He turned on the flashlight and scribbled the beam around for a moment, letting it play off the water and the planks.

'You're going to get us caught.'

Teddy placed the lens under his chin to monster up his face.

'Prepare to meet your doom,' he said in Karloff voice.

Susan ignored him as she sat on the edge of the pier. Teddy stared at the back of her head, thinking how easy it would be to shove her in the lake. That would be fairly fucking funny, seeing her soaked, especially the precious blond hair she'd blow-dried for Joel. She hated getting dunked. But if he pushed her he'd have Joel to answer to. So he simply sat next to her, carefully balancing the flashlight lens-down between them to create a subtle, undetectable glow.

'Quiet tonight,' Teddy said.

Susan remained silent. She really was on the fucking rag. He fired up a doobie, not even bothering to offer her any. A seed popped beneath the Cricket's flame shooting into the water like a dud missile. He looked back toward the Plaza. Joel would be here soon. Knowing that his novel was a no-go area, Teddy decided to pass the time by telling Susan about the article he'd been reading in *Scientific American*. It was about these things called black holes, which were actually dead stars. Incredibly interesting. Groundbreaking stuff. But he hadn't even got to the part about how their intense gravity literally crushed light when he caught her yawning.

'Am I boring you, Susan?'

'No more than usual,' she answered.

That was it. Enough was enough.

'I'll tell you what. How about I go call Joel and tell him that the whole thing's off? I doubt he's left the house yet.'

She stared at him for a long, angry moment. Hammering

began to echo across the black water from the hidden Pavilion.

'You really are a fucker,' she said.

'And a joker. And a smoker. And a midnight toker.'

'Well, enjoy it while you can, Teddy.'

'And what's that supposed to mean?'

At first, it looked like she wasn't going to tell him. But anger soon got the better of her.

'I'll tell you what it means, Tedward – Joel and I are going to run away together.'

Teddy felt a wave of fear pass through him. That invisible hammer continued to pound.

'Bullshit.'

'We decided it weeks ago, when we were in DC. In case Irma ever dropped the bomb. All we got left to do is iron out the details. Which is what we're going to do tonight. Tomorrow, we'll be gone.'

'No way.'

'You can think what you want. But you better find somebody else for your summer fun.'

Teddy stared down into the murky water for a moment. She was full of shit. There was no way they were going to bolt.

'Yeah, but where would you stay on this great adventure?'

'We got a place all worked out.'

Something about the way she said the words frightened him. She sounded too confident to be bullshitting him.

'Where? In DC?'

'I thought Joel tells you everything, Teddy.'

Her tone was mocking now.

'Come on, Susan.'

He could hear the urgency in his voice.

'Why should I tell you?' She smiled wickedly at him, her expression made crueler by the light leaking up from beneath her. 'You want to tag along?'

'Shut up.'

'Why should I shut up? What are you going to do? Call Joel? All right. Go ahead. And I'll stand right next to the phone and scream that you're a liar.'

'Maybe I'll tell Irma.'

'You wouldn't dare.'

The anger had taken him over now.

'Maybe I already have.'

She looked over at him sharply.

'What?'

He was the one who could smile smugly now. Figure that one out, bitch. She stared at him for a long moment. And then understanding flooded into her eyes. Teddy began to fear he'd pushed it too far. All of a sudden she seemed a lot older than him.

'You let it happen,' she said, her voice cold. 'You let my parents catch us. So we'd get into trouble and you could play your fucking games.'

Teddy felt his mouth starting to cotton up. This had definitely gone too far. The hammering stopped at the Pavilion, leaving the lake in absolute silence.

'Don't try to understand things that are beyond you,' he said without conviction.

'Oh, you think I can't see through you, Teddy? You think that just because you have a big brain that stupid people like me don't know you're a fem?'

'What did you call me?'

'You think Joel doesn't know?' she continued. 'You think he wants to hang around with you anymore? It didn't matter when you were kids. All boys are fems when they're fourteen. But it's getting real old, Teddy. Real old.'

'He never said that.'

'He's been saying it a lot recently. And he'll be saying it some more once I tell him what you did.'

Teddy stood. A circular saw began to howl at the Pavilion. It was a sound he'd always hated.

'You're not telling him shit.'

'You just wait.'

He could see by her expression that she wasn't bluffing. She really was going to do it. Tell Joel. Tell him that Teddy had betrayed him. And then Joel really would be gone. He'd never forgive Teddy for this.

They were going to ditch him.

'Susan – come on. Quit messing around.'

She stood, those silver bracelets jangling.

'Watch me, Tedward.'

She began to walk past him, her sandaled feet unsteady on the slanted planks. He grabbed her arm. She tried to pull away but his grip was too good. The saw's sound plummeted into a low growl as it bit into wood.

'Susan, I'm warning you – do *not* tell Joel about this.'

'Get *off* me.'

'You guys can't ditch me. You can't.'

She tried to struggle a moment longer. When it became clear he wasn't going to let her go she grew perfectly still, her eyes narrowing hatefully.

The saw stopped. Finally. The lake was silent.

'Faggot,' she said.

He lost it. He shoved her. Hard. She staggered backward, kicking over the flashlight. The slope made her travel faster than he'd intended. He reached out to reel her back in but she was long gone. And then she was falling, her face passing right through the toppled ray of light. In that brief moment of illumination Teddy saw her expression change from hate to fear as she disappeared into a black hole of his making. There was a sound and then a splash. It wasn't until after the splash had resolved itself that Teddy started thinking about that sound, the dull thud that seemed both silent and infinitely loud, like a whisper traveling across oceans. He stood perfectly still, waiting for Susan to start thrashing around, gurgling and spluttering and yelping in outrage. But there was nothing. Just silence. He moved to the edge of the pier, almost sliding down the slope into the water himself. The flashlight had managed to wedge itself against one of the jutting support beams. He picked it up and turned its beam onto the clay colored water. The turbulence was smoothing out. He stared at the sharp edge of the boat platform and remembered that dull sound.

The saw started shrieking again. It was the worst sound there was.

He said her name. There was no reply. After a few more seconds he lowered himself onto the platform and put the beam back on the water. There was still no sign of her.

'Susan, don't fuck around. This isn't funny.'

He checked under the pier to see if she was there. Crouching. Hiding. Having her little joke. But there was just a complicated web of shadow created by the timber pilings.

She was in the water. He shoved her and she busted her head and she was under there.

He placed the flashlight lengthwise on the boat platform so that its light played out over the dying ripples from Susan's fall. He peeled off his jacket and then his glasses. As he stripped down, the saw at the Pavilion once again bit into wood. God, how he hated that sound. Trying not to think about any of this, Teddy jumped. The water was warm and black. For a moment he couldn't even tell which direction the surface was. When he finally got his bearings he started to make his way toward the bottom, propelling himself with two strong scissors kicks. He couldn't believe how dark it was. Or how deep. He couldn't even see his hands, tearing at the water just a few inches in front of his face. Something brushed his shoulder. He reached for it but there was only more water. Fuck this, he thought. He turned toward what he thought was the surface and swam at it as fast as he could. But the surface wouldn't come. He saw a cloud of light and he headed toward that. Finally, just when his frail lungs were beginning to burn, he broke free of the water, only inches from where he'd jumped in. He gasped for air. It seemed darker now than when he'd first jumped in. The Pavilion was quiet. He wondered for a moment if the men there were watching this. But that was impossible. It was too far away. Those dense trees stood between them. He grabbed the edge of the platform and looked around. There was still no sign of Susan. Not floating on the surface. Not laughing at him from the pier.

Nowhere.

He took as big a breath as his narrow chest would allow and went back under. He only managed to find more darkness and more water. He surfaced and dove again. Each time he felt the same blind panic just seconds after going under.

Between the second and third dive he called her name. On the last descent he found the bottom, but that was just sucking clay and smooth rock. Touching it, he realized he would never find her. When he surfaced for the third time he knew he would not be going back under. His heart and lungs could no longer take it.

Susan was at the bottom of the lake. He'd shoved her and now she was gone.

He pulled himself spitting and gasping onto the boat platform. Why was it so fucking dark? And then he knew. The flashlight had gone out. He got down on his knees and groped for it along the redwood planks, finally finding it at the back of the platform. He worked the switch. It was dead. Everything was dead tonight.

Hammering started at the Pavilion. For some reason the noise made Teddy remember that Joel was due here any minute. He felt a sudden spurt of deep relief. Joel would know what to do. Joel could swim like a dolphin. His lungs could hold hours of air. He'd strip off his shirt and dive right in. He'd have Susan on the pier in no time flat.

The only problem was that she'd be dead.

Teddy grabbed his coat and his glasses and climbed back onto the pier. He looked back toward the Plaza. It remained empty. He had to get out of here. If he stayed here people would come and they would not understand. Before he did anything else, he had to go get his dad. The Swope would know what to do about this. He had to.

Teddy hobbled back along the slanting pier, his shoes squishing on the wood. Twice he almost slipped over. The sound of that fucking saw chased him. It seemed louder than ever, like it was trying to cut right through his skull. He was moving so fast by the time he hit the boardwalk that he almost slammed into that mound of fish. He hopped the fence and headed toward the Firebird. There was still nobody around. Just another quiet night in Newton. When he got to his car he sat behind the wheel for a moment, dripping on the customized leather seat.

Susan was in the lake. He'd put her there.

He fished his keys from his soggy pocket and slotted them into the ignition. But before he could turn over the motor he saw movement. He froze. Someone was coming along the boardwalk from the direction of Mystic Hills. He recognized the walk right away. Joel. He moved with the same loose-limbed confidence as he did back in school. Teddy checked his diver's watch. It was still working. Of course it was. It was a fucking diver's watch. And Joel was right on time.

Teddy waited until he'd disappeared over the fence before he started his car. He had to get out of here. He had to go talk with his dad.

The Swope was in his office. Working late, as usual. Teddy paused in the front hallway, trying to figure out what the fuck he was going to say, how he could make his father understand what had happened. Understand, so he could set things right. Like he always did. Though this was different from that DWI or the roust for that nickel bag down in College Park. This was for real.

But then his father summoned him to his office and Teddy knew there was nothing else to do but tell him exactly what had happened. The Swope sat behind his big oak desk, staring at him over the cradle's stilled spheres. A drained highball glass rested on the blotter; a stubbed Tiparillo smoldered in the ashtray.

Teddy could see his eyes flex in surprise.

'You've got to help me,' Teddy said, his voice sounding so small and weak that it almost wasn't his own.

'What is it? What's happened?'

'I was at the lake and . . .'

He didn't know where to start. The stupid girl. Why had she made him do this?

'Come in here,' his father was saying. 'Come in here and sit down.'

Teddy did as told, stepping up to one of the chairs facing the desk. He paused before dropping into it.

'I'm sort of soaked.'

'Teddy – sit.'

He sat.

355

'Now I want you to tell me right now what the hell is going on.'

Teddy felt his mouth form an unintended smile. His father was starting to get impatient. He knew he should start talking. But for some reason he couldn't find the right place to start.

'Wait a minute – where's Susan Truax? Weren't you supposed to be with her tonight?'

'She's in the lake.'

Something appeared on his father's face Teddy never thought he'd see. Fear.

'What does that mean, in the lake?'

Teddy looked at his father's desk. There were scribbles on the blotter.

'She's under the water, Dad.'

'Teddy, are you telling me Susan Truax has drowned?'

The word cut through him like the sound of that saw. For some reason he hadn't said it to himself yet. He nodded dully. His father stared at him for a moment, his eyes unblinking.

'My God. How did this happen?'

'We were waiting for Joel . . .'

'Joel?'

'I was letting them be together.'

His father accepted this, even though he didn't seem to understand.

'Go on.'

'Only Susan didn't get it. She's a stupid girl, Dad. She was going to screw the whole thing up. They were going to ditch me.' Teddy felt his voice catching in his throat. 'I shoved her. I mean, I just wanted her to shut up.'

'What exactly did you do, Edward? It's important that I know. I mean, if you hurt her or—'

'I shoved her, all right? Like, hardly at all. She was riding me so I gave her a little push. No big deal. I wasn't trying to hurt her or anything. Okay, maybe get her wet, but only to shut her the hell up. And then when she fell I guess she hit her head, 'cause she went under like a ton of bricks. I jumped in to get her but it's so dark in there . . .'

Teddy's father looked like he was trying to catch his breath for a moment.

'Where exactly did this happen?'

'You know the last pier?'

'The damaged one.'

'On that.'

'Did anybody see you?'

'No.'

'Teddy, listen to me. You have to understand this – are you sure that no one saw you?'

'They couldn't of. That was part of the plan.'

'Not Joel?'

'I split before he got there.'

'But you saw *him*?'

Teddy nodded.

'From my car. Right before I left.'

'But he didn't see you?'

Teddy shook his head. His father dipped his head, his eyes locking onto the blotter. For a moment Teddy thought that he was going to start yelling. But the only thing he did was stand and walk to the window overlooking the front yard. Teddy felt himself relax a little. This was what his father did when he had to solve a problem. He looked out a window. Here. At the office. It didn't matter. Almost like he was waiting for the solution to come into view. Teddy knew that he should keep quiet now. Let things run their course. But he had to ask.

'Am I in trouble, Dad?'

His father stared out the window a while longer before turning. His face was grim but there was no anger in it.

'No, Teddy.'

And then he spoke the words Teddy had heard so often when he was a boy, all those times he'd lost things or broken things. All those times people were mad at him. They were the best words there ever were.

'Leave it to me. It'll be all right.'

29

He had to act fast. If this was going to be handled, it had to be handled now, before police or parents or anyone else became involved. The girl was due home. Alarms might already be sounding. Something had to be done to stop the landslide rumbling down Prospero's Parade. Otherwise, his only child, his beloved son, the repository of every dream he'd mined from the grudging earth during a quarter century of mind-breaking work, would be buried without a trace.

Of course, the truth was not an option. Swope realized that before Teddy had even finished talking. A story had to be concocted, something that would remove the blame from his son's thin shoulders. And it was Swope who had to compose it. He had an hour, tops. After that it would be other people doing the writing. The cell door would slam. Twenty-two years of legal training had come down to a handful of minutes in the middle of a quiet Tuesday night, when his mind was already addled by a long day's work and those three shots of leftover rye.

'Dad?'

'Give me just a sec here, Edward,' he said gently.

Swope continued to peer through the window. His front yard was reassuringly quiet. Just trees and shrubs and mowed grass, all of it gently illuminated by the gaslight's pale radiance. No police cruisers or pack of reporters or sneering curious onlookers.

Not yet.

Start simply, he told himself. First principles. Construct

the case against Teddy. See what they got. Only then could he begin to pick it apart. Fact one – a girl is lying dead at the bottom of Lake Newton. What do they have to connect his son to this sad and weighty fact? Opportunity, for starters. It was no good arguing that Teddy hadn't been there. He'd taken the girl out on a date, for Christ's sake. And any number of passersby might have seen the Firebird in the Newton Plaza parking lot. Teddy was at the scene and very much with the victim. That much was undeniable. For a few seconds Swope toyed with the idea of claiming he'd abandoned her after a lover's spat on the darkened pier, where she then met a mysterious death. Maybe he could implicate one of those punks who'd tried to mug him the other night. But he knew before the thought was fully formed that it was no good. The story would raise more questions than it would answer. Girls didn't just happen to get killed by strangers moments after being ditched by an angry date. If it was just Chones, the story might wash. But Swope knew from experience that the sheriff had a tendency to call in the State Bureau of Investigation on major crimes. And those guys didn't owe Swope squat.

So Teddy was there and Susan was dead. These two facts were unavoidable. What Swope had to do was snap the causal link between them. An accident. Of course. That was the only way to go. She'd slipped on the slick and slanted pier, striking her head and drowning. Tough luck, but there you are. If it was anybody's fault it was Swope's for not getting the thing repaired. Without witnesses, the accident excuse was impossible to refute. He recalled the sardonic counsel of a criminal professor back at Michigan who claimed that if you wanted to get away with murder, the best thing to do was simply push your victim out a window when no one was looking. All Teddy would have to do was stick by the story. Folks had accidents all the time, especially on hazardous structures. They could have been messing around, like young lovers do, when she tumbled. Teddy jumped in to save her, but no soap. Especially given his medical history. Sure, Chones and the SBI might make him sweat that one a bit, but Swope would be there with him the whole time as guardian and lawyer. As long as the kid didn't crack, it would be all right.

So that was it. They'd rehearse the story and then call it in. The Truaxes would be crushed but manageable, especially after EarthWorks offered them a fat out-of-court settlement for not maintaining that pier. Teddy would have to spend a couple weeks under wraps, though by August the legal storm would have passed. Things would be back to normal.

Only, they wouldn't. Not at all. Because even if Teddy ducked a manslaughter charge, there would still be that noxious cumulonimbus hovering over him, a cloud which the crop dusters in the press would seed until it stormed all over the Swopes. Rich kid alone on first date with sexy girl who dies in mysterious circumstances. Powerful lawyer father gets him off with a handout to the deceased's family. The local rumor mill would run overtime. Harvard would hear about it. Potential employers. Even though he'd stay out of prison, Edward McDonald Swope would be damaged goods. The boy who beat the rap. And as the pressure built there was an increasingly good chance that he would crack, slipping up when Swope wasn't there to help him. As for himself, Swope could forget about city manager. Whatever leverage he'd gained over Wooten these past few days would disappear. The big, bad pendulum would swing right back and catch him in the nuts.

Come on, Swope told himself. You can do better than this. Think. Time is running out. Irma could be calling the cops right now. He looked over his shoulder at Teddy, damp and bedraggled and scared out of his wits. He stared hopefully back at his father, that sink-hole of a chest heaving in fear and exhaustion. Just as it had those first few incubated days of his life, when his father had been the only one there to save him. There had to be a better way for him now, just as there had been then. Something more than a besmirched and provisional innocence. Something that took the heat off him – immediately and permanently.

As he turned back to the window a white sedan passed the mouth of the cul-de-sac. It hesitated, looking like it was about to turn, and at that moment Swope felt a terror more intensely pure than any he'd ever experienced. So now it starts, he thought. The long slide into ignominy. But the car sped harmlessly on. They'd simply slowed to admire the house. As so many did.

When it was gone Swope knew what he had to do. The plan appeared suddenly, left behind in terror's wake. He was appalled by its terrible perfection, how it arrived fully faceted, all nuances and details utterly intact. And the fact that it was so awful did nothing to lessen its inevitability. Even as he told himself there was no way he could do this, he knew that he had no choice. It was this or lose Teddy. This, or watch his life slip away. There was no middle ground now. No easy out. They'd come too far.

He turned to his son.

'Tell me again about Joel,' he said.

'Joel?'

'I still don't understand his role in all this.'

Teddy looked at the desk, a nervous smile tugging at his blue lips. Swope felt an unwelcome pulse of anger. That girl could be floating in plain view by now and here his son was smirking.

'Teddy, for Christ's sake, you just confessed to murder,' he said, exasperation lacing his voice. 'Let's think about saving your own ass before we focus on loyalty to anybody else.'

Teddy glanced up at him and Swope instantly regretted his display of temper. That was not the way to move this thing along. Keep cool, he told himself. One step at a time. He smiled and nodded encouragement. Teddy took heart from this.

'I was just going him a favor,' he said after a moment. 'It was all a scam, me dating Susan. To get her out of the house. So she could see Joel.' He shook his head in a wronged sort of way. 'I was just doing him a favor.'

'But as far as anybody knows, you and Susan were on a date?'

'Except Joel.'

'And you said he didn't show up until after you left?'

Teddy nodded. Swope began to pace the room. His mind was racing now.

'Teddy, listen to me. Because there's not much time. We have to take care of this. Now.'

'All right.'

'I have to call Sheriff Chones. We must have a story for him.'

Teddy suddenly came to life.

'I was thinking about that on the way home. Maybe we could say it was an accident. You know, she just slipped . . .'

He stopped talking when he saw his father's shaking head.

'Why not, Dad? It'll be my word against hers. And she's . . . dead.'

'It'll be your word against everybody's,' Swope said.

'I don't understand.'

'What would you think if some boy you knew stepped out with a sexy girl on their first date and she wound up in the drink?'

Teddy shrugged.

'I don't know. That he'd offed her.'

'Damn right you would. Even if you couldn't prove it.'

Teddy said nothing. Swope could see he still needed a nudge to get with the program. A little white lie to push him toward the larger truth.

'I wish I could sit here and say that people would believe you if you told them it was an accident. But I can't. The county attorney will certainly charge you. And then it will be up to a jury. Twelve strangers, Teddy. Ordinary people with their ignorance and superstition and petty minds. People who would envy and hate a boy like you.'

'I barely touched her, Dad.'

'*I* know that. But you'll still be in trouble. Bad trouble. Trouble I cannot help you with.'

'What should I do, then?' Teddy asked, his voice getting weaker.

'You're going to have to tell one of your stories.'

Teddy perked up at the sound of that.

'Yeah. Cool.'

'Make it so nobody thinks about you and Susan anymore.'

'I could say I wasn't there.'

'No cigar, kiddo. Come on. Think.'

'What, then?'

Swope squatted, so that he was on his son's level.

'You're going to have to say you saw somebody else do it.'

'Yeah.' Teddy's eyes widened. 'I could make up this real bad mother. Some kind of demented hippie drifter. A cross between Manson and—'

'Teddy.'

His son stopped.

'It has to be somebody who exists. Someone the cops can get their hands on. Otherwise the focus will wind up right back on you.'

Teddy looked away, as if the words hurt him. He was getting it. The experts were right. The kid was no dummy.

'Who?' he asked finally.

'You know.'

'Not Joel.'

'Yes. Joel.'

Teddy shook his head.

'No way, Dad.'

Swope moved closer to him, placing a hand on his son's clammy forearm.

'Listen to me, Edward. You are looking at a dose of trouble right now that will completely ruin your life. I know you didn't mean to hurt that girl. I know it was an accident. But the law won't recognize these things.'

'But . . .'

'Look around this office. I know the law. Better than anyone you will ever meet – even at Harvard. And that law will make you pay. Do you understand what I'm saying?'

Teddy nodded dully.

'You will go to jail for what you did. Jail, Teddy. Not Harvard. But prison. With killers and rapists who will take advantage of you in the worst possible ways. For years and years you will be tortured and enslaved and spat upon. And when you finally come out there will be nothing for you. No Harvard and certainly no law school. Nothing. You will wash dishes, young man. You'll live alone in a cold-water flat above a Laundromat. There will be nothing left for you to do but count the days until they lower you into your grave, a forgotten ignominious failure.'

'But they might find me innocent. There's a chance of that, right?'

'Slim to none. But okay, let's say they did. For argument's sake. Even that wouldn't be much better. Because then you will simply be the boy who killed Susan Truax and got away with it. People will hate you even more. What do you think Harvard will say? They don't care about technical guilt at a place like that. They care about honor. *Honor*. That's who you'll be for the rest of your life – the kid who beat the rap.'

Teddy said nothing.

'There will only be one moment for you to get out of this. Now. Tomorrow morning or even an hour from now will be too late. And there's only one way. You must say that someone else did it.'

'But I can't say that. He's my friend. He's . . . innocent.'

Swope stood and walked back to his window, giving his head a sardonic shake.

'I'm surprised to hear you say that.'

'What?'

Swope turned back to his son.

'That the boy who used your goodwill to break the law – that this guy is innocent.'

'Joel didn't break the law.'

'How old is Susan?'

'Almost eighteen.'

'Then she's a minor, Teddy. If her parents say Joel can't see her, that's the law. Period. Jesus, even if this accident didn't happen you could still get in trouble for doing what you did. The last time I checked, aiding and abetting someone in the commission of a crime was deemed felonious.'

Which was bullshit, of course. No prosecutor in the world would go after his son for that. But Teddy had no way of knowing this. Not until he'd spent a few years in Cambridge.

'Really?'

'Yes, really.'

Teddy stared down at his soggy shoes. Swope knew he still

had a bit more to do to close this thing out. And he had to hurry.

'I'll make a deal with you,' he said. 'If you tell this story, then I'll guarantee you that Joel gets a very light sentence. I'll make sure they send him to one of those country club prisons. We're talking months, not years. You know the kind of pull I have with Spivey and Chones. And I'll also make sure he makes bail right away so he can stay at home while the grown-ups sort this mess out. He'll be home within hours. And when he gets out, nothing will have changed for him. Not really. He can still go to college. Get a job with his dad. Teddy, listen to me. If we don't fix this now, then your life will be over. The first story you tell is the only one they'll believe. After that no one will be paying attention. I know about these things. I know.'

'But Joel . . .' he protested, though without conviction this time.

'It'd be no different if he got hit by a car or came down with cancer. Just the Fickle Finger of Fate.'

Teddy stared at the desk for a long time. Swope could see that he was coming around.

'He was going to run away,' he said, his voice justifying.

'I'm sorry?'

'Joel and Susan were going to run away.'

Swope didn't understand the relevance of this. He nodded anyway. Anything to help his son over that last hurdle.

'Edward, nothing will be gained by your taking the blame for this. Susan will still be gone.' It was time to play his trump. 'And there's one more thing. I don't want to mention it because it seems selfish. But . . .'

'What?'

'What you've done will ruin me should it come to light.'

Teddy winced.

'Do you think I'll be able to be city manager with a son in jail? Or even with a son suspected of murder? And your mother. Do you think she'll be able to leave her bedroom, much less show her face in public?'

Teddy looked at his filthy hands.

'So what should I do?'

'Just agree to say what I tell you to say. That's all. A few dozen words and I swear to you no harm will come to any of us.'

'But what if the sheriff—'

'Ralph Chones will not come near you unless I'm sitting right by your side. If he tries any rough stuff I will cut off his balls with a rusty razor blade and shove them down his throat. Ditto for that pencil-neck piece of shit Lon Spivey.' Swope was speaking very quietly now, thrilling at the sound of his own words. 'This is *my* city, Teddy. No one will fuck with what is mine here. No one.'

Teddy's eyes had slowly closed during the speech. Swope waited for the answer upon which their lives now depended.

'I buried Paul,' he murmured after a long moment.

'What?'

Teddy's eyes snapped open.

'Okay. It's cool. I'll do it.'

Swope felt as if some passageway that had been clogged with a vile plaque suddenly disgorged deep within him. He stepped forward and placed a hand on the back of his son's neck. His skin was so cold. The water. The fear. He began to rub it, trying to knead in some warmth.

'I won't let you get hurt, Teddy. You know that, don't you?'

Teddy sniffled and nodded.

'Yeah.'

They honed the story as they drove to the lake. Anticipating questions. Cutting away extraneous details. Making sure of the sequence.

Getting it just right.

'Are you clear on all this?' Swope asked as Newton Plaza came into view.

'Sure. I mean, it's almost like the truth.'

'That it is,' Swope said. 'That it is.'

His relief deepened as they pulled into the lot. It was quiet and empty. No sirens. No crowds. Swope's eyes traveled down to the darkened pier as he pulled into his space.

'Could Joel still be there?'

Teddy shook his head.

'I told him if we didn't show by ten to go back home and wait for me to come by.'

'All right. You stay here. If you see anybody, don't panic. Tell them I'm here. I'll explain what's going on. Just don't say anything, all right? That's the cornerstone to this entire operation – sticking to the story. No improvising. No fine-tuning.'

Teddy snorted.

'Don't worry about it.'

Swope got his cell-battery flashlight from the trunk and made his way down to the waterfront. That dangling brass apple on the Gravity Tree never looked more imperiled. The only sounds were his footsteps and negligible waves lapping against the pilings. As he drew closer to the damaged pier he knew that this was it. The pivotal moment of his life. If he pulled it off, then everything would be fine. Teddy would be safe and their future intact.

If not, then it was all over.

Getting over the fence was a pain in the ass. That pile of dead fish stank to high heaven, casting a pall over the whole scene. As he moved along the pier he looked at the Pavilion's cloudlike canopy rising above the north shore's trees. He remembered authorizing some OT for the crew there, though there was no way the workers could have seen or heard anything. The pier began to angle to the left, forcing him to lean into the slope and modify his gait so he wouldn't slip. He stopped when he reached the point above the boat platform where Teddy said it happened. He stared down into the dark lake. The reality of the situation suddenly struck him, provoking an uprising of panic it took him several seconds to quell. He could feel it now. The death. His son's crime. It lingered in the air like the stink of those rotting fish. He thought about that dumb, pretty girl lying on the wet clay, all that water holding her down. He thought about John Truax, out there working for him. He thought about Irma, teetering unknowingly on the brink of a nightmare. And Wooten. About to be punished for his betrayal.

He thumbed on his light. The brown water was perfectly still, its smooth surface interrupted by a single dead fish, its silver skin as brilliant as chipped quartz. The flashlight caught its eye and, for a moment, it seemed to wink back up at him. He moved the beam around the surrounding pier, just to get the scene in his mind before the people came.

This was all right, he thought. This will work.

He jogged back to the lobby of Newton Plaza, pausing for a moment at the car to tell Teddy that everything was going according to plan. His son simply stared at him. The guard was at his desk, thumbing through a copy of *Hustler*. He hadn't seen anything unusual that night – except for Earl Wooten's son heading back toward Mystic Hills about an hour ago. He'd stopped him, thinking he might be one of those punks that had been running wild down here.

'How did he seem?' Swope asked.

The guard shrugged.

'Kind of distracted. When I found out he was Mr Wooten's kid I cut him loose.'

Perfect, Swope thought.

'All right.'

'Something wrong?' the guard asked, nervous now.

Swope didn't answer. He took his small address book from a coat pocket and looked up Chones's home number. He used the courtesy phone to make the call. The sheriff's voice was sleepy.

'Ralph, this is Austin. Look, there's been some trouble at the lake.'

The guard watched Swope with astonishment as he told Chones the story. After hanging up, Swope silenced the man's attempt at self-explanation with a raised finger. He had one more call to make.

The phone was answered before the first ring had even stopped.

'Irma, this is Austin Swope. Is John there?'

'John? Yes. I thought you were . . . here he is.'

Truax was on the phone immediately. He'd been standing right there.

'John, I need you to come down to Newton Plaza.'

There was a pause.

'Is something wrong with Susan?' Truax asked.

Irma was speaking German in the background.

'John, please, just come. Right away.'

After ordering the guard to remain at his post, Swope went back out to the Town Car. He lit a Tiparillo and leaned against the hood, looking everywhere but at that damaged pier. Teddy stayed in the passenger seat. Neither said a word. They avoided each other's eyes until sirens began to sound in the distance. Teddy looked up in near panic. Swope nodded.

'This is part of it,' he said. 'It's okay.'

As the sirens drew closer, he ran over the whole grisly mess in his mind. Everything had been accounted for. And even if there were some rough edges, he doubted anyone would be examining them too closely. A white girl was dead. The respected son of a prominent lawyer witnessed her murder by a black boy who'd been forbidden from seeing her following a pants-down confrontation with her parents. He didn't imagine the authorities would be looking for nuances on this one.

Two prowlers arrived, one after the other. Swope told the deputies Teddy's story. They wanted to question the boy but Swope explained that Chones was coming. They didn't press it. They knew who they were talking to. Swope led them down to the pier, the three of them clambering noisily over the fence. Teddy stayed in the car. One of the cops cracked a flare, planting it in the moist earth beside the pier's mouth. The cops stared wordlessly at the mound of dead fish for a moment, as if this might have some bearing on matters, then followed Swope down to the end of the pier. They lifted their arms for balance as they reached the sloped section, like pedestrians hitting a patch of unexpected ice.

'So this is where it happened?' the first cop asked, staring down at the boat platform.

'Yes, it is,' Swope said.

'Damn,' the second cop opined.

Chones arrived at the same time as the engine from the Cannon County VFD. They didn't have to climb the fence – a fireman snipped off its chain with some heavy-duty wire cutters. Swope and one of the deputies met Chones at the pier's mouth. The deputy gave him the canned version of the story. Swope let him talk without interruption – the story sounded more objective coming from the uniform. As he spoke the volunteers rolled aside the fifty-five-gallon drums, causing one of them to fall into the water beneath the deck. Everybody winced at the sound.

'Where's the boy?' Chones asked.

'Back up in my car. I thought it better that he wasn't here for . . .'

Swope let the sentence finish itself.

'We might need him to point out where she's at.'

'I know.'

Chones nodded sourly.

'Well, let's see what we got, then.'

He led everyone along the pier. With their hats and coats and big boots, the firemen looked outsized, bigger than ordinary men. Chones wore a black windbreaker with the word SHERIFF stenciled across its back. Everybody stared at him when they reached the end. For the moment, he seemed more interested in the slanted wood beneath him than the lake's still water.

'This thing ain't gonna fall down beneath us, is it?'

'No,' Swope said. 'It's stabilized. You could drive a truck on it.'

'In that case let's get this deal done.'

Swope lit a Tiparillo and stepped aside, letting it happen. One of the firemen went for a rental rowboat. Others toted portable arc lamps and a generator down from their engine. They attached the lights to the jutting support beams spaced at ten-foot intervals along the pier. Wires soon connected them to the generator. Someone cranked it up by pulling the cord, just like a Saturday-morning lawn mower. The lake quickly filled with its sound. The lights sputtered on, their beams angled down at the boat platform and the murky water surrounding it. Big police flashlights and the traffic flare added to the maelstrom of light.

A fireman with a pencil-thin mustache changed into diving gear that he pulled from a huge duffel bag on the boat platform. After donning the suit he slid into the lake as quietly as someone entering a hot bath. A few seconds later

370

the fireman in the rowboat arrived. He'd stripped to his T-shirt and suspenders, his thick arms laden with vivid tattoos. The frogman gripped the side of the boat, fixed something to his mouth, and then went under.

Nothing happened for the next few minutes. Swope looked at Chones – he stared at the boat with the neutral expression of a man watching his dog piss on public land. Diesel fumes leaked from the chugging generator, creating a cloud that hung just above the arc lights. Finally, the diver's slick, snorkeled head burst through the filmy surface. He grabbed the boat's aluminum hull and looked up at Chones, shaking his head tersely. Chones nodded to the man on the boat, who gently dipped his oars, pulling the diver to a new location, this one closer to the water-level platform. When the boat had come to a rest the diver slid back beneath the water.

Swope saw John and Irma Truax arrive just after he went under. He met them halfway along the pier and explained that the search was just a precaution. There was no reason for panic.

'No reason?' Irma asked, her voice shrill and bewildered.

'I'm taking care of this,' Swope said, meeting her eye. 'I promise you.'

They moved to the crowded end of the pier, joining the small crowd of firemen and cops who stood bracing themselves against the pitch. Chones saw them coming. He looked at Swope, raising his eyebrows slightly. Swope nodded. Irma's face was now drawn back into a frozen silent shriek. She held tightly to the sleeve of her husband's windbreaker, as if she were suddenly afraid of sliding off the tilted wood. Truax was as impassive as ever, his gloved hand hanging limply at his side. There was no question of him slipping.

There was a commotion in the lake. The diver emerged, more noisily than he had the first time, brown water streaming off his cowl. He held up his right thumb. Chones sighed and stared down at his shoe, which he kicked idly at the pier for a moment, as if trying to dislodge a piece of it. Finally, he looked at the Truaxes.

'Sir? Ma'am? I'd like for you to please step back to shore.'

Irma looked like she'd been slapped.

'No . . .'

'Ma'am, please. I'm just asking you to clear the immediate area for a bit.'

She looked at her husband. Truax stared at the sheriff for a moment, then turned to Swope, awaiting instruction. Swope nodded once. Truax muttered something to his wife and gently grasped her upper arm with his good left hand. Chones beckoned for a deputy to conduct them away. Irma was shaking her head now, looking over her shoulder with that shrieking expression. When the Truaxes were beyond the dome of light, Chones nodded to the fireman at the oars, who picked up a yellow cord from the boat's bottom. He tied it into a broad noose and handed it to the diver. He slid back into the water for a few long seconds. When he emerged the oarsman pulled the boat flush with the water-level platform, dragging the diver and his rope with him. Another fireman leaped down onto the platform, causing it to rock slightly. He took the cord from the oarsman and handed it up to the remaining firemen on the pier. They began to draw it in, leaning back into the pier's pitch. Slack was quickly taken up. Effort was now required. After they'd reeled in about ten yards the line caught. The firemen prepared to give it a greater tug but Chones said something sharp. Everybody waited as the diver went back under. The cord shimmered for a moment, then went slack.

The firemen resumed pulling. After a few long tugs something appeared just below the surface, a mass that began to resolve itself into features. An arm, hair, a shoulder. Susan Truax. Her body broke through. The rope was looped beneath her arms, pulling up her shoulders into a shrug. Her limp hair was streaked with clay. As they lifted her clear of the water she swung round and Swope could see her face. Her big eyes were hooded and her mouth slightly agape, a tip of pale tongue lolling through perfect teeth.

The fireman on the platform kneeled to hoist the body, guiding it over his head balletically as the men on the pier redoubled their efforts. It didn't take them long to get her up onto the pier. They placed her crossways, head above feet, so she wouldn't roll back into the lake. Chones moved in, muttering commands. Water cascaded from Susan's clothes and hair onto the wood. Some of it seeped through the cracks, hitting the lake below like rain. Her eyes were shut now. She looked beautiful, her face gathered into an almost pleasant expression.

And then the screaming began. Everyone turned to see Irma Truax running along the deck, her cork heels pounding unevenly on the angled planks. Her husband and the deputy followed, both holding up futile, beseeching hands. She ignored them. She ignored everything but the sight of the dead girl. She froze ten feet from the body and screamed again, a shrill exhalation that drowned out everything else. Truax caught up with her. He put his hands, good and bad, on her shoulders. She shrugged him off and lunged toward the body, stumbling on the slick and uneven surface. She landed heavily but did not stop moving, crawling the rest of the way on all fours, until she was close enough to collapse across her daughter's chest.

The men on the pier were transfixed by her muffled, watery screams. After a few seconds she was able to raise herself high enough to see her daughter's face. She grew suddenly silent, her eyes quizzical. She reached out and touched Susan's hair, as if surprised to find it wet? Slowly, carefully, she began to untangle the first of its many knots.

And then Swope was moving. He flicked his Tiparillo into the lake, where it died with a quick hiss. When he reached Irma he hiked up his trousers and squatted, placing a hand on her shoulder.

'Irma?'

She looked at him. They stared at each other for a moment and then she allowed herself to be raised to her feet. After one last look at her daughter she buried her face against Swope's shirt, smearing it with snot and mascara. Behind her, a fireman took the opportunity to place a gray blanket over the girl.

'I'm going to take care of this,' Swope said to her in a clear, soft voice. 'I promise you.'

A few minutes later Chones and Swope returned to the parking lot, leaving the Truaxes to stare at their daughter's blanketed body. Teddy told the sheriff his story from the back of the Town Car. Swope stood nearby, his eyes never leaving his son. Teddy started his account with a small confession. He had, it seemed, lied to Irma Truax earlier in the evening, telling her that he was taking Susan to see the new Bond film when he actually planned to bring her down to the lake to make out. Teddy knew it was wrong. But they never got a chance back at the Truax house. After what happened with Joel, Susan's parents watched her like hawks.

'What happened with Joel?' Chones asked quietly.

Teddy explained how Joel and Susan had been caught having sex in her bedroom. At this, Chones stole a quick glance at Swope, who gave him a terse nod. Teddy explained how he'd gone to see Susan to console her and they soon found themselves attracted to each other. Tonight was their first date. But Joel must have been spying on the Truax house or something, because he'd followed them, to find his ex-best friend kissing the girl he'd been forbidden from seeing.

He set upon them. Wordlessly. Like an animal. With sudden and absolute violence. He attacked Teddy first, striking him in the stomach with such force that he fell backward into the lake. The wind knocked out of him, Teddy almost drowned. Just as he finally struggled to the surface he saw Joel shove Susan. As she fell her head hit the side of the platform with a dull thud. Her body sank faster than he ever thought a body could. And then Joel was gone, racing back down the pier. Teddy frantically searched the murky water for Susan, diving time and again. But it was no use. Finally, realizing that there was nothing more he could do, he headed home to raise the alarm.

Chones was deeply impressed by Teddy's story. As was Swope. The boy's composure was remarkable. His grasp of detail and his sense of timing impeccable. By the time he was done Swope knew that Joel's contradictory, uncorroborated testimony didn't stand a chance.

Chones turned to one of his deputies.

'Go pick up Earl Wooten's boy,' he said, his voice level and low.

30

Wooten was fast asleep when the eagle-head knocker on his front door called, four sharp reports that sounded like a hunter's rifle on a frozen morning. He sat up before he was fully awake, wondering for a moment if the noise were part of a forgotten dream. But then it happened again. Four imperious knocks, more than a second between each of them. Wooten looked for his bedside clock but could only see unfamiliar things. He remembered that he was in the guest room. It took him a moment to find his watch. The luminous hands said that it was almost one.

He pulled his pants over his pajama bottoms and threw on the work shirt he'd worn earlier in the day. Yesterday. He listened for movement upstairs as he made his way toward the front door. It was quiet. That was good – the knocking hadn't woken anybody. There'd been enough disruption in this house recently. As he neared the door he could see a broad-brimmed hat hovering in the fan of windows, like a flying saucer in a UFO movie. Wooten recognized it right away as standard issue of the Cannon County sheriff's department.

Vota, he thought. Son of a bitch called the cops.

He opened his front door to two deputies. Their prowlers were parked on the circular drive. The cop on the porch was tall and fat. His shirt was too small, exaggerating the mounds of flesh beneath it. His hat had been pulled down so firmly that it seemed to shift his face right to the bottom of his head. The second cop was tall as well, but skinny. His hat rested on his long head like a bottle cap that hadn't been screwed on right. He remained in the driveway, one bony hand resting on the handle of his pistol.

'Gentlemen,' Wooten said.

'Earl Wooten?' the cop on the porch asked.

'That's right.'

'We have to see your son.'

Wooten hesitated, totally unprepared for the cop's words.

'My son?'

The fat cop on the porch was doing all the talking.

'We're going to need to take him down to Cannon City.'

'Why?'

'Because the sheriff asked us to.'

'No, I mean, what is it you want him down there for?'

'We're not at liberty to discuss that. Sheriff just told us to bring the boy in.'

'Well, that's simply not good enough.'

Wooten's words came out more vehemently than he'd intended. The two deputies stiffened.

'Mr Wooten, we *will* arrest your son unless you get him. Now.'

Arrest. The word turned Wooten's blood cold. He shook his head, less in defiance than disbelief.

'Now hold on a minute. You can't just barge in here without a better explanation than that.'

The deputies looked at each other and it was wordlessly decided that the skinny one would move onto the porch as well. Wooten stood his ground, wondering if he was really about to try to fend off two cops. But before anything further could happen there were footsteps on the stairs. Everyone looked. It was Ardelia. She stopped at the bottom step, pulling her robe close around her neck.

'Earl? What is it?'

'They want to talk to Joel.'

'Joel? What on earth for? He's asleep.'

As she spoke her eyes traveled from Wooten to the deputies. She noted their stony resolve.

'Maybe we should call Austin,' Ardelia said, her eyes fixed on the strangers.

'Ma'am, there'll be time for calling people later,' the fat deputy said. 'Right now we need your son.'

Wooten could see by his wife's expression that she'd read the situation. She may have been the owner of a five-bedroom house in an exclusive neighborhood, may have been the vice principal of a richly funded high school. But Ardelia Wooten was also a black woman born in prewar St Louis. She knew how quickly this sort of thing could go from bad to irretrievable.

'Earl, go get Joel.'

She was right. It was the only thing to do. He turned back to the deputies.

'Wait here,' he said in a voice that told them the subject wasn't open for debate.

As he climbed to the second floor he heard Ardelia speaking to the men. Inviting them in. Asking what this was all about. Wooten hesitated outside his son's door, listening for anything that would warrant this late-night intrusion. But it was silent. As he knew it would be. Chones was going to hear about this in the morning. He pushed into the bedroom without knocking. Though the light was off, the moonbeams that cut diagonals across his son's bed provided enough illumination to show that it was empty. Fully made. Undisturbed since morning.

The fear gathered in him now. He switched on the bedroom light and felt his heart leap when he saw Joel standing in the far corner, next to the window overlooking the backyard. He was wide awake and fully dressed. His sneakers were tied, his belt buckle fastened. There was a trapped look in his eyes.

'Joel, what are you doing? The police are here and they want to—'

'They found out, didn't they?'

His voice was charged with emotion. This wasn't what Wooten had been expecting to hear. Not at all.

'Joel, what's going on? Have you been out tonight?'

The boy simply stared at him.

'Son, listen to me – the police want to take you down to Cannon City. You've got to tell me what happened.'

377

'I don't know what happened.'

Wooten felt a presence behind him. He turned. It was the fat cop, filling the room's doorway with his girth and his equipment and the musky, impatient odor of a long shift. His eyes were hard and merciless.

'Sir, I'm going to have to ask you to stop talking to your son right now.' He turned his attention to Joel. 'Young man, come with me this moment or I *will* put the cuffs on you.'

'Now wait a minute . . .'

As he spoke Wooten raised his hands, palms forward. It was a gesture intended simply to suspend this whole process long enough to make some sense out of it. But the cop took it the wrong way. He moved quicker than Wooten would have guessed him capable, pulling his billy club from its sheath and placing the tip of it against Wooten's broad chest.

'Stand aside,' he said.

Wooten kept his eyes on the stick, afraid what might happen if he looked the man in the face.

'You best take that wood off my chest less you want to use it as a toothpick,' he said quietly.

The cop hesitated. Wooten could have taken away the man's stick in a heartbeat if he wanted. The question was where they went from there.

'Stop it,' Joel said in a querulous voice.

The two men looked at him.

'I'll go. All right?'

He was moving through the door before Wooten could respond. The cop pulled back the stick to make room for him to pass, then sheathed it as he set off close after the boy. Wooten was left to bring up the rear. Ardelia and the second cop waited silently in the front hall. Pleasantries had been exhausted. She searched Joel's face as he walked down the steps. Wooten could tell by her expression that he wasn't returning her gaze.

'What is it, honey?' she asked.

Joel walked right past her, leading the fat cop through the open front door. The second policeman fell in behind them. Wooten pursued them out into the night, desperately trying to figure out a way to stop this.

'Let me drive down with him,' he said at the backs of the cops' heads.

It was the skinny cop who answered this time. As he spoke he never took his eyes off Joel.

'You'll have to arrange your own transport.'

'Joel, don't do or say anything until I get down there,' Wooten said. 'You hear me?'

His son gave no sign of having registered the words as he lowered himself into the back of the cruiser. The fat deputy slammed the door; the skinny one headed back to his car, parked along the driveway's curve. Wooten pointed his finger at the fat deputy's chest before he could get behind the wheel.

'Tell Chones I'm coming right over. He is not to do a thing until I get there.'

The deputy stared at Wooten's finger until it was withdrawn, then slid into the car. Wooten took a step back as the motors started, one after the other, sudden and piercing, like a nighttime cough. Ardelia joined him, gripping his arm as their son's face flashed by.

'Earl?'

For the second time in a week, Wooten found himself calling Swope at a wrong hour. He used the kitchen phone this time. Sally answered, sounding wide awake.

'Sally, it's Earl. Look I'm sorry to call so late, but I need to speak to Austin.'

'He's not here.'

Wooten checked his watch. It was just after one-thirty.

'Really? Where is he?'

'I don't know. He went out a few hours ago.'

'All right. Do you know when he'll be back?'

'Late. Oh. Well. It is late. Later. Shall I have him call you?'

'Yes. I'll be down at the sheriff's office. He can reach me there.'

'All right.'

'I'm sorry for bothering you so late, Sal.'

'Don't worry,' she said, her voice ominous. 'I was already up.'

She hung up. Wooten tapped the phone against his

379

hip for a moment. Ardelia was standing in the kitchen door-way.

'What did he say?'

'He wasn't in.'

'Not in? Earl, what on earth is going on here?'

He replaced the receiver.

'I'm going to find out.'

It didn't take him long to get to Cannon City. He sped the whole way. They can pick me up if they want, he thought. I'm going there anyway. It was a six-mile journey down rural county roads lined by squat, indistinguishable brick houses and double-wides with cinder-block foundations. Lawn art and American flags decorated the yards. He passed the Cannon Baptist Church, where a sign warned that GOOD INTENTIONS DIE UNLESS THEY ARE EXECUTED. Just beyond that was the high school, home of the Bombardiers. Finally, he arrived at the town's square, a two-acre tract of trampled grass and spiked cannon. Diseased trees lined its edges, their branches pruned, their trunks painted a styptic white. The marquee on the old cinema advertised a flea market; the Woolworth's had gone out of business.

Wooten parked his Ranchero across the street from the two-story brick police station. There were three prowlers in the slant spaces out front. He knew this place well, having been here a half dozen times to help Chones catch a Florida gang who'd been rustling heavy machinery from Newton sites onto south-bound flatbeds. It was a building where he'd always felt welcome. But tonight, from the moment he stepped through the front door, he could feel the change of atmosphere, a barometric drop that warned of storms ahead. The duty sergeant, a short man with thick forearms and a shiny bald head, watched blankly as he approached the chicken-wired window. His expression suggested Wooten was a stranger, even though they had spoken cordially in the past. There was a puzzle book on the desk in front of him, something involving letters and boxes.

'I'm here to see my son.'

'You'll have to take a seat and wait 'til the sheriff gets here.'

380

'And when will that be?'

'When he's done doin' what he's doin'.'

Wooten looked into the open area of desks, cabinets and tacked-up posters behind the sergeant. There were several doors along the back wall. Two had the word HOLDING painted neatly across their heavy wood. Joel would be in one of those.

'Well, could you tell him to hurry it up, whatever he's doing?'

The sergeant stared at him for a moment.

'No,' he said finally.

'Excuse me?'

'No, I am not going to tell the sheriff to hurry it up.'

Wooten felt his temper rise. First the deputy pulling his club back at the house. And now this. He was tempted to ream the man out. Ask him if he knew who he was dealing with. But that was the thing. The man knew exactly who Wooten was. As if to reinforce his insolence, the sergeant pointed his chewed pencil nub at a bench beside a candy machine with an Out of Order notice taped across its money slot. The tape was yellow, like an old person's toenails.

'Take a seat, Mr Wooten.'

The anger left Wooten with unexpected suddenness, leaving him vaguely dizzy in the dusty air and harsh light. His stomach felt queasy, his mouth parched. He walked over to the fountain on the far side of the busted candy machine and took a long drink. The water was warm and bitter with minerals. He closed his eyes as the liquid settled into his stomach. When he opened them he noticed the sergeant staring at him through the wired glass. He looked distastefully from Wooten to the fountain, then returned his attention to whatever puzzle he was trying to solve.

Wooten lowered his big frame onto the bench's unadorned wood. This was all happening too quickly. He had to regroup. Get out ahead of this thing. Make sense of what was going on here. What the hell did Chones want with Joel that couldn't wait until morning? And why was his son dressed and wide awake so late, almost as if he expected that late-night knock on the door?

They found out, didn't they.

And then he understood. Of course. It was so obvious he couldn't believe he hadn't thought of it the moment he saw that hat on his porch. Joel had tried to see Susan. They'd attempted some sort of rendezvous and that insane Irma had sicced the police on him. Wooten relaxed. That was all it was. He wished the cops had explained back at the house. Saved everybody a lot of worry. Wooten was glad he hadn't got through to Austin. It would have been highly embarrassing to have hauled his friend all the way down here for some teenage foolishness, especially after last week's wake-up call. He stood and fished a dime from his pocket to phone Ardelia and set her mind at ease. But before he could start dialing Chones pushed through the front door, accompanied by a heavily muscled deputy. The sheriff looked weary and preoccupied as he approached the locked door leading to the inner station. Wooten hung up the unused phone and walked toward him, flashing a boys-will-be-boys smile, ready to authorize whatever fright the sheriff had in mind to make sure Joel stayed away from Susan Truax.

'Ralph . . .'

Chones turned. The moment Wooten saw his eyes he realized that he was dead wrong about what was going on. Whatever had happened was much worse than mere teenaged foolishness. There was no question of Chones offering his hand. The deputy moved forward, his neck muscles bunching and shimmering beneath pockmarked skin as he positioned himself between Wooten and the sheriff.

Chones pointed past the wired glass.

'Joel in there?'

'Yes. And I'd like to know why.'

'So you don't know what your son got up to tonight?'

'Sleeping, until a couple hours ago.'

'And you're sure about that?'

Wooten recalled Joel's moonlit bed, its covers as smooth as a parking lot covered by freshly fallen snow. He decided to take the initiative.

'Look, Ralph, if this is about Susan Truax, then I can assure you it won't happen again.'

Chones snorted. The big cop's neck continued to ripple.

'Damn right you can assure me that. Susan Truax was found dead in Lake Newton two hours ago.'

'Jesus Christ, Ralph. Susan drowned?'

Chones stared at him evenly.

'Maybe.'

'Hold on,' Wooten said. 'You think . . . was she killed?'

'Looks that way. The docs will have a look at her, but the story we're getting is it was no accident.'

'And you think Joel was there?'

'That's the way it's looking.'

'Let me see him,' Wooten said in his most businesslike voice. 'I'm sure we can straighten this out.'

'No-can-do, Earl. I got a call in to the SBI and the county attorney. Until they get here, we just all gotta hold back.'

Chones turned toward the door.

'Ralph.'

The sheriff stopped.

'You're not saying Joel hurt that girl.'

'I'm not saying anything, Mr Wooten. Not yet.'

'Because he wouldn't do something like that. Not in a million years.'

'Well, you're the first person I talked to tonight's said so.'

The sheriff and his deputy were buzzed through. Chones spoke to the duty sergeant for a moment, then walked to the closest of the two holding rooms, working a chin-level bolt to get in. Wooten tried to see inside but the door shut too quickly. The muscular deputy sat at one of the dozen desks and began to scroll paper into an ancient typewriter. The fluorescent light above him flickered for a few seconds before settling back into its monotonous brilliance. The desk sergeant returned to his puzzle.

Wooten stood in the middle of the scuffed tile floor, staring numbly at the holding room door. He could not comprehend what he'd just been told. Susan Truax was dead. That sweet, pretty girl. They found her in the lake. And they were saying Joel had something to do with it.

His son's words back at the house played through his mind. *They found out, didn't they.*

And then he heard a sharp cry coming from the holding room. Joel. His voice like Wooten had never heard it, and yet it was still his voice. The deputy and the sergeant both looked at the door, then turned to Wooten.

'What are they doing to my boy?' he asked loudly.

Neither answered. Wooten strode up to the buzzer door and grabbed the handle. It was locked.

'Sit down, Mr Wooten,' the sergeant said.

'I want to know what they're doing to Joel in there. Tell me now or I'll take this door apart.'

The sergeant tossed his pencil on the desk and stood. He stared at Wooten for a moment, then turned and walked slowly back to the holding room. He knocked softly. Chones answered after a few seconds. Wooten could see Joel this time. He sat at a table not much bigger than a school desk. His face was buried in his arms and his body shivered. Chones listened to the sergeant, then stepped wearily out of the room, making sure to work that bolt behind him. He looked at his shoes as he crossed the office. The deputy watched him pass, his crooked index fingers poised above the typewriter. Chones stopped a few feet from the glass.

'Nobody's hurting your son, Mr Wooten. I've just informed him that we'd like to question him about the death of Susan Truax. Only I can't get him to tell me if he wants a lawyer or not like the Supreme Court says I've got to.'

'You told him she was dead? Just like that?'

'Well, I'm not all that sure it was news to him.'

Wooten stared at Chones. The bastard had told Joel about Susan. Just like that.

'So?'

'What?' Wooten asked.

'Is your son going to want an attorney?'

'Damn straight he is, you acting like this.'

'Then I suggest you go ahead and arrange that. Unless you want me to call somebody on the state's dime.'

'I'll do it,' Wooten said coldly.

Chones walked away, heading not to the holding room this time but down the hallway leading to his office. Wooten realized that it was time to get Austin involved. He'd be able to sort this mess out. Find the fundamental mistake that was causing all this to happen. He went to the pay phone, fishing his dime from the change chute. A very awake Austin answered on the first ring.

'Austin, it's Earl.'

'Yes,' Swope said somberly.

'Look, you won't believe this, but they've got Joel—'

'Earl, I'm going to stop you right here.'

'Stop me?'

'Given the situation I think it's prudent that you and I have no further contact. Please don't call me again.'

And then he hung up. Without another word. Wooten held the phone to his ear until the line went dead, then replaced it on its hook. This was making no sense. Austin had just hung up on him. He'd asked the man for help and he'd put down the phone. First Chones comes out with this nonsense about Joel hurting Susan. And now his closest friend won't even talk to him.

Something shifted inside Wooten. An image of Joel standing in the corner of his darkened room flashed in his mind. With it came a faint echo of the fears he'd been having ever since he first laid eyes on Susan.

Maybe his son had done something.

No. That was impossible. Wooten took a deep breath. He had to calm down and start helping Joel. He needed a lawyer. Somebody entitled to get through that locked door. Somebody who could find out what Chones and Austin weren't telling him, so he could put an end to this nonsense once and for all.

Raymond McNutt. Of course. He knew these people. He'd know what to do. If Swope had some reason for not helping him then it would have to be McNutt. Trying to find anybody else would mean waiting until morning and then probably the better part of the next day. McNutt would know every inch of this building. There was a soggy-looking directory beneath the phone. Wooten dialed the number greedily, his big fingers clumsy in the small rotary holes. The lawyer answered on the seventh ring.

'Listen up,' he said when Wooten finished explaining the

situation. 'Sit tight. I'll be there within the hour. Nobody says anything until then. I'll call Chones right now and explain that I'm en route.'

He pronounced it 'in route.' Seconds after hanging up Wooten heard the duty sergeant's phone ring. The man put the call through with a sour twist of his lips.

Wooten phoned Ardelia, explaining what he knew. The words he spoke sounded like somebody else's sad story, the sort of thing you'd talk about with a wistful shake of your head, glad it wasn't you.

'Poor girl,' Ardelia said after he'd finished.

'I know.'

'But it's ridiculous. Joel was in his room all night.'

'I don't think he was, Ardelia.'

Another pause.

'What do you mean?'

'He was wide awake and fully dressed when I went up there. His bed hadn't been slept in at all. He said something, too. He asked me if they found out.'

'Who? What?'

'I don't know.'

'But wouldn't we have known if he left?'

Wooten remembered those faint noises he'd heard when he was in the guest room.

'Not if he didn't want us to.'

There was a long silence. Wooten had hoped his wife would say the words that would make sense of this thing and his growing suspicion go away. But now she seemed just as overwhelmed as him.

'Did our son do something, Ardelia?'

She didn't hesitate now.

'Don't even think that, Earl Wooten. If you think that even for a single moment I want you to come back here and let me handle this. They see doubt in you, and our boy is in big trouble.'

Wooten said nothing.

'Well?' she asked.

'No,' he said, though his voice sounded unconvincing to him. 'I don't believe it.'

'Protect him.'

'I will.'

After that, Wooten paced. He drank so much fountain water that it felt like his stomach was lined with lead. People began to arrive. First came a familiar woman in a lime-green outfit. Jill Van Riper. She worked for the county attorney. Wooten knew her a little, having helped her on that Florida case. She had a bland, pale face, slim shoulders and legs as stout as rain barrels. She glanced at Wooten and then turned quickly away. The sergeant let her through the locked door and she disappeared down the hallway. Next came two men he could see were detectives straight away. Both were white. The first was about fifty, with a puffy, dough-colored face. He held a nicked briefcase. His younger colleague looked like he wanted to be a TV cop but wasn't quite there. He had a Fu Manchu mustache and a shiny leather coat. They didn't look at Wooten as they made their way back to the sheriff's office.

Finally, McNutt arrived. He was dressed in a three-piece wool suit, Florsheim shoes and a silk tie held in place by a gold pin. His ironed hair glistened with fresh pomade. That keloid scar on his neck seemed darker, as if it had been dusted with a masking cosmetic. Wooten felt a moment's confused anger – why had the man taken the time to gussy himself up when he knew Joel was in trouble? It was three o'clock in the damned morning. McNutt nodded soberly, taking Wooten's proffered hand between both of his. A strong odor of lavender cologne emanated from his humid flesh. Something triumphant lurked behind his sympathetic expression.

'Earl,' he said. 'How are you holding up?'

Wooten shook off the question.

'They got Joel in there and they won't let me see him.'

'Well, that's not unusual. All right – tell me what you know.'

Wooten recited the litany of baffling facts. McNutt listened without comment, his thick brow slowly furrowing as the tale went on.

'How old is your Joel again?' he asked finally.

Wooten hesitated. It wasn't the question he'd expected.

'He was eighteen in May.'

'Ah.'

'Why?'

'Well, that means they'll be treating him like an adult.'

'Joel's no adult,' Wooten said. 'He's a good boy, but he's no man.'

'I understand. One more question. The deceased – she's white?'

The question scared Wooten as much as anything he'd heard all night. For a brief, crazy moment, he almost denied it.

'Well, yes.'

'I figured as much.'

'Why?'

'Chones wouldn't be out of bed at this hour if she was colored. All right. Let me have a word with the sheriff and then I'll talk to Joel. Get his side of things. You just sit tight. I'll be back soon as I can.'

Wooten watched as McNutt approached the desk sergeant. In the amount of time it took him to cross the small lobby his demeanor changed utterly. The sober complicity he'd shown Wooten gave way to a hale, almost jovial attitude. His voice grew louder; his right hand gesticulated as he explained that he represented Joel Wooten. The cop listened wearily before buzzing him through. As McNutt pushed through the door the sergeant watched him for a moment, then turned back to Wooten. His neck and shoulders contracted in a scoff. He returned to his puzzle.

McNutt disappeared down the hall, emerging a few moments later with the sheriff. The lawyer was talking, that shit-eating smile still frozen on his lips. Chones listened distractedly, his eyes on the floor. When the lawyer was done Chones shrugged with surpassing indifference, said a few words and opened the door. McNutt entered the holding room. The door closed before Wooten could catch another glimpse of his son.

He called Ardelia to tell her that a lawyer was with their boy. Things were happening now. The confusion was about to clear. She said that she wanted to come down but hadn't been able to find anyone to look after the twins. Wooten told her not to bother. He'd get this sorted out before long. If they weren't home for breakfast, they'd certainly be back for lunch. It was just a matter of time.

McNutt emerged a half hour later. He held up a finger to Wooten, then strolled back down to Chones's office. After a few minutes he came back through the locked door.

'Well, I've spoken to your son. As far as I can tell he's maintaining his innocence.'

'Innocence of what?'

'The charges.'

'What charges, exactly?'

'I thought they . . . Earl, they say Joel murdered that girl.'

Murdered. Everything left his head except that word. His vision tunneled into a long corridor with bloodred walls. At the end of that corridor was a swatch of dirty tile and nothing else.

'No.'

McNutt said nothing. Wooten cast about for something to grab on to to stop his mind from this free fall. But all he had were the words the lawyer had just spoken. He replayed them, searching for something that would make this thing end.

'What do you mean, as far as you can tell?' he asked after a moment.

'Joel's in an extremely agitated state just now. It was hard to get any sense out of him.'

'What did he say?' Wooten asked.

McNutt sighed.

'From what I can gather he'd arranged to meet the young lady at the lake. According to Joel, when he got there she was nowhere to be seen. He waited a bit, then returned home.'

'Well, there you go. He didn't do it.'

'I don't know, Earl. I think they have something they're not telling us.'

'What?'

McNutt spread his hands.

'Let me ask you this – is it correct that you had forbidden Joel from seeing Miss Truax?'

Wooten hesitated, once again tempted to deny the undeniable.

'Yes, that's right.'

'Why?'

'It was getting too serious.'

'So this was just a general feeling you had?'

'What are you asking?'

'Joel mentioned words to the effect of "ever since we got caught." '

Wooten hesitated.

'Look, Earl, if I'm to defend your son . . .'

Wooten took a deep breath.

'Her folks found them together. In the girl's room.'

'Together?'

Wooten nodded.

'Conjugating.'

'Yes.'

The two men stared at each other, joined by a knowledge that went far beyond the petty social divisions that had kept them apart these past five years.

'This looks bad, don't it,' Wooten said quietly.

'Prima facey, it don't look good.'

'Jesus. Give me something here, Raymond.'

McNutt shrugged.

'Like I said, I had a hard time getting your son to elaborate his account.'

'Which tells me it's the truth.'

McNutt grimaced and tilted his head.

'Others might not see it that way.'

'Let me see him,' Wooten commanded.

'Can't do that yet. Not until the state police have their turn.'

'When is that?'

'They want to do it now. Though I think it might be a good idea to wait.'

'No. Let them do it now. I want to get this whole mess over with. I want them to see he's innocent and let him go.'

'He's very agitated, Earl. It might be wiser to give him a while to simmer down.'

390

'You think he's going to get any less agitated sitting in some jail cell?'

'I just don't want him to say anything that makes all this worse.'

'There's nothing he can say if he didn't do it.'

McNutt sighed his unhappy assent.

'All right.'

'Go get them.'

McNutt nodded back through the wired glass.

'Oh, I don't have to get anybody, Earl.'

Wooten looked. The detectives, Van Riper and Chones were milling about the door to the holding room. The younger detective was staring at Wooten with pitiless, calculating eyes. Wooten started to return his gaze but realized there was nothing to be gained by such a showdown.

'Can I be in there?' he asked.

'I'm afraid not. Don't worry, though. I'll be right with him the whole time.'

Wooten wished the lawyer's words afforded him more comfort.

Dawn began to break while they talked to Joel. A woman arrived to take the place of the duty sergeant. She carried a tray of freshly baked cinnamon rolls. None were offered to Wooten. He sat on the bench, the same few thoughts roaming through his mind, like vehicles looking for spaces in a completely full lot. Joel had left the house without telling them. He was under arrest. They said he'd murdered pretty little Susan Truax.

They found out, didn't they.

McNutt finally emerged, looking grim. He told Wooten that Joel was being charged with the second-degree murder of Susan Truax.

'But I still don't understand what the cops are saying happened.'

'That Joel found Susan stepping out with another boy and attacked them.'

'What other boy?'

'Teddy Swope.'

391

The words left Wooten dumbfounded for several seconds.
'Teddy Swope?'
'That's right.'
'Was *he* hurt?'
'I don't think so. But he was assaulted.'
'Teddy?' Wooten repeated incredulously. 'Teddy and Joel are best friends.'
McNutt chucked his chin back toward the holding room.
'According to them there'd been trouble between the two of them about the girl recently.'
Wooten remembered Joel's return home last week with a bloody nose, his cryptic remarks about a fight with Teddy. He never had been able to figure out what it was all about, what with Chicago and then getting thrown out of the house.
'Yeah, they did have some sort of trouble last week.'
McNutt's expression somehow managed to get even more grave.
'Do you know what this altercation was about? Was it about Miss Truax?'
Wooten shook his head. Swope's behavior on the phone suddenly made sense. Teddy was the one saying Joel had hurt Susan.
'What did Joel say to all this?' Wooten asked.
'Some story about how Teddy was the one who'd arranged for him to be with Susan down there at the lake. It was sort of, well, hard to follow. I gotta tell you, I don't think it cut much ice with our friends in the State Bureau of Investigation.'
Wooten was silent for a while. This was starting to look very, very bad.
'So what do you think?' he asked, his voice sounded as desperate as he felt. 'Did my boy do something here?'
McNutt sighed.
'My client maintains his innocence so of course that's my position.'
'Cut the shit, Ray.'
McNutt stared evenly at Wooten.
'They have motive,' he said. 'They have opportunity. They have an eyewitness who happens to be the son of the most

important man in this county. We have a whole lot of I-don't-knows, a cock-and-bull story about some bizarre assignation and a dead white girl. You better hope I don't cut the shit, Earl. 'Cause it's gonna stink pretty damned bad.'

'Can I see him now?'

'After he's arraigned.'

'When will that be?'

'This afternoon at the earliest.'

'Can we get bail then?'

'I'll certainly try. It might be a bit steep but Spivey should go for it.'

'It doesn't matter how much it is. I just want him home.'

'All right. Look, I better get back in there. Let Joel know how the next few hours are going to play out.'

Wooten watched McNutt vanish back into that locked room, then collapsed onto the bench, searching for the one small thing that would stop the doubt hammering ever louder in his mind. Just a tiny, unnoticed fact he could build upon. A hard, immutable truth to which he could pin his son's innocence. But there was nothing like that. Everything pointed the other way. The fight with Teddy. Sneaking out of the house. Joel's own words.

And then a terrifying thought began to sound in Wooten's mind. Maybe there was no absolving fact, no alternative story to the one being told. Maybe Joel had done it. Wooten wasn't sure how and he wasn't even sure why. But suddenly, the idea that his son had hurt that girl started to look undeniable. The bad medicine had finally taken hold. He'd done it.

No, he told himself. It's too early to think these things. Let the sun shine on this whole mess for a few hours. See how it looks in the light of day.

It's too early to think it.

They brought Joel out a few minutes later, walking him toward that corridor. Going, Wooten knew, to the cells. He looked tired and confused. His shirt had come untucked at the back, his unlaced sneakers flapped awkwardly on the tile. Wooten raised his hands to attract his son's attention, but the boy disappeared without looking.

*　　*　　*

393

After that there was nothing left to do in Cannon City. There would be no visits, no intercessions. Not until the hearing that afternoon. McNutt left after explaining that he would meet with Joel later in the morning to prepare a plea. As of now he presumed it would be not guilty. Wooten nodded dully. And then the lawyer was gone, leaving behind a small cloud of lavender.

Wooten followed a few seconds later. He was surprised to discover upon coming through the station's heavy doors that it was a beautiful day. Birds, sun, fragrant air. People had begun to move through the square. Cars were now slotted into the slant spaces. As Wooten headed toward his Ranchero some men emerged from one of them, a dimpled Fury. They headed straight toward him. One was small and wore a corduroy suit. The other was tall and hairy and carried a camera.

'Mr Wooten?'

He kept walking toward his car.

'We're with the *Baltimore Sun*. Got a minute?'

The man in the corduroy suit was next to him now. The hairy man had moved in front walking backward as he took pictures. Wooten scowled at him but this only seemed to increase the shutter's clicking.

'Did your son kill Susan Truax, Mr Wooten?'

Just get to the car, he thought.

'Is it true they were lovers?'

Wooten looked at the man. Lovers. As if they were anything other than kids. He turned back toward the Ranchero, lowering his shoulder in the direction of the photographer. If the man got hit that would be his own damned fault. But he danced out of the way with surprising agility. Wooten dropped into the driver's seat. The camera was right against the window, its lens clicking against the glass like a trapped cricket. The reporter was still speaking. Just go, Wooten thought. He turned the engine over. There was a beastly growl that ended in a harsh choke. Don't do this to me now. He tried again. Once again, a growl, followed by silence.

Wooten looked around. Other people had begun to gather.

394

Citizens, on their way to work. They stood on the sidewalk, staring at him. A few whispered. They knew. There were other reporters as well, rushing toward him out of haphazardly parked cars. More cameras were wielded. Flashes began to strobe his tired eyes. Voices penetrated the sealed windows.

'How will your son plead?'

'Did he kill her?'

'Were they lovers?'

He gave the key a final, desperate twist. The engine turned over. Finally, some mercy. He checked the rearview mirror. People blocked the way. Wooten put the car in reverse and started to back out. But they wouldn't budge. It was as if they were deliberately trapping him. On the square in front of him there were some squirrels, some breakfasting birds. But no people. He dropped the car into drive and hit the gas pedal. It bumped hard over the curb and barely missed a parking meter. After that it was smooth going. Wooten could feel the tires bite into the damp ground. Divots filled his rearview mirror as he slalomed through the cannon and the trees. By the time he reached the far side of the square he was doing well over whatever the damned speed limit was out here.

31

He was in the basement when the screaming began. Steady, three-second howls, each of them followed by long intervals of echoing silence. The sound startled him when he first heard it. She wasn't supposed to be awake. She'd had enough of her pills and her booze to sleep until at least the afternoon. But her voice was clear and sharp, pouring beneath the doors and through the ducts like a gale. She was still on Susan's bed. He could tell by the way the sound moved down to him. She'd been lying there since seven, when they finally returned from the hospital in Cannon City, a flat brick building where they took Susan. Before that, she lay for what seemed like hours on the slanting redwood pier, covered by a blanket with the words CANNON COUNTY VFD dyed into its gray fabric. They had stood a few feet away, watching the water stain grow and then stop growing. Nothing happened until Swope returned from his conference with the sheriff in the parking lot. He was nodding grimly.

'They're arresting Joel Wooten,' he said.

Irma's eyes remained on the blanket.

'Teddy and Susan were down here and he attacked them,' Swope continued. 'Teddy tried to save her but it was . . . not feasible.'

When he heard this, Truax remembered Joel sneaking back into the house just a few hours earlier, the confused and worried look on his face, the way he'd crept up the steps. If he'd seen the boy sneaking out he would have followed him. But he'd dropped his guard. And now there was this.

Irma finally understood Swope's words.

'Joel? He did this?'

'The police are picking him up as we speak.'

She looked back at Susan's body.

'What if they can't find him?' she asked, her voice suddenly piercing.

Both men looked at her.

'What if he's gone? What if they're hiding him?' She was growing hysterical. 'They do that, you know. Hide them. They have places the police do not know about. Basements and hovels. What if this happens?'

Swope put his hand on her arm.

'There aren't places like that in Newton,' he said with a finality that silenced her. 'They'll find him.'

Moments later a van arrived from the coroner's office, driving along the dock and through the chain-link fence. It stopped at the mouth of the damaged pier. Two men emerged from it. One was fat, with red hair and a mincing walk. The other was a short, wiry black man who wouldn't meet anybody's eye. They peered beneath the blanket and wrote on clipboards. Muttering. Pointing things out. Knowing that everybody was watching them. After five minutes of this Chones spoke with them. Swope joined the conversation for a while, then returned to the Truaxes, explaining that the men would be taking their daughter to Cannon City.

'I want to go with her,' Irma said.

Her eyes were fixed on the two men as they loaded the body onto a retractable stretcher. The brakes on it were broken – they had to keep chocking it with their shoes so it wouldn't roll into the lake.

'Of course,' Swope turned to Truax. 'Are you all right or do you want me to arrange a ride?'

'No,' Truax answered, the first words he'd spoken since his arrival. 'I'm all right.'

They followed in the Cutlass. It was not quite dawn. For a short while a newspaper delivery truck got between them and the van. Irma started to whimper and so Truax sped up to pass it. He had no words for his wife. She wouldn't have heard him anyway. She was in the van with the girl.

There was nothing for them to do in Cannon City. The

people at the hospital were kind, offering them things. The autopsy wouldn't be until later in the morning, though the doctor who admitted the body said that it would be cursory. His initial examination suggested that Susan had drowned after being knocked unconscious. Which was why she sank. She'd breathed spasmodically and water filled her lungs. He used to work in Ocean City. He knew about these things.

Spasmodically, Truax thought.

They let them see her. She was on a stainless-steel gurney, a different blanket draped over her thin body. There were runnels. They were dry. Susan didn't look different yet. Death hadn't settled on her. Truax had seen so many like this, young faces still astonished to have lost a life that had seconds earlier been as easily held as a can of soda. The doctor assured Irma that they'd do everything they could to make sure she rested with dignity. The Truaxes sat on a bench for a while after that. Dawn broke. Robed sick people began to emerge from rooms around them, some pushing wheeled stands that held bags of liquid. A woman in a white uniform brought coffee that neither of them touched.

'We should go,' Truax said finally.

At home he woke Darryl and told her. She had slept, forgotten, through the night. Irma let him be the one to do it. She took her pills with three glasses of bourbon that might just as well have been tap water, then collapsed on Susan's bed. Truax could see her stockinged feet as he leaned over Darryl to shake her shoulder. She opened her eyes and stared up at him.

'What is it?'

He told her that Susan was gone, that she'd drowned in the lake. Darryl sat up and gathered a pillow to her stomach.

'So she's dead?'

'Yes.'

'Well, we have to pray.'

Truax looked at his daughter's coarse features for a moment, then peered across the hall at his wife's feet. The way her toes filled the ends of her nylons reminded him of the condom he'd seen on Joel Wooten. He stood.

'Dad?'

'You pray,' he said.

He went downstairs, a feeling of unfulfilled duty welling up from deep within him. There was no need to make funeral arrangements. Swope had said at the pier that he would handle all of that. But there were still people to call. Relatives. Friends at Meade.

And then he remembered he had to report in to Swope. He didn't know what the next move was. How this changed things. He dialed his home number. Sally answered on the second ring.

'John, we're so sorry.'

He nodded his head, not knowing what to say.

'John?'

'I need to speak with Mr Swope.'

'He's in the shower. I'll have him call you when he gets out.'

'All right.'

He hung up. The phone rang immediately. It was someone from the *Cannon County Courier*. Truax hung up before the man could finish asking his question. There were two more calls after that. The *Sun* and the *News American*. He hung up on them as well, then took the phone off the hook.

He'd call Swope later.

He sat at the kitchen table for a long time. There was a recorded voice on the phone and then some sort of beeper went off. After a while it stopped. He could hear Darryl dressing. She wept and then she sang. When she was done she went into Susan's room and said some things. Irma didn't reply. Darryl came down. She stood in the kitchen doorway, staring at Truax. He could hear her labored breath as it whistled through her braces.

'Why is the phone off the hook?'

'Because I don't want them to call.'

'Your hand smells bad, Daddy. You should change your dressing.'

'Yes. All right.'

She said something about Reverend Abernathy and the Interfaith Center. Truax let her go without a word. He went upstairs to check on his wife. She was still on the bed, her eyes closed, her breathing deep and even. Above her, Truax noticed that the glow-in-the-dark stars Susan had stuck to the ceiling had begun to come loose, their triangular edges dangling limply.

He went down to the basement, turning on the bulb above his workbench. His Sears Craftsman tools gleamed in the 80-watt glow. Irma and the girls had given him the complete set for his birthday last year, the idea being that once his hand was better he would start using them. But his hand wasn't better. It would never be better. The infection was crossing the lifeline. There was no denying it now. He'd peered beneath the dressing back at the hospital. So the tools would remain where they were, arranged on the Peg-Board according to size. Having built nothing. Having fixed nothing.

The key was hidden in a small drawer of twopenny nails. He had to dump them out and rummage before he found it. The cobweb-shrouded lockbox was slotted behind one of the bench's broad legs. He placed it on the work surface and opened the heavy lid. Oil had leaked into the wrapping. He laid the weapon on the bench, unfolding the cloth gingerly, like Christmas paper you might want to use again. He picked up the .45 with his left hand, feeling its weight. It was strange – he'd never wielded it with his left hand before. It was like nothing he'd ever held.

He put the weapon back on the bench and took the rest of the gear from the lockbox. The extra magazine, the spare rounds, the cleaning oils, the felt ball and brass brush. He laid them all out neatly, then sprang the magazine and thumbed out the rounds. He stacked these into a neat line and began to clean the weapon. He took his time, swabbing out the barrel twice. It was awkward, working with just one good hand.

Wooten had friends in Cannon City. The sheriff and the lawyers and the judges. Fellow thieves. People who couldn't be trusted. It was why Truax had been needed in the first place. And it was why he was needed now. To make sure that Wooten did not use his power to free his son. There was a law above the law and that was what Truax must now be. To make sure the boy was punished.

Irma began to scream just as he finished cleaning. He reloaded the first magazine and slotted it in, then held the weapon aloft, taking aim at various targets in the basement. The pressure meter on the hot water tank. A pair of goggles dangling from an old pair of skis. A chip on a cinder block. The box of left-handed gloves. He held a steady bead on each target for thirty seconds before squeezing the trigger. Not quite hard enough to fire. Seeking command and control. It was difficult. In the past, he had always used two hands. One on the trigger, the other cupping the magazine.

He placed the .45 back on the bench, then took his earplugs from the lockbox. They were regulation. Firing range specified. He buried them deep in each ear, drowning out his wife's ongoing screams. He retrieved his weapon, released the safety and chose a target – the VOC filtering unit on the opposite wall. It was the size and shape of a beer keg. White. There were three flanged holes at the top for the accordion tubes running up into the house. Trapdoors for the pleated filters cleansing the house of unwanted molds and free radicals were spaced evenly along the unit's housing. Truax drew a bead on a screw head just above the middle door. Command and control. He released his breath and squeezed the trigger. The gun kicked unexpectedly hard, causing him to fumble and almost drop it. The shot had pulled a few inches to the right but the level was good. The hole was jagged, as big as his fist. Dust wafted from it. Noxious particles. Freed radicals. He put the safety back on and slipped the weapon into his belt.

Irma had stopped screaming by the time he removed the earplugs. It reminded him of the way a single shot could silence an entire jungle. He loaded the second magazine, which he put into his pants pocket. Then he put everything else back in the box. He didn't bother to lock or hide it. There was no reason. There was a holster somewhere, in one of the trunks he'd brought home. He decided to leave it stowed. The weapon was enough.

He pulled the string next to the naked bulb and went upstairs. Irma was still on Susan's bed. The animals he'd brought his daughter surrounded her, strewn in lifeless array.

His wife looked at him and then looked at the weapon in his belt. She closed her eyes.

'I'm going to be out now,' he said. 'I have to work.'

She nodded. He turned to go.

'John?'

He stopped in the doorway.

'He's not going to get away with this, is he?'

He stood in silence for a moment.

'No. He's not.'

Part Seven

32

Swope stared at himself in the mirror's buttery light. Though his skin was a few shades too sallow and networks of pale veins cracked the whites of his eyes, he still appeared rested and in control. Anyone meeting him now would never guess that his mind had spent the last twelve hours churning at full throttle; never suspect that his guts were twisted into a constipated, percolating knot from the pressure of the worst night of his life. He dispensed some hot foam from the machine Sally had given him last Christmas. It felt good as he applied it to his stubbled cheeks, the molten warmth making him long momentarily for the comfort of his king-sized bed. But it was too early to rest. This thing still wasn't in the bag. He applied some cold steel to his face as an antidote to his momentary stupor, scraping a highway of flesh from his Adam's apple to his lower lip.

Teddy was going to be all right.

It was a new blade, opening a constellation of minute wounds that would begin healing before he'd even finished. He scraped off another line. He'd never stopped loving wet shaving. A lot of guys had given it up recently for Norelcos. The technology was getting so good that you could hardly tell the difference, especially with lightly bearded men like him. But Swope stuck with the old way. And not just for the ritual. He liked the cuts, the minute fissures that would hum with pain when he slapped on the English Leather. He wouldn't give that sensation up for all the electrics in Japan.

Teddy was going to be all right.

He pulled the remainder of the foam from his face. Row

after row, like mowing a lawn. There was something lulling in the motion. Exhaustion began to creep back into his mind. He shook it off, knowing that fatigue would open him up to sentimentality and self-doubt, making him question and then regret what he was doing. But those were feelings he could not afford. He couldn't afford to wonder if he'd pushed this all too far, couldn't let himself feel pity for Joel and his father. Because the price of indulging such emotions would be his son. And he was not willing to pay that. Not to a man who betrayed him.

He finished shaving and wiped away the residual cream, then took the English Leather from its sinkside perch and slapped it on his cheeks, neck and chin. Satisfying jolts radiated from his brain stem stright down to his nads.

Teddy was going to be all right. The news couldn't be better. It had been an amazing comeback – better than the Heidi Bowl. In just a few hours he'd managed to turn the whole mess around. Not only saving his son, but rescuing his own future as well. Joel had been charged. In a few hours he'd be arraigned. And it wasn't just Chones who was pointing the finger – the county attorney's office and the SBI were involved as well. Luckily, Byron Bench, the county attorney, was on vacation in Bermuda, leaving his young assistant, Jill Van Riper, in charge. Though Bench was a wily old country lawyer who was capable of standing up to Swope in the crunch, Van Riper was a humorless, none-too-bright drone with a University of Maryland law degree and the worst legs he'd ever seen. Swope always half suspected she had a crush on him. She'd be easily handled. Not that it mattered. Donald Duck could have prosecuted this one. The evidence was so strong as to constitute an open-and-shut case. Swope had learned in his 5 A.M. conversation with Van Riper that the deputies had arrived at the Wooten house in the still of the night to find Joel wide awake, fully dressed and clearly agitated. Better yet, he initially tried to deny having been out that evening, a position clearly contradicted by the Newton Plaza security guard who'd spotted him soon after Susan went into the drink.

They had their boy. And he wasn't Teddy.

After he finished shaving, Swope spent a few minutes massaging his gums with the rubberized prod at the base of his toothbrush. He then went back into the bedroom and put on the fresh suit Sally had laid out for him, a navy blue Brooks Brothers number with broad lapels and French cuffs. It was nearly one – the SBI men would be arriving soon to interview Teddy. Chones had called him at the office earlier to say that the detectives had a few small points to clear up with their star witness. Nothing major. They just wanted to dot their *i*'s and cross their *t*'s so they could get the hell out of Dodge. Nobody wanted to spend more time than they had to on a good-as-gold case. Chones wondered if Teddy might come down to Cannon City for the talk. Swope had politely told him that was out of the question. His son was still suffering from the trauma of last night's events. He wasn't going anywhere. If anybody wanted to talk to him they could come by the house and conduct their interview in Swope's presence.

That conversation had only been a small part of what had been a busy morning for Swope. He'd stayed at the lake until the girl's body had been carted off, then taken Teddy home, where he put him in his room and told him to stay put. A quick change of shirt and he was back at Newton Plaza to work the problem. He'd never been sharper than he was during that long morning. He was Don Shula, Gene Kranz and George Allen rolled into one. First, he placed a series of anonymous phone calls to area newspapers, many of them publications which had recently hitched on to the Wooten bandwagon, to let them know that the builder's son was in the Cannon City jail under suspicion of murdering a white girl. Sleepy editors had snapped to at that one. Then he woke Gus Savage at his Lake Shore Drive apartment. Their conversation had been short and sweet.

'Have you spoken with Earl?' Savage asked when Swope was through explaining the situation.

'He tried to call. I told him I didn't think it would be appropriate for us to have contact.'

'Should I talk to him?' Savage asked.

'Your call, Gus.'

'Maybe I'll just see how it pans out.'

'What I'd do.'

'Jesus. This is a real kick in the ass. So what do you think, Austin?'

'What do I think? I think the poor dumb kid's guilty as hell.'

'All right.' There was a short pause. 'Austin, listen to me. I want you to manage this. Limit the damage here. If it means distancing ourselves from Wooten, then so be it.'

'I'm on it, Gus.'

'Whatever it takes – I don't want the company's investment compromised.'

'Understood.'

After that he tracked down Van Riper. They spoke off the record, the prosecutor explaining that, after a phone call to Bench, she was leaning toward charging Joel with manslaughter. After all, it would be tough proving he'd intended to hurt the girl, much less kill her. Swope agreed. Nobody wanted to see Joel Wooten overly punished. Though he did have one idea. Wouldn't it be better to start out with murder two, then dangle a manslaughter plea in front of his parents? Make it seem like a way out of their bind. Let them know that Joel would get five years, max, with no more than eighteen months actually in the pokey. Provided, of course, the Wootens accepted the deal within, say, twenty-four hours, so there would be no time to bring in a real lawyer instead of the earnest-but-lightweight Raymond McNutt. They could easily get Spivey to withhold bail for the time being, just to keep the screws tight. Swope knew from experience that people were far more inclined to accept deals when the clock was ticking. When Van Riper hesitated, he mentioned that if she went to trial Wooten might be able to muster all sorts of black cronies to come to Cannon City, radical lawyers and protesters and civil rights leaders. The whole thing could turn into a circus. Van Riper saw the light after that, agreeing to run it by her boss.

A deep swell of relief had washed over him as he hung up the phone from that call. Getting the authorities to work for a guilty plea meant Teddy wouldn't have to take the stand.

Though the kid had been a rock so far, there was only so much pressure his young shoulders could bear. Besides, Swope knew that if it was handled right, then Wooten would bite. He was a realist. A man used to playing the hand dealt him. He'd know that it was time to cut his losses. Swope was sure of it.

The rest of the morning was spent tying off loose ends. After a few more calls to the papers, he summoned Holmes to his office and ordered him to draft a letter placing Earl Wooten on indefinite leave. And he wanted Holmes to deliver it himself by the close of business to allay suspicion that Swope was behind any of this. After he was gone Swope placed a call to Spivey, claiming that he'd just heard a rumor from somebody in Earl Wooten's office that he had been looking into one-way tickets to Liberia that morning. Spivey said nothing, though Swope could tell by the silence that he'd taken the bait. There'd definitely be no bail now. After one more call to Chones to make sure there were no more surprises coming down the pike, it was time to go home for a much-needed shower.

Sally was in the kitchen, cooking her homemade lentil soup. Teddy's favorite. Steam from the pan wafted through her stiff and flawless hair. She'd been shooting Swope somber looks ever since he got in, acting as if she sensed she wasn't being told the whole story.

'John Truax called while you were in the shower.'

Swope froze. Truax. In the morning's rush he'd forgotten all about him. He snatched the phone from the wall. As he dialed he was visited by an unwelcome image of the man's daughter breaking the lake's surface, though he used his mental discipline to push it gently back into the murk. The line was busy. Not surprisingly. He'd try again later. Or maybe swing by his house to offer condolences, help with arrangements and, most urgent, make sure Truax understood that he had to back off Wooten. Their mission was accomplished. The campaign was over.

'Teddy up?' Swope asked as he replaced the receiver.

'I don't think so.'

'I'll wake him.'

'Shouldn't he sleep?'

'The police want to talk to him.'

Sally turned from the stove with an alarmed expression.

'Don't sweat it, Sal. I'll be there.'

Their eyes held for a moment.

'What's going on here, Austin?' she asked, her voice almost a whisper.

For a moment he was tempted to tell her. Let her know what he was doing so she could say it was all right. Let her assure him that he was only being strong for his son. But then she would know. And he didn't want that. He wanted her safe. Just as he wanted Teddy to be safe.

'I don't understand what you mean,' he said evenly.

'I mean have you told me everything about what happened last night?'

'Of course I have.' He took a step toward her. 'Sal, what is it?'

Her eyes traveled back toward the swirling steam.

'I don't know. It just seems so out of character for Joel to have done something like this. And Teddy's acting so strange . . .'

'Well, obviously we never knew the whole story about Joel. And as for Teddy, that was an awful thing he went through.'

'I know that, Austin. That's not what I'm talking about.'

'Then what is it?'

'When I talked to him about it after you got home he just seemed so . . . reluctant. So unsure of everything. Almost like he was holding something back.'

Swope's mind raced. This would not do. He couldn't have her doubting the story. It would jeopardize everything.

'Sally, look at me.'

She did as he asked. He could see in her expression that she wanted to believe.

'The reason Teddy's being hesitant is because he doesn't want to tell the truth. He wants to protect Joel. You know how he feels about him. If he's acting strange, *that's* the reason. He feels guilty about being the one who witnessed this horrible crime. We start second-guessing him now and he just might start telling lies to shield his friend. And if that happens the cops are going to come down on him and there will be nothing I can do to help. Do you understand me?'

She mouthed a yes. He could see in her eyes that she still wasn't sure. But he could also see that there was no way she was going to press him any further. Not when Teddy's well-being was at stake.

'You have to trust me, Sally,' he continued. 'I'm going to make sure that everybody comes out of this terrible situation as well as they can. Including Joel. All right?'

She managed a weak smile.

'Now, let me go get him and we can all sit down to a nice meal together,' Swope said.

Swope knocked on Teddy's door. There was no answer. He pushed it open to find his son propped up in bed. Large black headphones covered his ears, music seeping from them like the noise of insects in a deep jungle. Though his eyes were firmly shut he was clearly awake. His long hair was plastered to his cheeks and neck. He'd changed clothes, though the new ones looked just as wrinkled and tattered as last night's drenched outfit. His gray T-shirt had the words PROPERTY OF ALCATRAZ stenciled across its chest.

Swope sat on the edge of the bed. Teddy's eyes fell open. They were listless and rheumy. He pulled off the headphones and dropped them on the floor, waiting to hear what his dad had to say. The bug music continued.

'How you doin', sport?' Swope asked.

Teddy stared at him, his eyes so bereft that Swope feared it was all over, right then and there. His son would no longer be able to stay the course. But then he shrugged and Swope knew that they were still in business. Pride ballooned within him. The boy had really showed him something last night. He'd learned a lesson they'd never teach him at Harvard Law – and learned it well.

'All right, I guess,' Teddy said.

411

'You're not losing heart on me here?'

'Losing heart? No.'

'You've got to talk to one more batch of cops today. You up for it?'

'You'll be there, right?'

'Absolutely. Just tell them what we told Chones last night and everything will be okay. Anything else comes up, I'll handle it.'

Teddy shrugged again. Swope stood and headed toward the door, turning back toward his son just before leaving the room.

'Oh, and Teddy? You might want to think about a different shirt.'

They ate in silence. Teddy, now wearing a respectable mauve Izod, barely touched his soup, much to Sally's chagrin. Every once in a while he'd smile to himself and mouth silent words. Swope watched him closely, wondering if he should call off the interview. But he knew that the sooner this thing was over, the better.

The doorbell rang just as Sally began to collect the plates.

'Ready?' Swope asked.

'Koo-koo-kachoo,' his son answered.

He deposited Teddy in his office, then greeted the cops at the front door. There were two of them. The older one carried a briefcase. His name was Roebling. The younger man was DeLisi. He had a Fu Manchu mustache, a shiny leather coat and what he thought must be a tough demeanor. We'll see about that, Swope thought as he led them to his office. The cops paused at the door.

'We were kind of hoping to talk to him alone,' Roebling explained.

'Why's that?' Swope asked, his voice stern but calm.

'No real reason,' the older cop continued. 'Just habit.'

'He's still pretty shaken up, guys,' Swope said. 'Any problem if I stay?'

Roebling shrugged.

'Why not,' he said.

Teddy sat slumped in one of the chairs facing the desk. He

didn't rise when he saw the two men. Swope handled the introductions; he arranged the furniture. DeLisi pulled a notepad from one of his side pockets.

'So why don't you tell us about last night?'

Teddy told his story. When he finished DeLisi wrote for a moment, catching up. He looked up when he realized everyone was staring at him.

'So, Teddy, one question – that your kick-ass Firebird out there?'

'That's right.'

'Bet it can book.'

Teddy shrugged.

'Sure.'

'And you were driving it last night, am I right?'

Swope's radar clicked on. This didn't sound good. His eyes flittered between his son and the young cop. Teddy nodded slowly, also sensing that something was amiss.

'Here's the thing,' DeLisi continued. 'According to the security guard, Joel was on foot. My question is, how was he able to follow you and Susan from her house all the way to the lake? I mean, the guy would have to be Bob Hayes on dexies to keep up with wheels like yours.'

Swope felt his heart begin to pound. Chilled sweat beaded on his just-scrubbed skin. Why the hell hadn't he thought of this? Joel following Teddy was a major point. A first principle. He should have seen it a mile away. This was just the sort of inconsistency that allowed a cop the opportunity to shoot their whole lumbering dirigible right out of the summer sky. He looked at his son, who met DeLisi's stony gaze over his tinted glasses. Teddy's eyes were utterly unreadable. He could be about to say anything. Swope's chest felt like it had been pumped full of helium. He wondered if anybody else could hear his heart pounding.

Finally, Teddy spoke.

'Joel knew that's where we'd go,' he said, his voice as flat and cold as a frozen lake. 'He didn't have to follow us.'

'Why's that?'

'Because that's where we partied, ever since the teen center closed. Joel and Susan and I always went there. It's the

413

only make-out place left in this freakin' town. You can ask anybody.'

DeLisi held Teddy's gaze for a moment, then flipped his pad shut and shrugged.

'Yeah,' he said. 'That's what I figured.'

'Anything else?' Swope asked quickly.

Roebling shrugged.

'Just putting Joel Wooten in Jessup.'

Swope got the cops out of there as soon as possible. When he returned to his office Teddy was still in his chair, one leg slung casually over its arm. Swope felt nothing but pride at the way he'd handled the unexpected question. The kid truly was a genius.

'Was that okay?'

'It was better than okay, Teddy.'

'Is that the sort of stuff I get to expect at the trial?'

'Don't worry. There won't be any trial. I've arranged it so Joel will have pled guilty by the weekend. Like I said last night, nobody wants this dragging on.'

Teddy nodded distantly. Something was clearly still bothering him.

'I've been thinking . . .'

He smiled, then frowned.

'Go ahead, Teddy.'

'Is there any way we can keep him from going to jail, you know, at all?'

Swope sucked in air.

'Not an option,' he said gently. 'But like I said last night, I'm working on a deal which will see him do as little time as possible.'

'How much?'

Swope snatched a number from the cool air.

'Three years as an absolute maximum. Almost certainly less.'

Teddy looked unhappy at this.

'Three years?'

'At the max. Probably closer to two. I'm sorry, Teddy, but given the circumstances, that's the best we can do.' Swope smiled tightly. 'Hey, kiddo, I thought we discussed this last night.'

414

'Yeah, I know. It's just the idea of him being in jail . . .'

'But that's the thing.' Swope decided a small, palliative fib was in order. 'He'll make bail today. And then he gets to stay at home until the judge decides what to do. It's really not that big of a deal.'

Teddy nodded distantly. Swope took a moment to examine his son. He could see in his twitching eyes and lips evidence of that big brain working overtime. He knew he'd better say something to put this to rest.

'Look, I know it's hard for you right now, thinking about Joel. You just have to keep focused on the important things. Your family and your future. Like I said last night, either you or Joel has to take responsibility for the problem he created through his reckless and selfish behavior, and, all things considered, it's better that it's him. I mean, I can help the guy a lot more than his father would ever be able to help *you*. Am I right, or am I right?'

Teddy stood.

'As always, you're right.'

Swope put a fatherly hand on his son's frail shoulder.

'You're tired and you just might be coming down with something. Go get some sleep. These things always look better on the other side of twelve hours of serious shut-eye. Believe me.'

After his son left Swope collapsed in his desk chair and cursed himself for not anticipating the Firebird question. Totally bush league. If Teddy weren't so damned smart then they'd both be taking a ride down to Cannon City with messieurs Roebling and DeLisi right about now. He'd have to do a better job staying sharp until Joel's plea had been entered. And Teddy was definitely remaining under wraps for the foreseeable future.

Swope leaned forward and set three balls of his Newton's cradle in motion, trying to think if there was anything else that needed to be taken care of. Just Truax. He reached for the phone and dialed the now familiar number.

Busy. It was time to pay the bereaved a visit.

* * *

Nobody answered the door. He rang, he knocked. Nothing. He was just about to leave when he saw movement through one of the glass panels. Irma, standing at the top of the stairs. She swayed slightly, her eyes focused on the empty air between them. Swope held up a hand to get her attention but she didn't seem to notice him. After a moment she disappeared back down the hallway.

Swope tried the handle. It was unlocked. He stepped into the house. It was cold – the air conditioner was on too high.

'John?'

There was no answer. He walked back to the kitchen, where the phone receiver dangled inches above the floor, like one of those lunatic jumpers from New Guinea you saw on *National Geographic* specials. He opened the basement door, thinking Truax might have fled down there. But it was dark. He was just about to shut the door when the smell wafted up to him. Gunpowder. There was a strange broken noise as well, the ruptured chug of some ruined machine. Swope felt his heart begin to pound as strongly as it had when the cops were questioning Teddy. An image of Truax with a gun in his mouth danced through his mind. He knew he had to go down. There might be some kind of note.

He hit the lights just inside the door and walked halfway down the steps. After a long, steeling pause, he took a deep breath and looked. There was an open toolbox on a large workbench; there were crates and bikes and toys. But no sergeant. Swope felt himself relax. Guys like Truax always seemed to snuff themselves at the workbench. If that was empty, then he was probably home clear. He walked down the remainder of the steps, quickly checking out the rest of the basement. No protruding shoes, no gathering puddles of dark blood. He discovered the source of that fractured sound – the VOC filter. Swope went to check it out. The gunpowder smell grew stronger as he passed the workbench. It didn't take him long to figure out what was wrong with the unit. Truax had shot it. Put an actual bullet into it. There was a small pile of dust on the floor. Other motes hovered. Swope looked around for some sort of switch but could see nothing.

He went back to the workbench, careful not to touch anything. The box he'd seen from the stairs turned out to be a gun case. There were bullets. Cleaning equipment. Some sort of rag. But no gun. Swope wondered if he should call Chones. He could simply say that he'd come over to condole and found this mess. But if they arrested Truax then he might talk about what he'd been doing the past week. All sorts of awkward questions could arise. Best to let the man be for now. He'd report in. He wouldn't do anything without Swope's approval. Besides, Joel was in prison. Nobody was going to hurt him there.

He went back upstairs, leaving everything the way he found it. He checked the garage – the Cutlass was gone. There was a glistening bruise of leaked oil on the swept concrete floor. Garden tools hung from hooks on a Peg-Board wall. A neat and orderly house. He remembered Irma, standing at the top of the steps. The way she'd clutched him last night, as if she were drowning, too. He went back inside and climbed to the second floor, checking the master bedroom first. There were some clothes on the bed, an array of photos of Truax. Swope started down the hallway, knowing from schematics that there were two more bedrooms at the end of the hall. Irma was in the one on the left. Susan's room. It had to be. Where this whole thing had started. There were posters and candles. Some sort of shining decals on the ceiling. She was on the bed, stretched out among a colony of stuffed animals. She stared at Swope, her eyes as glassy as those riveted into the dolls. Her skirt was hiked up above her knees – the loosened panty hose looked like a partially shed skin. Swope stared at her long, soft legs for a moment before meeting her eye.

'I was looking for John.'

'He had to work.'

Swope nodded, as if this was the answer he'd expected. The insistent rumble of that ruined machine filtered through a grill beside the bed.

'I came to see if you were all right,' he said softly. 'If there was anything you needed.'

Irma watched him without answering. Swope stepped into the room. The mirror above the dresser was flagged with curled snapshots. One of them showed Susan and Joel sitting by the Fogwood community pool. Teddy sat a few feet behind them, his eyes fixed on the entwined couple. Swope stepped to the edge of Susan's bed. Irma stared up at him. Moist mascara shadowed her big eyes. A complicated odor rose from her. Perfume and booze and sweat. Swope moved a grinning elephant out of the way and sat. Her left leg was turned outward, revealing the soft curve of her knee.

'I am so sorry, Irma,' he said. 'I would give anything for this not to have happened.'

'But it did.'

'I know.'

She closed her eyes and Swope could see her daughter in her. The way she was on those redwood planks. Her mouth slightly agape. The water draining off her into the invisible lake below, making a sound like rain.

'If there's anything . . .'

Her eyes snapped open.

'Our families,' she said hoarsely.

'What about them?' Swope asked.

'We were going to be friends. The Truaxes and the Swopes.'

'We *are* friends.'

'It will not be the same now.'

'No. Not the same. But we can still be friends.'

She closed her eyes.

'Not the same.'

Swope knew he had to get out of here. The woman had lost her mind. He put a comforting hand on her shoulder and searched for some final words.

'We're friends, Irma,' was all he could come up with.

He was just about to stand when she suddenly reached across her body with her left hand and grabbed his wrist. Her grip was as strong as a man's. Though her long nails were digging painfully into his flesh, he let her hold on to him, his eyes moving back to the curve of her knee. Her nails dug harder into the soft flesh beneath his wrist. The skin would break soon if he didn't do something. He looked back at her face just as her mouth fell open. Small mounds of lipstick clung to her teeth. Staring into her mouth Swope suddenly felt something come loose in him, the great reserve of terror and weakness he'd kept at bay these last hours. He bent over and their open mouths clamped together, Swope's tongue lashing the sweet pulpy mass of hers. Her right hand flew up against his stomach so hard that it almost knocked the wind out of him. She began to tug awkwardly at his belt. He put his hand on her knee and then ran it up her thigh, making her nylon hose crackle. She shouted and pulled her head back. Swope grabbed the top of her tights and yanked them down just as she freed his buckle. She tried to get his pants down but they were caught up on his erection. He stood and pulled them away, then moved back toward her.

She released his wrists as he entered her and began to claw at the middle of his back, pulling outward, as if trying to peel away the flesh and muscle to expose his spine. He pumped into her with violent thrusts, causing the bed to shudder against the wall. Stacked animals tumbled onto them. She made a guttural noise every time he moved into her, a revving, continual moan. He came quickly but kept on pounding into her, pouring out the black dread. He didn't look at her face because he didn't want to see the girl's face.

He only stopped when he heard the doorbell. There was no telling how long it had been ringing. She continued to convulse up into him, stopping only when he tried to pull free, tightening her already powerful grip on his back. Her face was frozen in the same grimace he'd seen on the damaged pier.

The doorbell rang again.

'Irma, let me go.'

She looked at him in confusion.

'People are here.'

She released him. Swope stood quickly, causing the animals that had been leaning against him to tumble onto her. Unicorns and zebras and koalas. Downstairs, they were knocking. They'd try the handle next. Find it open.

He had to get out of here.

*   *   *

He paused in the bathroom to check himself, straightening his clothes and tie. He combed his hair with his fingers. There were a few long scratches on his wrist but they weren't bleeding. He pulled his cuff over them, then switched off the light. The extractor fan continued to chug.

There were hairy heads on the front porch. Four of them by the look of it. Sure enough, somebody was trying the handle. A few seconds longer and they would have been in. He skipped down the last few steps and yanked open the door. The press. Two of them, reporter and photographer. They stepped back when he appeared, startled. The reporter, a short man in a corduroy coat, clearly recognized him. For an instant Swope wondered if they could read what had just happened in his eyes, on his livid flesh. He quickly cast the idea aside. No one would ever know anything about him. Not unless he wanted them to.

'May I help you gentlemen?'

'Are the Truaxes in?' the short man asked.

'And you are?'

'Andy Ackerman. *Baltimore Sun.*'

'We've spoken before, haven't we?'

'Yes, Mr Swope.'

'Look, you guys, the Truaxes aren't going to be able to talk to anybody just yet. They're pretty broken up. But they have asked me to make a statement.'

Pages flipped and a pen clicked. Swope waited until he was ready. A quick image flashed through his mind, an overhead camera shot of him standing at the scene of some disaster – tornado or flood or the tangle of a 707 – dealing coolly with the baying hounds of the press.

'John and Irma Truax would like to thank everyone for their thoughts and best wishes at this difficult time. They would also like to say that they are sure the Cannon County authorities will act quickly and decisively to ensure that justice is done to the young man responsible for this horrible crime.'

He paused. The reporter finished writing and looked up.

'Mr Swope, can you comment on Earl Wooten's future at EarthWorks, given the current situation?'

Swope considered mentioning Holmes's letter, due to

420

be delivered any minute. But he decided to let that be. The further he distanced himself from Wooten's fate, the better.

'Mr Wooten's future is no longer my responsibility.'

He excused himself with a curt nod and strode right through the men. He had to get back to the office. He had a city to run.

33

They had his boy in chains. A heavy set of dull iron shackles that connected Joel's wrists and ankles to his waist. When Wooten first saw the restraints he wanted to step over the dinky little courtroom fence and tear them off. It might take a few minutes and he would probably have to get his hands on some tools. Bolt cutters and maybe some needle-nosed pliers. But he could do it. They were, after all, only iron. Earl Wooten could take care of iron.

But he did nothing. Instead, he continued to sit dutifully in the place McNutt had reserved for him in the front row. The lawyer was at the table directly in front of him, rustling papers and clearing his throat. Ardelia was on Wooten's left, though she might just as well have been twenty miles away. They said nothing. They hadn't exchanged a word since the bitter argument over Joel's plea an hour earlier in McNutt's office. Seeing his son chained up like this, Wooten wanted to reach out and take her hand, though he knew it would be as unresponsive as that poor dead girl's.

The courtroom was so bland that it was hard to imagine anyone's fate could be decided here. The hardwood benches looked like pews. There were tall cloudy windows and the fake-lemon smell of furniture polish. Portraits of stern white men lined the walls. Bailiffs and clerks exchanged knowing, occasionally joking remarks, as if this were just another place to work, an insurance office or seed store. As everyone waited, McNutt would turn occasionally, his small hands gripping the fence separating them as he spoke. Though little more than two feet high, it seemed greater than any wall Wooten had ever known. He refused to look at the seats filling up behind him. If there were friends back there they would understand his stillness. To the others he would not give the satisfaction of showing his face.

And then his son was in the room, walking unannounced through the door just behind the empty jury box. He was flanked by two cops. The courtroom grew utterly silent as he shuffled toward the table, those ankle chains scraping the polished floor like unclipped claws. Although he had told himself to expect the worst, Wooten couldn't believe how bad Joel looked. His eyes were puffy with sleeplessness, his hair a bedraggled mess. His broad shoulders were bowed by some great internal weight. His expression was one of utter bewilderment, like the face of a refugee fleeing civil war. McNutt stood to greet him. Joel looked at the lawyer as if he'd never seen the man before in his life, then turned to his parents. First Wooten, then Ardelia. His eyes remained blank. Nothing moved in them. Ardelia began to stir, looking like she was going to reach for him. But she caught herself, remembering how McNutt had told her she must remain perfectly still during the hearing. No histrionics, he'd said. Guided by the cops, Joel lowered himself into the chair beside the lawyer. Wooten stared at the back of his son's head as it began to nod slowly forward, like that of a man falling asleep on a bus.

As he looked at his boy his mind replayed the painful meeting with McNutt an hour earlier. It had happened at his big, slightly shabby office overlooking the green's rusting cannon and shitting dogs. The news was bad, worse than it had been during those endless night hours Wooten had passed in the police station. The case against their son was formidable. For openers, Joel's presence at the murder scene was now a matter of fact, confirmed by a security guard as well as Teddy Swope. According to the prosecution, he'd killed Susan by throwing her from the pier into the water, where she drowned after knocking herself unconscious on a boat platform. The motive was jealousy – she had begun to see Teddy Swope. In fact, there had already been some sort of argument between the boys. As far as anyone could tell the formerly inseparable friends hadn't spoken for a week. Teddy had been thrown into the lake as well, though he'd managed to scramble to safety.

As he listened to McNutt laying it out for them, it began to occur to Wooten that he did not know his son at all. The deep reserve of familiar feelings and fatherly intuition about the boy he should have deployed against these facts was simply not available. Instead, there was a litany of misunderstanding. The recent arguments over songs and celebrities, the inability to find even a few feet of common ground over the girl. Wooten had no idea what lurked in Joel's heart. Two years ago he thought he knew; four years ago he was certain of it. But now Joel might just as well have been a stranger. God only knew what the two thugs from the SBI had turned up that morning when they searched his room. They'd arrived just after Wooten returned from Cannon City, demanding to be let in. Wooten left them cooling their heels as he called McNutt, who told him he might as well. These guys could get nasty if you made them get a warrant. Invade your house like termites. So Wooten stood helpless in the hallway as they rooted through Joel's things, packing the letters he had seen him reading just a few days ago into a big evidence bag. They also found a diary Wooten didn't even know existed, thereby taking possession of whatever unguarded and dangerous thoughts Joel had consigned to page. Thoughts Wooten had been too distracted by his own sins and ambition to try to understand.

After they left Wooten and Ardelia took the twins to stay with Richard Holmes's wife for the day, then headed down to Cannon City, where McNutt informed them that Joel was in a bad way. Susan's death, whatever the cause, had hit him hard. His story was still that he had never seen her and Teddy, who were supposedly performing some sort of pantomine of love in order to get Joel and the girl together. There had been no fight between the two friends, according to Joel. That was just part of the deception. If this kept up, McNutt confessed, he had no idea how he was going to mount an effective defense. In near desperation, he'd arranged for the Wootens to see him after the arraignment.

'I don't know,' he said. 'Maybe you can get some sense out of him.'

As the lawyer finished laying out his grim facts, a second realization began to blossom in Wooten's mind, this one infinitely more terrible than a mere acknowledgment of his son's estrangement. It was a thought he'd kept at bay since its first tentative appearance at dawn. But, sitting in that seedy office, drinking weak coffee served by a secretary who wouldn't meet his eye, he could no longer deny it. Joel was guilty. His son had done it. After a week of simmering anger and loneliness, he'd lashed out. Not meaning to do any real harm and certainly not meaning to do murder. But he'd lashed out nonetheless and now a girl was dead. Drowned in a lake Wooten had dug himself. With every grim fact McNutt presented, a terrible knowledge took hold in Wooten's mind, like an infection no drug would cure.

His son had done it.

He knew that no anger or blame should be directed at the boy. It was not his fault. It was Wooten's. He should have followed his instincts and stopped him seeing Susan months ago. Nipped it in the bud before it flowered into this evil thing, no matter what Ardelia said about times having changed or Newton being different. He'd listened to all those educated, optimistic voices when in fact it was crazy Irma Truax he should have been heeding all along. Joel and Susan had smelled like trouble from the first and now that's exactly what everybody had. Instead of doing what he knew to be right he let it go, ignoring the warning signs while he flew off to Chicago or passed long afternoons at unit 27. His own carnality and pride blinding him to his son's needs.

Joel did it. But it was Wooten's fault.

'There is one other thing,' McNutt said. 'I'm sure you won't even want to hear this, but as your attorney I am constrained to communicate it to you. I received a message from the prosecuting attorney just before your arrival. Although the state is publicly seeking a second-degree murder conviction, they would be willing to entertain a guilty plea on the charge of manslaughter. I of course responded

425

that my client is not guilty and we would be vigorously defending him against any charge.'

'Now hold on a minute,' Wooten said.

Ardelia and the lawyer looked at him.

'What exactly would that mean, manslaughter?'

'Earl . . .' Ardelia said in the voice she used on those rare occasions she got scared.

McNutt began to tap the table with the eraser end of his pencil.

'It could mean up to ten years, though from what I was able to glean from Miss Van Riper we would be looking at a sentence more in the neighborhood of five.'

'But it would wind up being less than that, right?' Wooten asked. 'I mean, that's how these things work.'

'Earl Wooten, you stop this talk right now,' Ardelia said, her voice even lower.

He turned to his wife.

'Why?' he asked with a bitterness that startled him. 'So we can spend the next few months going bankrupt to buy ourselves the privilege of watching a dozen Cannon County crackers send our boy off to Jessup for the rest of his natural life?'

The words silenced his wife.

'Have you been listening? He's going *down*, Ardelia. You remember down, don't you? We've come far, but not far enough to forget which way that is.'

Tears were welling in her green eyes. But she remained silent. Wooten turned back to McNutt.

'Well?'

'If I had to guess, I'd say you'd have Joel back home in about three years.'

'He'd be twenty-one.'

'Wait,' Ardelia said, outrage underpinning her voice now. 'Both of you stop this right now.'

Wooten and McNutt looked at her.

'Aren't you forgetting something here? *He didn't do it.*'

'And you know that?' Wooten asked.

'Well, yes. Of course I do.'

'How?'

'Because he's my son. Earl.'

'He's my son, too.'

She stood. Her eyes were flashing anger now.

'I do not believe this. Are you honestly going to sit there and tell me you think our son *did* this. Our son who never so much as struck another boy, much less some girl he loved?'

'It doesn't matter what I believe. The only thing that matters is what the man decides he's going to do with him. Ain't that right, Mr McNutt?'

McNutt looked like he wanted to be somewhere far away. He began to smooth his ironed hair with the heels of his hands. But he still wasn't contradicting Wooten. Ardelia stared at her husband for a moment, then turned to the lawyer.

'What does Joel want to do?' she asked.

'As far as I can ascertain, Joel will plead however you tell him to.'

Ardelia turned to her husband.

'Then he pleads not guilty,' she said, her voice cold as the prairie winds that used to blow over the ditches Wooten dug thirty years ago.

'And what if that's a gamble we lose?' Wooten asked.

She shook her head stubbornly.

'There's got to be something more to all of this,' she said. 'Before you two give up on my son, it would be nice if you could find out what that was.'

The county magistrate entered the chamber like a small mammal looking for food. The clerk instructed all those who had business before the court to rise and give their attention. Up until this moment. Wooten had viewed Lon Spivey as he did all the Cannon County grandees – as a vaguely comical figure who'd become rich on EarthWorks money and was now counting the days until he could start spending it. He was a small, scowling man, constantly trawling remarks made to him for submerged insult. His wife was confined to a wheelchair with chronically swollen feet. The last thing in the world Wooten was prepared to do was take him seriously. To see him decked out in a silk robe and sitting in judgment on Joel only added to the horror and unreality of the last few hours.

The hearing went quickly. Van Riper announced that the state was charging Joel Wooten with murder in the second degree. Spivey asked how the defendant pled. McNutt stood, then, almost as an afterthought, urged Joel to his feet. Everyone waited for the boy to speak. But he remained silent. Finally, McNutt pronounced the words not guilty in a reedy, inoffensive voice. Spivey accepted them with a sour, slightly surprised twist of his head. McNutt asked for bail and the judge denied him without explanation. A brief argument ensued – McNutt had been counting on bail. It was a fight that could end only one way. For now, Joel was to remain in custody.

And that was it. Everybody rose as Spivey scampered out of the room without so much as a glance over his shoulder. The cops led Joel away. McNutt turned to the Wootens, his usual cockiness gone.

'I don't understand about the bail,' Ardelia said. 'I thought we were going to get him home today.'

'They want us to take the plea,' McNutt said. 'Until then, we can expect no favors.'

A bailiff appeared.

'Five minutes,' he announced.

He led Earl and Ardelia into a dingy, rectangular room at the back of the courthouse. A long conference table occupied most of the space. The walls were bare; there were no windows. Wooten realized that it was the jury room. The place where Joel's fate would be decided. Unless he did something soon. His son sat at the head of the table, slumped sideways in his chair. His eyes were open but they might as well have been closed. A fat cop watched over him.

Ardelia went right over to her boy and gave him an awkward hug. The cop looked like he wanted to break it up, but relented when he saw this would entail tangling with Ardelia Wooten. He followed the bailiff out of the room. Wooten pulled two chairs from the dozen around the table and placed them to either side of Joel. He sat and after a

428

moment Ardelia did as well. Their son continued to stare down the length of the table, his eyes miles away.

'Joel, honey,' Ardelia said. 'Are you all right?'

For several seconds, Joel continued to look straight ahead. Finally, he turned toward his mother. His expression was quizzical, as if he were trying to figure out who she was.

'What is it?' she asked. 'Are they hurting you?'

His lips came apart with a dry, rending smack.

'Where's Susan?' he asked softly.

Ardelia recoiled. She looked at her son for a moment, then turned helplessly to her husband.

'Joel, Susan is gone,' Wooten said. 'They found her in the lake.'

'I know,' he said. 'Where is she *now*?'

'Oh. I don't . . . I imagine they have her over at the hospital. Earl?'

Wooten nodded, his eyes steady on his son. Joel looked back down at the table.

'I've been thinking something.'

'What's that?' Ardelia asked.

'The whole time I was sitting there. You know, at the lake? She was right below me. Musta been fifteen minutes. She . . .'

His words caught in his throat.

'Sweetness,' Ardelia said.

Wooten stared at his son for a moment longer before turning away. This was unbearable. He would not endure this. There was no way he was going to let Joel go to trial in this condition. They'd crucify him. Three years was the blink of an eye compared with what he would get if he fought them.

'Joel, listen to me, because we don't have long,' Ardelia said. 'You've got to start cooperating better with Mr McNutt if you're going to get out of this mess. Do you understand?'

Joel didn't react.

'You have to focus your mind, honey. They're saying you did something to Susan. If we're going to defend you then you must tell us more than you already have. Joel?'

Confusion danced across his son's brow for a moment.

'I told them everything,' he said.

'I know you *think* you have,' Ardelia continued, a teacher now. 'And that's good, that's real good. But we're going to need to know more.'

Joel shrugged.

'There is no more. I never saw anybody. I went down there but they never showed.'

'But Teddy's saying you did see them. He's saying you pushed them both in the water.'

Joel shook his head.

'You don't believe that shit, do you?' he asked, animated now. 'Teddy wouldn't lie like that. The cops are just saying that to trick me into confessing. That's how they do it, you know. They tell you your best friend's turning against you so you'll say anything. And that lawyer you got – he *believes* them. I don't want to have anything to do with that Tom. You should get the Swope in here, man. He'll sort this out.'

Earl and Ardelia exchanged their first look in two hours.

'Joel, look at me,' Ardelia said after a moment, her voice loud and clear, as if she were conducting a fire drill. 'Teddy Swope is telling the police that you did this. It's not a mistake. It's no trick. It's Teddy saying it. That's why you're here.'

Something in his mother's voice seemed to get through to him. He cast her an incredulous glance.

'No way.'

'Yes, Joel,' Ardelia said. 'Yes.'

'Teddy's really saying I killed Susan?'

'*Yes.*'

'Why would he do that?' Joel asked after a moment.

'I don't know. That's what you have to tell us.'

Joel looked down at the chain that snaked between his wrists.

'Are you sure?'

'Yes. Absolutely.'

'What else is he saying?'

'That he was on a date with the girl and you found them at the pier and attacked them.'

'Teddy wasn't on no date with Susan. He was just pre-

430

tending. To get her past her parents.' Joel's face twisted into a sour shape. 'Teddy going with Susan.'

'You weren't jealous of them?' Ardelia asked. 'That isn't what this is about?'

'Jealous? Why would I be jealous?'

'So there would have been no reason for you to attack them.'

Joel shook his head incredulously. Wooten remained silent. Not believing a word of this.

'But you told me you two boys had a fight earlier in the week,' Ardelia persisted, doubt in her voice as well.

'Nah, that was nothing. We were just scamming everybody that we were mad at each other. It was part of Teddy's plan.'

'Joel, let me get this straight – Teddy was pretending to go out with Susan so you could be with her?'

Joel nodded, as if this were the most obvious thing in the world.

Wooten couldn't take it anymore.

'Goddamn it!' he said, loud enough to cause his son to jump back, rattling his chains. 'What the hell are you talkin' here?'

Joel and Ardelia stared at him in astonishment.

'Do you expect anybody to *believe* this bullshit?'

'Earl!'

'But it's true.'

'True? Are you really going to sit there and tell me you spent the last few days scheming against your mother and me, lying like a dog on a fireside rug, and then expect us to take what you say as the gospel *truth*?'

'Earl . . .'

'No, Ardelia. Time is running out. We take this weak-ass lie up before the judge, it's all over. They'll laugh this boy right down to Jessup.'

'But it's the truth,' Joel persisted weakly. 'Teddy would do anything for me.'

'Then why's he got you looking at a life sentence?'

Joel had no answer for that.

'Just be a man, Joel. 'Fess up to what you've done and take your punishment. They're willing to let you off light, probably because Austin is telling them to. But you got to tell the truth. If you come back at them with this *nonsense*, then it's all going to go away.'

'Dad, I didn't do anything,' Joel said, his voice small.

That was it. Before he knew what was happening, Wooten was on his feet, his hand reaching for the boy's neck. Joel raised his arms to defend himself and somehow Wooten found himself holding those chains. He pulled them upward, causing Joel to rise a few inches out of the chair.

'Earl!'

Ardelia was on her feet, her strong hands grasping Wooten's wrists.

'You have to do what they say!' He was shouting now. 'Do what they say!'

Ardelia began to pull harder at her husband's arms. Joel had gone limp, his head twisting down and away. Wooten continued to shake those chains, causing his son to flop around like an empty sack.

' 'Fess up, goddamn you. 'Fess up!'

The door opened and the bailiff rushed in, followed by the fat cop. They were on Wooten in a heartbeat, their practiced hands pulling him back toward the door before he'd even felt their force. He tried to shout one last command at his son but a forearm had closed off his windpipe. And then he was out the door, back in the courtroom, where a few stragglers watched him in astonishment. The last thing he saw before the door slammed shut was his son's face, closing in anguish, oblivious to his mother's comforting touch.

34

The Wooten house was quiet. It had been empty since late morning, when Truax had parked the Cutlass on Rhiannon's Rest and made his way through the inconsequential foliage to his post in the treehouse. Unlike his stumbling progress at Renaissance Heights in the first days of the operation, he made almost no sound at all now, his footfalls no louder than the scavenging rustle of squirrels. The things he'd learned in war had come back to him. The rust was gone. He was ready.

He wasn't surprised to find the house empty. They would have gone down to Cannon City to be with their son. The same journey Truax had taken a few hours earlier. Only, they would bring their child home alive. Walk him up the driveway and through the front door and into his room. Feed him and protect him and keep the harm away. Wooten would bribe the people down there to get his son free. That was how he worked. If not tonight then tomorrow. Or the next day. Whenever it happened, Truax would be here. He would stay as long as it took.

Although it had been over two days since he'd closed his eyes, he felt as alert as he had during those long nights on the wire at My Song. He noted every dappled shadow and shimmering leaf; his ears marked birdsong and wind. Nothing would come to this house without him seeing it. Provisions weren't a problem. That morning he'd stopped at the 7-Eleven to refill his big tartan thermos and empty the Hostess rack. Nobody seemed to mind him moving to the front of the line. They made space, some of them looking at his slick

433

glove as they moved away. He handed the woman all the change in his pocket. She put the money into the register without counting. Not once meeting his eye.

Cars had begun coming up the Wootens' driveway soon after Truax had taken up his position. Most appeared to be reporters, though there were also friends, coming to offer support. They would ring the bell – some even called out. One of them, a long-haired man with cowboy boots and a camera dangling from his neck, walked around back. He stepped up onto the redwood deck and peered through the kitchen's sliding-glass door for a long while, using cupped hands to stop the glare. Then he knocked with his palm, making a noise that echoed like distant splashes. When it became clear that no one was home he left, leaving behind a cloud of breath on the window that took minutes to fade. They all went. Leaving only Truax behind. By midafternoon they'd stopped coming. The house's shadow crept across the backyard until it joined the shade where Truax hid. He continued to hold his position. His body had settled into itself. His sidearm was on the untreated wood just a few inches to his left. The spare clip was in his pants pocket, no more bulky than a set of keys. Occasionally he'd reach into the paper bag stuffed with Ho Ho's and Sno-Balls and Twinkies. But the moment he felt their cool cellophane the sickness swelled, causing him to leave them uneaten. Instead, he sipped lukewarm coffee from the plastic thermos cup and waited. Later he could piss it back into the thermos and then, if it was necessary, he would drink it again. The one thing he would not do was leave this position. Not until he was sure the boy would be punished.

She'd breathed spasmodically and water filled her lungs. That was how the doctor said she'd died. He wondered if there had been a moment when she woke, a brief eternity of lucidity before everything stopped. A second or two after her mind overcame the blow it had suffered. She would have tried to find the air her lungs needed but there would have been only the cold, muddy water. And then she would have known. He'd seen that happen. Men whose hearts or guts had been ripped to shreds – men who had no business being

434

awake – suddenly blinking into startled consciousness. Just long enough to know, and take that knowledge with them. With Susan there would have been the impenetrable murk of that dirty water. The cold. There would have been fear and panic but those would have quickly given way to loneliness. That was the thing Truax couldn't accept. The loneliness that would have been the last thing she'd known.

While Joel Wooten fled to this safe home.

Swope had said that the boy would be punished. And Truax knew that he would try to make that happen. Swope was a man of honor. But a deeper part of him knew that sometimes Swope's law didn't work. He had seen this in the war. Every day, at the end. Almost every hour. Times when you had to make sure for yourself that it worked. That was why he was here. In case the law didn't work.

Sometime during the afternoon his wrist began to ache. He wished he'd remembered to bring his first aid kit. The smell was becoming rank. Though he knew the problem was more than just the smell. The infection was traveling into his body. That explained the pain. Good nerves were being assaulted. He could feel the faint fever pricks along his arm and shoulder. Sweat collecting in the valley of his spine. The bubbling acid in his guts that made eating impossible. This was how the fever had started last time. He should go to a doctor and get something for it. But that would mean abandoning his position. He'd done that once already and Joel had escaped to kill his daughter. He would not do it again. Not until he was sure the boy had been punished.

The dreams began to come in the late afternoon, providing him blessed relief from thoughts about Susan lonely in the water and Susan on that steel gurney. He never stopped watching the Wooten house as he dreamed, the images layered over reality, like a photograph that had come back wrong from the developers. Making love with Irma back in Germany that first winter, seeing her perfect snowy breasts and feeling her talcy flesh. His young daughters in his arms, their surging weak limbs entwining him. One by one, un-willed, the same dreams that had carried him through the long nights in My Song played through his mind. Breaking the shell of time and allowing him to float freely in the eternal liquid that spilled through the cracks.

The dreams vanished when the Wootens arrived home at dusk, Ardelia's Le Sabre bouncing over the curb. Before she'd even come to a stop Truax was ready, feeling as alert as if he'd slept for ten hours. His left hand reached out instinctively for his weapon as he watched the front door open and the hall light flicker on. It was just Wooten and his wife. No Joel. That meant nothing. This thing was still not over. He watched as the couple walked into the kitchen. They looked tired. It must be bad, having a son who is a killer. In other circumstances Truax might have even felt sorry for them. But this was different. They were his enemies now. They would try to make Joel free and Truax would stop them. Ardelia filled a copper kettle from the sink and put it on the stove. Blue flame winked beneath it. Wooten started to speak. After a few seconds she turned and said something back to him. Her words appeared to be angry. Wooten bowed his head as he listened.

John Truax, spiking fever but ready, watched them from his dark fort.

35

Ardelia turned away from the stove, her eyes as hot as its blue flame.

'So what exactly are you saying, Earl?'

'I'm saying we better come to a decision about this before they pull the rug out first thing tomorrow morning.'

She began to shake her head slowly.

'How many times do I have to tell you?' she asked. 'He didn't do it. He's as innocent as the day he was born. That's the only decision there is.'

'And you know that for a fact.'

'An absolute fact.'

Now Wooten shook his head.

'I wish I could be as sure as you.'

'I wish you could as well.' Ardelia's voice was sharp. 'I also wish I knew what it was about our son that makes you think he could have done this thing.'

'He's a boy, Ardelia. A confused, unhappy boy.'

'A boy who'd never hurt so much as a flea in his entire life. And now you're calling him a violent criminal. A killer. Why is that, Earl? What is this quality in our son that makes you believe the worst of him? For heaven's sake, the child just looked you in the eye and said he didn't do it.'

'He lied before,' Wooten said. 'He tried to meet with her, didn't he?'

'Oh, and everybody knows that breaking curfew to be with your sweetheart leads directly to homicide.'

They waited out an ominous spell of silence.

'It's because he's black, isn't it?'

It took several seconds for Wooten to register what she'd said.

'That's ridiculous.'

'Is it? I've been wracking my brain all day trying to understand where you are on this. I mean, where is all this rage and deceitfulness supposed to come from?'

'Ardelia . . .'

'Don't Ardelia me. Explain to me how eighteen years of careful tutelage and character building can disappear in the course of a summer's night. What is it, Earl? Juju magic? Schizophrenia?'

Wooten said nothing.

'Which leaves one thing,' she continued. 'Because he's black.'

Wooten looked down at the big pine table separating them. There were unreadable words gouged in its surface, remnants of Joel's homework. Wooten tried to think of a way to express the feeling he'd had ever since first seeing Joel with Susan. The wicked foreboding that was now coming true.

'I'm not saying he set out to kill the girl,' he said slowly. 'I'm not even saying he wanted to hurt her. Something happened and he . . . lashed out.'

'Lashed out? Now when's the last time you saw Joel lash out? I seem to remember him being about two, though perhaps you may possess knowledge to which I'm not privy.'

'This is different.'

'Why? Because there's a white girl involved?'

'It's not that simple.'

'Oh, it's simple, all right. And now I suppose you're going to start spouting all that nonsense about the evil magic between black boys and white girls those Bama kin of yours put into your thick head forty years ago.'

'Ardelia . . .'

'No, Earl. No sale.' She put a hand on her cocked hip. 'That's not how it works. All my life I've been hearing this trash about how you black men have some wild beast in you that we have to be careful to keep under lock and key. Keep the white women away else the colored boys start swinging in the trees! Well, let me ask you – where was that in my

438

father? Or his father? Or yours? Where was it in my sweet brother Wyatt? And where the hell is it in *you*?'

Wooten remembered his hands on Vota's collar. The anger he'd felt at his own son just an hour ago, so intense it took strangers to pull him away from it. He knew where it was in him. About an inch below the surface.

'Joel wouldn't have hurt that poor child any more than you would have,' Ardelia persisted. 'And if some kind of terrible accident did happen, then he would have walked right up to you, looked you in the eye and told you about it. Long before any redneck deputy showed up at our door. And then he would have waited for you to help him.' Her voice had grown terribly quiet. 'Look inside yourself, Earl. Not the self a bunch of superstitious people conjured up in your fool mind but the *real* you. Look inside yourself and then look inside your son. Now, I ask you – is there killing there?'

Wooten looked away from his wife's intense glare. The old copper coffeepot began to rattle behind her. Her words were so strong and right. He wasn't so sure anymore. He wished there were some way he could see what had happened down at the lake. Some way he could peel back the misunderstanding and hostility and look into his son's heart.

Ardelia was still talking.

'You know, doubting Joel and going down to that woman – they're the same thing. The same damned thing. It's like you wake up every morning and can't believe you aren't as weak as they told you you were. So you got to go out and prove it.'

'All right,' he said wearily. 'Let's say you're right. Let's say he isn't guilty. We still have a problem.'

'What's that?'

'Proving it.' Wooten shook his head. 'The evidence is just too strong.'

'Something will turn up,' Ardelia said, her voice less confident now.

'What?' Wooten asked.

'I don't know. I mean, for one thing, it's pretty clear to *me* at least that Teddy Swope isn't telling the whole story about what happened down there.'

'But why wouldn't he? Why would he wreck Joel's life? He worships him. They're best friends.'

'Earl, please, let's not waste our valuable time trying to get inside *that* boy's head. There's things going on in there that you and I couldn't even guess at. He has an IQ of one seventy-seven, Earl. That's about forty points higher than me, and I ain't simple. I saw the results. We all stood around the teacher's lounge with our mouths hanging open. We don't even *have* the tests that can accurately measure that boy's mind. Iowa, SAT – I don't care. And you put that with his childish personality, well, it's like having a nuclear reactor in a Volkswagen.'

Wooten began to see what she was driving at – that what had happened to Susan was some sort of bad accident and now Teddy was telling stories to get himself out from beneath it. But this was just a theory, little more than wishful thinking. He'd seen Joel back in his bedroom; he'd heard the words he'd said when the police came. The boy had been desperate and distraught. He'd done something wrong. Trying to pin this horrible thing on Teddy would only ensure that Joel's life was wrecked. Wooten's job here wasn't to go chasing after pipe dreams and thin theories. It was to help his boy. To take the best offer the man had and run with it.

'We don't have time,' he said.

'I'm sorry?'

'We don't have the time to be messing around with what Teddy said or what Joel thinks. We have to decide about that plea. Tonight.'

'There's nothing to decide. We say not guilty and fight like trapped cats.'

'And what if we lose?'

'We won't. We can't.'

Ardelia met his gaze defiantly. They were going round and round now. He knew she would never agree. But he also knew that she was not the one who would have to provide the final answer here. McNutt and Van Riper – it was Wooten they wanted to hear. It would have to be him. Alone. Because Joel would do what his father told him. Despite the recent friction between them, that was how it would play. It was how he'd been raised. Wooten would have to sit across from his son and tell him his only choice was to say what the man wanted him to say and then do his years. Otherwise, he would lose his life. Lose it in a slow drip of wasted days and prison bitterness that would leave him shucked and shelled by the time he was thirty.

So there was no reason to argue with Ardelia about it, no reason to let her turn him around with conjectures that might sound good even while they were nothing more than smoke and air. There was only one thing to do. Make the plea. Wooten decided that he would tell her nothing for now. Let it ride. And then, in the morning, he would drive down to Cannon City and tell his son how it had to be.

'All right,' he said.

'All right we plead not guilty or all right we send our boy to jail?'

Wooten ran his hands over his scalp.

'I don't know. I just . . . don't know.'

She shook her head.

'You amaze me, Earl Wooten. You really do.'

She began to gather her things to go out.

'Well, I don't know about you, but I'm going back to Cannon City to sit with our boy – *if* they'll let me. And then I have to pick up the twins. In the meantime I suggest you have a good hard think about how we're going to fight this. Open up that pig head of yours and entertain the possibility that your son is telling you the truth. Just do that much for me and our twenty years together. Because if you cave in on this, on the back of everything else that has happened this week, then you and I are through. *Through.*'

And then she was gone, her heels clicking angrily on the polished floor as she stormed toward the front door. Though she was walking fast, it still took her a long time to cross the house Wooten had built to keep his family safe.

When she was gone he realized he was hungry. It had been almost twenty-four hours since he'd eaten. If he didn't get something into his stomach soon the panic would come. And then it would be impossible to think at all. He walked

441

over to the big fridge, pulling the door free of its suction strip. Cool air and cool light washed over him. He looked at the countless things inside, the half-empty pickle jars and vacuum-wrapped packets of lunch meat, the split lettuce and Tupperware containers. There was a shriveled lime on the door. Mason jars of preserves no one would ever eat. The back wall was covered with a pall of condensation. Beyond that the motor chugged, replacing escaping frost.

The phone rang. Wooten was tempted not to answer. But it might be about Joel. He swung the door shut and went over to it.

'Mr Wooten, this is Andy Ackerman from the *Baltimore Sun*. I was wondering if you might answer a few—'

He hung up. It rang again, so quickly that he knew it couldn't be the same caller. It was a woman's voice this time. Her age was easy to guess. Three hundred years.

'Fucking nigger. They should lynch your son for what he did to that bitch. Not that she didn't deserve it.'

'I'm hungry,' Wooten said.

There was a moment of stupefied silence on the other end of the line. Wooten continued to hold the phone to his ear.

'Then why don't you eat my shit, you black fuck—'

He hung up the phone and stared at it for a moment. When it didn't ring he crossed the kitchen to the walk-in pantry, a room he'd designed large enough to hold more food than his family would ever need. He pulled the cord to the overhead bulb and looked at the rows of cans and cartons, the restaurant-sized boxes and sixty-four-ounce jars. The phone rang again. Wooten began to move toward it but then stopped. It wouldn't be Joel. Nor McNutt. They weren't going to call. They weren't going to be doing anything until he decided. A sudden stab of pain moved through his guts, a vivid combination of dread and hunger that almost doubled him over. It was unexpectedly intense, like the twist of a knife. Wooten took a sharp breath but it did no good. The pain held its ground, caught in some intestinal switchback.

The phone continued to ring, echoing loudly through the kitchen. Ice dropped noisily in the freezer. The cooling kettle gave out one last desultory rattle. Wooten knew that he had to get out of here. They would not leave him alone if he stayed. They would call and they would come. His wife would keep on him to say no, everyone else to say yes. He had to get out of this house. Go somewhere he could get some thinking done. Get some food in his stomach to stop this pain.

There was a knock on the front door, the sort of bold-timid rap that would not be denied. Wooten set off toward it, still half stooped from the pain in his guts. The knocking sounded again just as he reached the door. Suddenly furious, he jerked the handle so hard that he could feel something break beneath his closed fist. The lock. He'd forgotten to twist it open before turning the knob. And now it was broken.

Richard Holmes was in the process of taking a protective step backward when the door flew open. His Vega idled in the driveway behind Wooten's Ranchero. The unlit mahogany pipe was in its usual place between his clenched teeth. His usually serene eyes were blinking nervously as they stared at the ruined doorknob. There was an EarthWorks envelope in his right hand.

'Richard. What is it? The twins . . .'

'No, they're fine. Crystal took them to Swensen's.'

Wooten waited as Holmes blinked a few more times, his lips nervously working the chewed stem. Then he handed Wooten the envelope.

'I'm sorry, Earl.'

Wooten took it from him. The letter was terse. A single paragraph, informing him that he was on indefinite leave as of immediately.

'It's not a personnel decision, Earl. It comes straight from Chicago.'

Wooten folded the letter and placed it in his back pocket. He crumpled the envelope and let it fall into the perfectly manicured shrubs surrounding his front porch. Straight from Chicago. Although he should have anticipated this, it still came as a shock. He was out of a job. For the first time in over thirty years. There would be no AmericaWorks now. No percentage. No piece of the pie. He wouldn't even be able to finish the city.

Holmes plucked the pipe from his mouth.

'I feel bad about this, Earl.'

'Not bad enough to let somebody else write the letter,' Wooten said, though he couldn't bring himself to feel the anger his words implied.

'That's not fair.'

Wooten had to smile at that one.

'Fair?' he asked. 'You want fair, son, you best take your show on the road.'

Holmes stared at him helplessly for a moment, then took the bigger man's advice and walked quickly back to his idling car.

She still wore her uniform. Mookie was in his corner, making noises. She stepped aside to let him pass, her eyes tracking him closely. It was strange to think how furious he'd been with her a few days ago. And now it meant nothing. He collapsed on her busted couch, the pangs still gnawing at his guts. She stood uncertainly above him. Mookie gargled a few seconds of meaningless laughter.

'I heard about your son,' she said softly.

He looked up at her.

'I had a cousin raped a white girl down in DC. Man didn't get him until he was in Lorton. They said he hung hisself.'

'I'm hungry,' Wooten said.

She accepted this as a natural progression in the conversation.

'I'll fix you something up. You want eggs? I ain't got no bacon.'

'Yeah,' he said. 'Eggs.'

She went into the kitchen and pulled a pan from the sink's stagnant puddle. He stood unsteadily and followed her. She was wiping it clean with a paper towel.

'You look bad, Earl,' she said.

'Why did you do it?' he asked wearily.

'Do what?'

'Tell about us.'

'I didn't have no choice.'

'No choice?'

444

'He told me he would throw us out back to Anacostia.'

Wooten stared at her a moment.

'Who?'

'What?'

'Who told you he'd throw you out?'

She turned to look at him.

'Mr Swope. Who you think?'

'Austin Swope talked to you?'

'Uh hunh. Came here last Thursday and told me I best tell him what was what atween us else he'd cancel my lease and tell the clinic not to see Mookie no more.'

The pain in Wooten's guts was radiating to his legs and chest. His head felt light.

'I don't understand. Did you write Swope a letter as well as Ardelia?'

She was holding the pan at her side. Water ran from it onto the blistered floor.

'What letter?' she asked. 'I ain't write no letter.'

On the other side of the apartment, the boy started laughing again. Wooten became aware of another sound. A siren, somewhere in the city.

Swope had been here.

He stood and walked over to her phone, the pain once again almost doubling him over. Sally answered on the twelfth ring. There was a vague, underwater quality to her voice.

'Oh. Earl. Austin's not here.'

'Do you know where he is?'

'He went to Newton Plaza to deal with the emergency.'

So that's what they were calling it now. He began to hang up.

'Earl?'

He put the phone back to his ear.

'Yes?'

'I'm sorry. About how things have turned out. You know?'

Wooten hung up without another word. She was still watching him from the gallery kitchen. Mookie had begun to rock. It would be hours until he stopped.

Swope had been here. Swope knew.

445

'I have to go,' Wooten said.

'You don't want no eggs?'

'No,' he said softly. 'I'm not so hungry now.'

'You gonna be back?'

Wooten stared at her for a long moment.

'I don't know what I'm going to be.'

As he stepped out onto the concrete landing the siren's wail seemed to grow louder. It was heading into the heart of Fogwood. Wooten tracked it heedlessly, still trying to make sense of what he'd just discovered. Swope had been to unit 27. He knew. Which meant that whoever had sent the letter had made good their threat to contact others. Wooten wracked his brain to think of who it could have been. One of the other cafeteria women. Though Alice swore they didn't know. And the neighbors – Wooten couldn't even remember setting eyes on a single one during the entire course of his visits. Whoever it was, they'd told Austin, who'd come down to find out for himself.

Wooten gave his head a rueful shake. Funny how long he'd feared just this happening. People finding out. But now that it was known it didn't matter. He might as well have been caught jaywalking. Because there was only one thing in his life now. His son was behind bars and he still didn't know what he was going to do about it.

A second siren joined the first, this one coming to life somewhere beyond the city limits. Wooten walked heavily down the concrete steps, picturing the moment tomorrow when his son stood before Spivey and admitted his guilt. At least they'd have him home before long. Though what kind of home it would be was anybody's guess. His father out of work and probably out of the house, permanently unforgiven by Ardelia.

How did it get so bad, so fast?

A third siren began to sound as he reached the Ranchero. A fire at somebody's house, he thought idly. Probably nothing. Some grease flared up or an appliance started smoking. By tomorrow it would be forgotten. He opened the door and lowered himself into the car. But before he could slot the key into the ignition, it occurred to him that he didn't know where to go. Home was no good and he would never go back to 27. There was Cannon City, of course, though they would want him to decide down there and he wasn't ready for that. Mary's Bar BQ, the office – suddenly, everywhere seemed off limits to him. You spend five years building a city and then in the course of a few days you become a pariah in it.

A noise startled him. Shouts and curses. A half dozen boys had emerged from a stairwell, laughing and hollering as they tore across the parking lot. They were black. Joel's age. The fisted handle of a pick stuck up from the leader's head. They moved as if they'd been summoned by the gathering sirens. Wooten watched as they tore past the Dumpsters, joining the bike path for a few yards before turning off into the thin scrim of woods guarding Zeno's Way. He slotted his key into the ignition. But before he could turn the motor over his arm froze, paralyzed by a sudden realization that caused his heart to start pounding in the great cavity of his chest.

She'd said Thursday. Swope had come by the apartment on Thursday. But Ardelia didn't get the letter until Friday. Wooten had talked to her late Thursday night and she clearly hadn't read it, bidding him a sweet good night after quiet talk about daily things. There was no chance Swope would have heard from the mysterious author before her – whoever wrote the letter had said he or she was only thinking about telling others. Which meant that Austin must have found out some other way. Maybe he'd known for weeks. Months. But then why had he chosen just a few hours before Ardelia was told to visit the apartment? And why had he threatened Alice with expulsion unless she told him the truth? It was almost as if his visit was the cause of the letter, rather than the other way around.

Suddenly, Wooten understood. In one of those thudding beats of his heart, everything became clear. Swope had heard the rumor. Of course. This was Austin Swope. Nothing happened in this city without him knowing about it. He'd heard the rumor that Earl Wooten was about to be named city manager and he'd believed it. Just like Wooten had. And he'd found out about the Chicago trip – Wooten remembered turning aside some vague question at the party about his meeting with Savage. Which must have been Swope's way of probing him. And Wooten had lied. So Swope had hurt him. Found out about 27 and used it. Got someone to write the letter or maybe even done it himself. Thinking he was fighting back. He knew how Swope could be when he was crossed. Dangerous as a rabid animal. He'd seen it a dozen times, watched in awe as he turned his enemies to dust.

Which meant that it was Swope who'd been responsible for the dozen other small catastrophes that had plagued Wooten this past week. They were no coincidences, no run of bad luck brought on by his infidelity. Swope had been doing this to him. Probably using a security guard or off-duty deputy. All because of a rumor started by Savage to put the fear in Swope and placate the boys in Afro-Am. He'd put the fear in him all right. And Swope sent it right back at Wooten.

This had to be true. It was the only way the insanity of the last few days made sense.

Oh, sweet Jesus, Wooten thought. Joel. Swope had done that as well. He'd put Joel behind bars. For some reason Teddy had caused that girl to drown and now his father, possessed by a sudden hatred for Wooten, was making it seem like Joel had killed her. Saving his son and destroying Wooten at the same time. It explained everything. Why he wouldn't help. Why Teddy had turned against Joel. Why the authorities were so eager for him to plead guilty. Swope had thought he was being betrayed and so he fought back. Wooten was sure of it. He knew how the man thought.

He started his car and gunned the engine. He had to get over to Newton Plaza and straighten this out before it was too late. Have Swope call off whatever dogs he'd loosed. Let him know that he had nothing to fear. Because that's all this was. Misunderstanding and fear. There was nothing here that couldn't be fixed once the truth was out.

He almost sideswiped a state police cruiser hauling ass toward Fogwood as he pulled onto the pike. Wooten fell in behind it, using its speed to mask his own. He became aware of more sirens, at least a dozen of them now swirling around Newton. He made a bend and the Pavilion's canopy came into view. Just ahead the cruiser turned abruptly off the pike onto one of the residential streets lining the lake's north shore. Wooten looked down the street as he came parallel to it. Flame hovered over somebody's perfect lawn. A dozen people had gathered around. The police car's headlights illuminated a man in the process of pulling a garden hose toward the burning lamp. Which would only make it worse. Fool'd wind up knocking off the housing and then there'd be no getting near it. Wooten pulled over to the shoulder, knowing that he had to double back and help these people.

But a thought struck him as his tires crackled to a stop on the shoulder's gravel. He was suspended. His son was in prison. There was no time to help anybody. They'd have to figure out how to quench the fire for themselves. His foot found the gas pedal. Tonight, they were on their own. Just like him.

He passed another fire a few blocks later, this one attended by the same loose congregation of impotent onlookers. There was a Cannon County deputy in attendance, though his activity seemed limited to keeping people out of harm's way. Once again Wooten felt himself lured toward the crisis, though the feeling was weaker this time, easier to deny. As he passed a third fire at the northwestern corner of the lake he knew that the system was failing. The egghead from Chicago was right. It was in the design. Valves would keep popping now like buttons on a fat man's shirt until somebody turned off the main trunk line. And even then there would be additional fires as the gas already in the system bled off. The blazes would go on until after midnight.

He saw the burning man just before he reached the mall. The terrifying image flashed by so quickly it was hard to be sure that it was real. A flaming human figure, arms spread wide as it raced along a small cul-de-sac. Cyclonic after-images marked its course. Wooten slammed on the brakes and reversed back to the street's entrance. But by the time he got there the figure was gone. The only movement was a sole ruptured gaslight, burning unattended in front of the street's last house.

Just go, Wooten said. Save your boy.

Newton Plaza came into view. Although it was almost nine o'clock, lights shone right across the wall of glass. Everybody would be there. Including Swope. Wooten realized he hadn't figured out what he was going to say when he saw him. If he was going to confront him with the truth or try to outfox him. Though he quickly realized there was no choice. He could never contend with Swope at deception. The last few days had proven that. The truth was the only way. It was all he had left.

The wild boys reappeared just before he turned into the Plaza's parking lot, streaking directly in front of the speeding Ranchero. They were still laughing and hollering, giddy with the night's anarchy. Some carried looted things, radios and clothes. Wooten slammed on his brakes and swerved hard to the left, almost losing control as he wrestled the car into the parking lot. Haphazardly parked sedans blocked the way to his space. He left the Ranchero at a far corner and jogged to the main entrance. The security guard rose from his desk when he saw Wooten crossing the lobby, nervously wiping the palms of his hands on his polyester trousers.

'Mr Wooten, I have instructions that you are not to be admitted,' he said uncertainly.

Wooten stopped and stared at the man. Getting by him would be no problem. But that would be foolish. It would give Swope the excuse he needed to let others handle this for him.

'I've been reinstated to deal with the crisis,' he said sternly.

'Really? Nobody called down.'

'They haven't had time.'

The guard hesitated.

'Look,' Wooten continued, 'you hear the sirens? They got a new fire every two minutes out there. You want to be responsible for a few more houses burning down or you want to let me through so I can tell them where the goddamned off switch is?'

'Go,' the guard said, moving aside, even though he wasn't in the way.

An elevator door opened the moment he touched the

arrow. The ride up seemed to take no time at all. The door to the executive suite had been propped open with a flower pot. Wooten passed the empty reception desk and quickly crossed the shadowy expanse of the secretarial bullpen. Track lighting burned in the corridor leading to Swope's office. He could hear voices. The door of the hallway's first office was open, its floor-to-ceiling window affording a view of the northern and eastern parts of the city. Despite his urgency, what he saw stopped Wooten in his tracks. After several long seconds he crossed the empty office to get a better look.

The city was in flames. There were at least fifty gaslight fires burning in every occupied neighborhood. The sight reminded him of an East Texas oil field he'd once seen during his road-laying days. The main concentration of fire seemed to be on the trunk line running through Fogwood and Mystic Hills, the flickering flames configured like stars on the belt of some celestial entity. The jagged line of fire crossed Merlin's Way, where a lamp he guessed to be Martin O'Brien's burned just a hundred yards away from his own house. There were red and blue lights of emergency vehicles everywhere, moving helplessly among the fires. Wooten began to detect other flames in the city, structural fires whose existence could not be explained by the gas surge. The frames of two unfinished houses. Dumpsters at Fogwood Center and Renaissance Heights. He remembered that rampaging pack, roaming the city with the knowledge that the police had greater things on their minds.

Urgent voices sounded in the hall, moving quickly away from Swope's office. Wooten remembered why he was here. He waited in the darkness as a group of men passed. They were mostly engineers, though there were also a few familiar faces from Wooten's own construction gang. Their voices were both grim and thrilled, like a team about to take the field. When they were gone he stepped back into the hallway and walked silently down to Evelyn's anteroom. As he entered he could hear a familiar voice speaking behind Swope's half-open door. He stepped into a dark corner just as Chad Sherman emerged.

'Oh, and Chad,' Swope called after him.

He wheeled.

'No need to say anything about that guy who got himself burned.'

'Yes, sir.'

'And make sure you emphasize that the problem is being dealt with by the county authorities. Let people draw their own conclusions about where the blame lies.'

'Gotcha.'

After Sherman disappeared Wooten listened for a moment to make sure no one had been left behind. There was only silence. He stepped into the doorway. Swope stood at the far side of the model, staring out the window at the pulsing lights. Smoke from a recently lit Tiparillo wreathed his head.

'Austin.'

He turned quickly, his blue-gray eyes flexing in quickly mastered surprise.

'Earl,' Swope said, his voice free of emotion. 'Didn't Holmes contact you?'

'Yeah,' Wooten said. 'He contacted me.'

'Well, then, I appreciate your coming in to lend a hand, but we've got things under control. I think it's for the better that you weren't on the premises.'

There was no malevolence in Swope's voice. No aggression. Just the slight weariness of a man absolutely in the right.

'We have to talk.'

Swope took a quick drag of his cigarillo, its end pulsing like one of those fires behind him.

'Now's not good.'

Wooten said nothing. He just stood there, massive and undeniable.

'If this is about your suspension, Earl, I have to tell you that you better take it up with Savage.'

'You know what this is about.'

Swope held his ground behind the model. Waiting.

'You sent the letter to Ardelia.'

Swope exhaled, masking his face with smoke.

'Earl, I'm afraid I'm going to have to insist you leave.'

'What happened at the lake, Austin?'

452

'You know what happened.'

'Teddy did something to that poor girl and you're pinning it on Joel.'

Swope stared evenly at him. Not answering. Neither affirming nor denying. Suddenly, Wooten saw his opening. The man was simply afraid for his boy. All he had to do was let him know that he'd never do anything to harm Teddy. Just make him understand that he'd be willing to do whatever it took to help Swope protect his son. After all, they were friends. They'd built a city together. They could overcome this.

'Come on, Austin,' he said gently. 'It doesn't have to be like this. Listen, whatever happened, let's just you and me sit down and decide on a way out. To hell with Chones and Savage and everybody else. Let's just protect our families here. I'll do whatever it takes. Get Joel to say it was an accident. You know I will. You know that about me.'

Swope continued to stare at him, those small, colorless eyes unreadable.

'Look, they never even offered me the job,' Wooten continued. 'That's the thing you've got to understand. It was all a crock. Not that I would have taken it anyway. They want me to build an amusement park down in Virginia. It was supposed to be a big secret. You see? We're not against each other here. I know why you think we were but it's all right. It's always been all right.'

Finally, there was a break in the impenetrable facade of Swope's face. Worry creased his brow. His thin lips parted slightly. Wooten pressed on. Sensing victory now.

'Call Gus if you don't believe me. Ask him. And then let's get our boys out of this trouble.'

Swope absently flicked ash onto his carpet. For a moment he looked ready to agree. But then something happened. Slowly, his expression hardened. That coldness returned to his eyes.

'I don't know what you're talking about,' he said softly.

'Austin . . .'

'Earl, you're under a lot of pressure. That's understandable. No one will blame you for flying off on tangents like this.'

'They aren't tangents, Austin. They're the dead center.'

'I strongly urge you to take the plea bargain on offer. Otherwise Joel is in grave jeopardy.'

Wooten realized there would be no appealing to their friendship, to past heroics or a sense of camaraderie. All that was as dead as Susan Truax. Killed by a single malignant drop of suspicion.

He took a step forward, anger boiling up in him.

'What happened on that pier, Austin? Did Teddy try to rape her? Is that it?'

Swope gave a disgusted shake of his head. But there was no conviction in his scorn.

'You're so wrong . . .'

'What I can't believe is that you've done all this about a job. A goddamned *job*.'

'It's not about a job, Earl,' Swope said with a bitterness Wooten had never before heard.

'No,' Wooten answered slowly. 'I guess it isn't.'

'Take the plea, Earl.'

'I'll tell . . .'

'What? That you weren't putting the wood to that pathetic junkie down at Renaissance Heights? That you didn't lay hands on Joe Vota? That your son didn't hump that girl in her father's house?' Swope paused to allow the remainder of his confidence to return. 'What, Earl, are you going to tell the jury down in Cannon City that Joel isn't *black*?'

Wooten took a step forward.

'You motherfucker.'

Swope pointed a thin finger at him.

'Stand back. Or this is going to get a lot worse for you.'

Wooten continued to move forward.

'See, that's your mistake. You've made it so it can't get any worse for me. But I'm still standing. I'm still able to come at you.'

He reached the edge of the model. Swope's eyes began to flutter, looking for a way out of this. Vast tracts of carpet lay on either side of him. It was clear that Wooten could easily catch him if he tried to flee.

'What, you afraid now?' Wooten asked.

454

Swope's eyes dropped to the model. As if that were some sort of protection. Some sort of barrier. Wooten gripped its edge. It would be easy to flip it over, pinning Swope against that tinted glass, maybe even pushing him through. But he knew before the thought was even complete that he wouldn't do it. Not because he didn't want to. But because it was what was expected of him. And he was done with what was expected of him.

'I'm going to fight you on this, Austin.'

'You'll lose.'

'Probably. But I get the feeling you will, too, once I start talking. First I'm going to call Gus and the papers and everybody else. Give them my side of this. And then I'm going to make Teddy tell his lies to the whole world. I'm going to hire the best lawyer they got and he's going to put your son on the stand. For days. Weeks, if he can. I'm going to fight you, Austin. I'm going to keep the pressure on you until something breaks.'

Before Swope could respond there was a sound, the fleshy arrival of another body. The fear left Swope's face. Wooten turned. It was Chones. There was a walkie-talkie in his hammy right hand. He pointed it at Wooten.

'Should he be in here?'

'Not really,' Swope said.

'You want me to put him out?'

'There's no need for that,' Wooten said. 'I'm not the dangerous one here.'

He turned back to Swope.

'It's not over.'

'Whatever you say, Earl,' Swope said, though there was no ease in his voice.

Wooten turned and walked out of the office, careful to avoid the beefy shoulder Chones left in his way.

He saw the boys just before he got to his car. The same pack he'd already seen twice tonight. Two were leaning through the just broken window of an LTD. Wooten recognized the car by its faded PEACE WITH HONOR bumper sticker – it belonged to Chad Sherman. The third boy, the lookout, was tracking a flashing siren as it raced by on Newton Pike. Nobody had seen Wooten.

He walked over to them, his footfalls deliberately silent on the asphalt. It wasn't until he was three car lengths away that the sentinel finally spotted him. He grabbed the T-shirt of the nearest looter and pulled him backward. The boy turned to protest but then saw Wooten. He bolted without a word. The lookout followed, leaving the third boy behind. A swatch of underwear showed above his pants, its Fruit of the Loom label visible in the artificial light. Wooten was suddenly struck by an image of some loving, futile mother buying this hoodlum a pair of boxers. And with it came the realization that the boy was, like everybody else out here, nothing more than somebody's son.

The looter finally rose out of the car, an eight-track player in his hands. Wires dangled from it like the roots of some tenacious plant. The fisted pick Wooten had seen earlier had slumped to an unmenacing angle. The boy looked around for the others. Then he saw Wooten. His eyes briefly widened, then quickly hardened into their customary defiance.

'Go ahead,' Wooten said. 'Tear it up. Take it all.'

The boy stared at Wooten for a long moment. Then he snorted silently, a bitter, knowing smile tugging at his cracked lips. He turned and strutted off slowly, certain that no one would touch him tonight.

36

Teddy was getting a cold. Typical. This happened every time he went into the water. And this one was gearing up to be a real doozy – clogged sinuses, throbbing headache and a low-grade fever that no amount of Bayer would chase away. By tomorrow morning he'd be sick as your proverbial dog. Which meant three days of sucking Sucrets and trying to avoid his mother's stifling ministrations. Summer colds were the pits. He'd have to keep the air conditioner jacked up to cool out the fever, which would in turn make his head ten times worse. Bebe Rebozo would definitely not be able to blow his nose-oh. This was why he never went in the pool. Not because he was ashamed of his 'bod,' as Susan so artlessly maintained. He just didn't want to have to deal with the inevitable sickness immersion brought.

Susan. The name rang through his mind like an explosion in a slumbering city. He wasn't supposed to mention it. He'd made a deal with himself to keep her exiled in the oblivion she'd joined the previous night. It was the only way he was going to get through the next few days.

He checked his bedside clock: 9:34. Which meant he'd been trapped in his room for almost eight hours, trying to figure a way out of this mess. Normally, that would have been more than enough time. But no matter how hard he focused today, he couldn't seem to get anywhere. Whichever mental route he took, he always seemed to wind up back at square one. Half-formed thoughts swam elusively through his mind, like answers on Eight Ball that never adhered to the window. Each time he'd begin to come up with a new plan its evil twin would loom in his mind, contradicting and nullifying it. Yin kicks the shit out of Yang. Fischer draws with Spassky. McCartney smothers Lennon's poetry with a glib tune.

It was his interview with the two meatheads from the SBI that finally brought home the gravity of the situation. In the hour before that, he'd been able to kid himself that the whole rotten episode was in some way provisional, just another pickle for his father to jar. But when he was confronted by those two slouching, unintimidated cops, he finally knew that this was for real. The lie he was telling was going to have serious consequences. If he didn't do something, Joel was history. Through the dawn hours it had been easy to think his dad would sort it all out with no harm done to anybody. But not now. There were some things even he couldn't control.

So it was down to Edward M. Swope to find a way to get Joel out of this jam without frying his own ass in the process. After the cops left, he cloistered himself in his room and got to work. His imagination fired by a steady stream of bong hits and Lennon tunes, he began to run through all the permutations. First, he dispensed with the moves that were obviously wrong. Confessing, for openers. Not an option. It would only bring ruination on himself and his family. Besides, he hadn't done anything that needed expiation. His dad understood that and Joel ultimately would. What happened was an accident. There was no way Teddy was going to put his faith in some jury.

The first option he came up with was helping Joel escape. Bust him out of that podunk jail. Getting his hands on a gun would be hard but not beyond his capabilities. They could be in West Virginia within the hour, Mexico in two days. But it didn't take long to realize that escape was no good. Although a jail break was not without its visceral attractions for a guy who'd sat through Butch and Sundance three times one rainy afternoon, it was simply too fraught with risk. And then there was Harvard. As Swope pointed out Tuesday night, unless you were Ellsberg, Leary or Kissinger, they tended to frown upon blatant criminality up there.

He could always change his story. Say that the whole thing

had been a terrible accident that happened while they were messing around at the end of the pier. Joel had playfully pushed the girl, who'd fallen in the water and drowned. After that the two friends panicked and tried to cover it up. If they were guilty of anything it was rampant immaturity. But he soon realized that this wouldn't cut it, either. It was too late to change his story. It had already gone to press. The big ugly printing machine was up and rolling. You only had to take a look at those two cops to see that. The questions would be too knotty for even Teddy to answer, much less a dazed and confused Joel. Why hadn't they simply admitted it was an accident in the first place? Why hadn't Joel, the better swimmer, gone in the water to rescue the woman he loved? And why had Teddy turned against his friend? Even the dolts in Cannon City would see through that one. There was no changing his story. There would be no escape and certainly no confession. The dice had been rolled. Joel was going to jail. Like the Swope said, it was fate.

This is how it went, all afternoon. Round and round. And now night had arrived, bringing with it a bad cold. If only there was some way to effect a brief suspension of the space-time continuum so he could undo that insignificant little nudge. It would make things so simple. The Truaxes and the Wootens and the Swopes would all be happy citizens once again. Joel would be free and the mental snot clogging Teddy's brain would finally clear. This was what he didn't get. Why was this thing that everybody wanted so impossible? Why did that silly girl have to hit her vacant head and screw everything up?

'Teddy?'

His mother stood in the doorway.

'Hey, Ma.'

'Do you need anything?'

'The powers of resurrection.'

Her eyes narrowed.

'Teddy, listen . . .'

'Yeah?'

'If there's anything you want to talk to me about, I mean, you can. Whatever you want to tell me, it'll be all right.'

'No, Ma. I'm cool. Dad's been a big help.'

'I know he has, sweetheart. But your father sometimes asks a lot of people. And if you start to feel that it's all too much, I want you to know you can come to me.'

Teddy looked up at her. For a moment he wondered if maybe he should talk to her. She might have some ideas on what he could do. She could be a pretty sensible woman. But then he remembered what his father had said. No one should ever know. Not even her.

'Right, Mom. Sure. Appreciate it.'

After hovering for a few more seconds she disappeared. Teddy checked the clock: 9:41. He donned his headphones and punched on his customized Lennon tape for the umpteenth time. He considered firing up yet another bowl but decided against it. Better to lay off the herb until he sorted this one out. Toking now would only bring on coughing fits, amp his headache and make his schnoz run like Victoria Falls. Instead, he reached for the bottle of prescription cough syrup he'd found in the medicine chest earlier that evening. He'd got it from the family doc for his last bad cold after he announced that he categorically refused to fuck around with Vicks. It was the good stuff, codeine based, dispensed with great reluctance by a doctor who couldn't afford to lose Sally Swope's business. The dosage was written in big, cautionary letters on a label that was so soggy with red liquid it looked like a dressing to a fatal wound. Do not exceed two teaspoons. Blah blah blah. Teddy exceeded, downing a quarter of the bottle, enough to provide a sufficient buzz to get him through the night.

The tape's first song came on, that supremely meaningless ditty Teddy usually fast-forwarded right through. Not Lennon's finest hour. But still, it was part of the man's oeuvre. You had to take the good with the bad. That was how genius worked. After last night, Teddy should know.

And then, suddenly, it happened. Straight out of the blue. Just as the backing brass went through their first rendition of those five familiar notes, his answer came. Without even thinking about it, Teddy understood what had to be done. Jesus, it was right there in the song. John Himself providing

the answer in his shallowest-ever tune. Teddy rewound and
ran through the stanza again.

No one you can save that can't be saved.
Nothing you can do, but you can learn how to be you in time.
It's easy.

And it was. Easy. Teddy couldn't believe he hadn't thought
of it earlier. Joel was already saved. Nothing had to be done.
He just had to learn how to be himself in time. The answer
wasn't in keeping him out of jail. It was too late for that. A
certain stupid girl who shall remain forever nameless had
settled that matter when she started running her mouth last
night. The thing to do was to make sure the right stuff
happened to Joel *while he was there*. It was after he was in
prison that Teddy would save him. In fact, when he thought
about it, incarceration would be good for Joel. It would focus
him on what was important. He'd have time to read and
think and understand the things Teddy had been trying to tell
him these past few years, when the world's distractions had
begun to lure him away. He'd be able to forget about you
know who and learn how to be himself in time. Best of all,
there would be no more of this running away talk. Never
again was Teddy going to get ditched.
    So there it was. Teddy would look after Joel in jail. Look
after him like no friend had ever done. And, to do so, he
was going to make the ultimate sacrifice. He'd bag Harvard
and transfer to Hopkins. Maybe even Maryland, if that
made things easier. This is what he would do for his friend.
Give up his place at the best college in the world so that he
could be near Joel. And if they transferred him to some prison
out of state, Teddy would follow him there. With visits and
letters and phone calls, he could bring Joel around to see how
last night's accident was a good thing, saving him from a life
of mediocrity and drudgery, enabling him to go through this
rite of purification that would lead to a higher state of
consciousness. Teddy could give him countless books. Hesse
and Suzuki and Laing. Gandhi and George Jackson and
Huey Newton. He knew it wouldn't be easy. Joel's mind was

good, but it lacked discipline. There'd been too many years in which he'd been allowed to limp along on the crutches of charm and good looks. But Teddy would have time on his side now. Joel wasn't going anywhere. He would be rapt.

And it wouldn't be long until he was free. The Swope had mentioned something like three years, though with Teddy's tireless campaigning it would be way less. People would have to be impressed by the sight of one of Joel's victims fighting so hard on his behalf. He'd be out in less time than it would have taken him to get some useless diploma. And when he finally walked he'd be smarter than Bucknell could have ever made him, his mind running in perfect sync with Teddy's. They could get a place together up in Cambridge, where Teddy would finally be able to attend Harvard. Joel could enroll in some local school. BC. BU. The place was stinking with colleges. Like the Swope had said, nobody would hold a few years in the stir against a smart black kid. And they could be students together again. Freshmen. House jumpers.

All he had to do was let Joel know that it was cool. And he had to do it tonight. Otherwise he might not take the deal. Teddy knew that was the key to this whole thing. Because if Joel tried to fight the charge then he'd wind up getting twenty years and there'd be no saving him. The question was how to let him know. There was no way they'd put a call through to him in jail. And Teddy wasn't about to go down to Cannon City. One brush with authority was sufficient unto the day. Then he remembered what his father had said about arranging for Joel to get bail. There had been some sort of hearing that afternoon – they'd probably already cut him loose. Which meant that Joel was no doubt sitting at home this very minute, just waiting for his friend to come by and sort things out. All he had to do was pay him a visit.

Teddy's triumphant thinking was cut short by the most horrible noise he'd ever heard. It came roaring down the headphones, a bedlam of dying screeches and slow-motion moans, the din of a trillion souls being sucked into some fathomless abyss. He tore the headphones from his ears and looked for whatever howling chorus of demons had arrived to damn him to eternal torture. But his room was empty. It was just him and his Lennon posters. He checked his tape player. The wheel had slowed to a churning, erratic tumble. He punched stop and eject, then pulled the cassette from the slot, revealing a glistening, gutted tangle of ruined tape. He stuck his pinkie in the hole and began to rewind it. But it was no good. It had been shredded and twisted into an insoluble thread.

He chucked the busted cassette into his trash bin and looked at the clock: 10:01. Time to get over to the Wootens'. He downed another big swig of cough syrup and slid on his Keds. This was going to work. He was sure of it. Just before leaving the room he remembered something. Joel's visor. The perfect ice breaker. He plucked it from the bedstead where it had rested this past week and headed out into the Newton night.

He vacated the premises the back way, just to make sure he didn't run into his father, who'd categorically forbidden him from leaving the house until further notice. Though Teddy had heard him hurrying off an hour ago, there was no telling when he'd be back. His mother had no doubt already gone to bed. She wouldn't be a problem.

He heard the siren the moment he stepped through the sliding-glass door onto the back porch. He froze in his tracks, one hand still gripping the handle. His heart began to pound in his thin chest; blood coursed through his already dizzy head. The siren was moving south along Newton Pike. Which meant it was heading his way. This was it. They were coming for him. His story had fallen to pieces. Some crucial flaw had been detected by those two SBI thugs. Which was why his father had to rush from the house – to try to forestall the inevitable. But not even the Swope could prevent the shitstorm now gathering on the horizon. Teddy was going down. His whole beautiful plan was about to be flushed down the crapper. He'd never be able to show Joel the sacrifices he was prepared to make, never have the chance to explain how things would be.

He leaned against the house's cool wood shingles for support, wondering how long he would get. His dad had said just a few years. But that was for Joel. They wouldn't go so easy on Teddy. There were lies involved. Trickery and deceit. And then there was the jealousy his father had spoken of last night. Those twelve spiteful gentlemen of the jury would be sure to throw the book at him. He just hoped they'd let him have his tunes. Lennon would help him get through. He'd write to him at this Dakota place he'd just moved to in Manhattan. They could get a correspondence going. The Swope-Lennon Prison Letters. That would be intense. There could even be a visit and then maybe a song on the next album. He'd written one for Angela, after all. John Sinclair. 'Attica State.' Surely Teddy would rate. If not a song then at least a few lines.

He was snapped from his reverie by the realization that the siren had come to a halt down near the north shore of Lake Newton. Which meant he wasn't going to be busted after all. Which meant there was still time to save Joel. Energized by his reprieve, Teddy bolted down the steps and headed around the side of the house, wondering if maybe he should drive. But that would be too risky. The Swope would know he was gone for sure if he saw the Firebird missing. Better to walk.

Other sirens had begun to sound as he climbed to the top of Prospero's Parade. There were a half dozen of them, zigzagging all over the place. Teddy wondered what it could possibly mean. Maybe the restless natives at Renaissance Heights had finally gone on the rampage. He turned onto Merlin's Way, but only got a few steps before he was hit by a sucker-punching spell of dizziness that snipped the strings holding his body aloft and sent him crashing into the Bartelts' carefully trimmed shrubbery. Twigs shattered beneath him and then the sweet smell of peat filled his nostrils. Bummer. He rolled onto his back and took a few deep breaths, his vision tunneling into a star-sized dot, his head so light it felt like a weather balloon. Perhaps he'd ingested a tad too much of that syrup. It took him a while to remember the exact procedure for standing. When finally on his feet he allowed himself a minute or two to get his gyroscope up and running, then attempted a few tentative steps. Left, right, left. That was better. He noticed something in his right hand. The visor. He settled it onto his head. It felt good to be wearing something of Joel's. Even though he knew it must make him look like a complete nimrod.

He continued down Merlin's Way, taking deep breaths in an effort to clear his mind before arriving at the Wooten house. He'd have to be at his most articulate to pull this one off. He wasn't about to kid himself here. It would be hard to make Joel see past his undoubtedly grim short-term prospects. And then there was the thorny subject of a certain blond girl's demise. There might be some bad scenes on that score. But it was cool. Teddy was ready for any eventuality. He'd hang with his friend as long as it took for him to see that there was only one future for him. Teddy's future.

The fire appeared the moment he turned the last sharp bend before the Wooten house. At first he thought it was some sort of neo-biblical visitation, a burning bush or flaming angel come to cast light upon his crime. Or maybe it was simply a hallucination, fueled by stress, sleeplessness and his unwise consumption of that codeine. Whatever it was, it was spooky, the way the fire just hovered there in the darkness. Teddy was sorely tempted to turn around and bolt for the sanctuary of his room. That horrible music and the sirens and now this – it was looking like a bad night to be out and about. But he had a mission. He'd just have to brave it. Joel had to be told to take the plea.

He took a bracing breath and walked on. As he drew closer to the fire he relaxed, realizing that it wasn't some disembodied spectral conflagration after all, but simply a ruptured gaslight. Urgent blue flame poured through the shattered iron assembly, hissing with a wicked and insinuating sibilance. The lamp belonged to Something-or-Other O'Brien, a lawyer who worked down in DC and regularly came by the house to borrow the Swope's legal tomes. A crowd had gathered on the stretch of lawn between the lamp and the house. As he approached unseen Teddy realized that he knew these people. In addition to Mr and Mrs O'Brien and their dickhead son Chris, there were the Parkers and the Bartelts, into whose shrubbery Teddy had just tumbled. O'Brien and Parker held something over their crotched arms; Chris, who'd captained Newton High's 1–11 football team, balanced a baseball bat on his shoulder. The women and kids stood behind them, up by the porch.

Just as Teddy reached the edge of the property the O'Briens' Jack Russell bolted from among the knot of men. Teddy, who had tangled with this dog in the past, stood his ground, not wanting to add a bite to the day's catalog of woe. Somebody whistled and the dog froze. There was another whistle and it retreated, casting resentful glares over its shoulder. Teddy pressed on, vectoring across the lawn toward the small assembly of citizens. Everyone was staring at him now. Light and shadow danced across their faces, making them look like they were grimacing. Bits of broken glass littered the sod beneath the burning lamp. He could now see that O'Brien and Parker held shotguns.

'*Hola*, citizens,' Teddy said, his voice sounding like it was coming from a point just beyond his right ear. 'What gives?'

For a moment the only reply was the gaslight's exaggerated hiss. It was O'Brien, a fat man whose flaxen hair looked like it should have surrounded a corncob, who finally spoke.

'Haven't you heard? These damned things have been blowing up all over town.'

'Really?' Teddy said. 'Golly.'

They all watched the flame for a moment.

'You gonna shoot it out or something?' he asked, nodding to the gun resting on O'Brien's arm.

'Word is they've been taking advantage of the trouble to break into houses over in Fogwood,' Parker explained. 'Guy over on Zeno's Way said a bunch of them just walked right in and took his TV.'

'They being . . .' Teddy wondered.

'*Them*,' Parker said.

'Ah.'

'We're just making sure they don't try anything up here,' O'Brien added.

'I *wish* the fuckers'd come.'

That was Chris speaking. Teddy nodded a sober hello. Last fall, Chris had given him a mega-wedgie after gym class, hanging him like curing meat on the edge of a locker. It had been ten gonad-crushing minutes before Joel had found him and let him down. Teddy immediately told Ardelia, who suspended Chris for the next game, which turned out to be the team's only win of the season. But all that seemed to be forgotten in the current emergency.

'Does your dad know about this?' O'Brien asked.

'He left home for Newton Plaza almost an hour ago.'

They waited, clearly in need of further reassurance. Teddy's head suddenly began to swim. Out beyond the dome of light, the darkness was spinning cyclonically. He hoped he wasn't about to fall again. That glass looked sharp.

'Contingencies are being hammered out as we speak,' he heard himself saying. 'Stay close to your telephones and make sure you have plenty of fresh drinking water stored. Above all else, defend your property.'

Was he actually saying this? The words came without thought or intention. And yet the ad-hoc suburban posse accepted his counsel with sober, appreciative nods. Women were on the scene now, having migrated down from the porch. They stared at him with the blank expectancy of refugees. Even the fucking dog seemed to be mollified by Teddy's presence.

'Moments like these test our mettle,' he continued. 'They force us to decide what kind of community we're going to become. Whether law and justice will prevail or its idiot sibling, anarchy, will rule the day.'

This sounded good, though Teddy wondered if it might not be wasted on this particular crowd. Chris seemed especially at sea, a quizzical look twisting his thick features. In the ensuing silence the men began shifting their weaponry from crook to crook; the women hiked their draped sweaters onto frail shoulders. Teddy, champion debater, Robespierre of the Newton High student council, knew when he was on the verge of losing an audience. He decided to get while the getting was good.

'Well, good night,' he said pleasantly. 'I'll make sure Dad knows what's up.'

He didn't wait for their response, heading without further comment back along Merlin's Way. He could feel his body sway as the codeine washed sluggishly through him. He was beginning to wish he hadn't taken so much. He walked on, step after step, yard after yard. He passed one last copse of trees and then the Wooten house came into view. The windows were dark. Teddy swore beneath his breath – he hadn't counted on them being in bed for the night. But when he reached the bottom of the driveway he saw that both the Ranchero and the Le Sabre were gone. They must all still be down in Cannon City. Which was excellent news – he could wait in Joel's room. This way, he would be free to explain the future to his friend without having to run the gauntlet of Ardelia and the Earl.

The only problem was getting inside. On those nights that Teddy and Joel had to sneak in after staying out too late they used the guest room window around back. Because it was ten feet off the ground, nobody bothered to lock it. But they needed each other to do that, Teddy standing on Joel's broad shoulders and piling through, then creeping around to the kitchen's sliding-glass door to let his friend in. It would never work on his own. He walked around the back of the house anyway, trying every door he passed, hoping to get lucky. Garage, basement. No soap. He stepped up onto the deck and jiggled the sliding door. Locked. The guest room window hovered tantalizingly beyond reach. And of course there was no ladder in sight. Teddy went back around to the front of the house, trying more windows and doors as he went. But the place was locked down tight. The Earl's years in the badlands of St Louis had made him ridiculously security conscious. As if anybody was going to bust into his house out here. Well, all right, Teddy was, but that was different. He was a friend of the family, whether anybody knew it or not. By the time he reached the front porch he'd reconciled himself to waiting in the shadows for their return and then resorting to the hoary convention of tossing pebbles against Joel's window. For no good reason, he stepped up to the front door and gave the knob a hopeless little twist.

It opened. He couldn't believe his luck. The lock was broken. The pigs must have done it when they busted Joel. Typical. He stepped into the house, making sure to pull the

468

door shut behind him. It was completely dark. He hit a light to get his bearings and almost leapt out of his skin when he saw the deep and unreadable eyes of Joel's slave ancestor on the wall. Teddy could never get used to that guy. After quickly charting a course up to Joel's room, he turned off the lights and plunged into the welcoming darkness.

37

Dreams filled the night. They played across the back of Wooten's house like the outsized projections of a drive-in movie. Bad dreams this time, disconnected fragments that were nothing like the peaceful apparitions of the long My Song nights. The first was the most complete, recalling the chaotic moments after a napalm drop during his last tour. Truax himself had called for the raid after his platoon had been pinned down by an ambush. F-4s had responded almost immediately, lighting up the jungle a few hundred yards ahead. The ensuing rumble and crackle was broken after thirty seconds by a screeching sound high in the triple canopy, a noise so unexpectedly bizarre that most of the men began to smile in bewilderment. But the smiles quickly faded as the source became apparent – a stampede of macaque monkeys fleeing the explosion through the thick liana. They were burning, every one of them wreathed in haloes of blue flame that set small fires in their wake. The first of them began to drop just before they reached the hunkered-down patrol, screaming and writhing in the swampy earth like children playing in the rain. A new guy lowered his M-16 to put the closest out of its misery but Truax ordered him to shoulder his weapon. Mercy too often meant death out here. The monkey could die in his own time.

That dream was followed by a quick image of a ville that had been sacked by a platoon of renegade marines. Truax's patrol arrived to find the place in ruins. Hooches had been burned, locals and animals slaughtered. Most of the bodies had been dumped in a well, though one girl – she couldn't have been more than twelve, Susan's age – was curled on the floor of a hooch, a plastic bag clinging amniotically to her face, the legs of a Barbie emerging from her bloodied vagina. In the dream the doll's legs began to scissor and Truax found himself reaching to pull them out, only to find they were too slick to grasp. After that came a vision of the tax collector who'd been staked to the ground by VC in a paddy just off Route 4. He was a gnarled old Chinaman who stared at Truax with milky, beseeching eyes. At first he seemed to be miraculously unharmed. After checking him for booby traps they cut him loose. It was then that Truax discovered the writhing colony of maggots his captors had spread beneath him like spring seeds. The parasites had eaten through the flesh around his ribs and were nibbling at the edge of his liver. This time, Truax didn't worry about alerting the enemy. They knew exactly where he was. He took his .45 from its holster and put a round through the man's right eye, leaving him to the maggots who'd already claimed his flesh as their due.

Truax shook himself awake after that one, frightened that the dreams would suck his fevered mind into a pit from which he might never emerge. He couldn't let the night get the better of him. He had to stay clear. Wooten was down in Cannon City, arranging his son's freedom with lies and bribes. Truax could not let that happen. He would have to stay alert to be sure the boy was punished.

He began to perform the long-familiar series of stretches and twists that ushered blood into his tired muscles. The only resistance came when he tried to move the fingers of his right hand. They responded listlessly, wriggling just a few unpredictable centimeters. The hand was dying now. Some time in the late afternoon he had removed the glove and the bandages to look. The first whiff of unfettered rot drove him to the treehouse's rear window, where he'd vomited out a stream of still-hot coffee. When he held the hand up to the last of the day's sunlight he could see that the flesh was cracked and inflamed all the way to the veins of his wrist. Waves of fever pulsed from it toward every precinct of his exhausted body. And now, as he struck the flattened palm against a two-by-four, he felt only a faint telegraphic hum. Soon his hand would no longer be part of him. Once he was sure Joel had been punished he would go back to that old doctor at Bethesda and let him saw it off. Truax had known so many men who'd lost so much of themselves that forfeiting a hand seemed almost insignificant.

A siren began to wail in the distance, drifting up from the northern edge of the city, beyond the lake where they had found his daughter. At first Truax thought nothing of it, though after a few seconds he realized that it was moving into Fogwood. He reached down to make sure his weapon was where he'd left it. The fever spiked, bringing another dew of sweat to his skin just as more sirens began to sound, coming from various directions now, all of them heading toward the city. Some choked off abruptly just as others materialized. The night seemed to be built of their howls.

And then he understood. Joel. He'd escaped. Wooten had paid off someone at the jail; a door had been left open. And now the boy was back in Newton. Chones and others were making a show of looking for him, though of course he would never be found. Not unless Truax did it himself. His eyes instinctively sought out that near-invisible patch of graffiti in the treehouse's corner. *Joels. dick.*

Suddenly, as if summoned by the sirens, firelight began to flicker through the trees to the northeast of Wooten's house. No sound accompanied its appearance, no explosion or combustive sigh. Truax leaned forward to get a better look. The fire was only a couple hundred yards away. There was no way to be sure what was burning. A car. Debris. Shadowy human forms began to arrive at the scene; there were urgent shouts. Although the flames seemed to possess great energy, the fire itself wasn't growing any bigger. Truax was tempted to go check it out but that would mean leaving the house. And he couldn't do that. The house was all he had.

After a few minutes he looked away from the fire to find that the slope of that snowy hill at Fort Bragg had appeared on Wooten's back wall. Truax felt something slacken in him. The good dreams had finally returned. Susan was a little girl and she was alive and they were racing down that hill. The cold and the speed quickly soothed his fever. As long as he could stay like this then everything would be all right.

But it didn't last – after just a few seconds he sensed that the dream was going wrong. The hour was too late, dusk giving way to darkness. And there were no other racers on the slope, just the mangled frames of Flexible Flyers that had been crushed against evil-looking boulders. Silent figures watched from the side of the hill, heads bloodied, arms and legs splinted. There were no cheers and laughter, just weak shouted warnings telling Truax that he should get his daughter out of harm's way. Worst of all, the forgiving plain at the hill's bottom was veiled by a blackness so absolute that it was impossible to know what it hid. Another voice began to cut through the howling winter air – a terrified Susan, telling him she didn't want to do this. Begging him to stop. But he was powerless. They were going too fast. Racing down a slope that was about to enter the darkness.

And then, just seconds before they reached the bottom, the dream vanished, leaving only the sirens and the cicada and Truax's own rapid breathing. That flame still pulsed steadily beyond the trees. It took him a moment to realize why he was awake and when he did he felt a clarity of mind more intense than anything he'd known since My Song.

Someone had come around the side of Wooten's house.

It was a single figure, moving in silence and stealth. A boy. A man. The backyard was too dark to make out who he was. Truax's first temptation was to leap from the treehouse and challenge him. But it was too soon. It might be another of those reporters. He had to be certain before he acted. Whoever it was climbed onto the deck and tugged at the sliding glass door. Truax snatched the .45 from the smooth plywood, his eyes never leaving the figure as it walked back down the porch steps and disappeared around the side of the house. A few seconds later the front door opened. A silhouette was briefly framed in the doorway before being swallowed in darkness. Two seconds later a light flashed on and off in the front hall, so quick that it was impossible to make out anything except the familiar leather visor shielding the interloper's face. Truax was tempted to rush the house straight away, but his discipline kept him sitting perfectly still, in case there were others. Nothing happened for ten seconds. Joel was alone. And then another light flashed. This one in the boy's bedroom window.

He had come home to get money or a car. Wooten must have bought off the whole county to keep the cops away this long. Truax dropped through the hatch onto the peaty ground and headed toward the deck, moving in a half crouch, the weapon held in front of him. His feet made no sound on the thick sod. The sirens continued to wail. When he reached the bottom of the redwood steps he paused to hear if anyone else was approaching. But there was no one. The house was empty. There was only Joel.

He took the steps three at a time. He paused for a cautious moment at the sliding-glass door, then slammed the stock of his weapon against one of the flower decals. There was a soft, hollow sound as the safety glass puckered. Truax had to strike it three more times to punch all the way through. The reports of his blows were no louder than a child's cough. Bits of honeycombed glass fell silently on a dimpled rubber mat bearing the word WELCOME! Truax used his bad hand to widen the hole, chopping away at the shattered edges. He knew he must be cutting himself but there was no longer any feeling. When the hole was big enough he stuck his weapon in his belt and reached in with his left hand. The lock opened with a gentle click.

The ice machine gave raucous birth to a few crescents just as he stepped into the kitchen. He walked quickly across the tiled floor, his shoulder setting a row of hanging pots gently ringing, a sound that reminded him of the matin bells of a Delta monastery that always told him the night's danger had passed. He moved down the hallway, wondering if he should call Swope. But there was no time. He had to secure the boy first. Then they would take him somewhere where he could be punished. Baltimore or, better, Washington. Somewhere the law still held.

At the bottom of the steps he listened. There was only silence. He started to climb, working a round into the breech and then clicking off the safety. They might have given the boy a gun. Truax did not want to hurt him but there was always the chance he'd have to. It took him a moment at the top of the steps to figure out which door was Joel's. Last on the left. Just like Susan's. He headed toward it, raising his weapon to a ready position. Command and control. He placed his ear to the door's cool wood. There was a wheezing breath inside. Truax placed his bad hand on the knob. Getting a grip was impossible – his flesh was too slick with blood and rot. So he put the .45 into his belt and gave the handle a slight twist with his good hand. It was unlocked. He took a deep breath and entered the room.

Earl Wooten was driving fast. He was going thirty as he left the Newton Plaza parking lot, sixty by the time he reached Mystic Hills. Twice he passed speeding state police prowlers. Neither bothered him. They had bigger things to worry about. As did Wooten. He had to get home and let Ardelia know about Swope's lies. Tell her what she'd known from the minute the police knocked on the door. Joel was innocent. Their son was not guilty. And then he would call McNutt and tell him to stop everything. There would be no deal with the State. The plea would remain as it was. After that, Wooten would go down to Cannon City and demand to see his son so he could let him know that the doubting was over. They would fight this. Van Riper and Chones and Swope would never win. It might take everything they had but Joel would not be punished for what had happened to Susan.

Wooten cursed his stupidity as he drove, the swamp-blind, hanky-headed stubbornness that had enabled Swope to play him like a stride piano. That was the most galling thing. Not the man's trickery or his sheer evil. But the fact that his schemes had stood upon a single foundation – Earl Wooten's brittle spine. Swope had known that Wooten would be so grateful to a high-powered white man for befriending him that he would never think to doubt him, that he would believe the worst about his own son before suspecting some scrawny and strange white boy. He had been weak and because of that Joel was being hurt.

No more. From now on, Wooten would challenge Swope

every step of the way. He knew it wouldn't be easy. Swope's smug expression at his office told him all he needed to know about that. The man had worked the angles. Every plank and nail in his house of lies was in place. But Wooten also knew that once he removed the foundation Swope had laid – his own blind Tommery – the whole rotten edifice would begin to tumble. Maybe not right away and maybe not in one great surge. But it would come down. Swope might be able to take away his job and wreck his marriage. Bankrupt him and even take away his house. But he would not get his son. Too many boys had already been taken. Joel would not be one more.

He raced up Merlin's Way, the thought of Joel locked in some cramped cell making him push the gas pedal right down to the floor. He could tell that his own house was empty as he bumped over the driveway's undulant curb. Which meant Ardelia was still down with Joel. Not that it mattered. McNutt could break the news to her. It didn't matter. Nothing mattered but his boy's freedom. He pulled himself out of the rocking car and strode through the front door, that broken lock rattling in his fist like cracking knuckles.

The worst thing he'd ever smelled froze him in the middle of the hallway. It was as if someone had pumped in a distillation of all the unholy stinks Wooten had ever unearthed: dead animals and ruptured sewer lines and festering clots of Mississippi peat. It was not a smell that belonged in his house.

And then, before Wooten could even ask himself what the hell was going on, a familiar voice sounded upstairs.

Teddy was trying to stop his head from spinning. It was worse now than it had been back on Merlin's Way. He'd gone through all the usual sobering drills to bring himself down, taking deep breaths and trying to focus on specific objects, though all he'd been able to accomplish was to let that bad noise sneak back into his head. Only this time it was trapped inside his brain and there was no way to turn it off, no headphones to remove or button to punch. It was as if the shrieks and wails had been permanently embedded in his cerebrum. He tried to conjure other tunes to crowd them out.

'Revolution.' 'Helter Skelter.' 'Instant Karma!' 'Power to the People!' None of them stuck. After just a few bars they would fade into that howling, churning stew of sound.

So he tried to drown it out with good thoughts. And there was only one of those worth thinking – that this was going to work out. Now that he was in Joel's room, he was certain of it. All those years and all those times together had to mean more than some stupid accident at a fake lake. Friends made sacrifices for each other all the time. Took bullets and fell on grenades. Kept their counsel in the face of torture and prison. Sacrifice was the anvil on which friendship was forged. Teddy couldn't remember if he'd read that or made it up. Either way, it was true. Joel would have to understand. Now that a certain party was out of the way, there was nothing stopping him.

As if in answer to these positive vibes, the noise stopped abruptly, cut off like a lifted needle. And then he saw why. The bedroom door was opening. The racket in his brain must have stopped him from hearing them return. He stood too quickly, causing his vision to tunnel into a narrow corridor populated by dozens of brilliant floaters. The door came all the way open and there was a silhouette. Joel. It had to be.

'Hey, man, it's me,' Teddy said.

In response Joel raised a hand. Just like he used to in those empty houses, right before they would jump. Teddy relaxed. Everything was cool. Nothing would have to be explained. Nothing else mattered. He took a step forward, reaching out to grasp his friend's hand.

And then the room was filled with light and the air was gone from his frail lungs and he was falling; falling before he'd had a chance to grab hold.

The boy rose from the bed and came at him, saying words he could not understand. Truax pulled the weapon quickly from his belt. His grip was clumsy, his finger too low on the trigger. The boy took another step and raised his hand just as Truax moved his finger to a better position. His actions sent a tiny spasm of adrenalized energy along Truax's arm, causing his finger to twitch before it was settled. The weapon discharged. The round caught the boy a few inches right of center, spinning him into the darkness. He flipped back over the bed and hit the window frame, bringing down curtains. After that there was no sound in the room, no light. Just this thing he had done.

He stood perfectly still for a long moment. This was not right. He had only wanted to secure the boy and then take him to Swope. He reached blindly for a light switch with his bad hand but couldn't feel anything. His eyes remained on the body heaving beneath the curtain. This was not right. He had to call Swope. He'd know what to do. How to make people understand about the gun going off. He'd told Truax from the beginning that if anything happened he would handle it. All he had to do was call.

The boy began to breathe fast and shallow. Truax knew what that meant. He'd seen it so many times. It would not be long. But it was all right. Swope would make everyone understand. Truax had only meant to stop him. The boy had come forward and raised his hand. No one would blame him for this.

Light erupted behind him. Truax wheeled. The shadow of a man's head was growing larger on the floor. No, Truax thought. It's too early. He hadn't called Swope yet.

He tightened his grip on his weapon. This time he would be ready.

The explosion happened at the same instant Wooten realized that it was Teddy who had spoken. He knew it was a gun immediately. He'd heard plenty of them in his day, fired in anger and celebration and even jest. Though none of them had the same thunderous authority as the one that rolled down the broad staircase. He hesitated for a moment, an infinite number of grisly scenarios playing through his mind. Each worse than the last. Each involving Joel and Teddy. But none of them could be right. Joel was in jail. And Teddy was huddling under his father's protection back on Prospero's Parade.

Wooten shook away his indecision and raced up the stairs. That beastly smell grew stronger with every step he took. He paused at the top, looking down the hall. It was dark down there, the explosion's echo making the air seem blacker still. He hit the hall light. Ten long steps took him to the door, that dead meat smell mixing with the unmistakable tang of gunpowder as he drew closer.

At first he could see nothing but the darkened shapes of his son's furniture. He reached in and turned on the light. Wooten understood nothing about the sight that greeted him. John Truax stood in the middle of the room, a large pistol in his hand. Teddy Swope lay to his right, crumpled at the foot of the bed, his tangled body shrouded with fallen curtains, Joel's visor at a jaunty angle on his head. More blood than that skinny body should have ever contained leaked into the fabric covering him, staining it a lucent black. His eyes were closed, their lids fluttering. His mouth labored for air, each breath accompanied by an evil-sounding suck from his chest. Twin bubbles, pink with oxygenated blood, expanded and contracted in his nostrils, like the exposed lungs of some frail mammal.

Wooten looked back at Truax just as he raised the gun. It shook like an insect's wing.

'John, no.'

'He was going to get away.'

'Teddy? From what?'

Truax didn't seem to hear what he was saying. And then Wooten understood. He thought he'd done this thing to Joel.

'John, what have you done?'

Truax pulled back the gun's hammer. His hand shook even harder.

'Look. Just . . . look.'

Wooten pointed at Teddy. The boy's breathing grew even more tremulous.

'Look what you've done,' he said, almost shouting now.

Truax blinked and then he understood. Without lowering the gun he looked down at the boy he'd shot. He stared at Teddy for a long time without expression.

'He's the one who killed your girl,' Wooten said. 'Teddy did it. And his father is covering it up.'

Truax looked up at Wooten.

'Why do you think he's here?' he continued, pointing to Teddy. 'He's guilty, John. He's the one.'

Something shifted in Truax's eyes. He nodded once. Wooten let himself breathe. The poor man understood. This could end now. Bad as it was, it was about to be over.

'All right,' Truax said wearily. 'All right.'

And then he put the shivering gun in his mouth. As it passed his lips his hand stopped shaking. His eyes fell shut and a stillness settled over his whole body. Wooten began to shout but before he could utter a word the room was filled with a terrible sound. Truax dropped heavily onto the bed, his arms flopping lazily to his sides. His left foot gave a few weak kicks, then settled. Mist and smoke hung where he'd stood. There was a pattern on the wall behind him. Whatever noise was left from the explosion was swallowed by the ringing that now filled Wooten's ears. He took a step forward but stopped when he realized there was nothing he could do.

The boy, he thought. Help him. He crossed the room and kneeled by Teddy. Do not look at the other thing, he told himself. Just let it be. That is for others. Look to the boy now. There's a chance for him. He peeled back the bloody drapery. Teddy's T-shirt looked like it had been used to mop up motor oil. The wound was just below his right clavicle, a second concavity in his woebegone chest. Lessening waves of blood pumped from it. Wooten gathered the end of Joel's comforter into a ball and pressed it against the hole. Knowing even as he did that it was too late.

Teddy's eyes fell open. They were badly dilated, though he seemed to recognize Wooten. There was an interruption in his breathing. His dry lips smacked. He was trying to say something. Wooten leaned forward, putting his cheek next to the boy's mouth. It was hard to hear through the ringing.

'Tell Joel it's cool,' Teddy gasped. 'I got it all figured.'

Wooten pulled back. The boy's eyes closed and a small, angelic smile twisted his lips. The flutter of his chest stopped and then a last gargle of blood seeped from the wound. Wooten knew there were things he should do to the boy's chest and his mouth to help him, though he knew even more deeply that there was no use.

480

Voices and footsteps began to penetrate the sound in his ears. It was Ardelia, home with the girls. He could tell by the way she was speaking that they'd heard none of this. Wooten stood. He looked down one last time at Teddy and then turned away, careful not to look at the body on the bed. He was moving quickly now. He had to get out of here. He had to be with his family. He had to protect them from this.

38

Austin Swope placed his palms on the cool membrane of glass that protected him from the elements and looked out over the city below. He had to admit – Newton was beautiful on fire. Most of the forty-three gaslights that had erupted before they turned off the trunk line still burned, as did the scattering of arson jobs set by kids taking advantage of the temporary confusion. Luckily, these were limited to uninhabited structures. House frames. Dumpsters. Some portable toilets at the Pavilion, whose chemically treated shit burned like Sterno canisters at a buffet. Chones had picked up most of the troublemakers and was holding them in the gym at Newton High. They'd be released without charge later, when things were quiet. There'd been enough arrests for one summer. Blue lights from prowlers and fire trucks strobed the city's houses and trees, though they lacked the urgency of an hour earlier, when the crisis was in full swing and it looked like this whole business might get out of hand.

But now, the party was just about over. Thank Christ. There would be no more gas fires. Those currently burning would soon die when the system finally bled out. The unaffected lamps had already begun to flicker into oblivion. All in all, the night had not been the disaster it first seemed. When the call had come to his home about multiple explosions, Swope had experienced a few minutes of un-controlled dread. This was too much. Things had finally swirled beyond his control. First the job and then Teddy and now a con- flagration that would engulf them all. The drive over to Newton Plaza had only made his panic worse as he passed fire after fire, most of them attended by clusters of terrified citizenry. Everything was falling apart. By dawn the city would be ruined and he would be exposed as a liar and a fraud.

But when he was greeted in his office by the anxious, dependent faces of a dozen good men, each of them needing his counsel and strength, he knew that everything was going to be all right. He was back in his element. He soon lost himself in the crisis, just as he had when a soaked and terrified Teddy had walked through the door twenty-four hours earlier. Emergency responses were coordinated. Chones was called. Engineers were summoned, many of them redolent of dinners they would never finish. Citizens were mollified and the press kept at bay. Within an hour of his arrival the main gas trunk line had been closed. As far as anybody could tell there had only been one major injury, some fool homeowner who'd tried to deal with things himself. He was currently on his way to Hopkins with third-degree burns. Which meant another reach into the company's deep pockets. But still, it could have been a lot worse.

Soon it would be over and the cleanup could start. Maintenance crews were already assembling in various sheds and garages throughout town. They'd be rolling by midnight, weeding out the ruined hulks of erupted lamps. Dozers would level the burned structures, flatbeds cart off the charred Dumpsters and toilets. By dawn you would have to look twice to see the trouble's remains. The vultures of the press would find the carrion picked clean. To the citizens, the sirens would seem like nothing more than an irksome dream.

Looking over the dying fires, Swope felt a sudden, fathomless pride at the horizon-to-horizon panorama of houses and roads and schools; the mall and the lake and the concert park. Pride, because the city was now his, promised to him just a few minutes ago, when he'd called Savage to give him the all-clear. They had been in constant contact throughout the day, first about Joel and then the gaslights.

'You've handled this well, Austin,' Savage said soberly as the call came to an end.

483

'Thanks.'

Swope realized that the moment had come to finally grasp what was his.

'Listen, Gus, there's one more thing. I'd like a decision on city manager.'

'Tonight?'

'It's crazy, me having to call you on every nickel-and-dime decision. The situation out here is fluid. I got a hundred kids locked up at the high school and a couple thousand pissed-off citizens with no gas. I really think I've earned the right to manage matters as I see fit.'

The ensuing silence was shorter than Swope had thought it would be.

'Of course you have. All right. Austin, congratulations – as of now you are the city manager.'

'Full term?'

'Sure. I'll make some calls and get the board to rubber-stamp it in the morning. But you're the man.'

'Can I announce it out here? It might soothe jangled nerves.'

'You can shout it in the trees. Just keep the lid on. Whatever it takes. We've still got two thousand units to sell.'

'Oh, we'll move units, Gus. Don't worry about that.'

'I look forward to hearing your ideas on the subject.'

'That you will.'

After hanging up his eyes shifted focus from the fires to the damaged pier. The cops had ringed it off with yellow tape earlier in the day, when he was at home dealing with Teddy. It suddenly occurred to Swope that he could have it pulled down. There was no need to clear it with anyone. All he had to do was give the order. Once the cops released the scene he'd dispatch a wrecking crew. Damn thing was jinxed anyway. He'd characterize the dismantling as a tribute to the city's first murder victim. Use the wood to build a playground nearby. The Susan Truax Memorial Tot Lot. On second thought, maybe he'd wait on that one. The thing about memorials was that they made it hard to forget. Better to restrict his beneficence to a healthy chunk of change for John and Irma.

Irma. Jesus, that had been insane. He still couldn't believe he'd let it happen. Complete loss of control. Not that he blamed himself. That soft flesh and those expert hands. And her eyes, so crazy with desire. But still. He couldn't let that happen again. It was lucky that John hadn't walked in on them. Swope thought about Truax for a moment. Although he'd entertained thoughts of cutting him loose after seeing that mess in his basement, as the day wore on he realized that the soldier would be a useful man to have on board. To keep him quiet, yes, but also because there would doubtless be moments ahead when his help might be useful. Besides, he owed him now. If he kept him close then he'd be able to start repaying that debt.

He broke free of the window and returned to his desk, where that afternoon's copy of the *News American* lay across his blotter. Their coverage of the Truax killing ran just beneath the fold, superseded only by the latest batch of skulduggery from down Washington way. SON OF PROMINENT BUILDER HELD IN SLAYING OF NEW CITY TEEN. Swope had just about written the article himself in an off-the-record call to the reporter early that morning. In addition to the hard facts, it spoke of Joel's simmering anger at being forbidden from seeing Susan and his jealousy at finding she was now dating another boy. The parents of neither the victim nor the accused could be reached for comment, though Swope had gone on record as saying that it was 'a tragedy for everyone involved.' Teddy's name was not reported. Nor would it be, if Swope had his way. Accompanying the story were three photos. The first was a yearbook picture of Susan Truax, looking heart-stoppingly beautiful. Next to her was a very dark Joel. Last came the same photo of Wooten that had appeared in the recent laudatory articles about him. As he studied that final picture Swope recalled their confrontation a half hour earlier. He'd hoped Wooten wouldn't find out about his visit to unit 27 until after he'd taken the plea, though in the end it didn't matter. Even knowing Swope was behind it, he still had no choice. The only surprise came with that cock-and-bull story about the amusement park. As Wooten spoke, Swope seemed to remember some vague company scuttlebutt about a mysterious land grab in western Virginia. For a horrible moment, doubt entered his mind. Maybe Wooten was telling the truth and the whole thing was a mistake. But he quickly regained his composure. Wooten was just trying to cloud the issue. Buy some time for his son. He'd already shown himself to be an inveterate schemer. Nothing he said could be trusted. If only he hadn't over-reached, none of this would have had to happen. Nobody would have to pay. But he'd tried to get his big hands on what wasn't his. His betrayal had led to his own destruction. That little display of defiance he'd put on before leaving the office would of course come to nothing. Earl Wooten was a reasonable man. He knew the score. After all, it's how he got so far in a world which was never his. When the time came he'd take the deal.

'Mr Swope?'

Chad Sherman stood in the doorway. Swope chucked a grim, fraternal chin at him. The kid had been a rock all night, running point with the bumptious citizenry as well as the press.

'The state police are standing down. They'll leave a few cruisers behind for routine patrol but otherwise they're outta here.'

'That's fine, Chad. Have you spoken with those night editors yet?'

'I was just about to.'

'You might want to tell them that I've just been named city manager.'

Sherman's eyes pulsed in surprise.

'Just now?' he asked.

'That's right. Effective immediately, for a full, three-year-term.'

The kid smiled broadly.

'That's great. I . . . that's just great.'

'Thanks.'

'You want me to use the press release we prepared? Or I could write up a new one . . .'

'Let me have another peek at it, but sure. Tell them if they want to call me for their morning editions that will be fine. I'll be at my desk all night.'

486

Sherman nodded. There was a barely detectable mist in his eyes. He started to go but then turned back.

'Mr Swope, I just want to tell you . . .'

'Yes?'

'This is going to make a lot of people happy around here. I think, you know, we're over the worst of it.'

'Good of you to say that, Chad.'

'I'll report back after making those calls.'

'You do that,' Swope said, his voice thick with benevolent authority. 'And then I want you to knock off. You should be home with your family.'

When the kid was gone Swope thought for a moment about the Shermans. They were typical Newtonians. His wife was a former hippie who'd recently started to shave her legs and wear a little Cover Girl. They lived in an aluminum starter-home in Juniper Bend but had their eye on Mystic Hills. Once old Chad's college loan was paid off it would be time to bite off a man-sized mortgage. Grab himself a second set of wheels, maybe one of those Datsuns you were starting to see around. The week in Ocean City would stretch into two on Hilton Head. Chad would trade in those Montgomery Ward off-the-racks for some European threads. These were Swope's people. He was here to serve them now, to help the Shermans of the world create their modest American paradises. They no longer had anything to worry about. With Wooten and Barnaby out of the picture, the more outlandish strands of the new city experiment could wither and die, leaving behind only that which was solid and prosperous and good. He'd finally be allowed to get some cops on the streets. Privatize the HUD projects. The bureaucrats inside the Beltway would piss and moan about that, though he'd already prepared a few preemptive injunctions in case they got frisky. Besides, the Nixon gang was going so spectacularly bellyup that a little Chapter IX reneging wouldn't even raise an eyebrow.

Swope checked his watch. It was getting late. He wondered if Wooten had taken that plea yet. He decided to call Van Riper to make sure she was still on the ball. It took a while to track her down – she was up to her ass in looters. She reported that McNutt had called earlier in the evening to schedule a meeting for first thing the following morning. Swope smiled as he hung up the phone. For all his earlier swagger, Wooten had taken the bait.

Before leaving his desk he called home to pass on the news about the job.

'What are all those sirens?' Sally asked.

'Oh, just a couple of fires. Don't worry. Everything's under control.'

'Everything?'

'Yes. Everything. How is he?'

'I think he's getting a cold. I was just about to go check on him.'

'That's probably not such a bad thing, a cold. Keep him home until this all blows over.'

'Austin?'

'Yes?'

'He still doesn't seem right.'

If only you knew, he thought.

'Sal, you're just going to have to give him some time. He'll work it out.'

She didn't answer.

'Look, once this settles, we'll get out of here for a while. The three of us. Maybe hit Bermuda. What do you say?'

'That would be nice,' she said distantly.

He'd almost forgotten his news.

'Hey, guess what? It's official. Savage just named me city manager.'

'That's wonderful, honey. You were silly to ever doubt it.'

Swope didn't say anything for a moment, annoyed at her lack of excitement. But he quickly dismissed the feeling. There was no way she could have known how close he'd come to losing the job – or how much he'd done to rescue it. There was no way anyone would ever know.

'Yes. I was. Look, I better go. Tell Teddy if he wants to talk or anything, he should call me. I'll be right here.'

After hanging up he strolled over to the city model, contemplating it for a long time, taking his usual solace from its elegant symmetry. His eyes followed the shapes of the wooded hills and winding streets, the bike paths and parks. He slowly allowed himself to start thinking the thought he'd kept at bay all day. He'd done it. He'd won. The job was his. Teddy was safe. What had seemed like absolute ruin and certain defeat just twenty-four hours earlier had worked out perfectly. Yes, he'd had to push the envelope this time. But he'd done it.

The city was his.

And then his eyes washed over Mystic Hills and a strange and unwelcome memory flashed through his mind, a rogue scrap of nostalgia he could have easily lived without, especially tonight. It was from the year they'd moved out here. The city's first Fourth of July. The Wootens had invited the Swopes over for a barbecue. This was back when there was no one else around – they might as well have been neighbors in 1880s Oklahoma, separated by a couple thousand acres of Indian country. What had Ardelia called their house? Fort Apache. Wooten had really gone the whole hog for the feast, custom-building a barbecue by slicing open a fifty-five-gallon drum lengthways and propping it on a portable cement mixer's stand. For the rack he used a big piece of framed chicken wire. By the time the Swopes arrived the fire looked like it had been burning for a week. Wooten had ribs and chicken going, hot dogs and burgers. All of it smothered with his special sauce. There were baked potatoes wrapped in aluminum foil and, in the kitchen, a vat of simmering corncobs. Sally had brought macaroni salad and strawberry shortcake. Miller for the men, iced Taylor Lake Country for the ladies. Joel and Teddy disappeared immediately to the treehouse Wooten had recently built, concocting some elaborate game that had them both jumping through its hatch into a pile of dry leaves. The twins stuck shyly to Ardelia. After stuffing themselves with Wooten's miraculous food, the four adults gathered in a laager of lawn chairs protected by bug lamps. It was the first time they had all relaxed together like this. And it was good. Sally and Ardelia hitting it off. Earl and Austin lapsing into silences that were half satisfied by what they had accomplished and half dreading the task ahead. Night fell and Wooten announced that he had a surprise. Ardelia rolled her eyes as he disappeared into the garage, returning with a burlap sack full of fireworks a masonry supplier had picked up for him at South of the Border. There were bandoleers of firecrackers, bottle rockets and Roman candles, sparklers and even a few M80s. Wooten announced that since the town fathers had neglected to set up a fireworks display, he'd decided to do one himself.

'Hey,' Swope cried. 'We *are* the damned town fathers.'

The boys came crashing out of the woods at the sound of the first rocket's whistle. The twins clung even tighter to Ardelia's skirts. Teddy and Joel begged to be allowed to set something off. Their fathers agreed, though only under the strictest supervision. And so the Wootens and the Swopes had a fireworks display. There were a few duds and the M80s had to be abandoned when their first sonic boom sent the twins into fits of tears, but otherwise it was as good a show as any currently erupting beside the Potomac.

It was the last bottle rocket that started the fire. Teddy set it off. Though he later claimed he'd done nothing wrong, Swope had seen him mischievously lower its trajectory just before lighting the fuse. It hit the upper branch of a tree at the yard's border and ricocheted into the surrounding woods. Wooten and Swope raced in after it, though by the time they got to the crash site the rocket's spewing exhaust had set alight a patch of undergrowth. They began to stamp and kick the flaming leaves, but this only spread the fire farther. Just as the situation looked like it was going to get out of hand a cool blessing of water rained on them. Only it wasn't rain. It was Ardelia, wielding the hose she'd pulled across the yard. She didn't worry too much about soaking her husband or Swope as she doused the flames. In fact, once the fire was out she continued to irrigate them. They stood there and took it. Finally, she released the nozzle.

'Next time either of you jeopardize my house with your foolishness, I'm going to take some lye and a wire brush to you as well.'

They tramped out of the smoky, dripping woods, laughing and swearing mildly. Swope caught his son's eye. Teddy was clearly petrified that he was going to be blamed. But his father merely smiled and nodded. No harm done. It would be yet another of their little secrets.

'Well,' Wooten announced as he opened a cold Miller for Swope. 'I do believe we just inaugurated the Newton Volunteer Fire department.'

Just when he was about to start feeling something suspiciously like remorse, Swope yanked himself out of this unwelcome reverie. There was no use in thinking such thoughts. Especially now. Wooten had played his hand and lost. If something good had been destroyed in the process then it was his own fault. Swope was only doing what he'd taught himself to do since the beginning, when he dragged himself out of frozen, impoverished Grand Rapids or spent those long nights by his son's hospital bed or moved to Newton. Claim what was his. Claim it, and protect it.

Something flashed in the corner of his eye. Another blue light. It took him a moment to realize that this one was different from the others. It was in the wrong part of town, racing down Merlin's Way, straight for his house. Swope stepped over to the east-facing window to chart its progress. Dread moved through his guts as it approached Prospero's Parade. He'd relaxed his guard too soon. Something had cracked. The truth was out. But the fear vanished the moment the prowler passed his street and moved on toward Wooten's end of the neighborhood. It was nothing. Just the cops, mopping up.

And then the phone began to ring. That would be the papers, wanting to know what it felt like to be the man in charge of the new city. After one last look at the darkening plain below him, Austin Swope took a deep breath and went to answer his future.

THE END

Acknowledgments

I am deeply indebted to Gerry Howard, whose acute editing made this novel better than it should have been; Henry Dunow, whose passionate agency placed it where it was supposed to be; Sarah Westcott, whose keen British eye added much-needed perspective to the whole enterprise; and the sublime, ever-calm Rachel Calder, who believed from the first and for some reason has never stopped.

But most of all my wife Caryl Casson, who continues to make it all possible.

A WIDOW FOR ONE YEAR

John Irving

'IRVING'S MOST ENTERTAINING AND PERSUASIVE
NOVEL SINCE *THE WORLD ACCORDING TO GARP*'
The New York Times

'GRIPPING, FULL OF HORROR AND HUMOUR'
Katherine Knorr, *Literary Review*

Ruth Cole is a complex, often self-contradictory character – a
'difficult' woman. By no means is she conventionally 'nice', but she
will never be forgotten. Her story is told in three parts, each focusing
on a critical time in her life. When we first meet her – on Long
Island in the summer of 1958 – Ruth is only four.

The second time we meet Ruth it is 1990, when she is an unmarried
woman whose personal life is not nearly as successful as her literary
career. She distrusts her judgement in men, for good reason. The
book closes in 1995 when Ruth is forty-one years old, a widow and a
mother. She's about to fall in love for the first time.

Richly comic, as well as deeply disturbing, *A Widow for One Year* is a
multilayered love story of astonishing emotional force. Both ribald
and erotic, it is also a brilliant novel about the passage of time and
the relentlessness of grief.

'HIS BEST SINCE *GARP*'
Time

'WICKEDLY KNOWING, MISCHIEVOUSLY
POST-MODERN AND MAGICAL REALIST ALONG THE
LINES OF GUNTER GRASS, GABRIEL GARCIA
MARQUEZ AND ROBERTSON DAVIES'
Maxim Jakubowski, *Time Out*

'A JOY TO READ'
Evening Standard

0 552 99796 X

BLACK SWAN

EDDIE'S BASTARD

William Kowalski

'A REMARKABLE DEBUT'
Time Out

Billy was deposited as an infant on the doorstep of Thomas Mann's
home in a simple wicker basket with a plain two-word message
pinned to his shawl reading 'Eddie's Bastard'. Eddie, Thomas's son,
had been killed in Vietnam three months earlier, and his father had
given up on life, having lost his only son. But now, suddenly,
Thomas has a grandson and an heir – if not to the once-vast Mann
fortune (for Thomas recklessly squandered that in a foolhardy
enterprise involving ostriches just after his heroic return from the
Second World War), then at least to the long legacy of the Mann
family stories, stretching back to the Civil War.

In this rich, deeply resonant literary début, William Kowalski
explores the power of family, the meaning of history, and the bonds
of individuals united and divided by love. By turns hilarious, thrilling
and heart-breaking, *Eddie's Bastard* is a novel that stays in the mind
long after the reading is over.

'CLEVER, EMOTIONAL STORYTELLING WITH LAUGHS,
TEARS, AND LOVE'
The Times

'A BOOK WRITTEN WITH SUCH ELEGANCE, MATURITY
AND HUMOUR IT IS DIFFICULT TO BELIEVE THAT
THE AUTHOR IS ONLY 28 YEARS OLD'
The Good Book Guide

'WICKEDLY FUNNY AND GENUINELY MOVING'
Attitude

0 552 99859 1

BLACK SWAN

A SELECTED LIST OF FINE WRITING
AVAILABLE FROM BLACK SWAN

99313	1	OF LOVE AND SHADOWS	*Isabel Allende*	£6.99
99820	6	FLANDERS	*Patricia Anthony*	£6.99
99619	X	HUMAN CROQUET	*Kate Atkinson*	£6.99
99824	9	THE DANDELION CLOCK	*Guy Burt*	£6.99
99686	6	BEACH MUSIC	*Pat Conroy*	£7.99
99715	3	BEACHCOMBING FOR A SHIPWRECKED GOD		
			Joe Coomer	£6.99
14698	6	INCONCEIVABLE	*Ben Elton*	£6.99
99587	8	LIKE WATER FOR CHOCOLATE	*Laura Esquivel*	£6.99
99721	8	BEFORE WOMEN HAD WINGS	*Connie May Fowler*	£6.99
99801	X	THE SHORT HISTORY OF A PRINCE	*Jane Hamilton*	£6.99
99848	6	CHOCOLAT	*Joanne Harris*	£6.99
99796	X	A WIDOW FOR ONE YEAR	*John Irving*	£7.99
99758	7	FRIEDA AND MIN	*Pamela Jooste*	£6.99
99859	1	EDDIE'S BASTARD	*William Kowalski*	£6.99
99807	9	MONTENEGRO	*Starling Lawrence*	£6.99
99580	0	CAIRO TRILOGY I: PALACE WALK	*Naguib Mahfouz*	£7.99
99552	5	TALES OF THE CITY	*Armistead Maupin*	£6.99
99762	5	THE LACK BROTHERS	*Malcolm McKay*	£6.99
99785	4	GOODNIGHT, NEBRASKA	*Tom McNeal*	£6.99
99718	8	IN A LAND OF PLENTY	*Tim Pears*	£6.99
99817	6	INK	*John Preston*	£6.99
99810	9	THE JUKEBOX QUEEN OF MALTA	*Nicholas Rinaldi*	£6.99
99813	3	MOUNT MISERY	*Samuel Shem*	£7.99
99846	X	THE WAR ZONE	*Alexander Stuart*	£6.99
99780	3	KNOWLEDGE OF ANGELS	*Jill Paton Walsh*	£6.99
99366	2	THE ELECTRIC KOOL AID ACID TEST	*Tom Woolfe*	£7.99